Takane &

3

STORY AND ART BY
Yuki Shiwasu

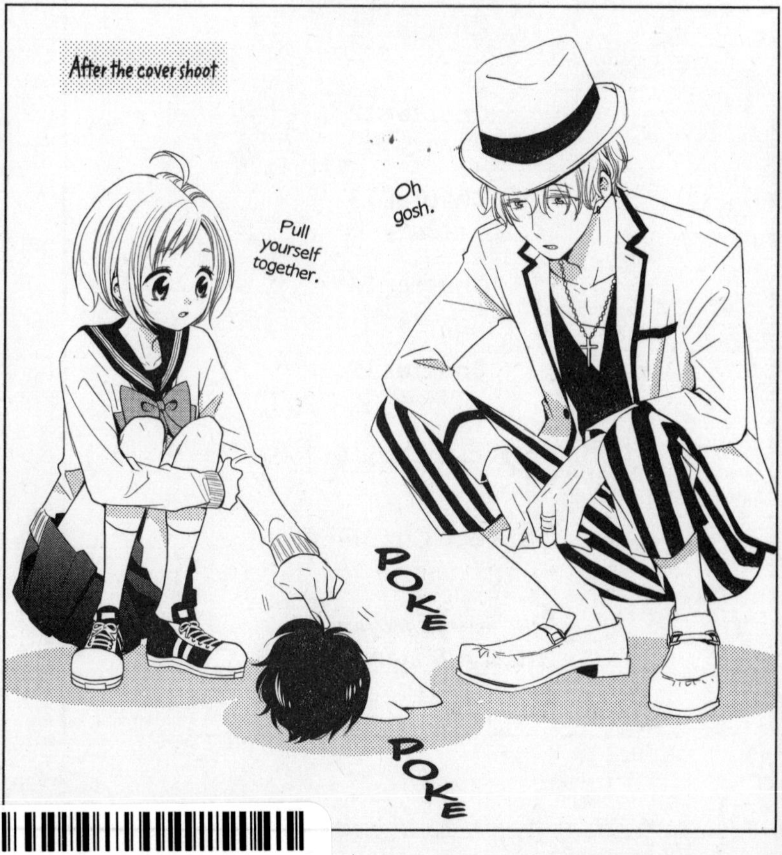
After the cover shoot
Oh gosh.
Pull yourself together.
POKE
POKE

Takane &✿Hana

3

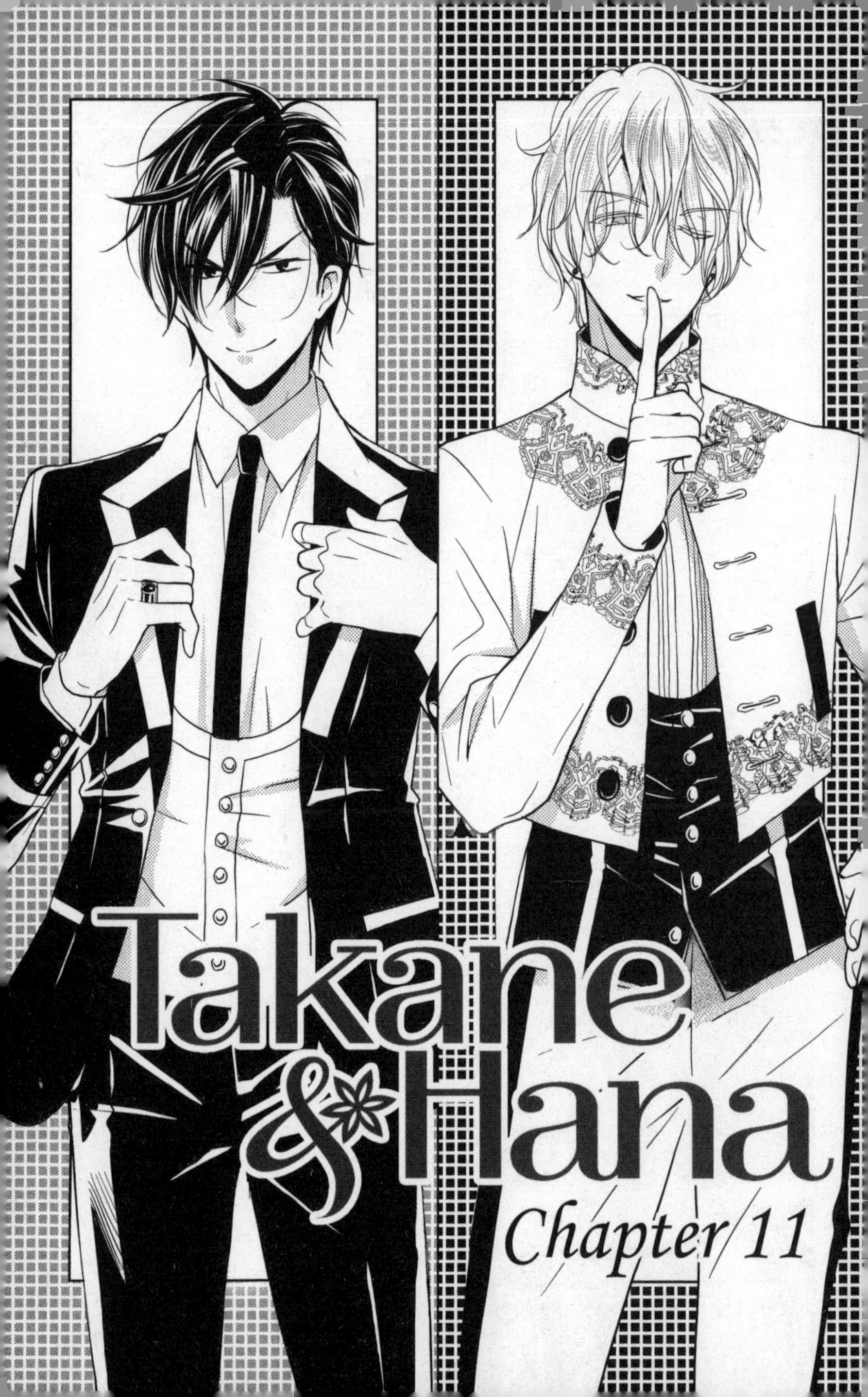
Takane & Hana
Chapter 11

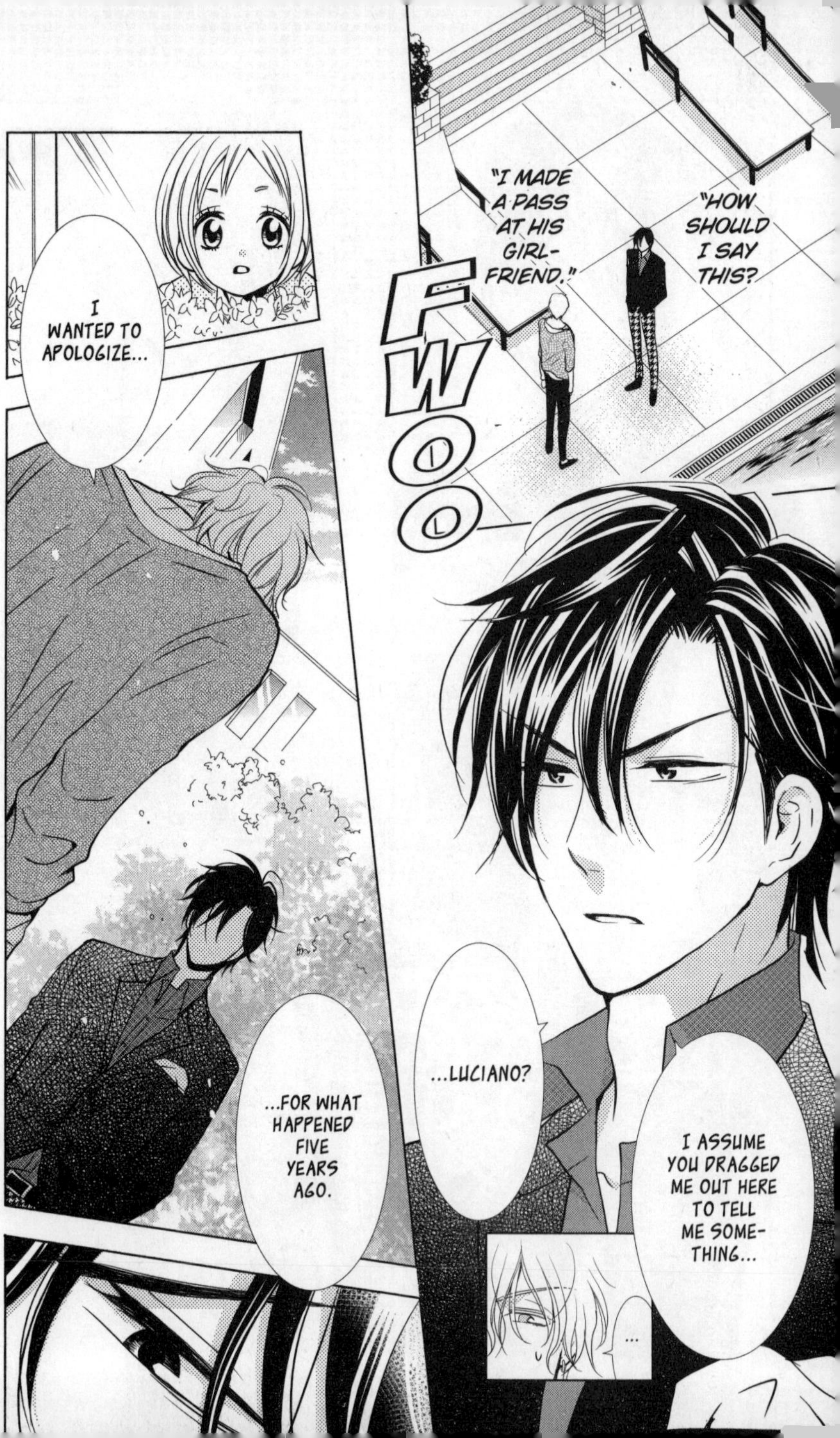
"HOW SHOULD I SAY THIS?
"I MADE A PASS AT HIS GIRLFRIEND."
FWOOL
...LUCIANO?
I ASSUME YOU DRAGGED ME OUT HERE TO TELL ME SOMETHING...
...
I WANTED TO APOLOGIZE...
...FOR WHAT HAPPENED FIVE YEARS AGO.

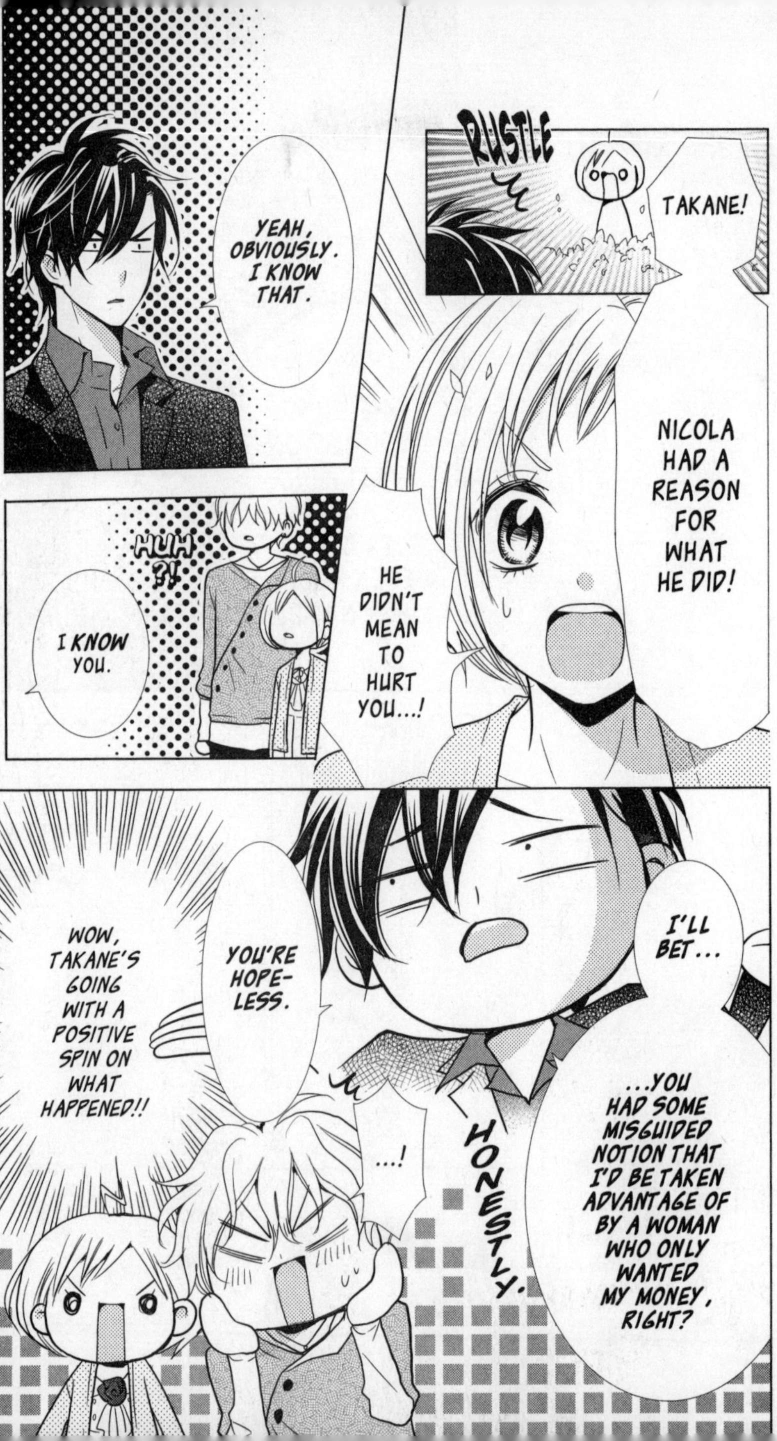
RUSTLE
TAKANE!
YEAH, OBVIOUSLY. I KNOW THAT.
NICOLA HAD A REASON FOR WHAT HE DID!
HE DIDN'T MEAN TO HURT YOU...!
HUH ?!
I KNOW YOU.
I'LL BET...
...YOU HAD SOME MISGUIDED NOTION THAT I'D BE TAKEN ADVANTAGE OF BY A WOMAN WHO ONLY WANTED MY MONEY, RIGHT?
HONESTLY.
YOU'RE HOPE-LESS.
...!
WOW, TAKANE'S GOING WITH A POSITIVE SPIN ON WHAT HAPPENED!!

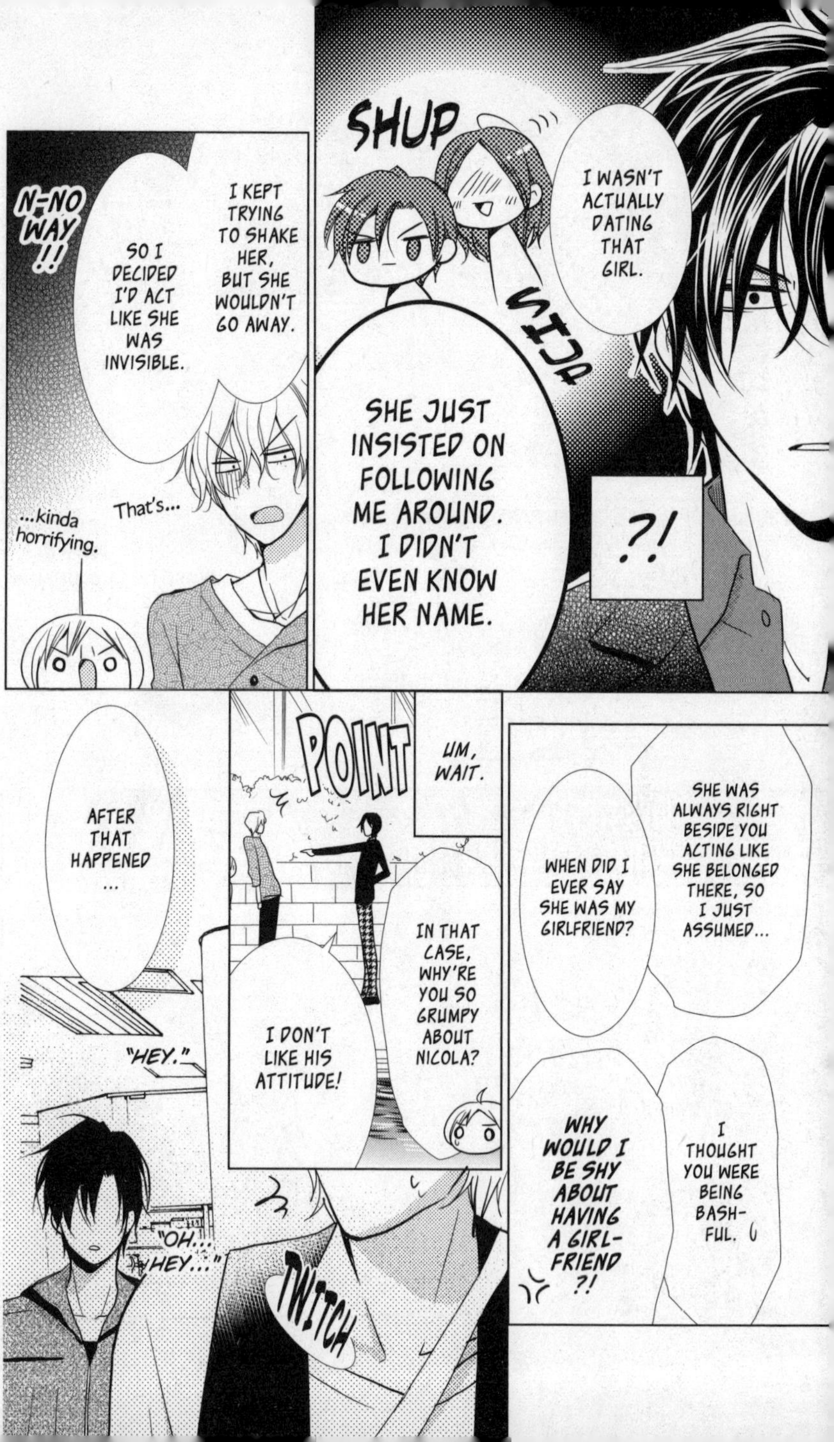
I WASN'T ACTUALLY DATING THAT GIRL.
SHUP
SHE JUST INSISTED ON FOLLOWING ME AROUND. I DIDN'T EVEN KNOW HER NAME.
?!
I KEPT TRYING TO SHAKE HER, BUT SHE WOULDN'T GO AWAY.
SO I DECIDED I'D ACT LIKE SHE WAS INVISIBLE.
N-NO WAY!!
That's...
...kinda horrifying.
SHE WAS ALWAYS RIGHT BESIDE YOU ACTING LIKE SHE BELONGED THERE, SO I JUST ASSUMED...
WHEN DID I EVER SAY SHE WAS MY GIRLFRIEND?
I THOUGHT YOU WERE BEING BASH-FUL.
WHY WOULD I BE SHY ABOUT HAVING A GIRL-FRIEND?!
UM, WAIT.
POINT
IN THAT CASE, WHY'RE YOU SO GRUMPY ABOUT NICOLA?
I DON'T LIKE HIS ATTITUDE!
AFTER THAT HAPPENED ...
"HEY."
"OH... HEY..."
TWITCH

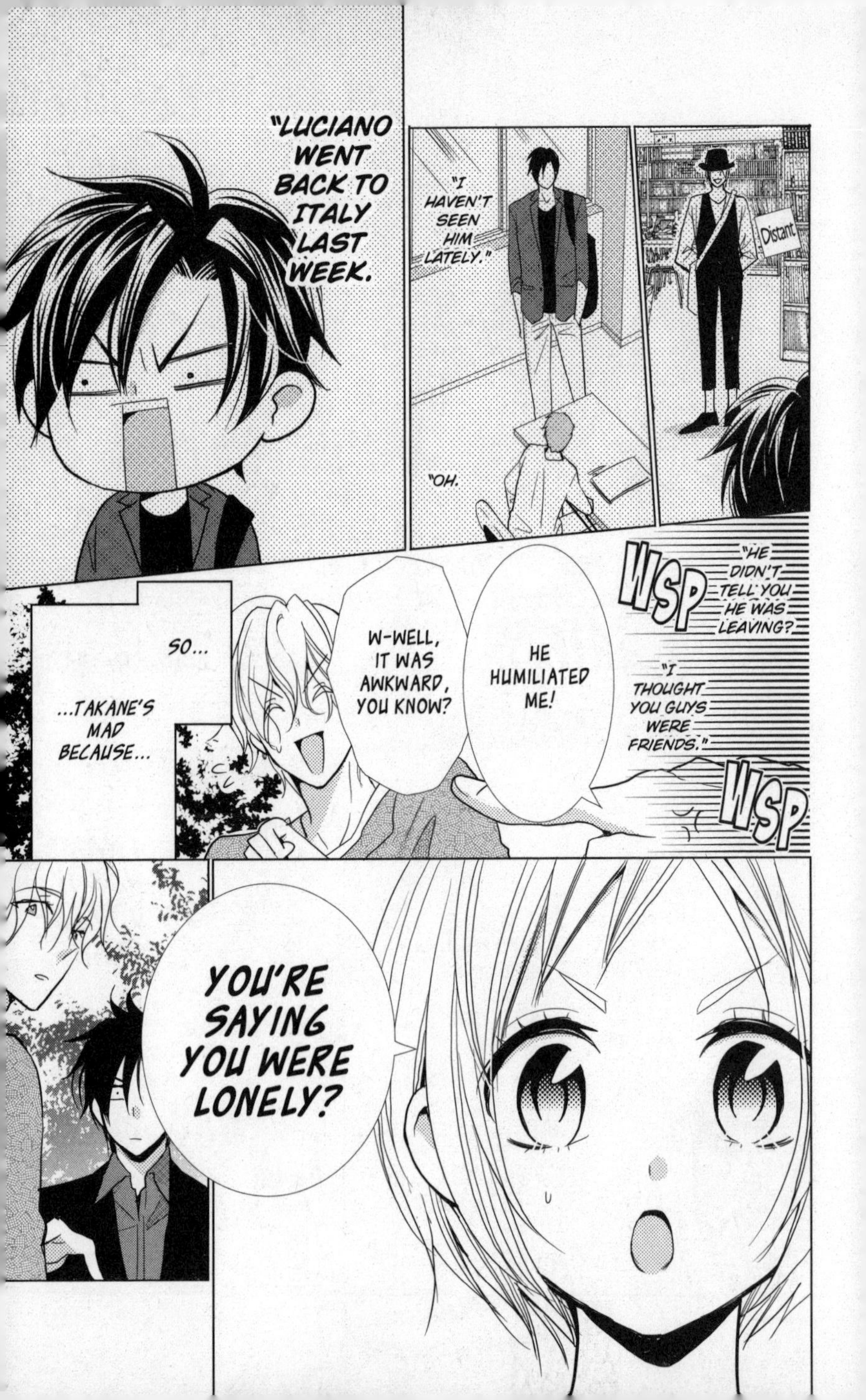
Distant
"I HAVEN'T SEEN HIM LATELY."
"OH.
"LUCIANO WENT BACK TO ITALY LAST WEEK.
WSP
"HE DIDN'T TELL YOU HE WAS LEAVING?
"I THOUGHT YOU GUYS WERE FRIENDS."
WSP
HE HUMILIATED ME!
W-WELL, IT WAS AWKWARD, YOU KNOW?
SO...
...TAKANE'S MAD BECAUSE...
YOU'RE SAYING YOU WERE LONELY?

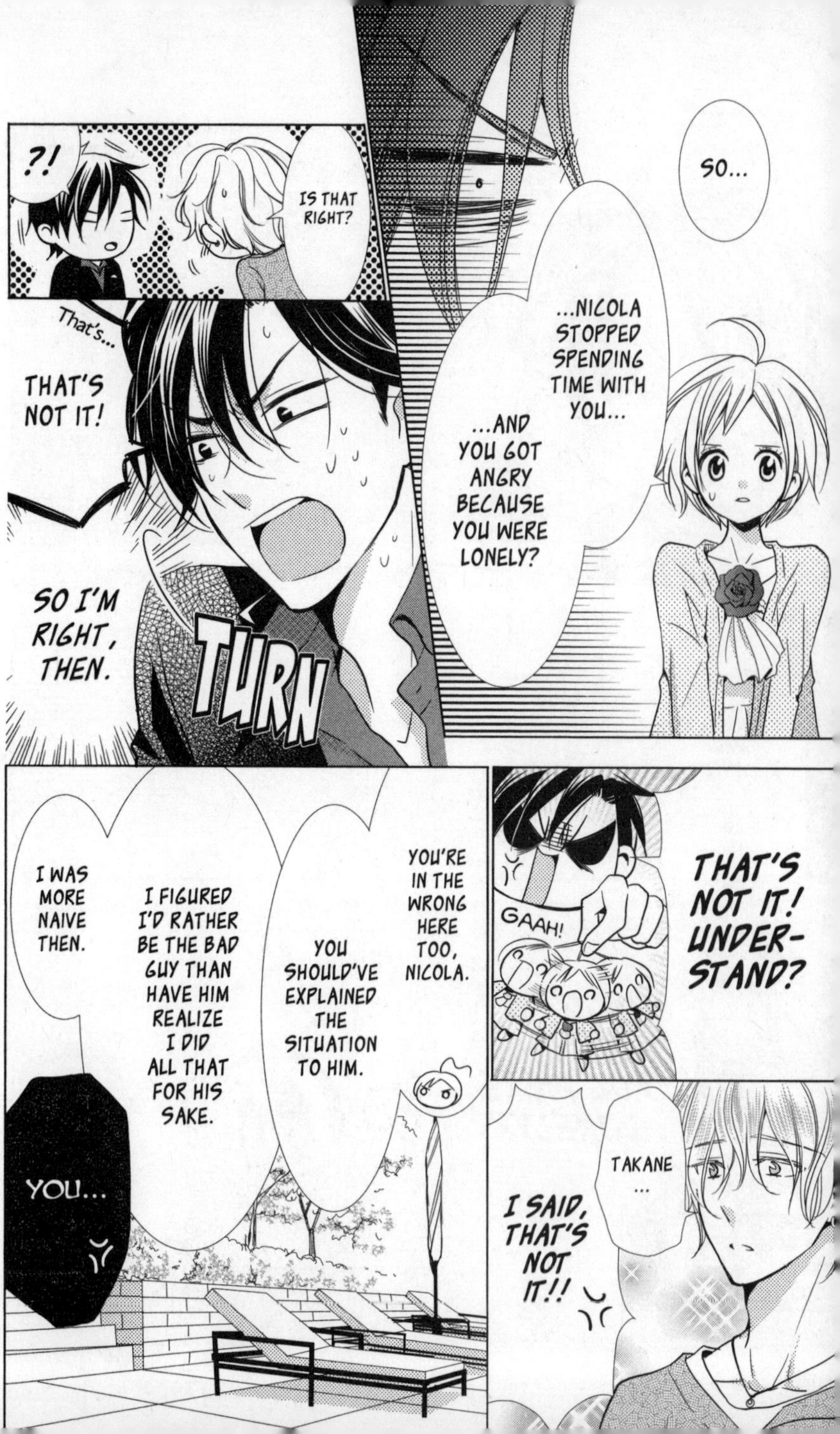
So...
...Nicola stopped spending time with you...
...And you got angry because you were lonely?
Is that right?
?!
That's...
That's not it!
So I'm right, then.
TURN
That's not it! Under-stand?
GAAH!
Takane...
I said, that's not it!!
You're in the wrong here too, Nicola.
You should've explained the situation to him.
I figured I'd rather be the bad guy than have him realize I did all that for his sake.
I was more naive then.
You...

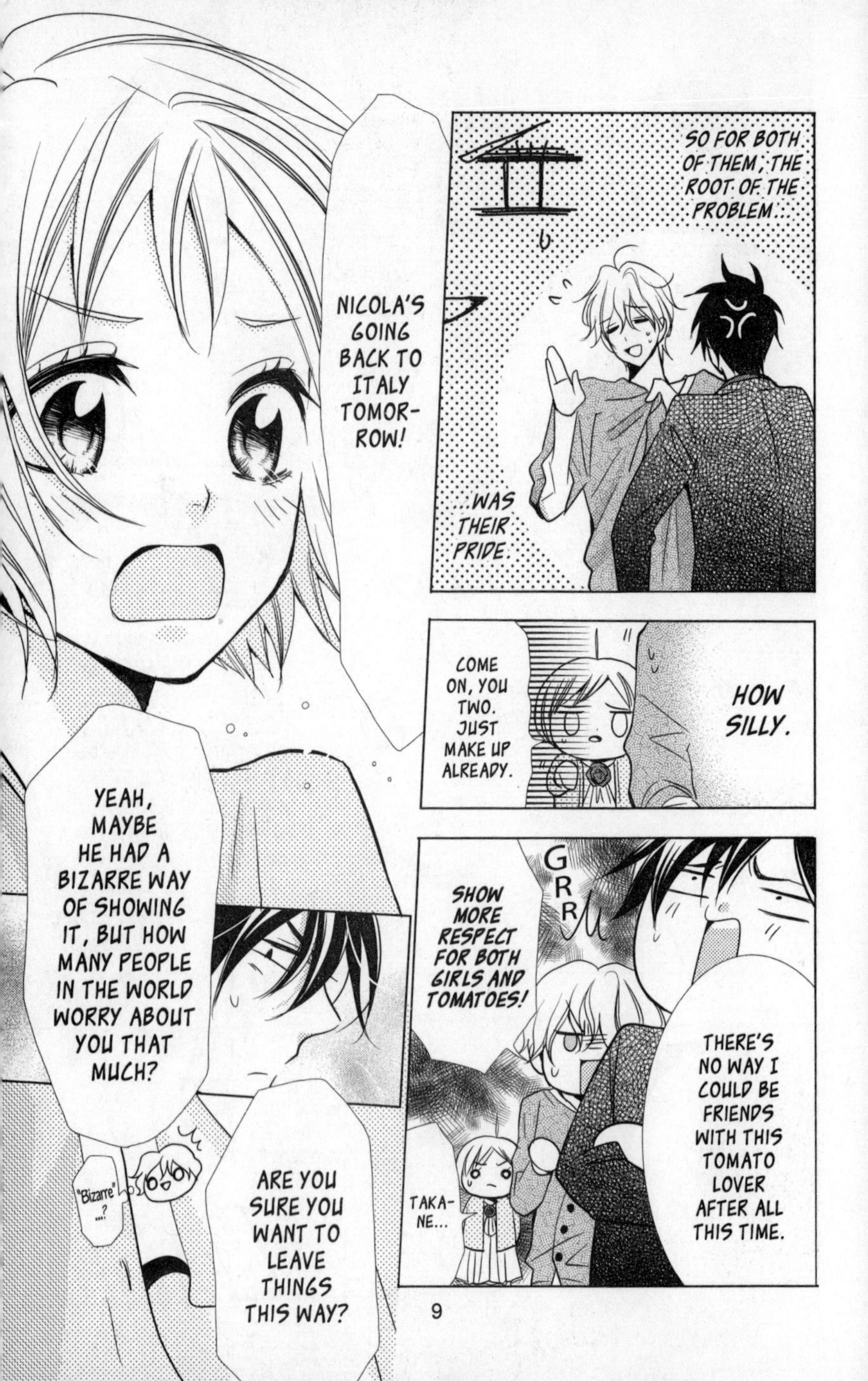
SO FOR BOTH OF THEM, THE ROOT OF THE PROBLEM...
...WAS THEIR PRIDE.
HOW SILLY.
COME ON, YOU TWO. JUST MAKE UP ALREADY.
GRR
SHOW MORE RESPECT FOR BOTH GIRLS AND TOMATOES!
THERE'S NO WAY I COULD BE FRIENDS WITH THIS TOMATO LOVER AFTER ALL THIS TIME.
TAKA-NE...
NICOLA'S GOING BACK TO ITALY TOMORROW!
YEAH, MAYBE HE HAD A BIZARRE WAY OF SHOWING IT, BUT HOW MANY PEOPLE IN THE WORLD WORRY ABOUT YOU THAT MUCH?
"Bizarre"...?
ARE YOU SURE YOU WANT TO LEAVE THINGS THIS WAY?

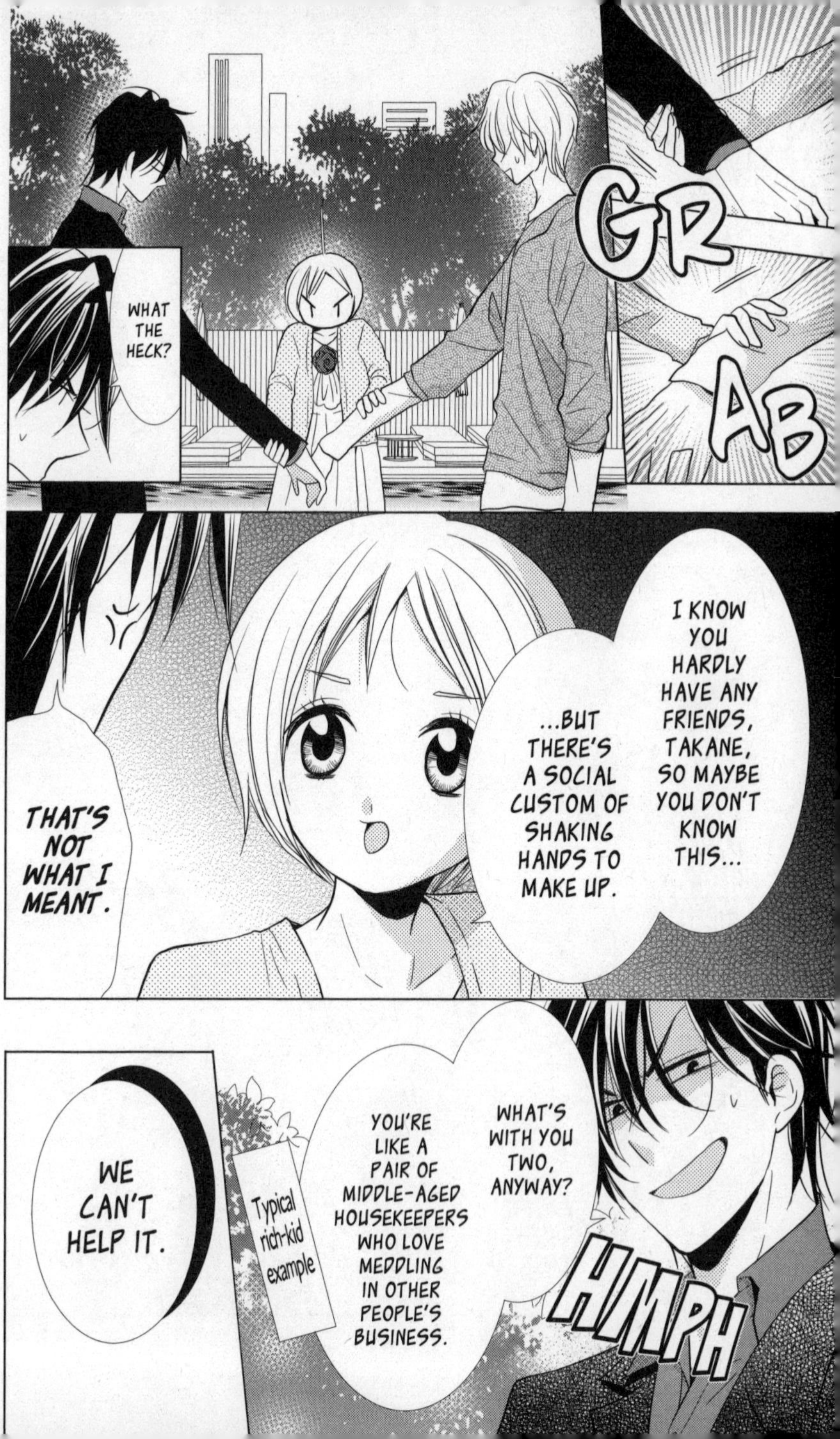
GRAB
WHAT THE HECK?
I KNOW YOU HARDLY HAVE ANY FRIENDS, TAKANE, SO MAYBE YOU DON'T KNOW THIS...
...BUT THERE'S A SOCIAL CUSTOM OF SHAKING HANDS TO MAKE UP.
THAT'S NOT WHAT I MEANT.
WHAT'S WITH YOU TWO, ANYWAY?
YOU'RE LIKE A PAIR OF MIDDLE-AGED HOUSEKEEPERS WHO LOVE MEDDLING IN OTHER PEOPLE'S BUSINESS.
HMPH
Typical rich-kid example
WE CAN'T HELP IT.

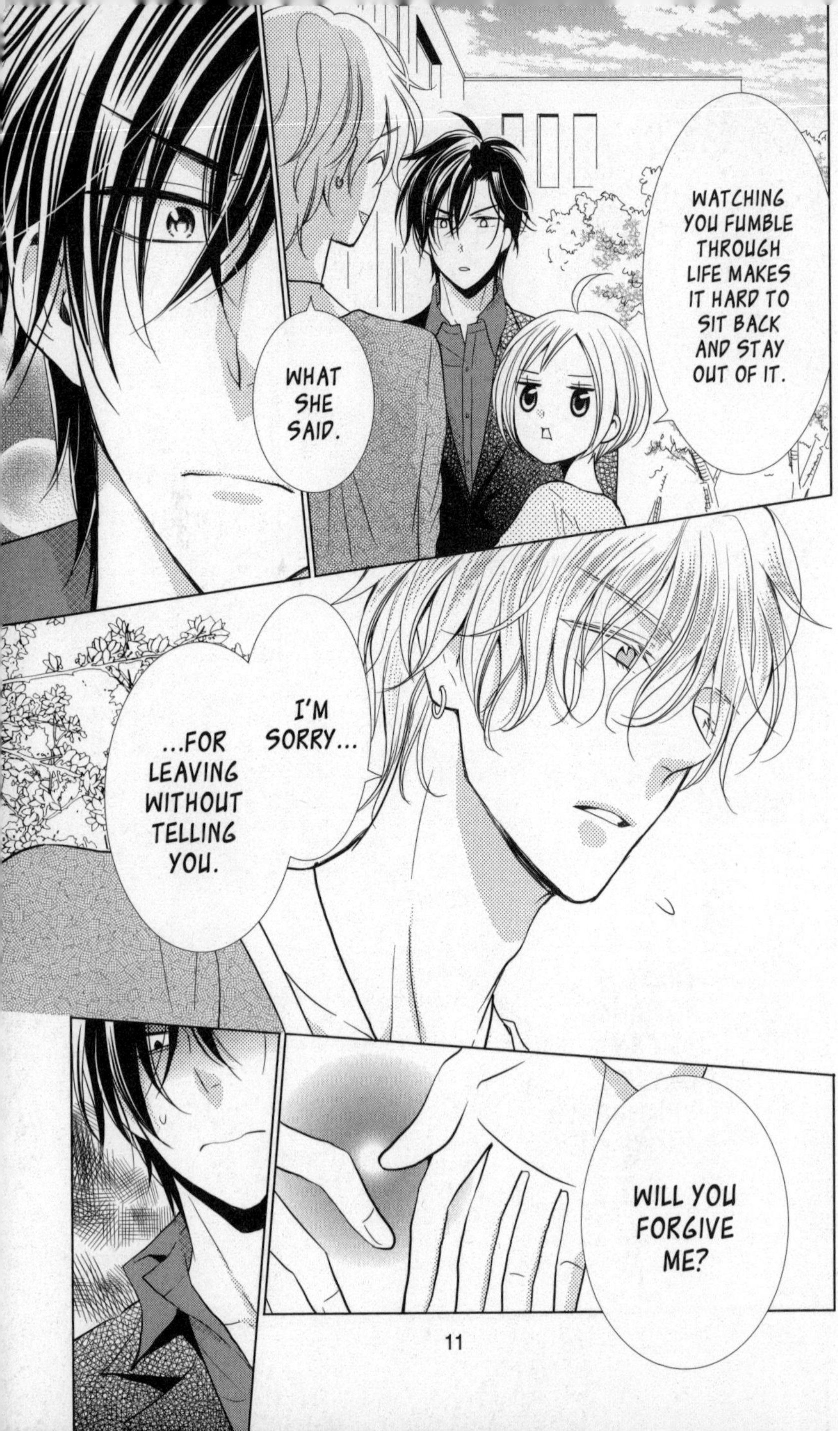
WATCHING YOU FUMBLE THROUGH LIFE MAKES IT HARD TO SIT BACK AND STAY OUT OF IT.
WHAT SHE SAID.
I'M SORRY...
...FOR LEAVING WITHOUT TELLING YOU.
WILL YOU FORGIVE ME?

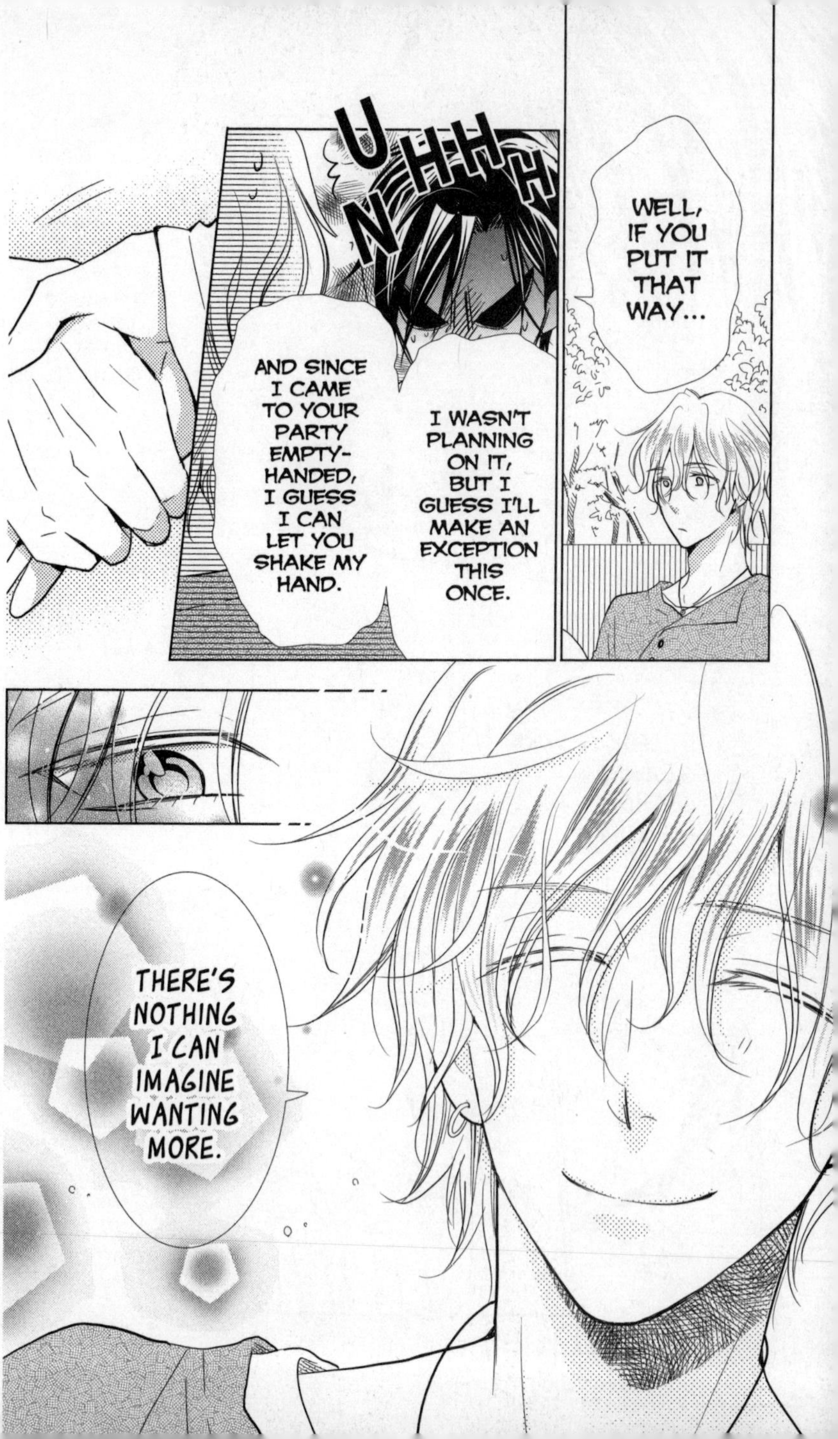
WELL, IF YOU PUT IT THAT WAY...
UHHHN
I WASN'T PLANNING ON IT, BUT I GUESS I'LL MAKE AN EXCEPTION THIS ONCE.
AND SINCE I CAME TO YOUR PARTY EMPTY-HANDED, I GUESS I CAN LET YOU SHAKE MY HAND.
THERE'S NOTHING I CAN IMAGINE WANTING MORE.

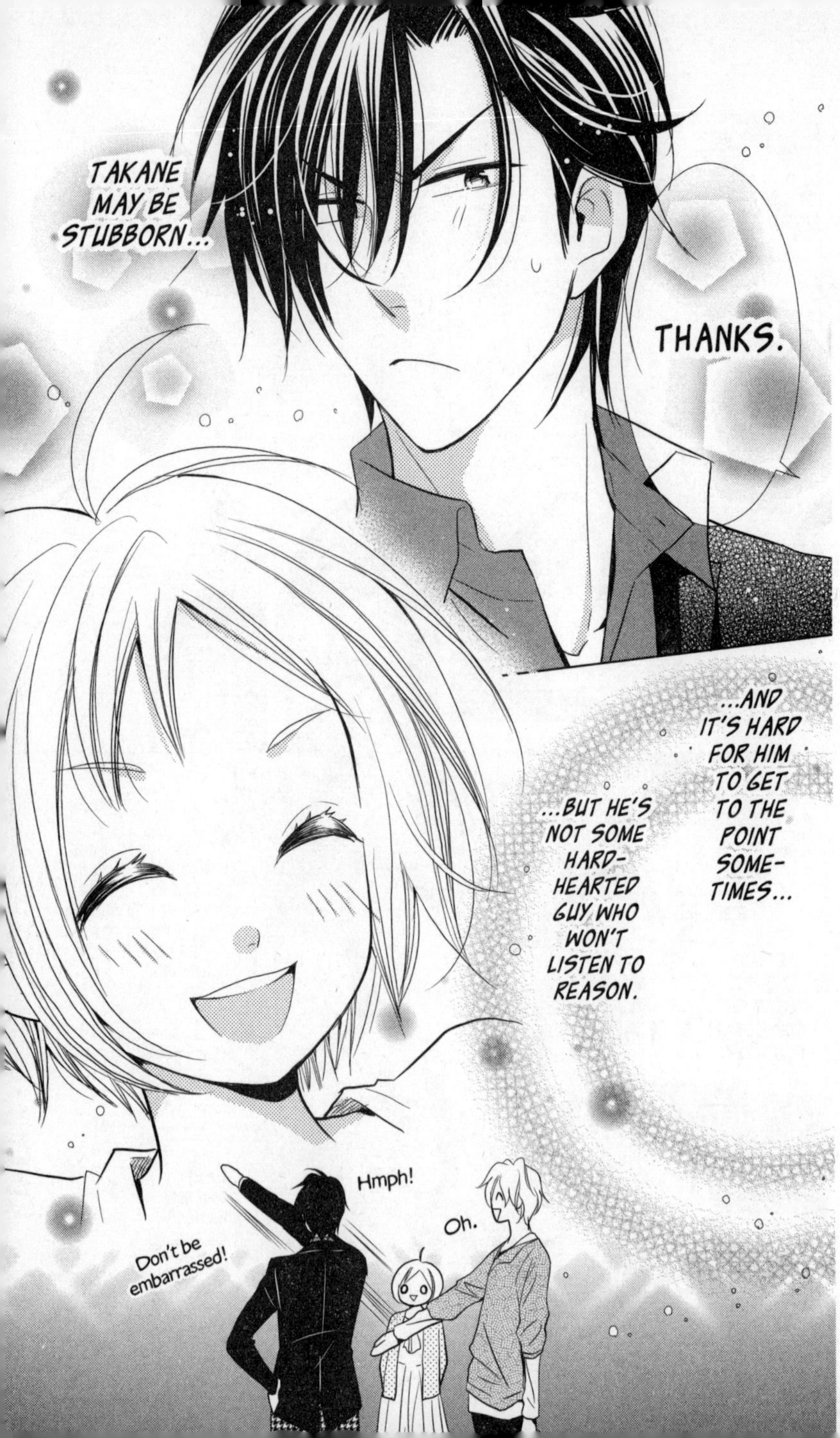
THANKS.
TAKANE MAY BE STUBBORN...
...AND IT'S HARD FOR HIM TO GET TO THE POINT SOME-TIMES...
...BUT HE'S NOT SOME HARD-HEARTED GUY WHO WON'T LISTEN TO REASON.
Hmph!
Oh.
Don't be embarrassed!

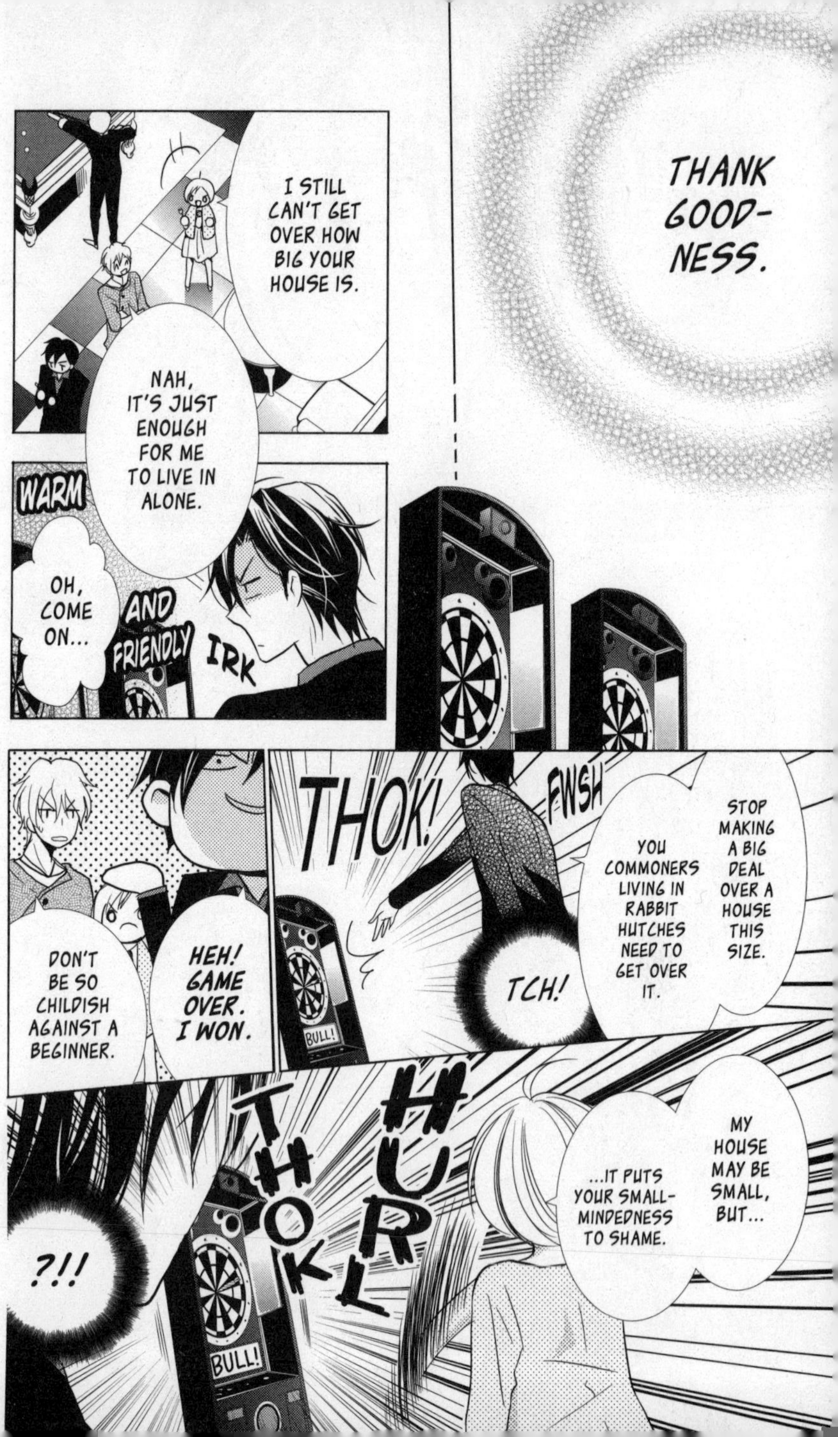
THANK GOOD-NESS.
I STILL CAN'T GET OVER HOW BIG YOUR HOUSE IS.
NAH, IT'S JUST ENOUGH FOR ME TO LIVE IN ALONE.
WARM
AND FRIENDLY
IRK
OH, COME ON...
THOK!
FWSH
STOP MAKING A BIG DEAL OVER A HOUSE THIS SIZE.
YOU COMMONERS LIVING IN RABBIT HUTCHES NEED TO GET OVER IT.
TCH!
BULL!
HEH! GAME OVER. I WON.
DON'T BE SO CHILDISH AGAINST A BEGINNER.
MY HOUSE MAY BE SMALL, BUT...
...IT PUTS YOUR SMALL-MINDEDNESS TO SHAME.
HURL
THOK
BULL!
?!!

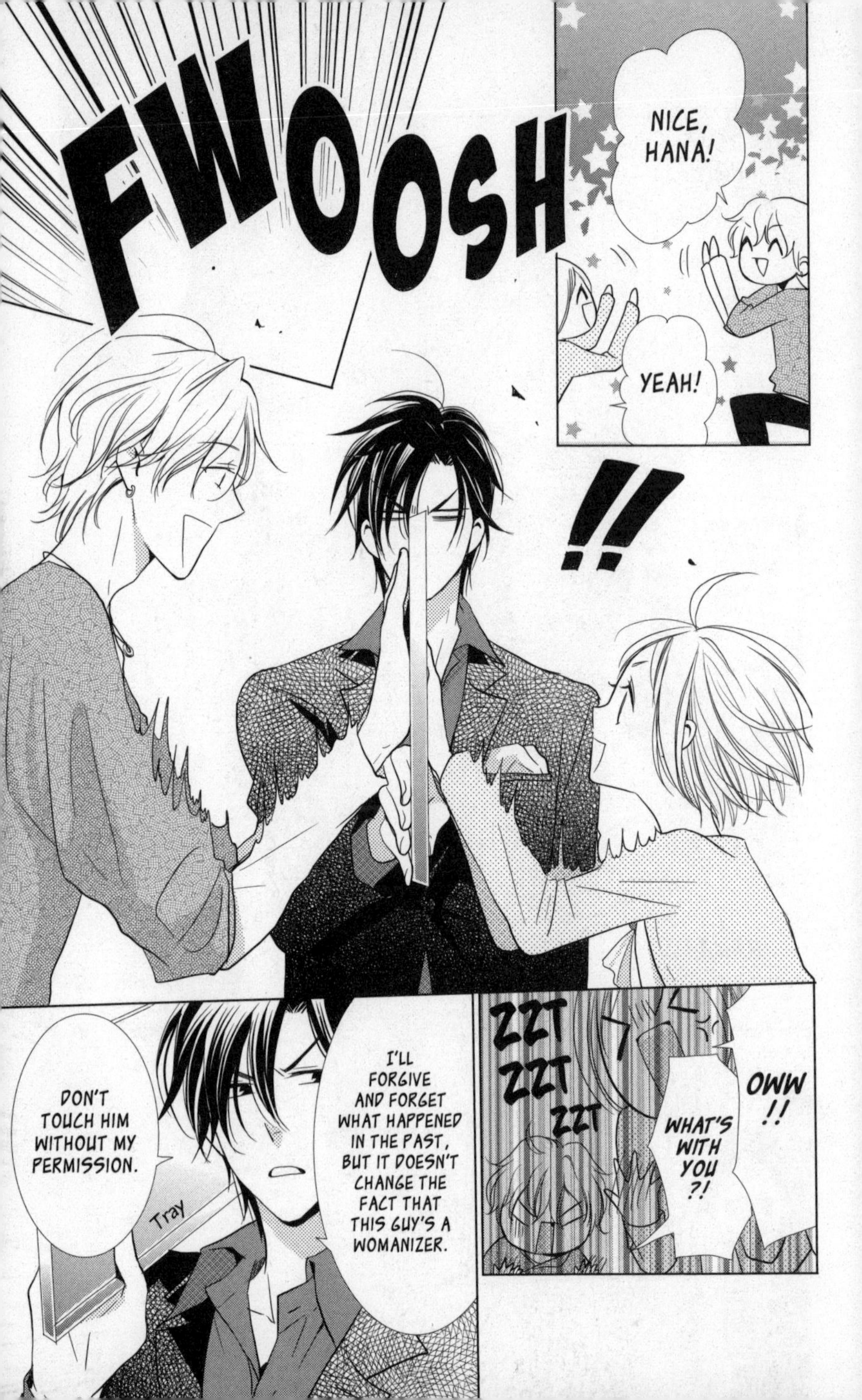
NICE, HANA!
YEAH!
FWOOSH
!!
ZZT ZZT ZZT
OWW !!
WHAT'S WITH YOU ?!
I'LL FORGIVE AND FORGET WHAT HAPPENED IN THE PAST, BUT IT DOESN'T CHANGE THE FACT THAT THIS GUY'S A WOMANIZER.
DON'T TOUCH HIM WITHOUT MY PERMISSION.
Tray

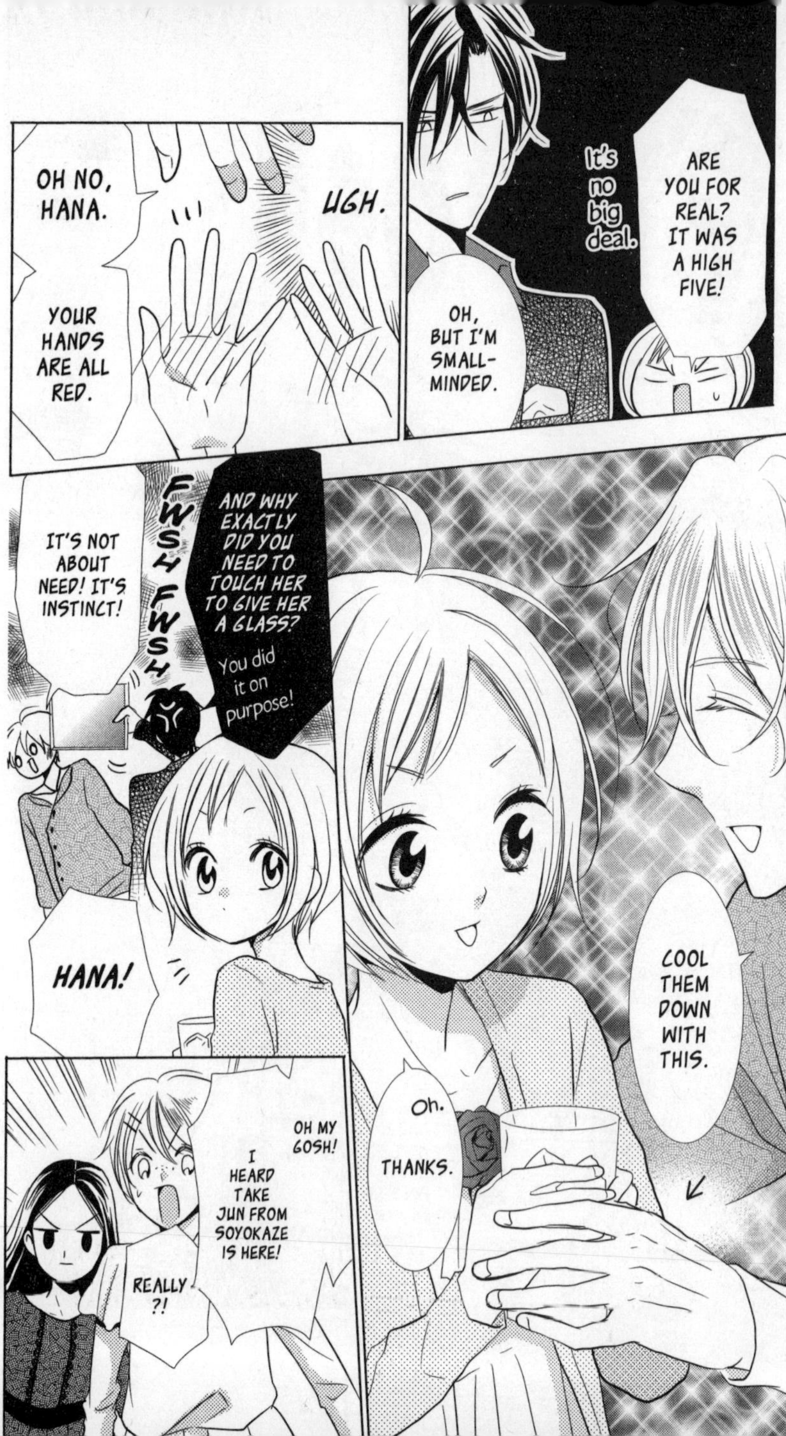
ARE YOU FOR REAL? IT WAS A HIGH FIVE!
It's no big deal.
OH, BUT I'M SMALL-MINDED.
UGH.
OH NO, HANA.
YOUR HANDS ARE ALL RED.
COOL THEM DOWN WITH THIS.
Oh.
THANKS.
AND WHY EXACTLY DID YOU NEED TO TOUCH HER TO GIVE HER A GLASS?
You did it on purpose!
FWSH FWSH
IT'S NOT ABOUT NEED! IT'S INSTINCT!
HANA!
OH MY GOSH!
I HEARD TAKE JUN FROM SOYOKAZE IS HERE!
REALLY?!

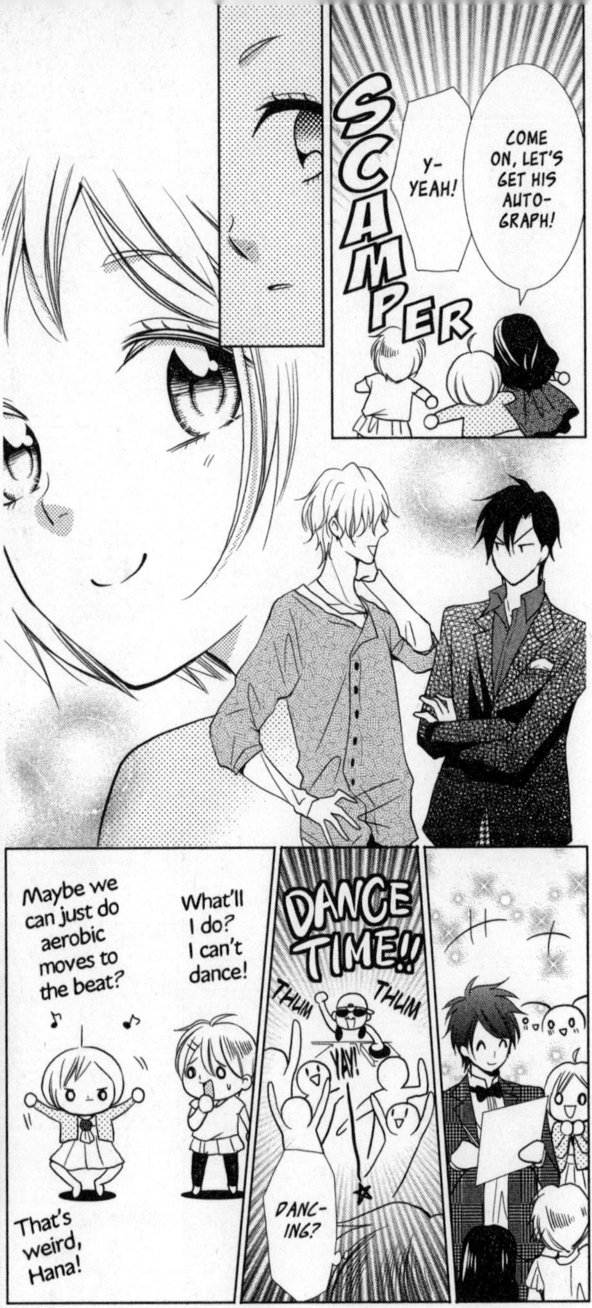
COME ON, LET'S GET HIS AUTO-GRAPH!
Y-YEAH!
SCAMPER
DANCE TIME!!
THUM THUM
YAY!
DANCING?
What'll I do? I can't dance!
Maybe we can just do aerobic moves to the beat?
That's weird, Hana!

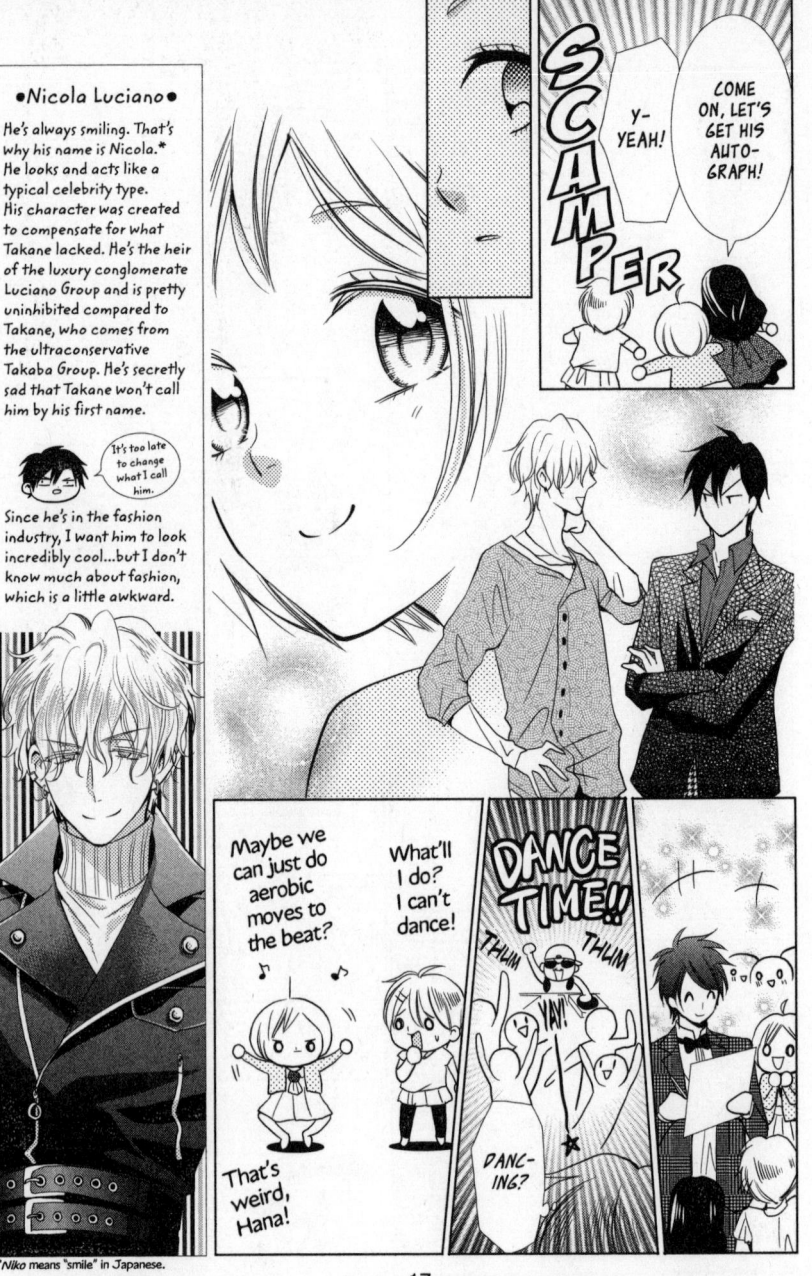

●Nicola Luciano●

He's always smiling. That's why his name is Nicola.* He looks and acts like a typical celebrity type. His character was created to compensate for what Takane lacked. He's the heir of the luxury conglomerate Luciano Group and is pretty uninhibited compared to Takane, who comes from the ultraconservative Takaba Group. He's secretly sad that Takane won't call him by his first name.

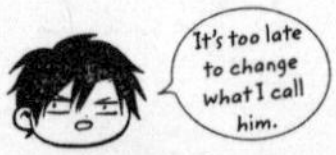
It's too late to change what I call him.

Since he's in the fashion industry, I want him to look incredibly cool...but I don't know much about fashion, which is a little awkward.

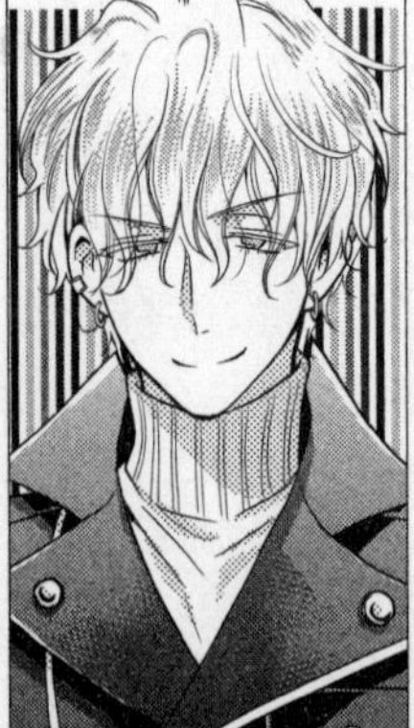

*Niko means "smile" in Japanese.

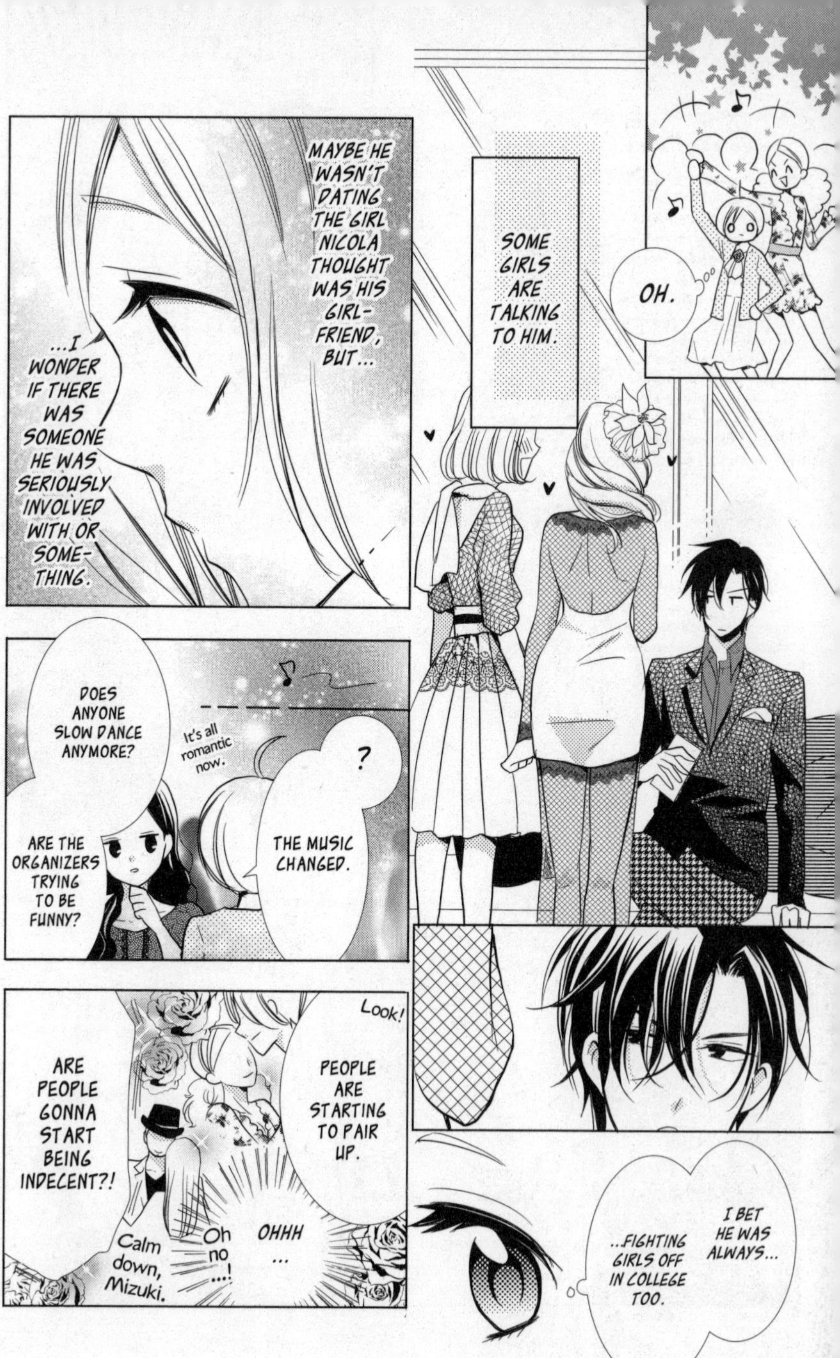
OH.
SOME GIRLS ARE TALKING TO HIM.
I BET HE WAS ALWAYS...
...FIGHTING GIRLS OFF IN COLLEGE TOO.
MAYBE HE WASN'T DATING THE GIRL NICOLA THOUGHT WAS HIS GIRL-FRIEND, BUT...
...I WONDER IF THERE WAS SOMEONE HE WAS SERIOUSLY INVOLVED WITH OR SOME-THING.
?
THE MUSIC CHANGED.
It's all romantic now.
DOES ANYONE SLOW DANCE ANYMORE?
ARE THE ORGANIZERS TRYING TO BE FUNNY?
Look!
PEOPLE ARE STARTING TO PAIR UP.
OHHH ...
Oh no ...!
ARE PEOPLE GONNA START BEING INDECENT?!
Calm down, Mizuki.

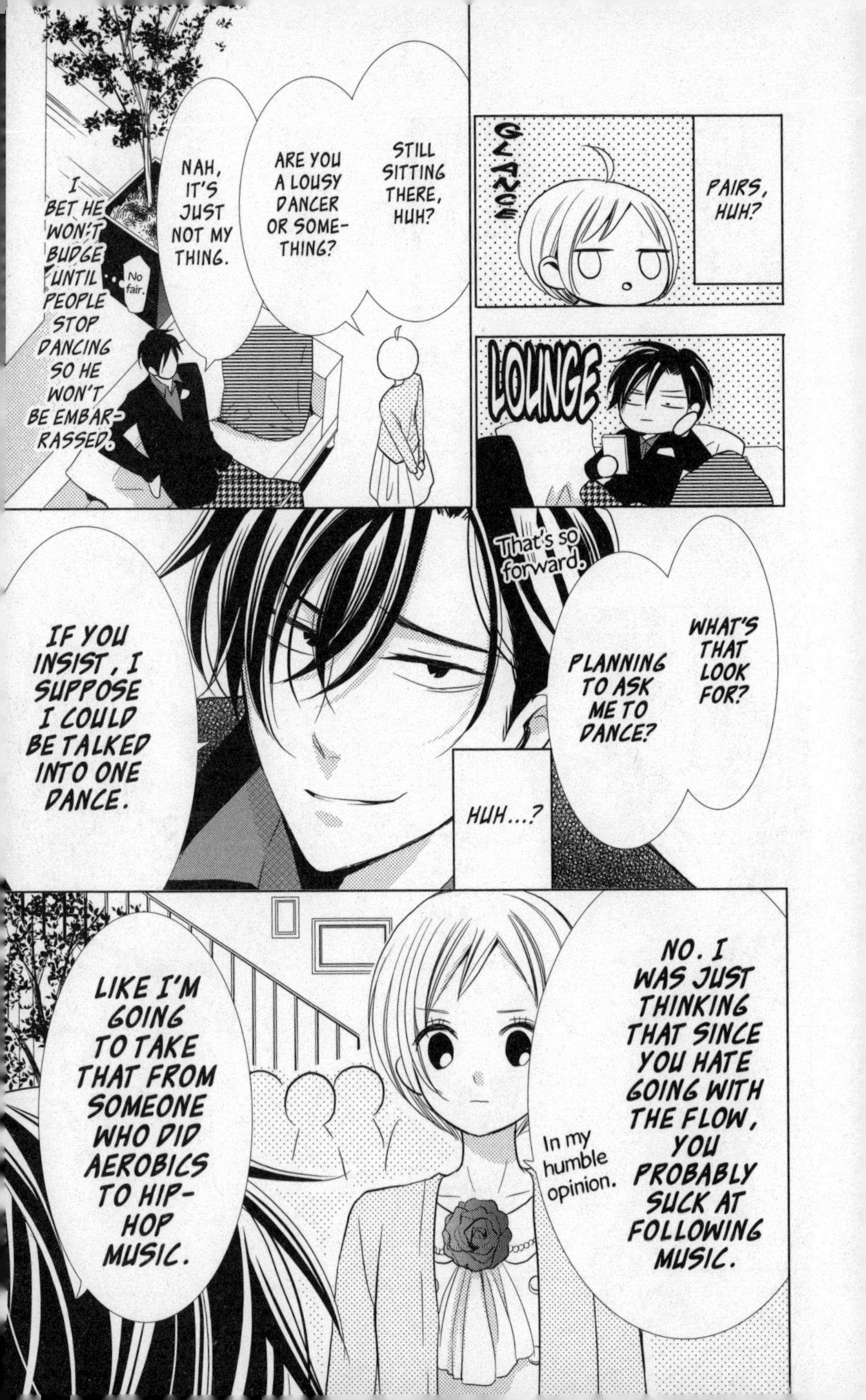
PAIRS, HUH?
GLANCE
LOUNGE
STILL SITTING THERE, HUH?
ARE YOU A LOUSY DANCER OR SOMETHING?
NAH, IT'S JUST NOT MY THING.
I BET HE WON'T BUDGE UNTIL PEOPLE STOP DANCING SO HE WON'T BE EMBARRASSED.
No fair.
WHAT'S THAT LOOK FOR?
PLANNING TO ASK ME TO DANCE?
That's so forward.
HUH...?
IF YOU INSIST, I SUPPOSE I COULD BE TALKED INTO ONE DANCE.
NO. I WAS JUST THINKING THAT SINCE YOU HATE GOING WITH THE FLOW, YOU PROBABLY SUCK AT FOLLOWING MUSIC.
In my humble opinion.
LIKE I'M GOING TO TAKE THAT FROM SOMEONE WHO DID AEROBICS TO HIP-HOP MUSIC.

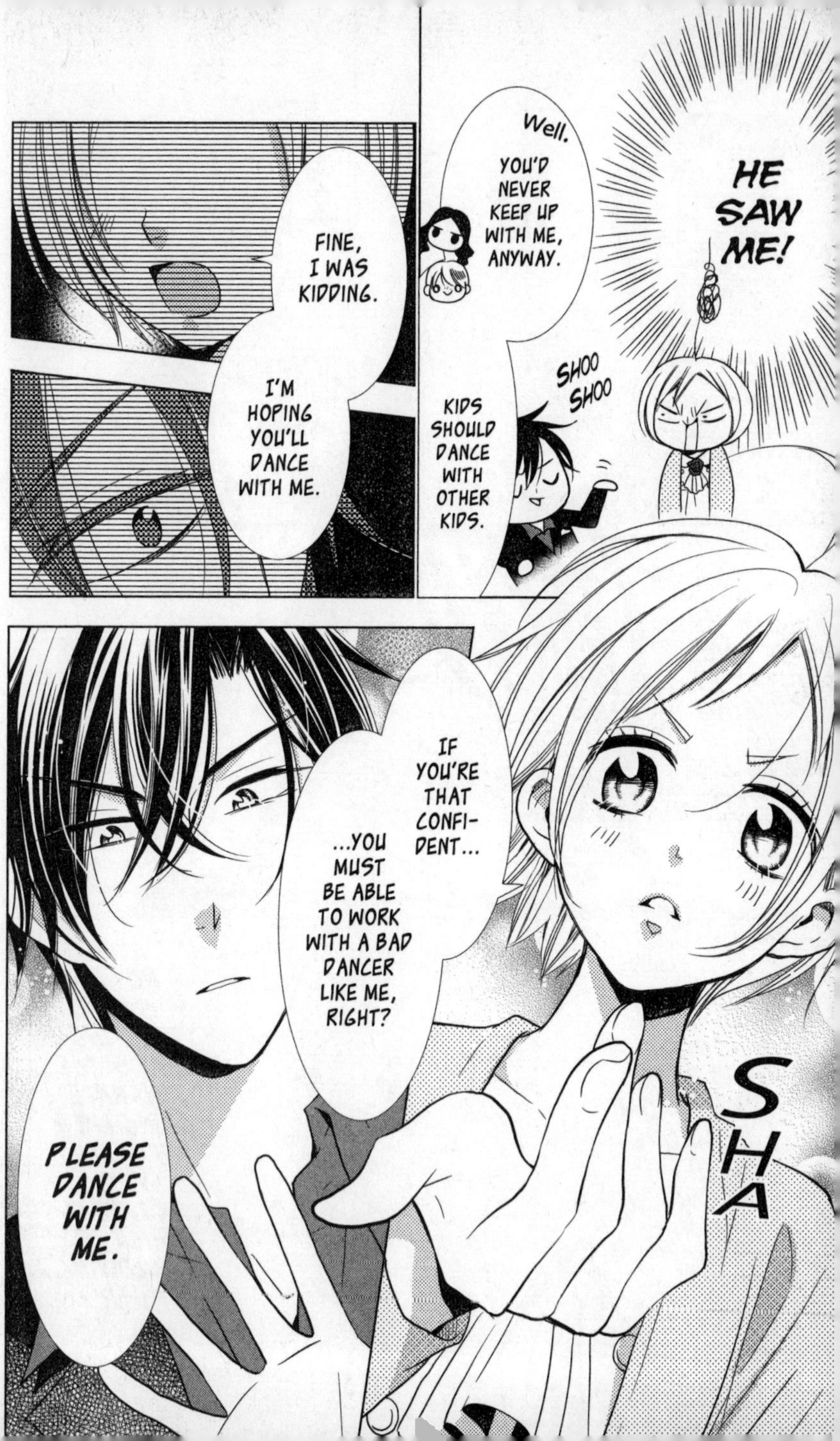
HE SAW ME!
Well.
YOU'D NEVER KEEP UP WITH ME, ANYWAY.
SHOO SHOO
KIDS SHOULD DANCE WITH OTHER KIDS.
FINE, I WAS KIDDING.
I'M HOPING YOU'LL DANCE WITH ME.
SHA
IF YOU'RE THAT CONFIDENT...
...YOU MUST BE ABLE TO WORK WITH A BAD DANCER LIKE ME, RIGHT?
PLEASE DANCE WITH ME.

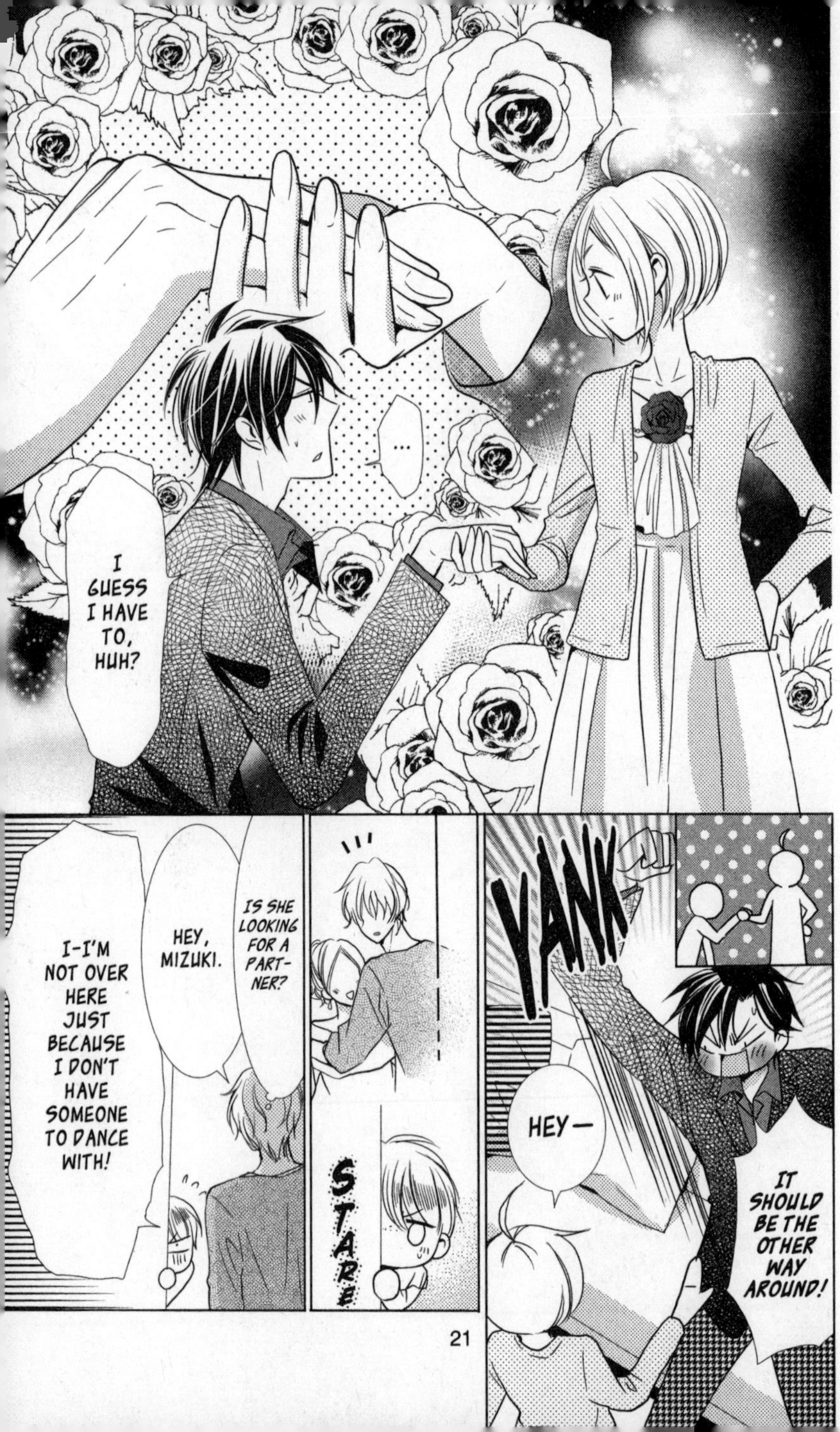
...
I GUESS I HAVE TO, HUH?
YANK
HEY—
IT SHOULD BE THE OTHER WAY AROUND!
IS SHE LOOKING FOR A PART- NER?
STARE
HEY, MIZUKI.
I-I'M NOT OVER HERE JUST BECAUSE I DON'T HAVE SOMEONE TO DANCE WITH!

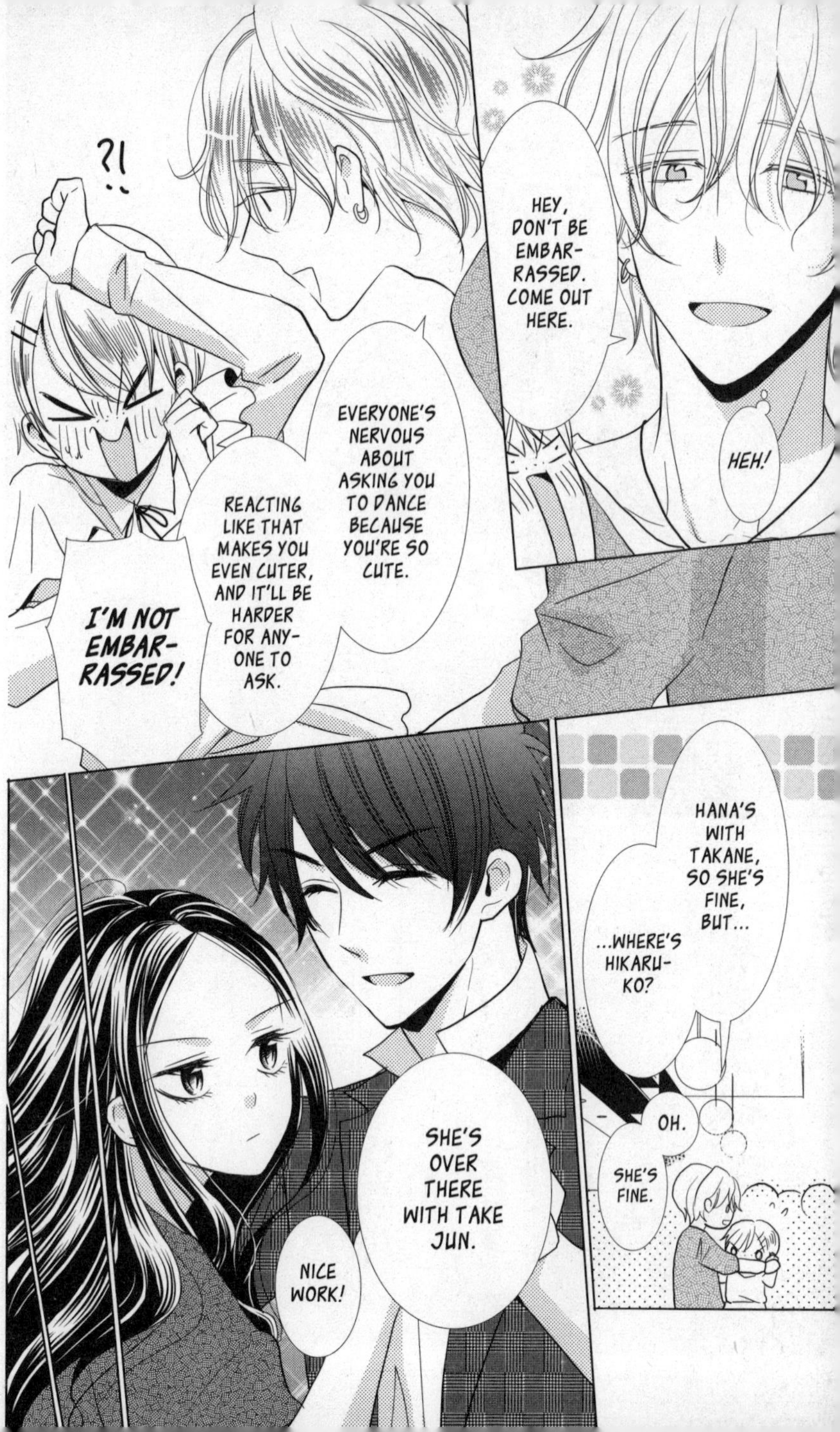
HEY, DON'T BE EMBARRASSED. COME OUT HERE.
HEH!
EVERYONE'S NERVOUS ABOUT ASKING YOU TO DANCE BECAUSE YOU'RE SO CUTE.
REACTING LIKE THAT MAKES YOU EVEN CUTER, AND IT'LL BE HARDER FOR ANYONE TO ASK.
?!
I'M NOT EMBARRASSED!
HANA'S WITH TAKANE, SO SHE'S FINE, BUT...
...WHERE'S HIKARUKO?
OH.
SHE'S FINE.
SHE'S OVER THERE WITH TAKE JUN.
NICE WORK!

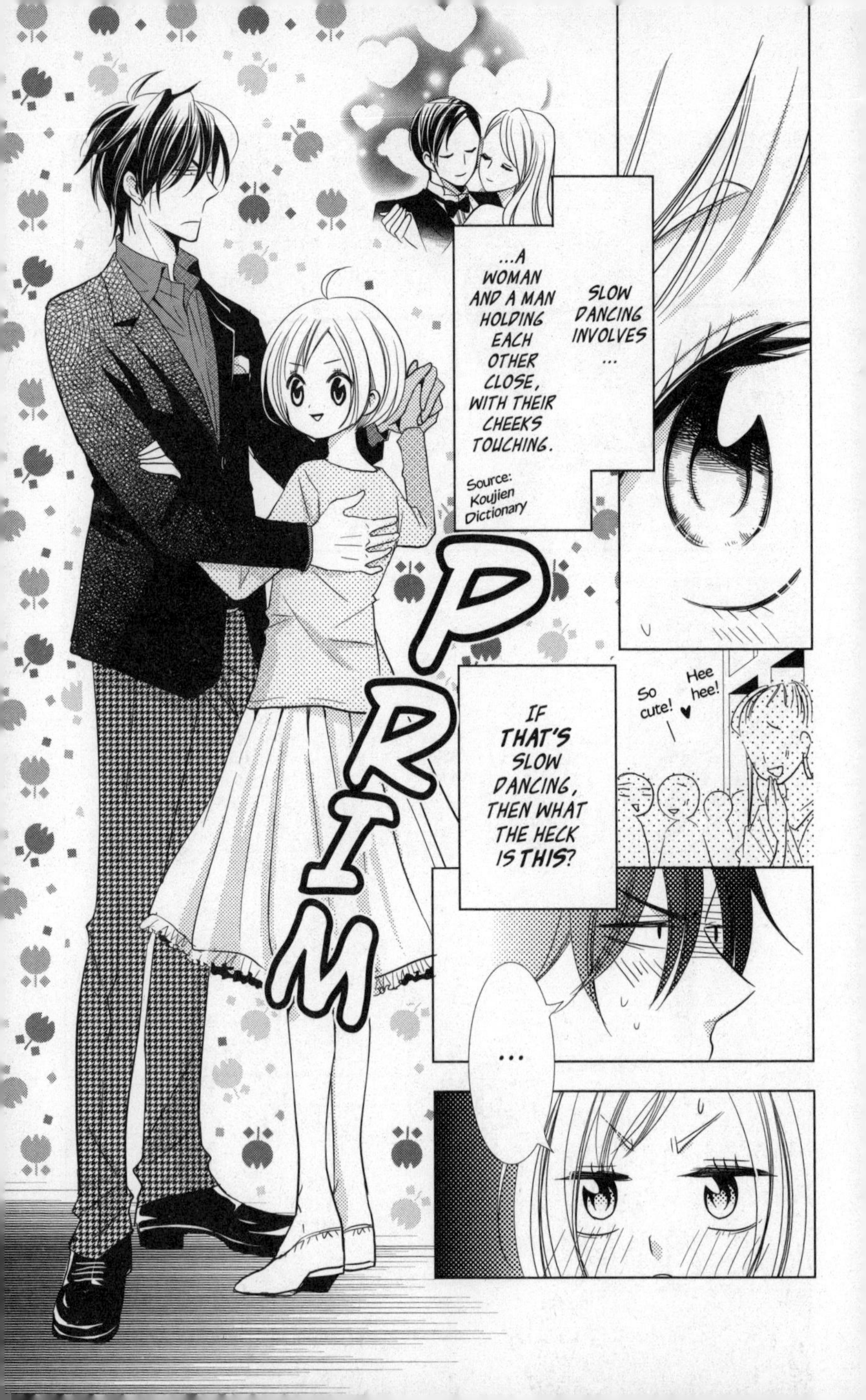
SLOW DANCING INVOLVES ...
...A WOMAN AND A MAN HOLDING EACH OTHER CLOSE, WITH THEIR CHEEKS TOUCHING.
Source: Koujien Dictionary
Hee hee!
So cute!
IF THAT'S SLOW DANCING, THEN WHAT THE HECK IS THIS?
PRIM
...

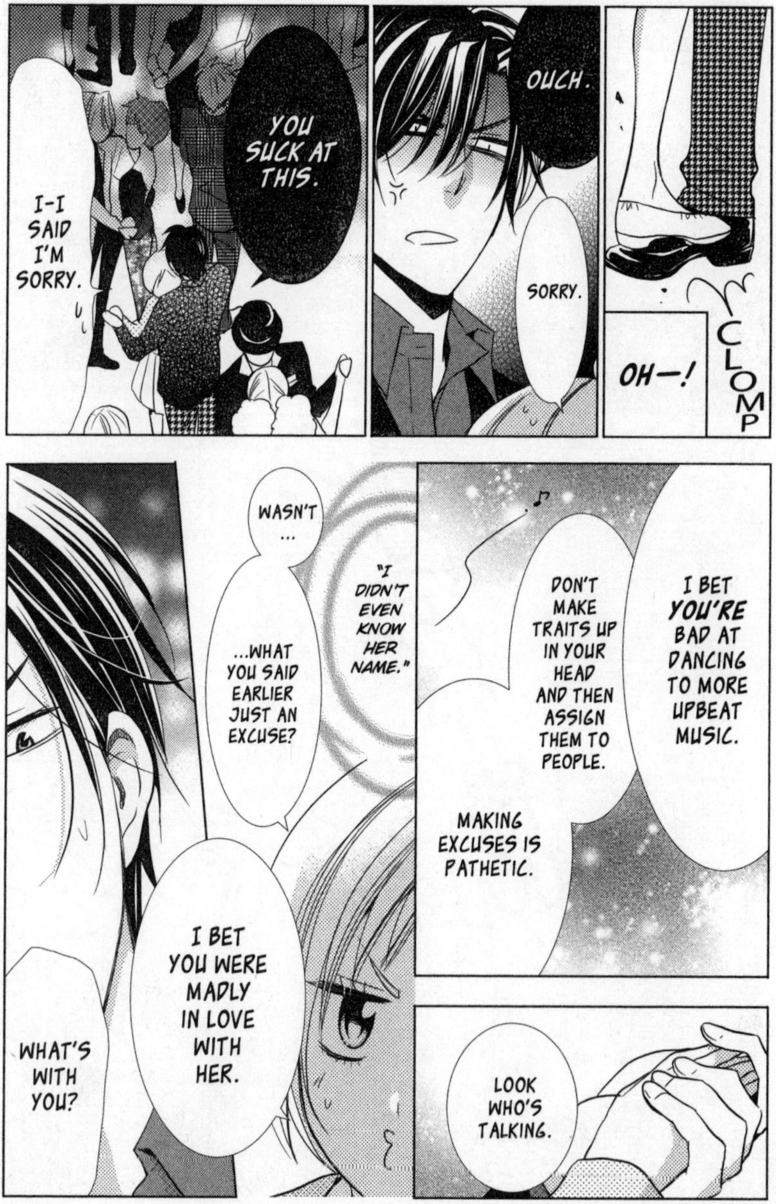
CLOMP
OH—!
OUCH.
SORRY.
YOU SUCK AT THIS.
I-I SAID I'M SORRY.
I BET *YOU'RE* BAD AT DANCING TO MORE UPBEAT MUSIC.
DON'T MAKE TRAITS UP IN YOUR HEAD AND THEN ASSIGN THEM TO PEOPLE.
MAKING EXCUSES IS PATHETIC.
LOOK WHO'S TALKING.
"I DIDN'T EVEN KNOW HER NAME."
WASN'T ...
...WHAT YOU SAID EARLIER JUST AN EXCUSE?
I BET YOU WERE MADLY IN LOVE WITH HER.
WHAT'S WITH YOU?

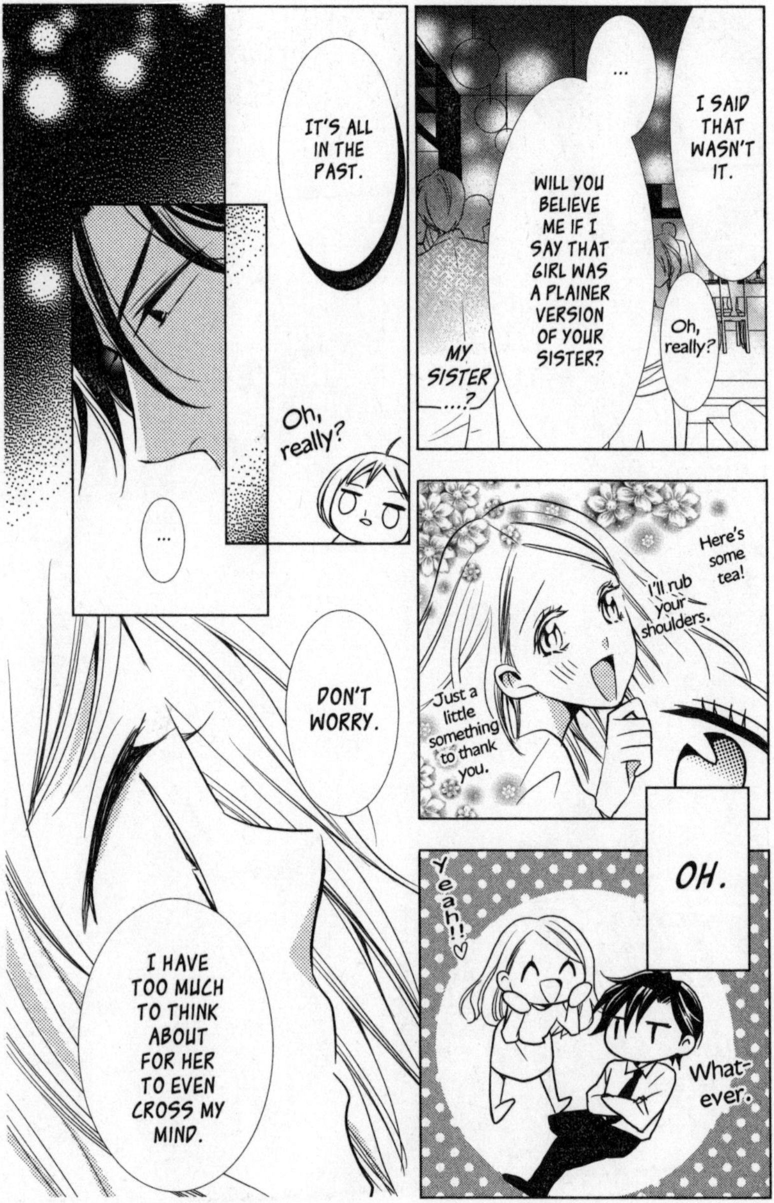
I SAID THAT WASN'T IT.
...
WILL YOU BELIEVE ME IF I SAY THAT GIRL WAS A PLAINER VERSION OF YOUR SISTER?
Oh, really?
MY SISTER ....?
Here's some tea!
I'll rub your shoulders.
Just a little something to thank you.
OH.
Yeah!!♥
What-ever.
IT'S ALL IN THE PAST.
Oh, really?
...
DON'T WORRY.
I HAVE TOO MUCH TO THINK ABOUT FOR HER TO EVEN CROSS MY MIND.

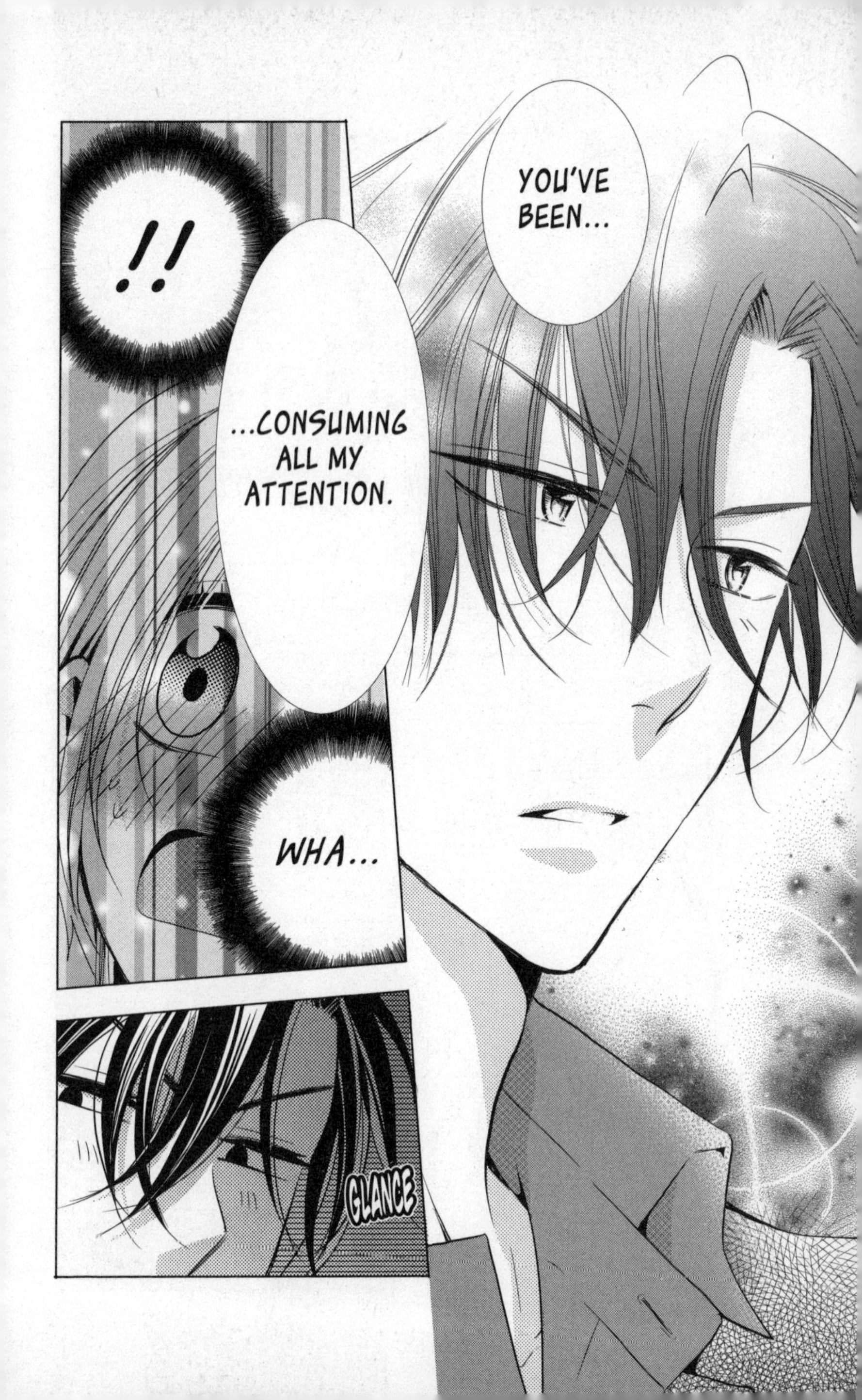
YOU'VE BEEN...
...CONSUMING ALL MY ATTENTION.
!!
WHA...
GLANCE

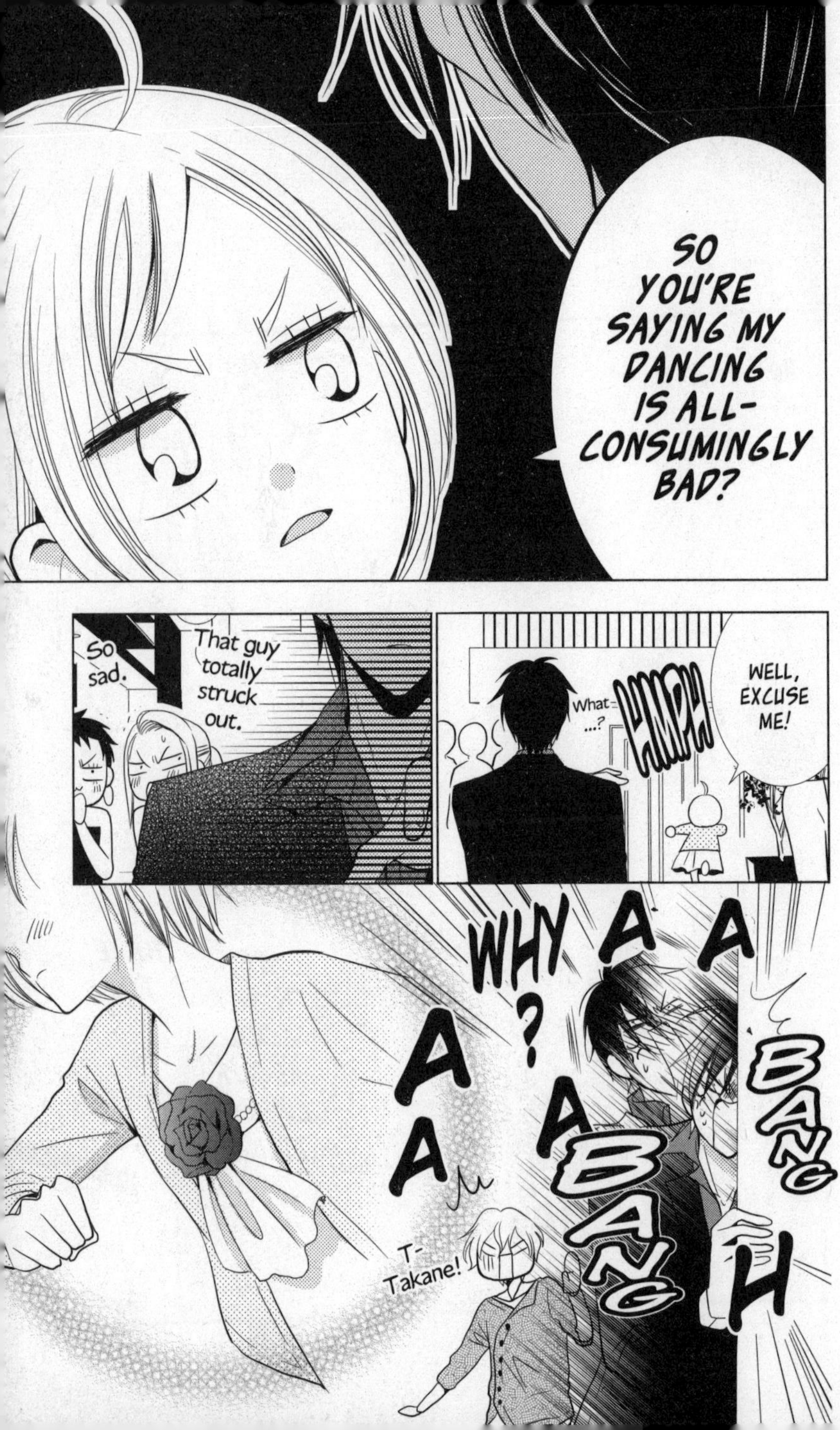
SO YOU'RE SAYING MY DANCING IS ALL-CONSUMINGLY BAD?
WELL, EXCUSE ME!
What ...?
That guy totally struck out.
So sad.
WHY A A A A A H
BANG BANG BANG
T-Takane!

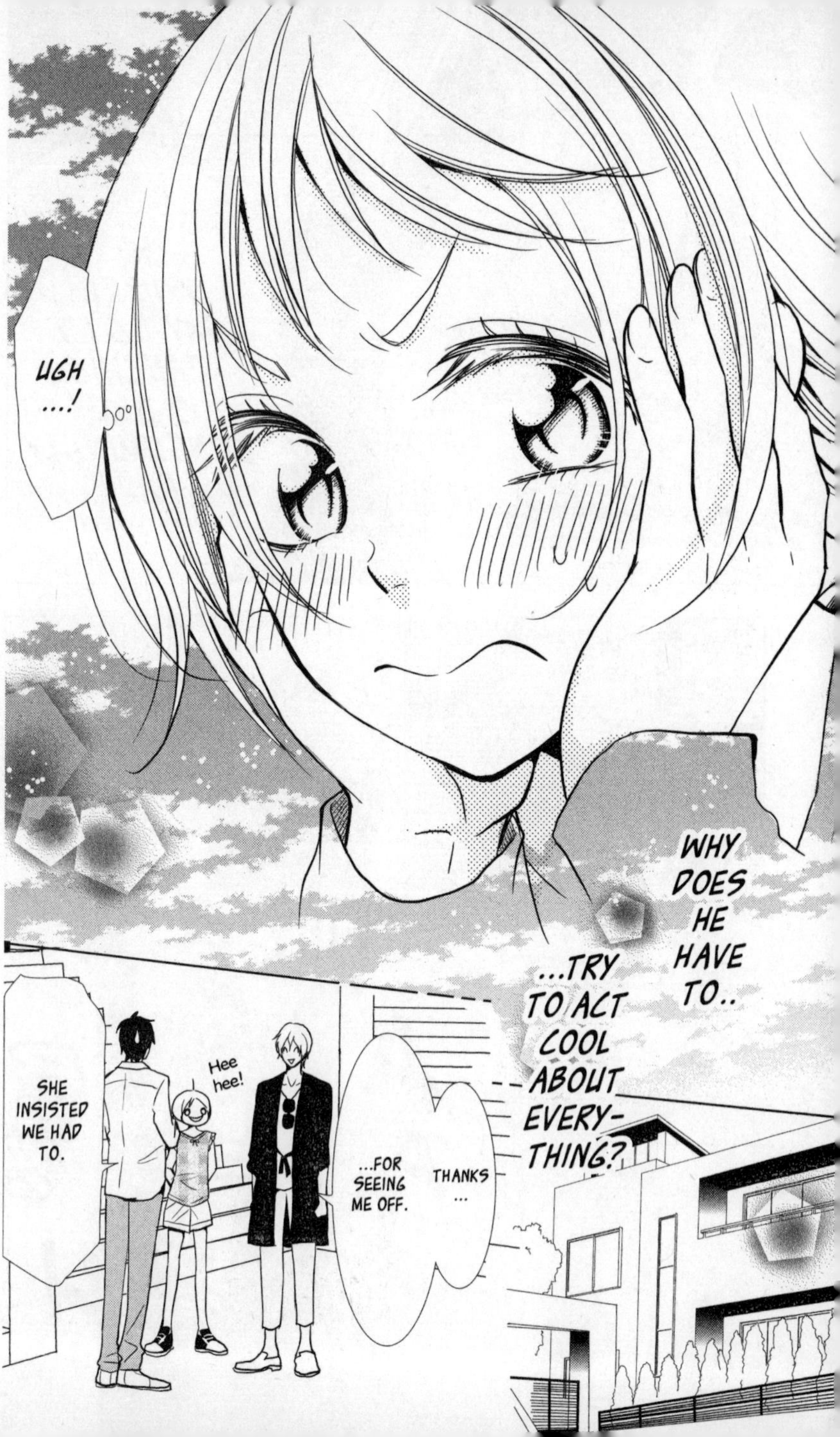
UGH ...!
WHY DOES HE HAVE TO..
...TRY TO ACT COOL ABOUT EVERY-THING?
THANKS ...
...FOR SEEING ME OFF.
Hee hee!
SHE INSISTED WE HAD TO.

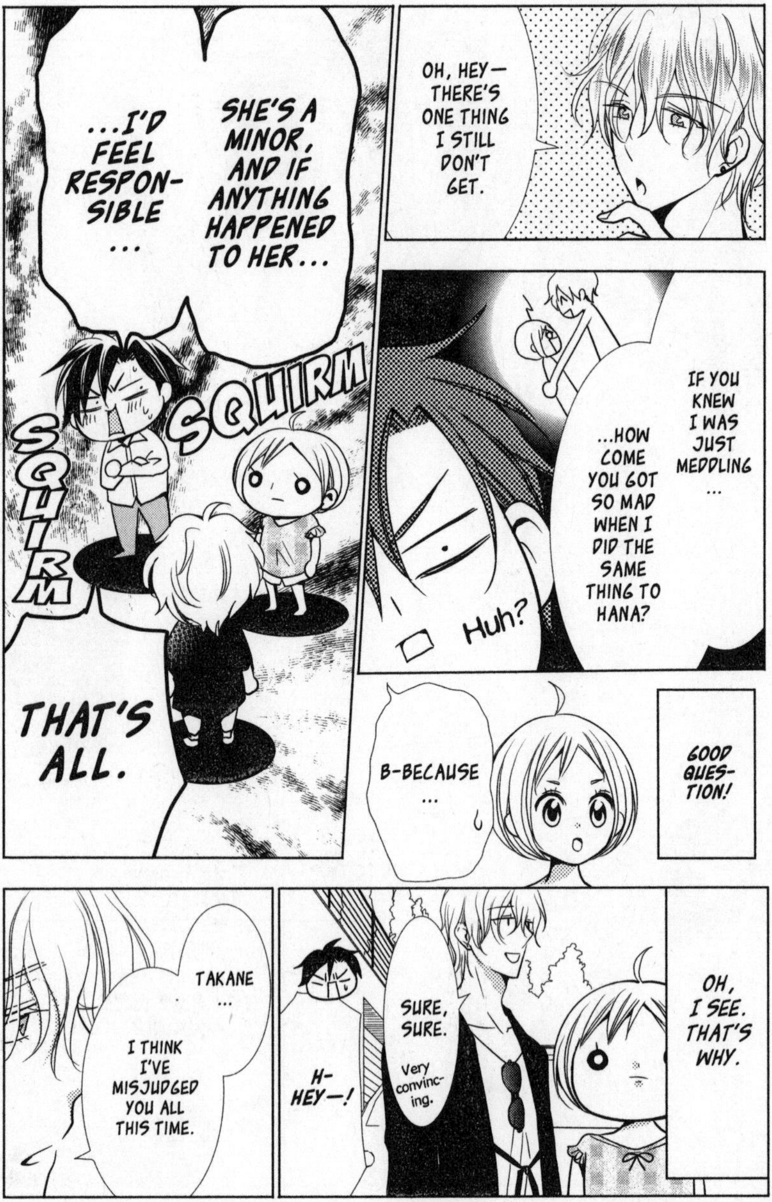
OH, HEY—THERE'S ONE THING I STILL DON'T GET.
IF YOU KNEW I WAS JUST MEDDLING...
...HOW COME YOU GOT SO MAD WHEN I DID THE SAME THING TO HANA?
Huh?
GOOD QUES-TION!
B-BECAUSE...
SHE'S A MINOR, AND IF ANYTHING HAPPENED TO HER...
...I'D FEEL RESPON-SIBLE...
SQUIRM
SQUIRM
THAT'S ALL.
OH, I SEE. THAT'S WHY.
SURE, SURE.
Very convinc-ing.
H-HEY—!
TAKANE...
I THINK I'VE MISJUDGED YOU ALL THIS TIME.

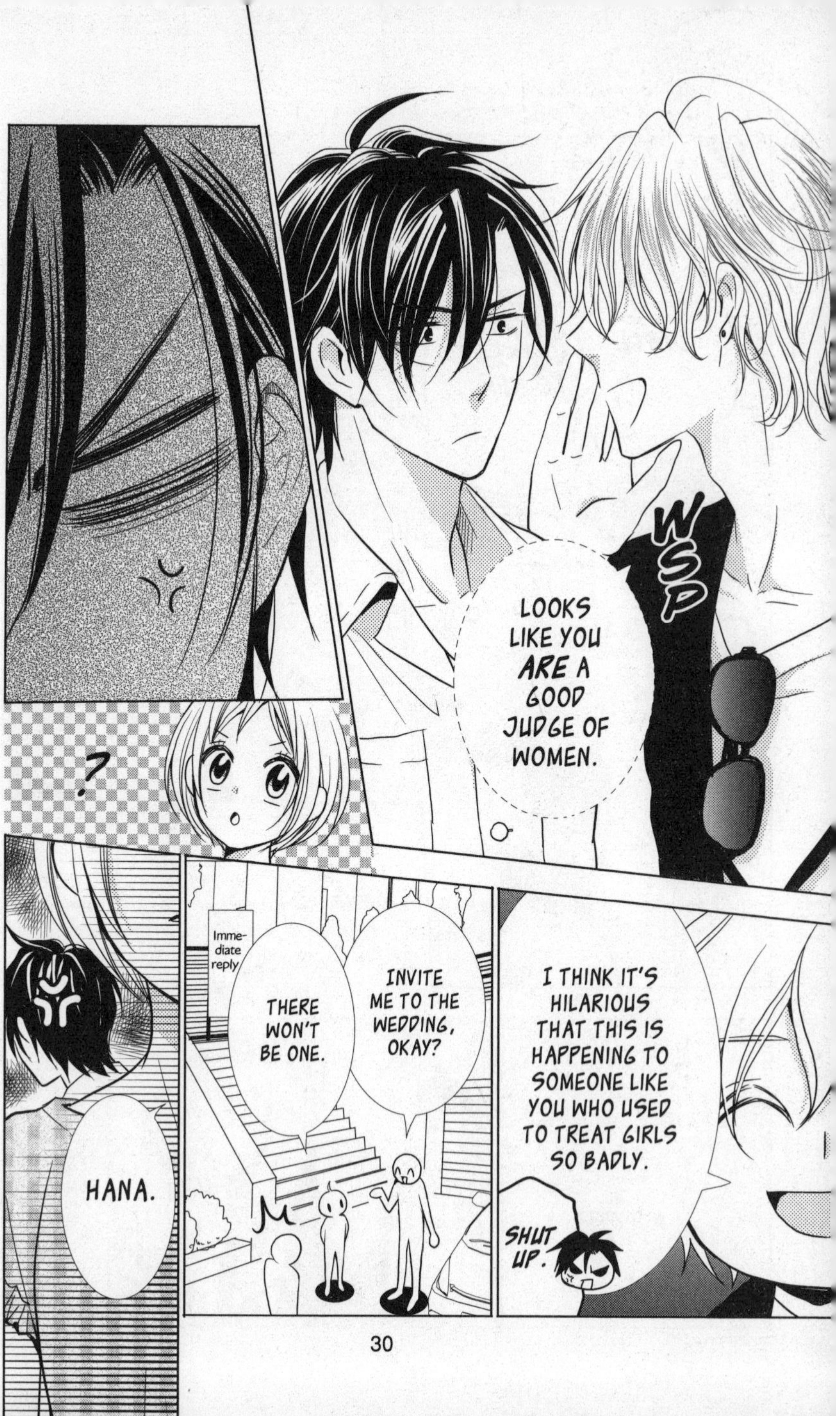
LOOKS LIKE YOU ARE A GOOD JUDGE OF WOMEN.
?
I THINK IT'S HILARIOUS THAT THIS IS HAPPENING TO SOMEONE LIKE YOU WHO USED TO TREAT GIRLS SO BADLY.
SHUT UP.
INVITE ME TO THE WEDDING, OKAY?
THERE WON'T BE ONE.
Immediate reply
HANA.

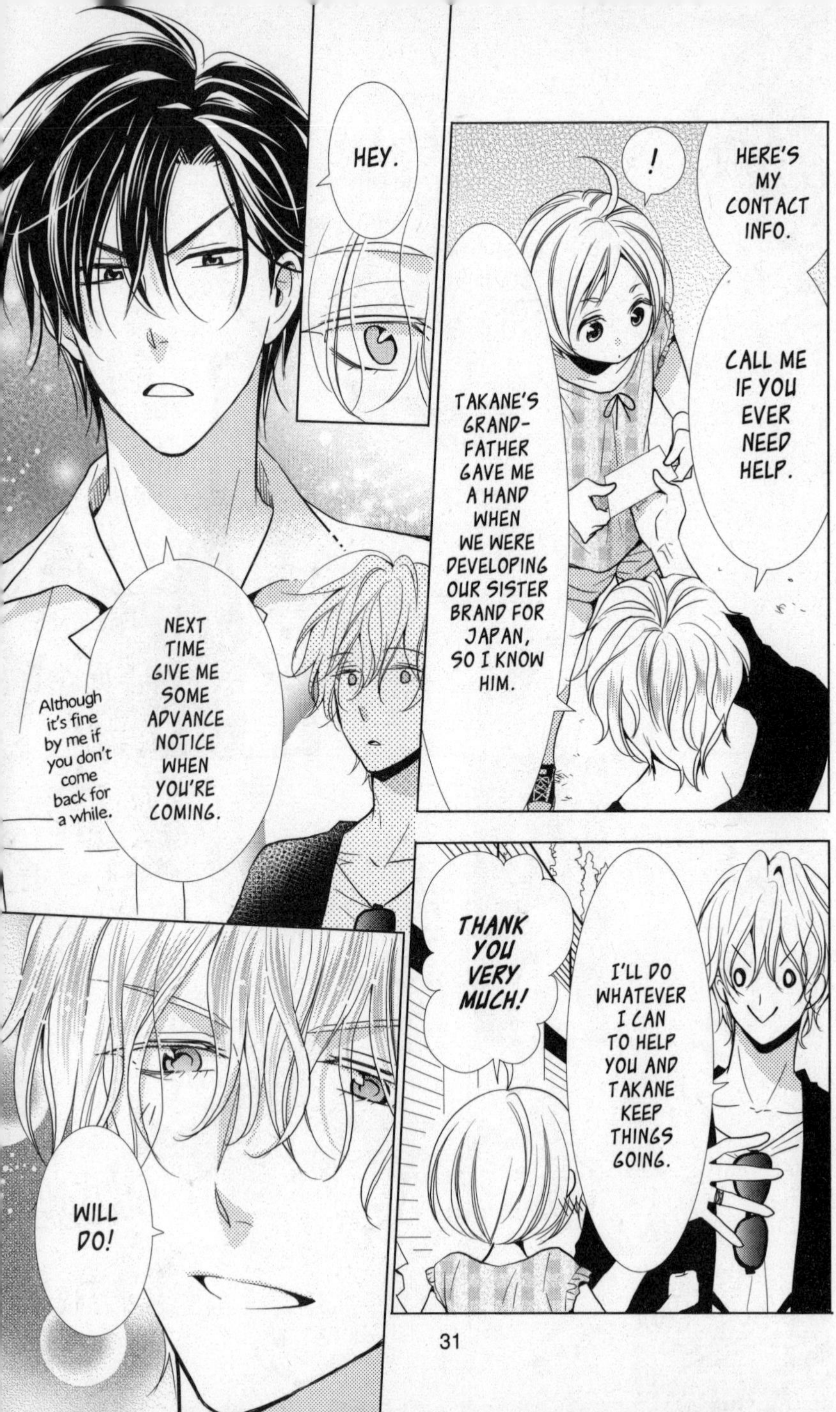
HERE'S MY CONTACT INFO.
!
TAKANE'S GRAND-FATHER GAVE ME A HAND WHEN WE WERE DEVELOPING OUR SISTER BRAND FOR JAPAN, SO I KNOW HIM.
CALL ME IF YOU EVER NEED HELP.
HEY.
NEXT TIME GIVE ME SOME ADVANCE NOTICE WHEN YOU'RE COMING.
Although it's fine by me if you don't come back for a while.
I'LL DO WHATEVER I CAN TO HELP YOU AND TAKANE KEEP THINGS GOING.
THANK YOU VERY MUCH!
WILL DO!

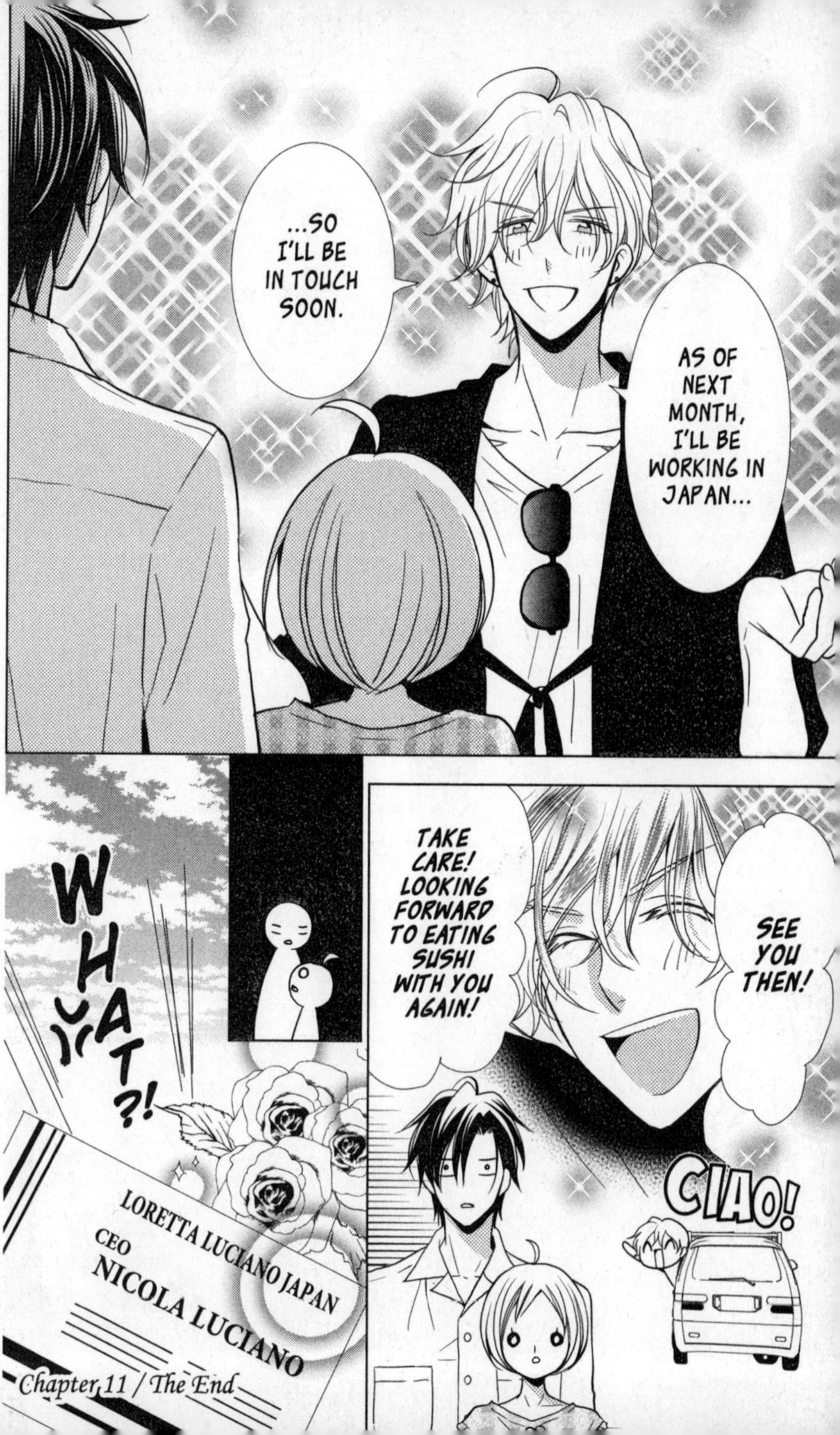
AS OF NEXT MONTH, I'LL BE WORKING IN JAPAN...
...SO I'LL BE IN TOUCH SOON.
SEE YOU THEN!
TAKE CARE! LOOKING FORWARD TO EATING SUSHI WITH YOU AGAIN!
CIAO!
WHAT?!
LORETTA LUCIANO JAPAN
CEO
NICOLA LUCIANO
Chapter 11 / The End

Chapter 12

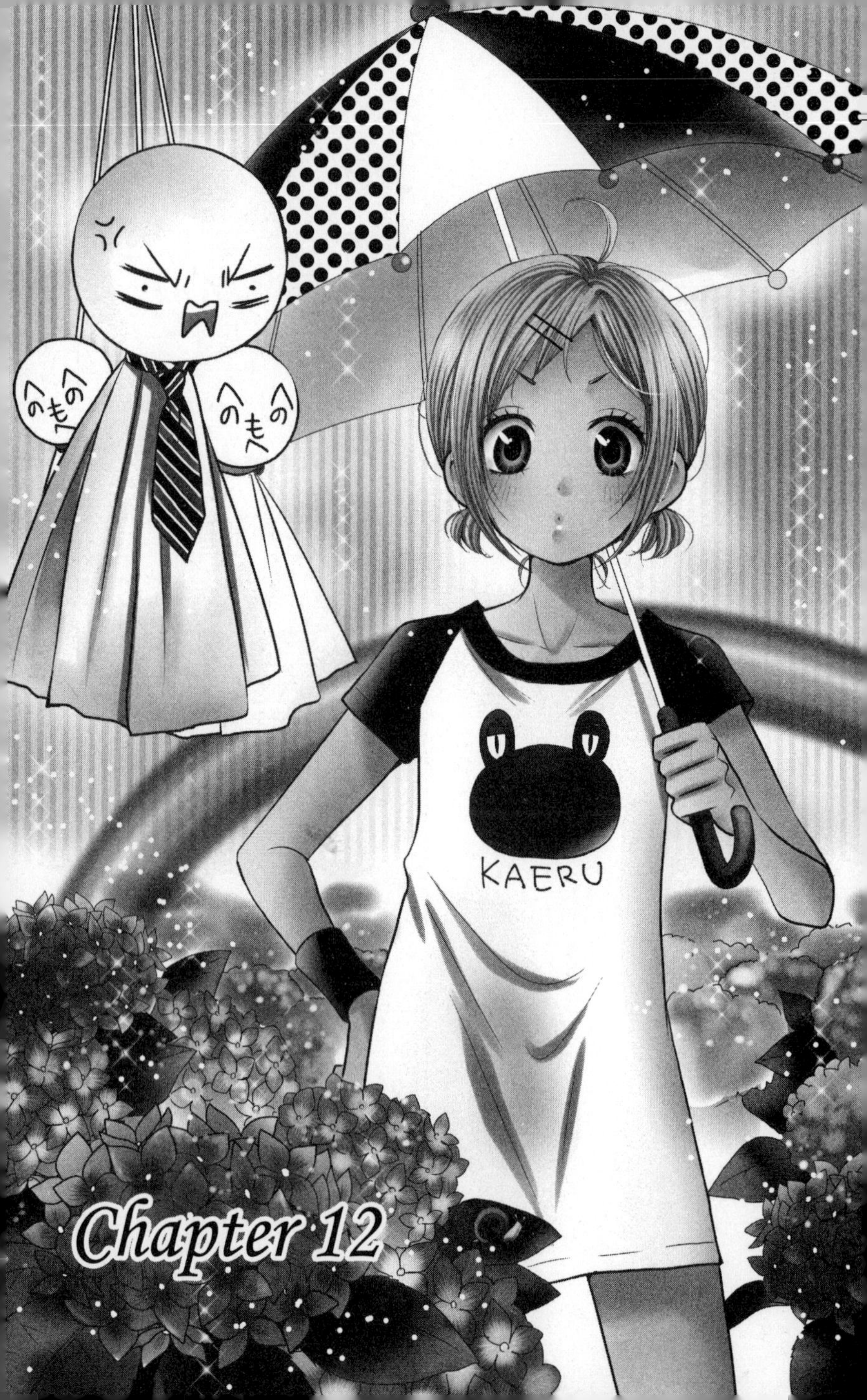
KAERU

A Professional Italian

NICOLA LUCIANO HAS JUST ARRIVED IN JAPAN!
LET'S TRY TO CHAT WITH HIM.
EEE !!
Nicola!
Over here!
EEEE!!
LOTS OF FANS ARE HERE TODAY!
YEAH.
I'M ECSTATIC THAT ALL THESE ANGELS CAME TO GREET ME.
I THOUGHT I MADE A MISTAKE AND BOARDED A FLIGHT TO HEAVEN.
EEEE
YOU SURE I'M OKAY? AM I REALLY ALIVE?
CAN YOU PINCH ME?
SQUEEZE
HE LIVES UP TO HIS REPUTA-TION, FOLKS!

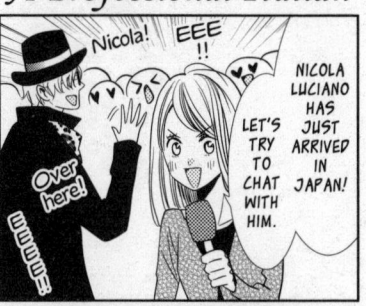

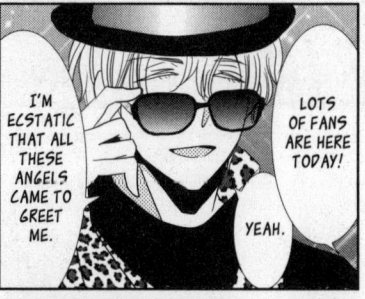

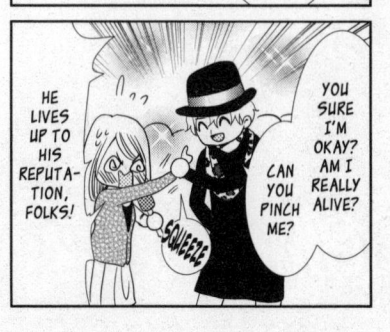

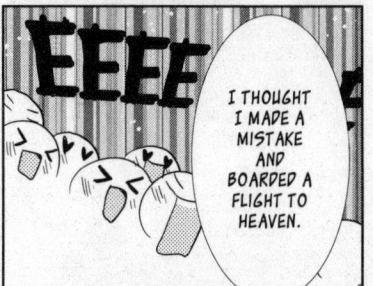

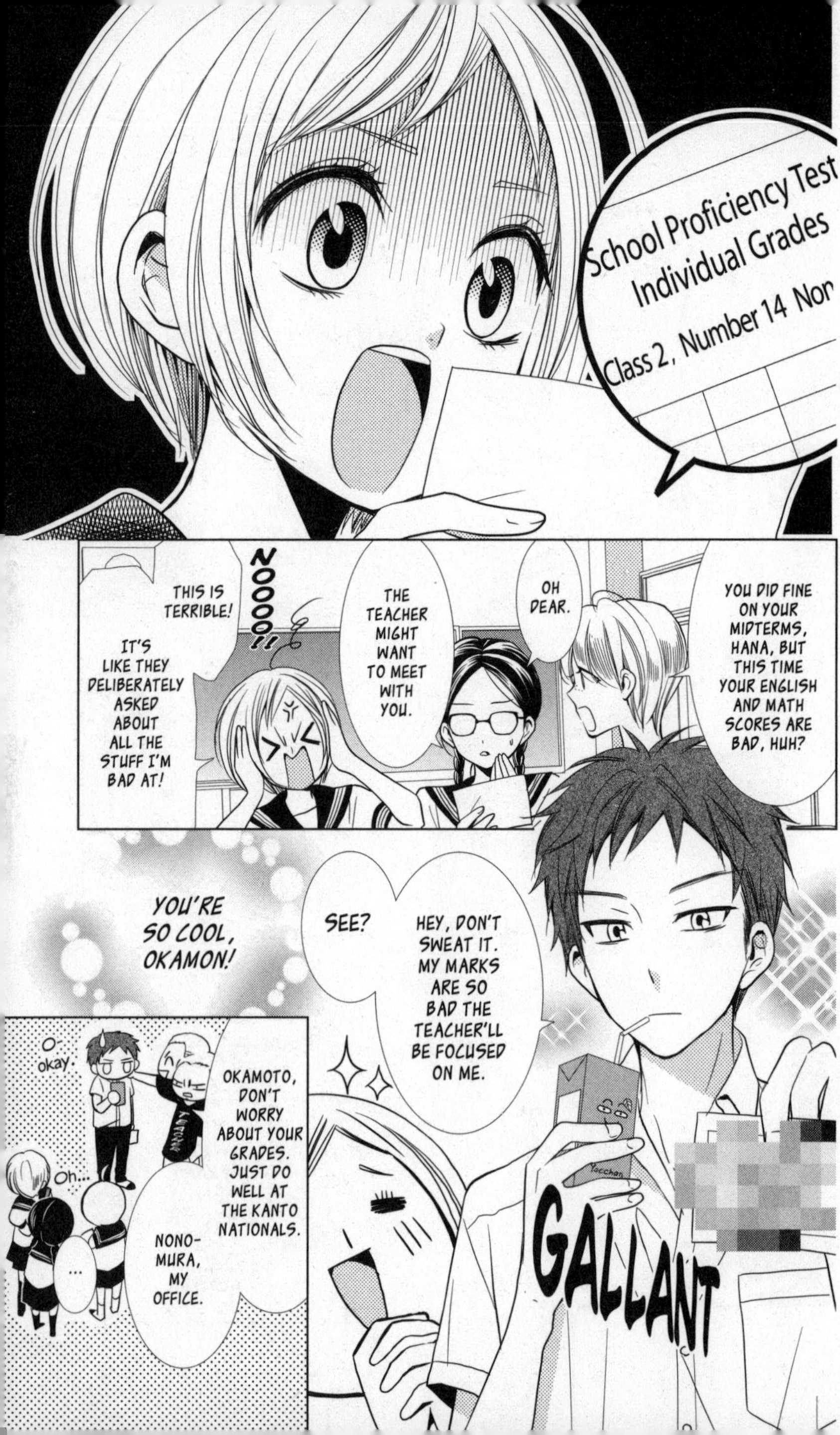
School Proficiency Test Individual Grades
Class 2, Number 14 Non
You did fine on your midterms, Hana, but this time your English and math scores are bad, huh?
Oh dear.
The teacher might want to meet with you.
NOOOOO!!
This is terrible!
It's like they deliberately asked about all the stuff I'm bad at!
Hey, don't sweat it. My marks are so bad the teacher'll be focused on me.
See?
You're so cool, Okamon!
GALLANT
Okamoto, don't worry about your grades. Just do well at the Kanto nationals.
Nonomura, my office.
O-okay.
Oh...
...

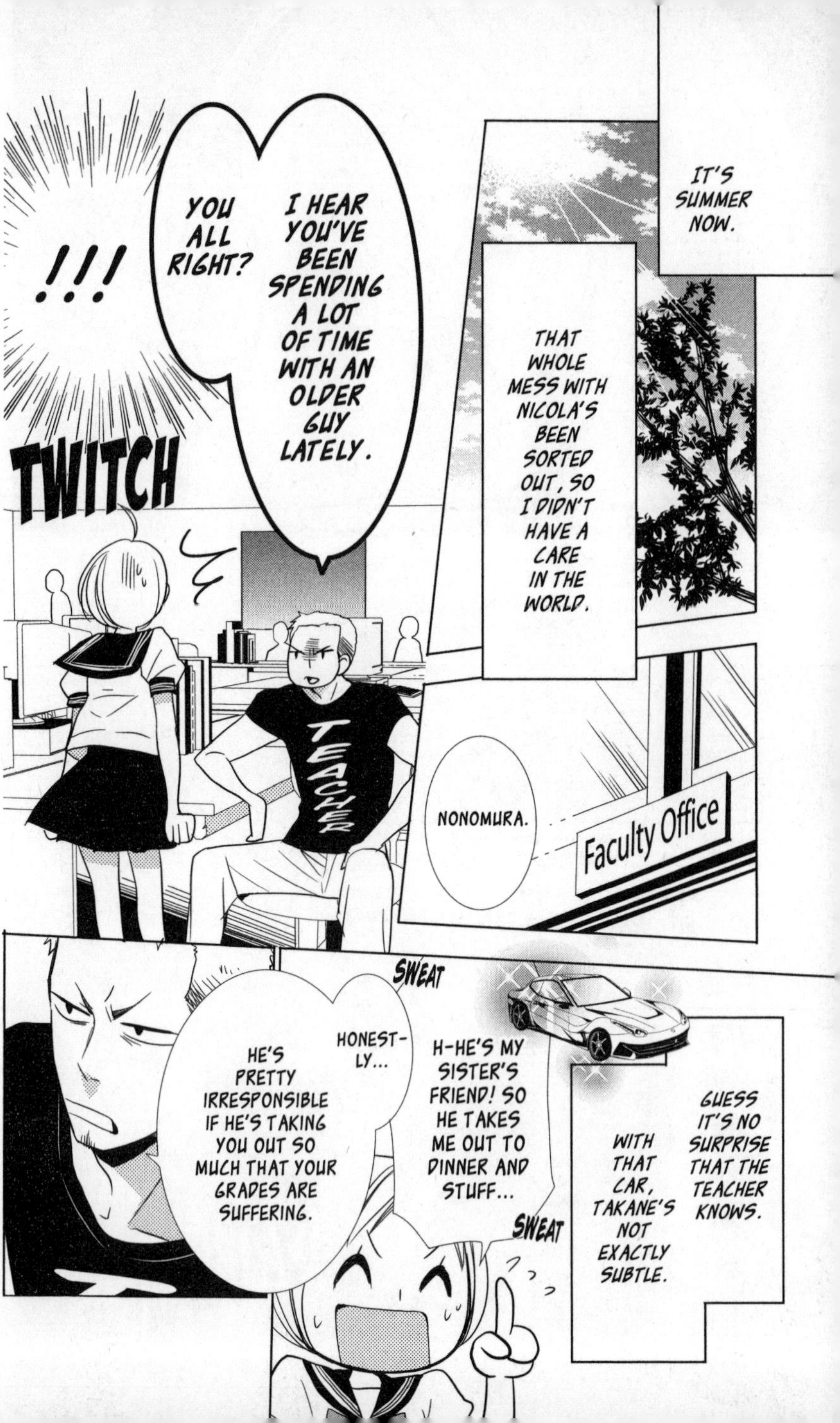
IT'S SUMMER NOW.
THAT WHOLE MESS WITH NICOLA'S BEEN SORTED OUT, SO I DIDN'T HAVE A CARE IN THE WORLD.
Faculty Office
NONOMURA.
I HEAR YOU'VE BEEN SPENDING A LOT OF TIME WITH AN OLDER GUY LATELY.
YOU ALL RIGHT?
!!!
TWITCH
TEACHER
GUESS IT'S NO SURPRISE THAT THE TEACHER KNOWS.
WITH THAT CAR, TAKANE'S NOT EXACTLY SUBTLE.
SWEAT
H-HE'S MY SISTER'S FRIEND! SO HE TAKES ME OUT TO DINNER AND STUFF...
SWEAT
HONEST-LY...
HE'S PRETTY IRRESPONSIBLE IF HE'S TAKING YOU OUT SO MUCH THAT YOUR GRADES ARE SUFFERING.

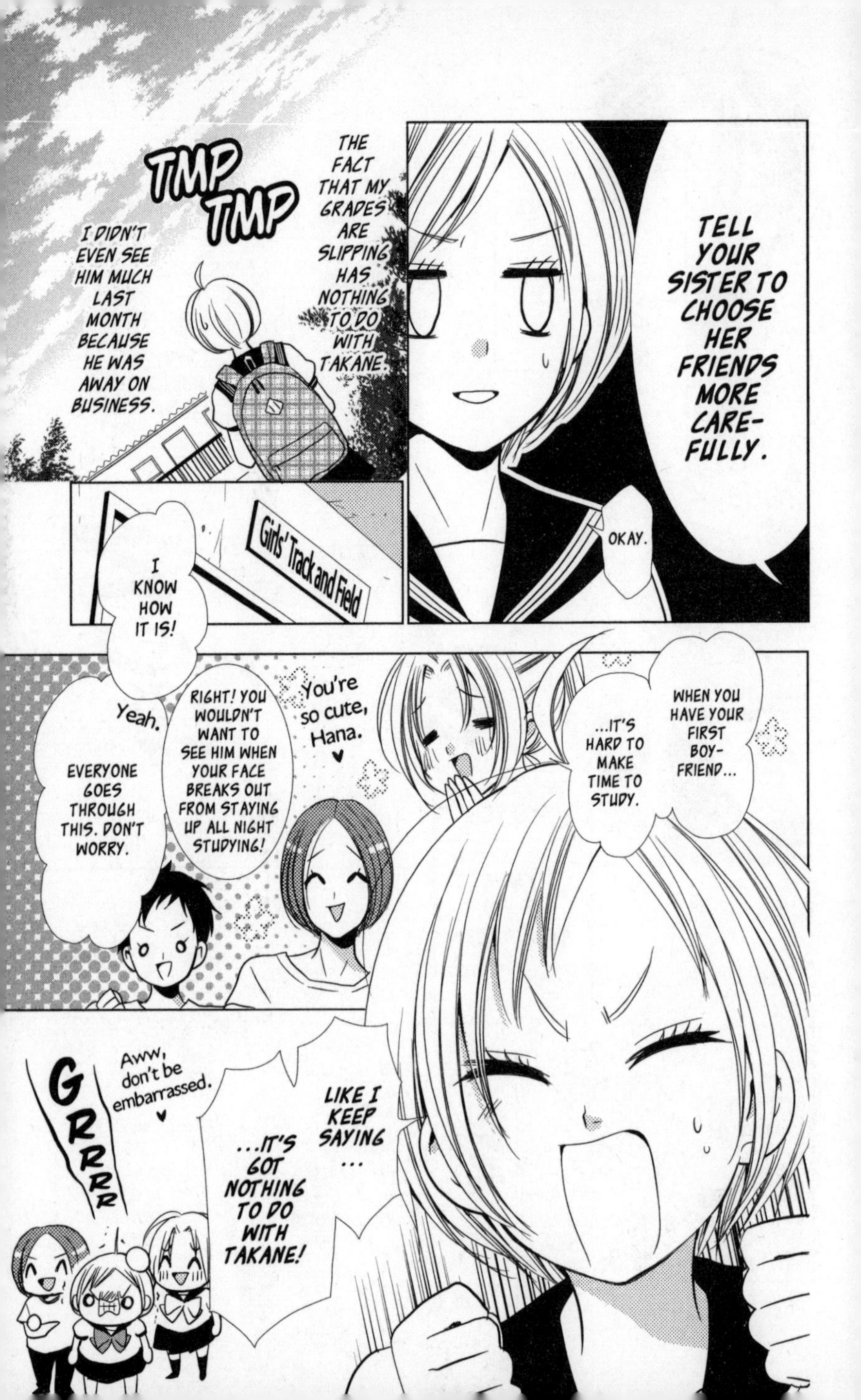
TELL YOUR SISTER TO CHOOSE HER FRIENDS MORE CARE-FULLY.
OKAY.
THE FACT THAT MY GRADES ARE SLIPPING HAS NOTHING TO DO WITH TAKANE.
TMP TMP
I DIDN'T EVEN SEE HIM MUCH LAST MONTH BECAUSE HE WAS AWAY ON BUSINESS.
Girls' Track and Field
I KNOW HOW IT IS!
WHEN YOU HAVE YOUR FIRST BOY-FRIEND...
...IT'S HARD TO MAKE TIME TO STUDY.
You're so cute, Hana.
RIGHT! YOU WOULDN'T WANT TO SEE HIM WHEN YOUR FACE BREAKS OUT FROM STAYING UP ALL NIGHT STUDYING!
Yeah.
EVERYONE GOES THROUGH THIS. DON'T WORRY.
LIKE I KEEP SAYING...
...IT'S GOT NOTHING TO DO WITH TAKANE!
Aww, don't be embarrassed.
GRRRR

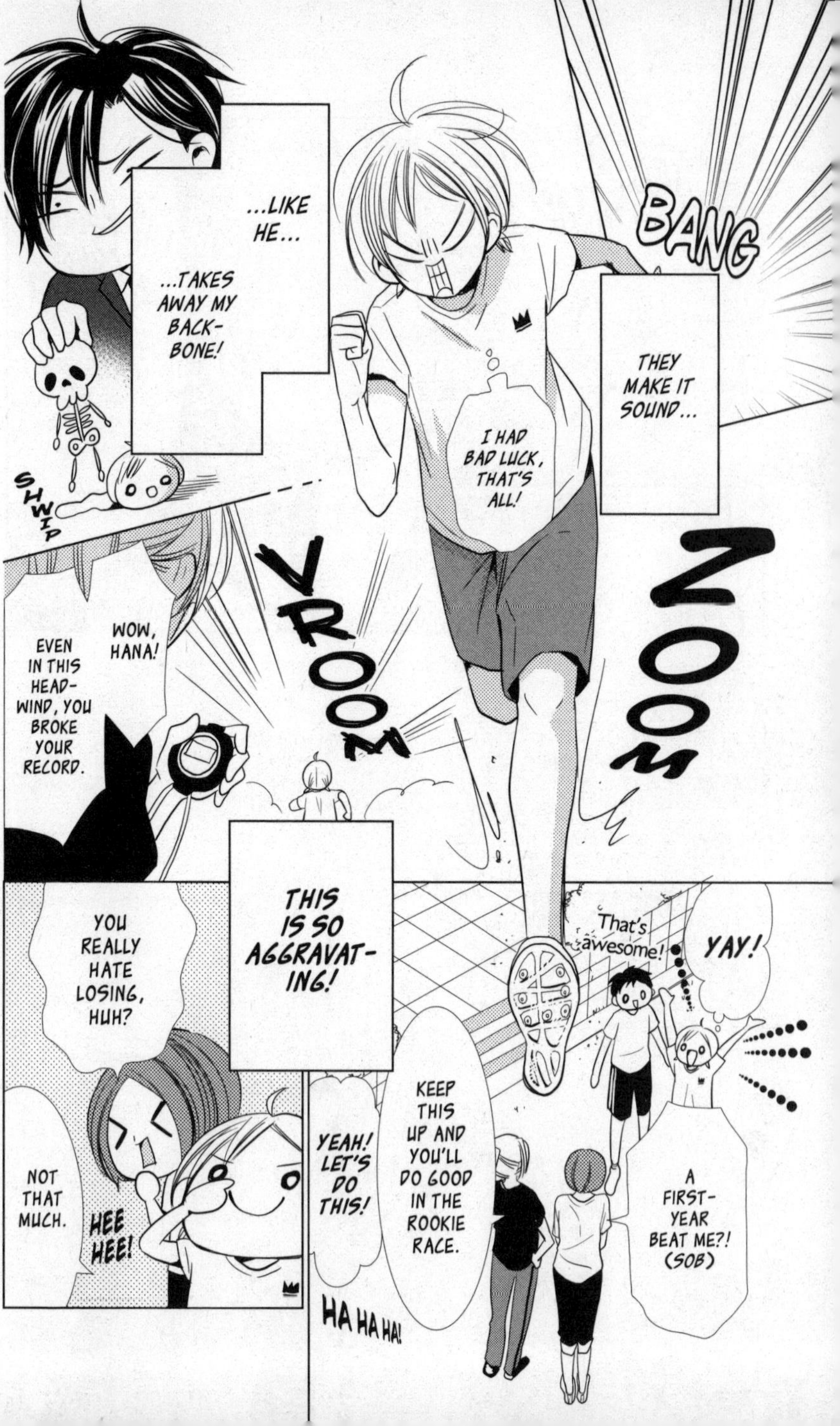
BANG
THEY MAKE IT SOUND...
I HAD BAD LUCK, THAT'S ALL!
...LIKE HE...
...TAKES AWAY MY BACK-BONE!
SHWIP
ZOOM
VROOM
WOW, HANA!
EVEN IN THIS HEAD-WIND, YOU BROKE YOUR RECORD.
YAY!
That's awesome!
A FIRST-YEAR BEAT ME?! (SOB)
KEEP THIS UP AND YOU'LL DO GOOD IN THE ROOKIE RACE.
YEAH! LET'S DO THIS!
HA HA HA!
THIS IS SO AGGRAVAT-ING!
YOU REALLY HATE LOSING, HUH?
NOT THAT MUCH.
HEE HEE!

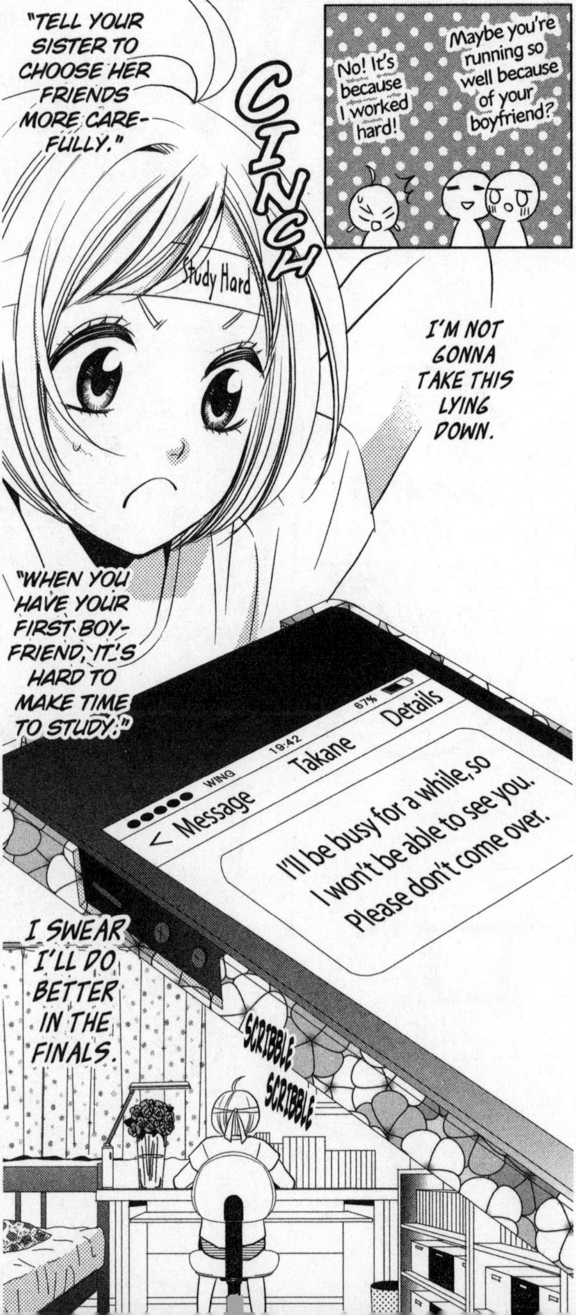
Maybe you're running so well because of your boyfriend?
No! It's because I worked hard!
I'M NOT GONNA TAKE THIS LYING DOWN.
CINCH
Study Hard
"TELL YOUR SISTER TO CHOOSE HER FRIENDS MORE CAREFULLY."
"WHEN YOU HAVE YOUR FIRST BOYFRIEND, IT'S HARD TO MAKE TIME TO STUDY."
WING 19:42 67%
< Message Takane Details
I'll be busy for a while, so
I won't be able to see you.
Please don't come over.
I SWEAR I'LL DO BETTER IN THE FINALS.
SCRIBBLE SCRIBBLE

•Souma Okamoto•

I haven't had a chance to mention his full name in the story, so I'll do it here. He was originally called Hayate.

Even when he was younger, he was athletic and took good care of younger kids. He even helped out in the family restaurant. Basically he's different from Takane, the book-smart rich boy, in every way.

He's only a first-year, but he's a starter on the school soccer team. Since I'm always drawing boys with long, annoying bangs, it's nice to have a chance to draw short hair!

I haven't been able to draw him like this very much, since Takane hogs the spotlight in this manga. ↴

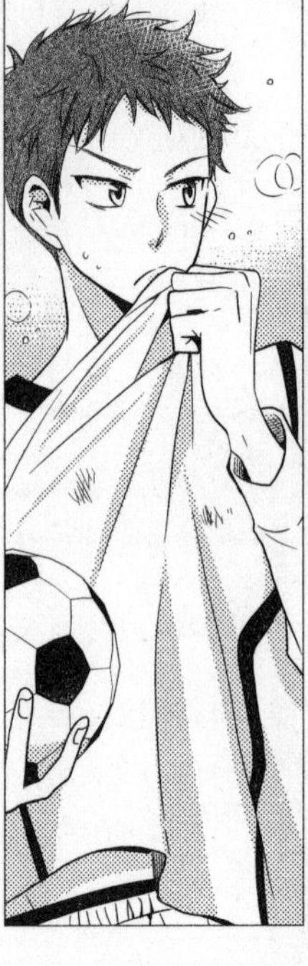

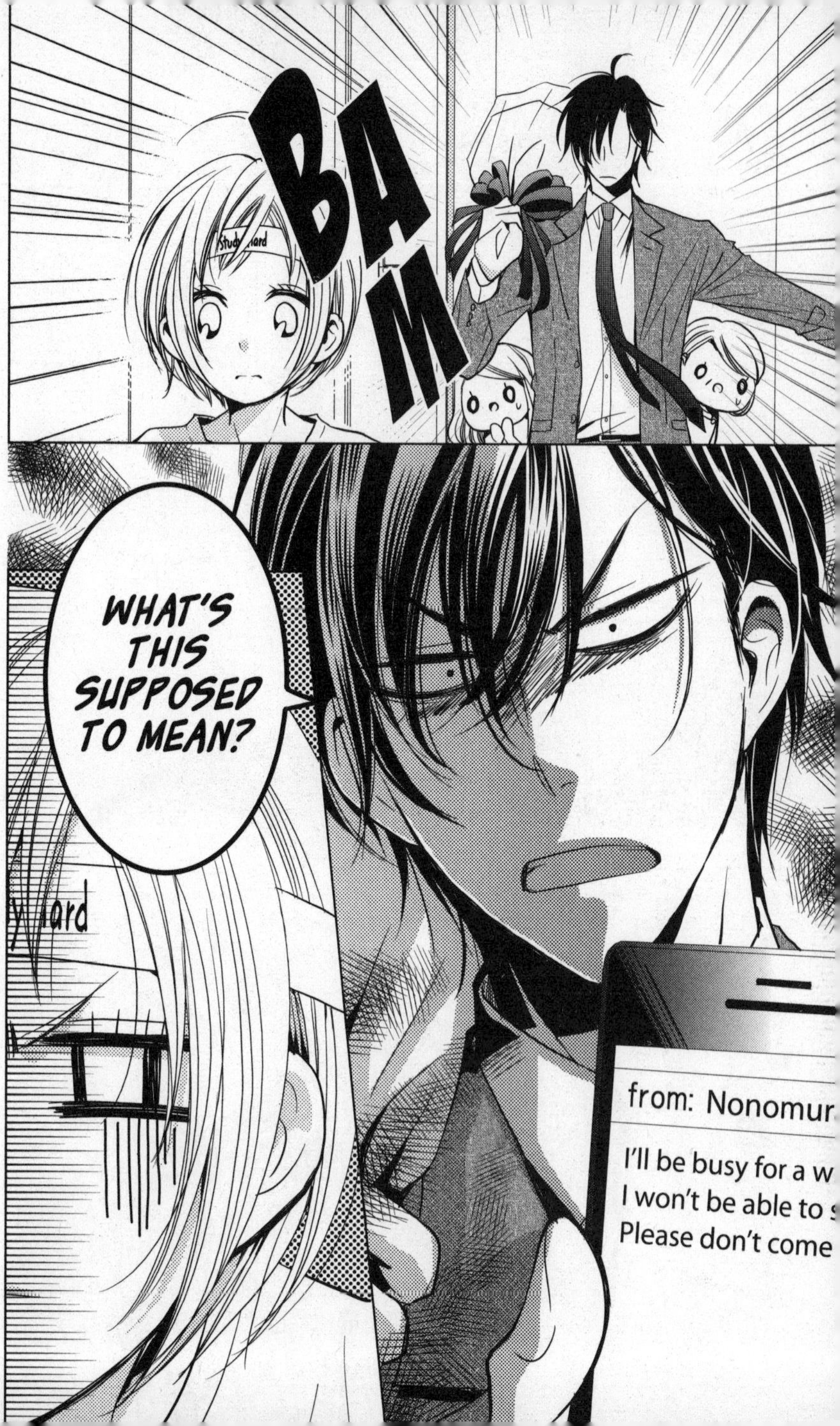
BAM
WHAT'S THIS SUPPOSED TO MEAN?
from: Nonomur
I'll be busy for a w
I won't be able to
Please don't come

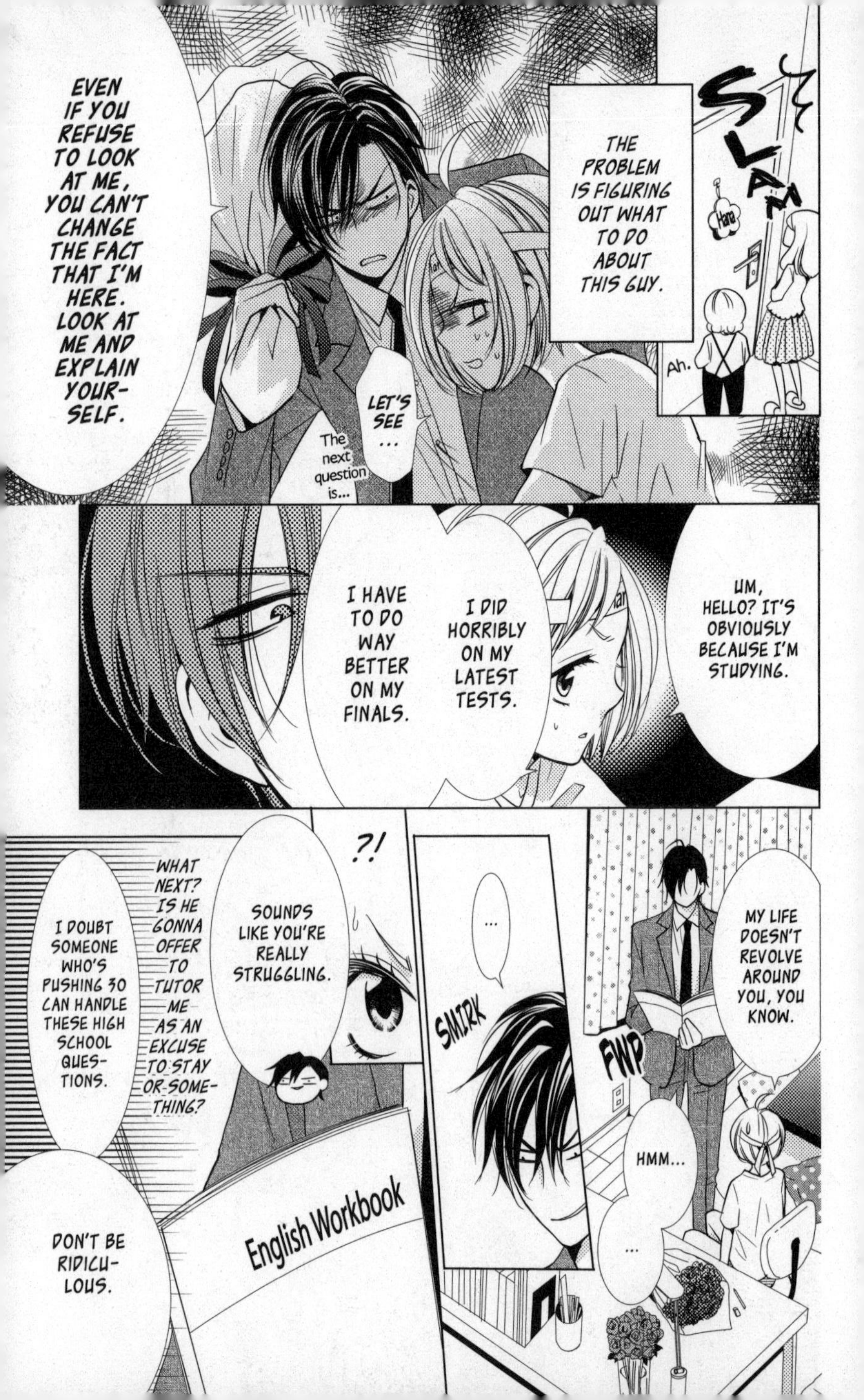
SLAM
Hana
Ah.
THE PROBLEM IS FIGURING OUT WHAT TO DO ABOUT THIS GUY.
EVEN IF YOU REFUSE TO LOOK AT ME, YOU CAN'T CHANGE THE FACT THAT I'M HERE. LOOK AT ME AND EXPLAIN YOURSELF.
LET'S SEE...
The next question is...
UM, HELLO? IT'S OBVIOUSLY BECAUSE I'M STUDYING.
I DID HORRIBLY ON MY LATEST TESTS.
I HAVE TO DO WAY BETTER ON MY FINALS.
MY LIFE DOESN'T REVOLVE AROUND YOU, YOU KNOW.
FWP
HMM...
...
...
SMIRK
?!
SOUNDS LIKE YOU'RE REALLY STRUGGLING.
WHAT NEXT? IS HE GONNA OFFER TO TUTOR ME AS AN EXCUSE TO STAY OR SOMETHING?
I DOUBT SOMEONE WHO'S PUSHING 30 CAN HANDLE THESE HIGH SCHOOL QUESTIONS.
English Workbook
DON'T BE RIDICULOUS.

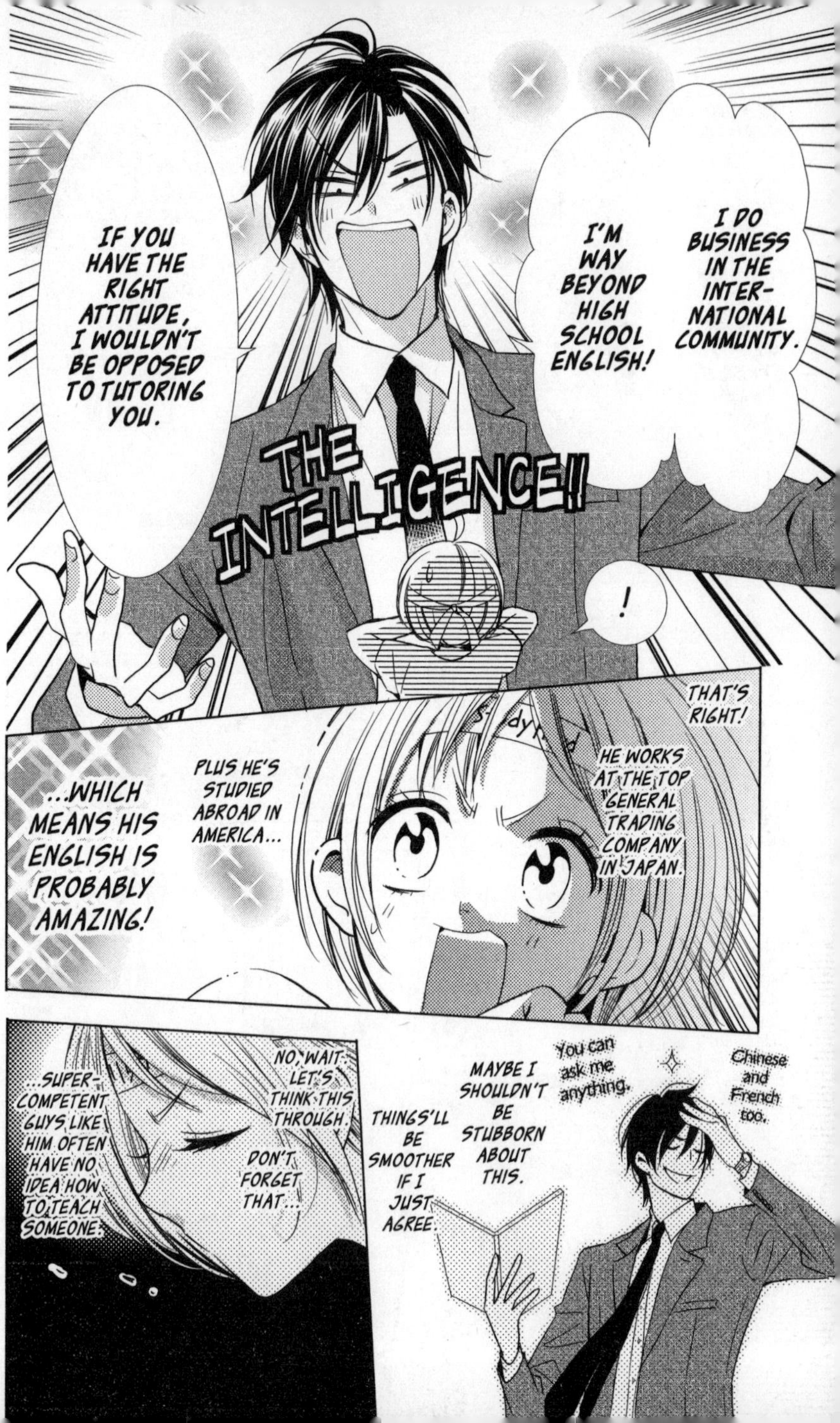
I DO BUSINESS IN THE INTER-NATIONAL COMMUNITY.
I'M WAY BEYOND HIGH SCHOOL ENGLISH!
IF YOU HAVE THE RIGHT ATTITUDE, I WOULDN'T BE OPPOSED TO TUTORING YOU.
THE INTELLIGENCE!!
!
THAT'S RIGHT!
HE WORKS AT THE TOP GENERAL TRADING COMPANY IN JAPAN.
PLUS HE'S STUDIED ABROAD IN AMERICA...
...WHICH MEANS HIS ENGLISH IS PROBABLY AMAZING!
Chinese and French too.
You can ask me anything.
MAYBE I SHOULDN'T BE STUBBORN ABOUT THIS.
THINGS'LL BE SMOOTHER IF I JUST AGREE.
NO, WAIT LET'S THINK THIS THROUGH.
DON'T FORGET THAT...
...SUPER-COMPETENT GUYS LIKE HIM OFTEN HAVE NO IDEA HOW TO TEACH SOMEONE.

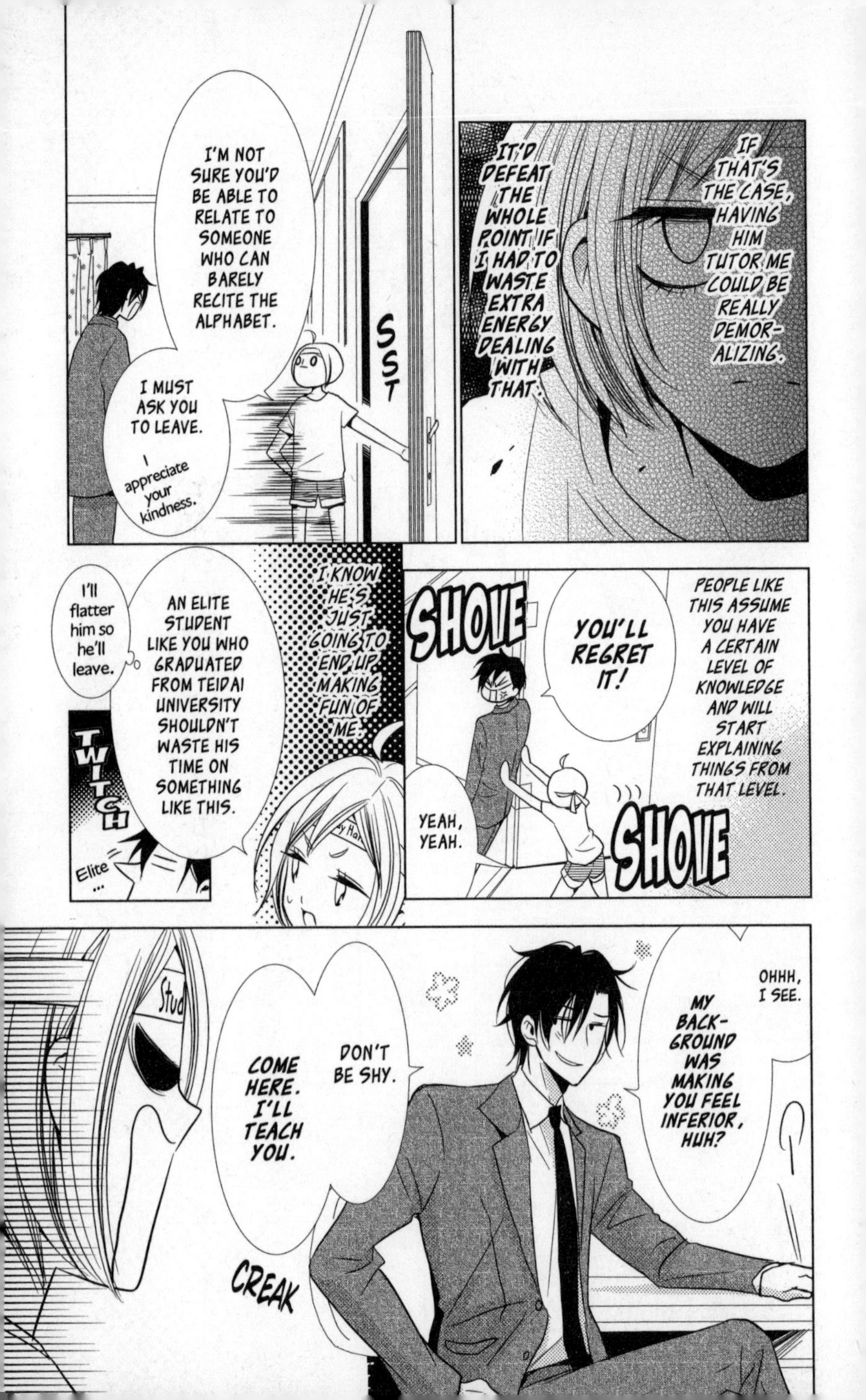
IF THAT'S THE CASE, HAVING HIM TUTOR ME COULD BE REALLY DEMOR-ALIZING.
IT'D DEFEAT THE WHOLE POINT IF I HAD TO WASTE EXTRA ENERGY DEALING WITH THAT.
I'M NOT SURE YOU'D BE ABLE TO RELATE TO SOMEONE WHO CAN BARELY RECITE THE ALPHABET.
SST
I MUST ASK YOU TO LEAVE.
I appreciate your kindness.
PEOPLE LIKE THIS ASSUME YOU HAVE A CERTAIN LEVEL OF KNOWLEDGE AND WILL START EXPLAINING THINGS FROM THAT LEVEL.
SHOVE
YOU'LL REGRET IT!
SHOVE
YEAH, YEAH.
I KNOW HE'S JUST GOING TO END UP MAKING FUN OF ME.
AN ELITE STUDENT LIKE YOU WHO GRADUATED FROM TEIDAI UNIVERSITY SHOULDN'T WASTE HIS TIME ON SOMETHING LIKE THIS.
I'll flatter him so he'll leave.
TWITCH
Elite...
OHHH, I SEE.
MY BACK-GROUND WAS MAKING YOU FEEL INFERIOR, HUH?
DON'T BE SHY.
COME HERE. I'LL TEACH YOU.
CREAK

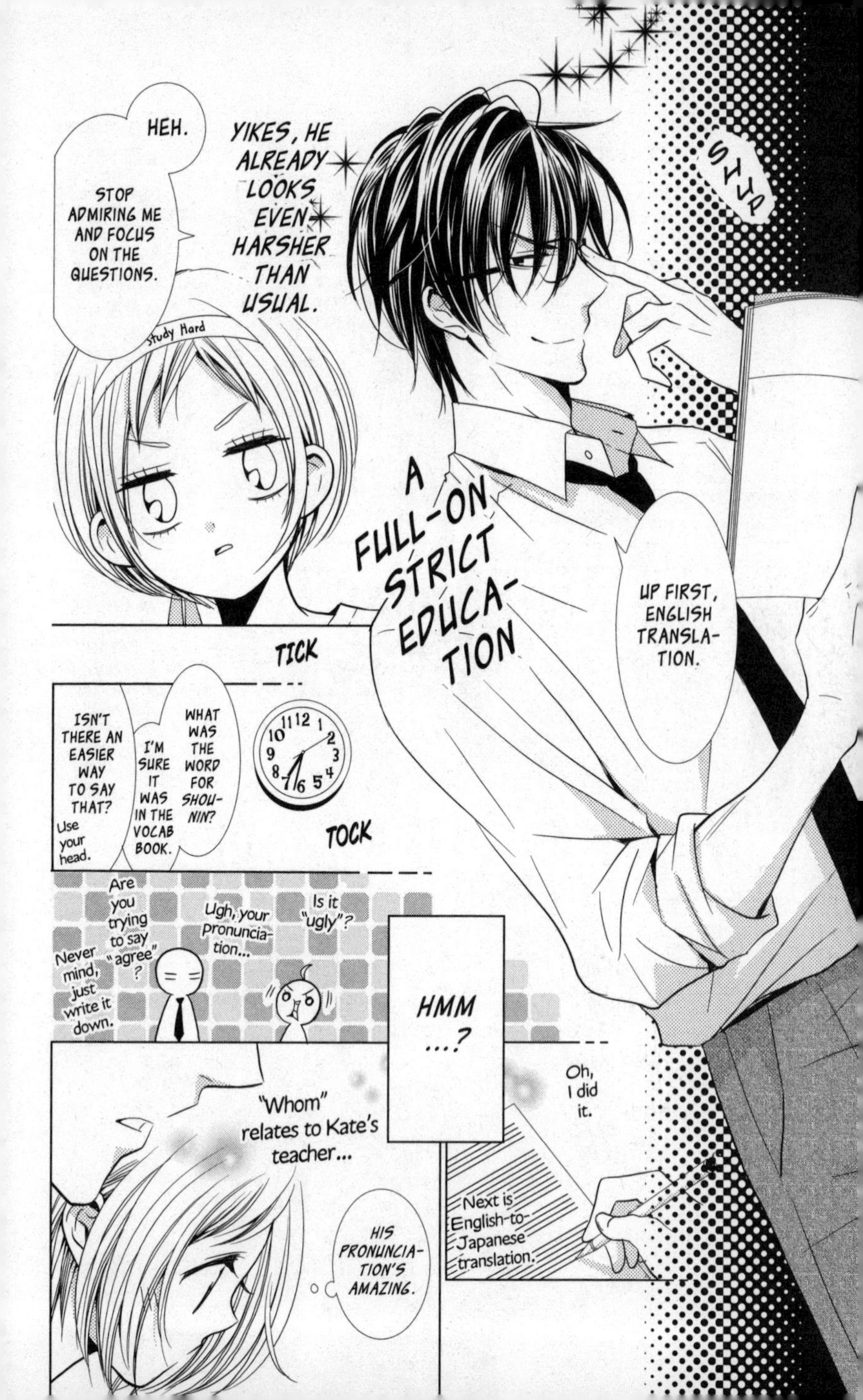
SHUP
YIKES, HE ALREADY LOOKS EVEN HARSHER THAN USUAL.
HEH.
STOP ADMIRING ME AND FOCUS ON THE QUESTIONS.
Study Hard
A FULL-ON STRICT EDUCATION
UP FIRST, ENGLISH TRANSLATION.
TICK
TOCK
WHAT WAS THE WORD FOR SHOUNIN?
I'M SURE IT WAS IN THE VOCAB BOOK.
ISN'T THERE AN EASIER WAY TO SAY THAT?
Use your head.
Is it "ugly"?
Ugh, your pronunciation...
Are you trying to say "agree"?
Never mind, just write it down.
HMM ...?
Oh, I did it.
Next is English-to-Japanese translation.
"Whom" relates to Kate's teacher...
HIS PRONUNCIATION'S AMAZING.

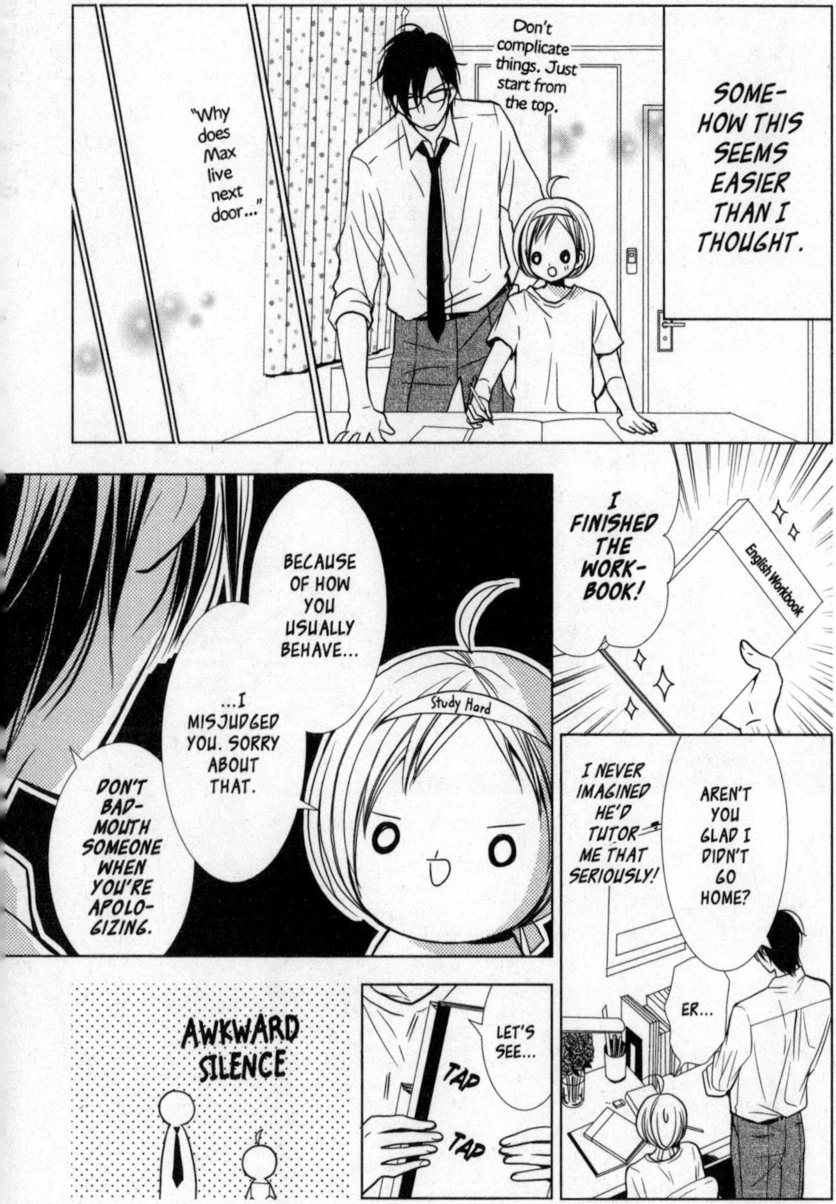
SOME-HOW THIS SEEMS EASIER THAN I THOUGHT.
Don't complicate things. Just start from the top.
"Why does Max live next door..."
I FINISHED THE WORK-BOOK!
English Workbook
I NEVER IMAGINED HE'D TUTOR ME THAT SERIOUSLY!
AREN'T YOU GLAD I DIDN'T GO HOME?
ER...
BECAUSE OF HOW YOU USUALLY BEHAVE...
...I MISJUDGED YOU. SORRY ABOUT THAT.
Study Hard
DON'T BAD-MOUTH SOMEONE WHEN YOU'RE APOLO-GIZING.
LET'S SEE...
TAP
TAP
AWKWARD SILENCE

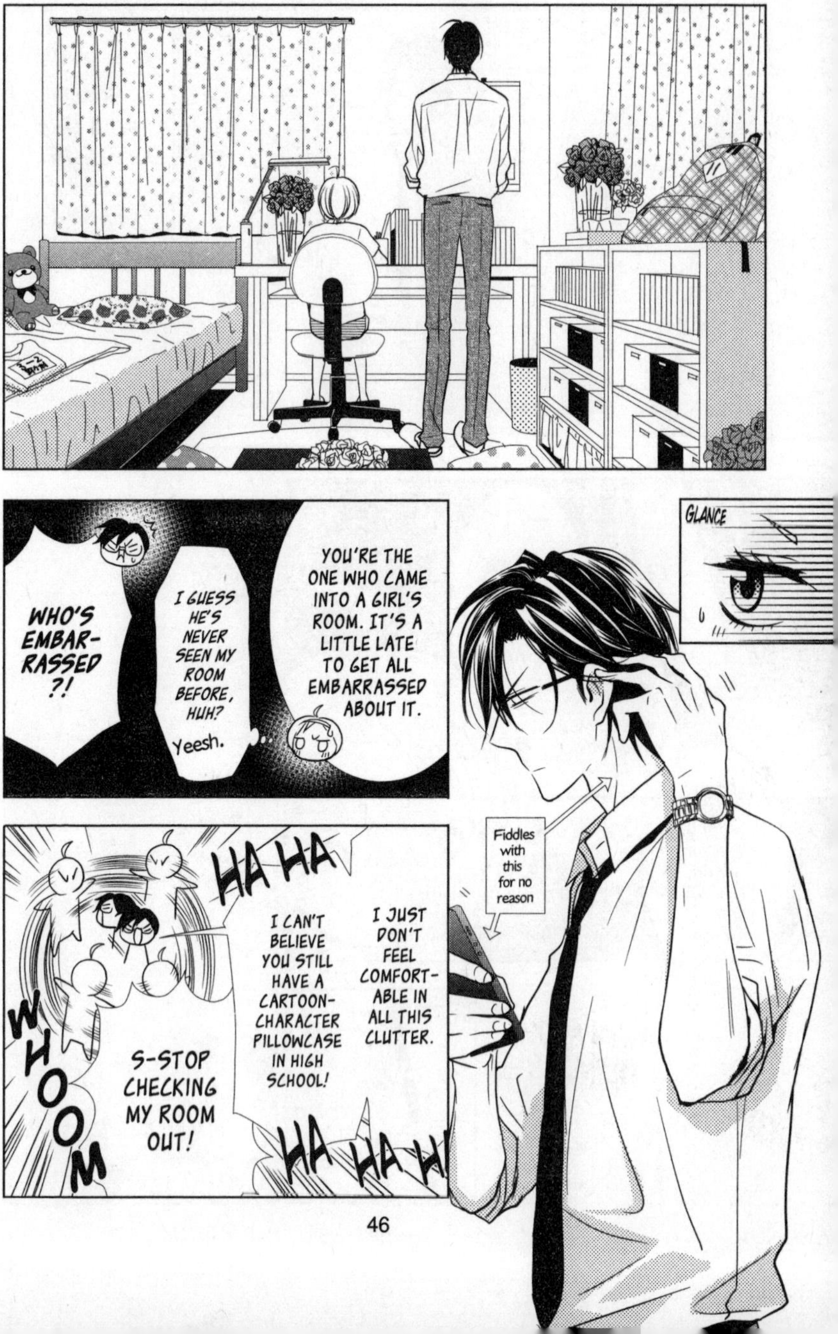
GLANCE
Fiddles with this for no reason
YOU'RE THE ONE WHO CAME INTO A GIRL'S ROOM. IT'S A LITTLE LATE TO GET ALL EMBARRASSED ABOUT IT.
I GUESS HE'S NEVER SEEN MY ROOM BEFORE, HUH?
Yeesh.
WHO'S EMBARRASSED?!
HA HA
I JUST DON'T FEEL COMFORTABLE IN ALL THIS CLUTTER.
I CAN'T BELIEVE YOU STILL HAVE A CARTOON-CHARACTER PILLOWCASE IN HIGH SCHOOL!
S-STOP CHECKING MY ROOM OUT!
WHOOM
HA HA H

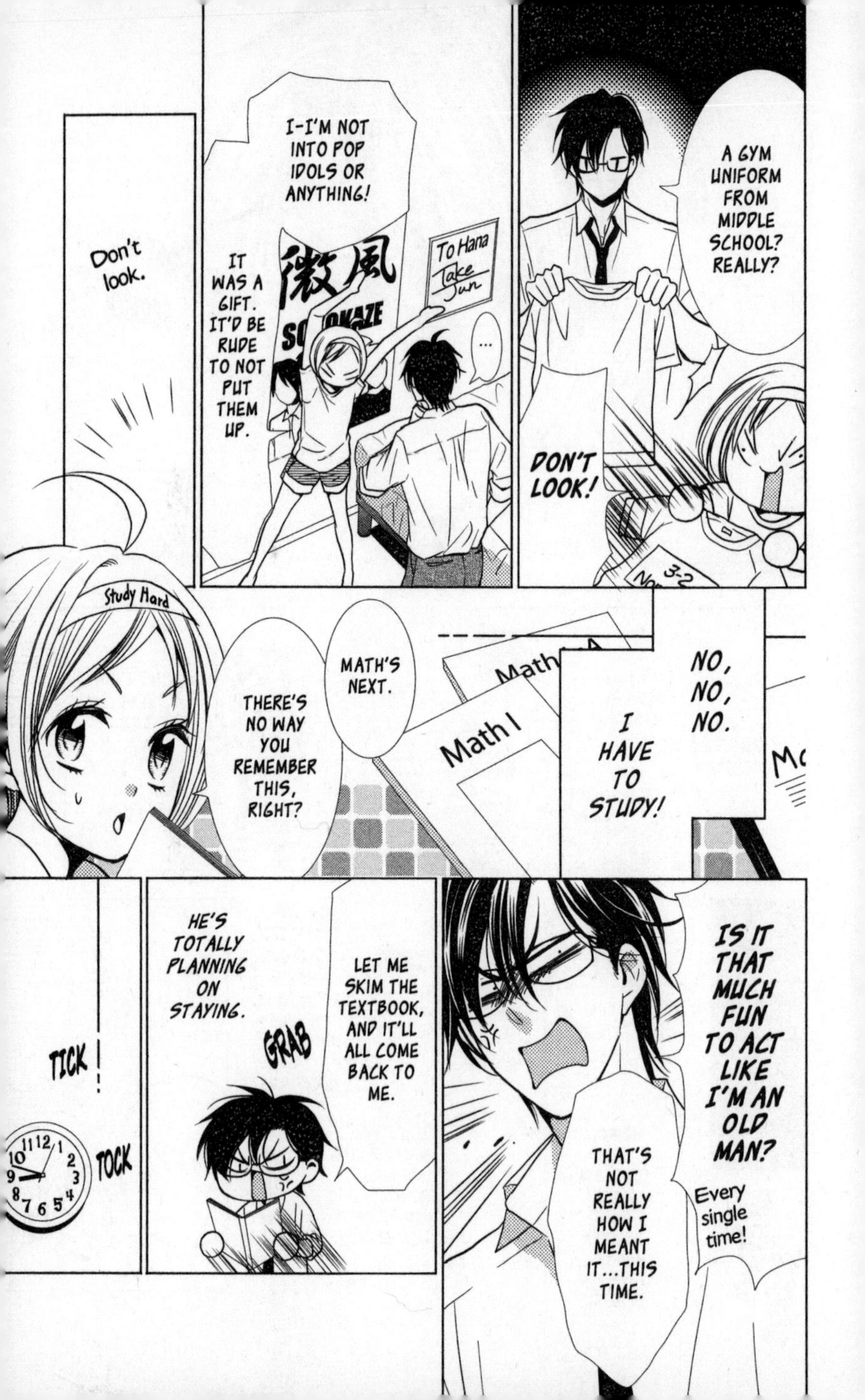
A GYM UNIFORM FROM MIDDLE SCHOOL? REALLY?
DON'T LOOK!
3-2
I-I'M NOT INTO POP IDOLS OR ANYTHING!
IT WAS A GIFT. IT'D BE RUDE TO NOT PUT THEM UP.
To Hana Take Jun
...
Don't look.
NO, NO, NO.
I HAVE TO STUDY!
Math I
MATH'S NEXT.
THERE'S NO WAY YOU REMEMBER THIS, RIGHT?
Study Hard
IS IT THAT MUCH FUN TO ACT LIKE I'M AN OLD MAN?
Every single time!
THAT'S NOT REALLY HOW I MEANT IT...THIS TIME.
LET ME SKIM THE TEXTBOOK, AND IT'LL ALL COME BACK TO ME.
GRAB
HE'S TOTALLY PLANNING ON STAYING.
TICK
TOCK

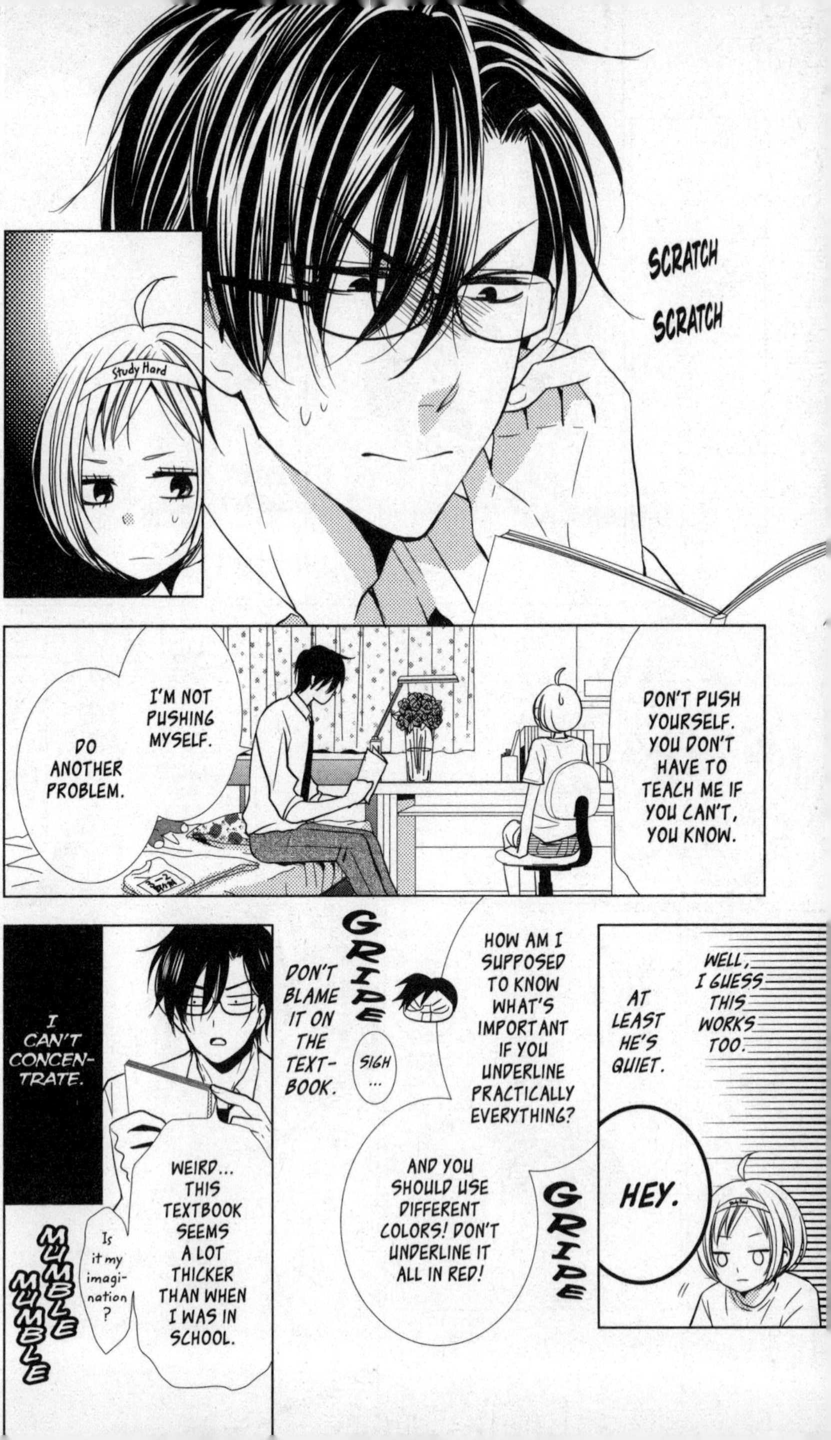
SCRATCH
SCRATCH
Study Hard
DON'T PUSH YOURSELF. YOU DON'T HAVE TO TEACH ME IF YOU CAN'T, YOU KNOW.
I'M NOT PUSHING MYSELF.
DO ANOTHER PROBLEM.
WELL, I GUESS THIS WORKS TOO.
AT LEAST HE'S QUIET.
HEY.
HOW AM I SUPPOSED TO KNOW WHAT'S IMPORTANT IF YOU UNDERLINE PRACTICALLY EVERYTHING?
GRIPE
AND YOU SHOULD USE DIFFERENT COLORS! DON'T UNDERLINE IT ALL IN RED!
GRIPE
SIGH ...
DON'T BLAME IT ON THE TEXT-BOOK.
I CAN'T CONCEN-TRATE.
WEIRD... THIS TEXTBOOK SEEMS A LOT THICKER THAN WHEN I WAS IN SCHOOL.
Is it my imagi-nation?
MUMBLE MUMBLE

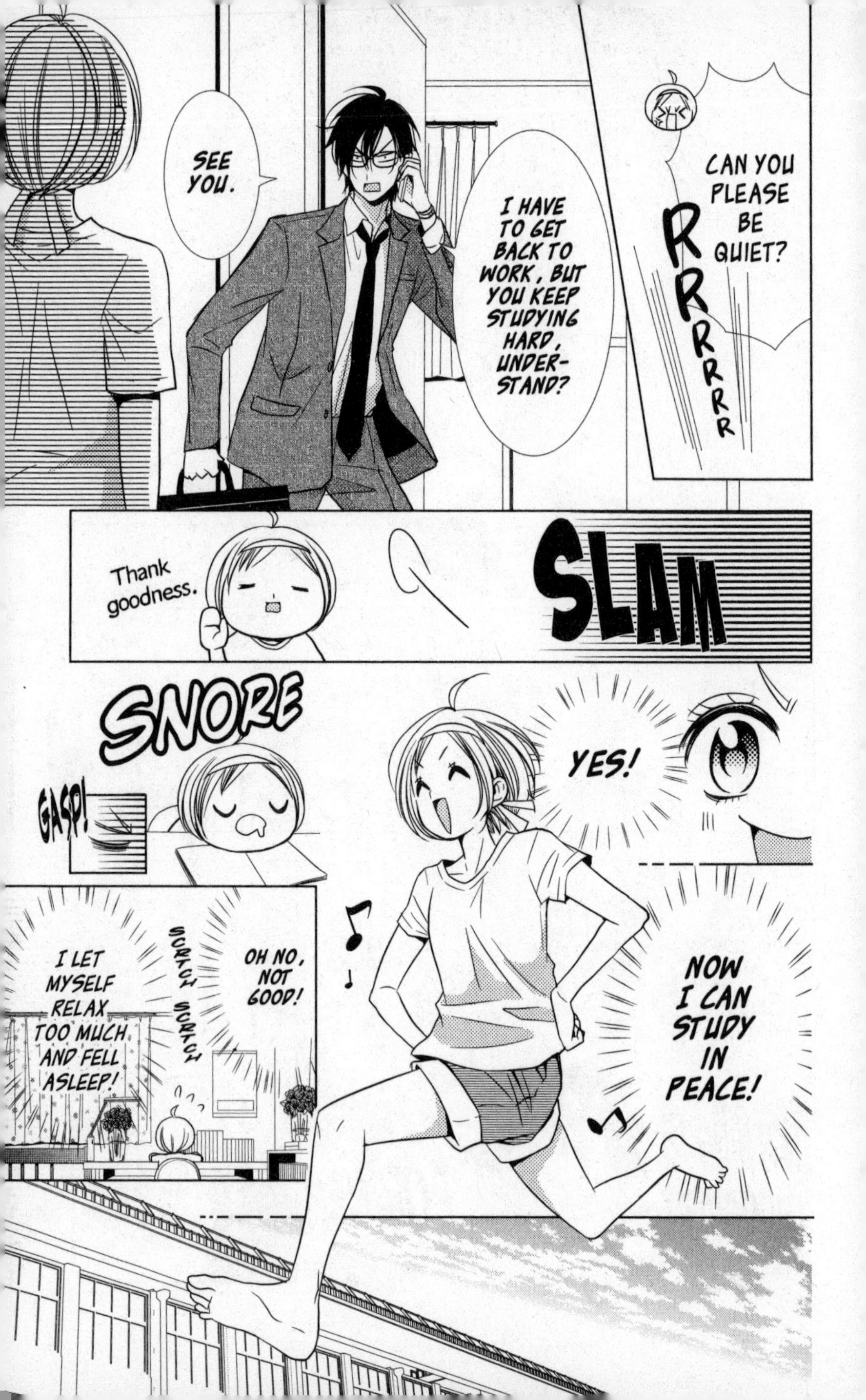
CAN YOU PLEASE BE QUIET?
RRRRRRR
I HAVE TO GET BACK TO WORK, BUT YOU KEEP STUDYING HARD, UNDERSTAND?
SEE YOU.
SLAM
Thank goodness.
YES!
SNORE
GASP!
NOW I CAN STUDY IN PEACE!
OH NO, NOT GOOD!
SCRTCH SCRTCH
I LET MYSELF RELAX TOO MUCH AND FELL ASLEEP!

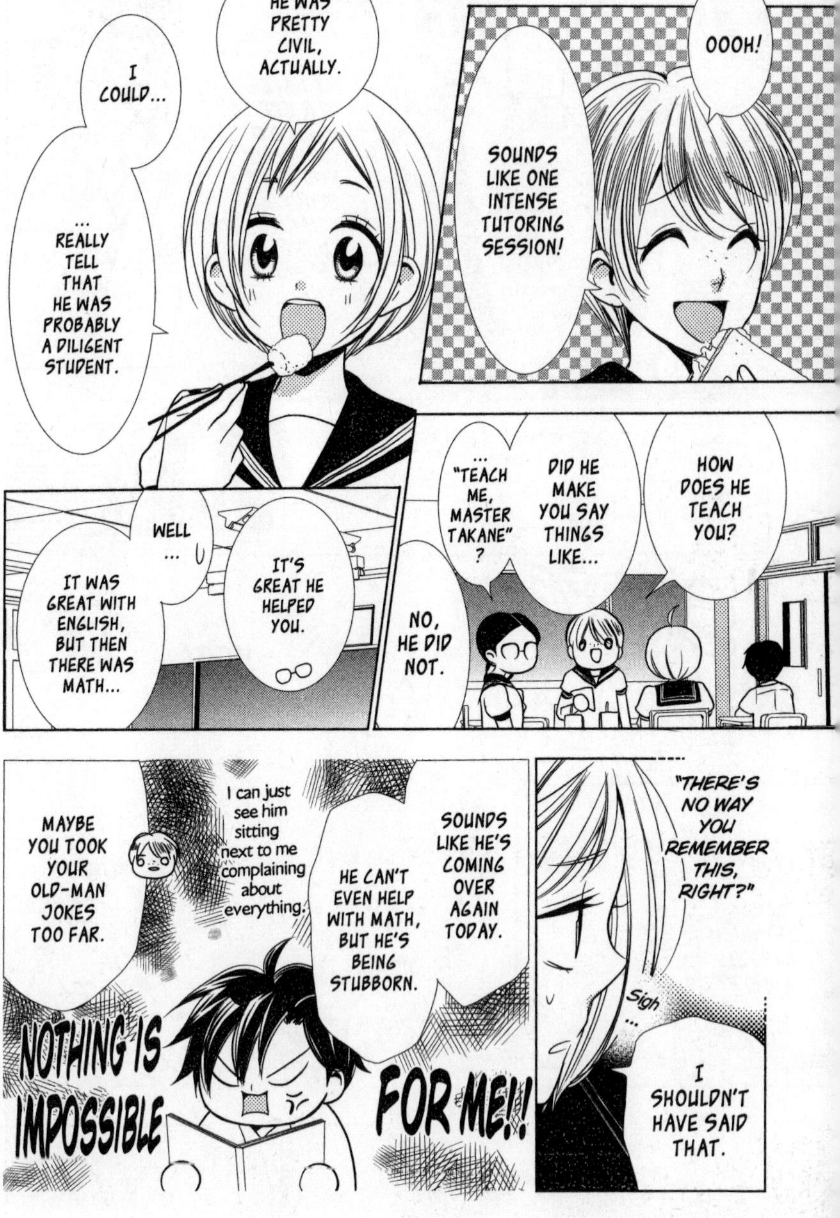
OOOH!
SOUNDS LIKE ONE INTENSE TUTORING SESSION!
HE WAS PRETTY CIVIL, ACTUALLY.
I COULD...
...REALLY TELL THAT HE WAS PROBABLY A DILIGENT STUDENT.
HOW DOES HE TEACH YOU?
DID HE MAKE YOU SAY THINGS LIKE...
..."TEACH ME, MASTER TAKANE"?
NO, HE DID NOT.
IT'S GREAT HE HELPED YOU.
WELL...
IT WAS GREAT WITH ENGLISH, BUT THEN THERE WAS MATH...
"THERE'S NO WAY YOU REMEMBER THIS, RIGHT?"
Sigh...
I SHOULDN'T HAVE SAID THAT.
SOUNDS LIKE HE'S COMING OVER AGAIN TODAY.
HE CAN'T EVEN HELP WITH MATH, BUT HE'S BEING STUBBORN.
I can just see him sitting next to me complaining about everything.
MAYBE YOU TOOK YOUR OLD-MAN JOKES TOO FAR.
NOTHING IS IMPOSSIBLE
FOR ME!!

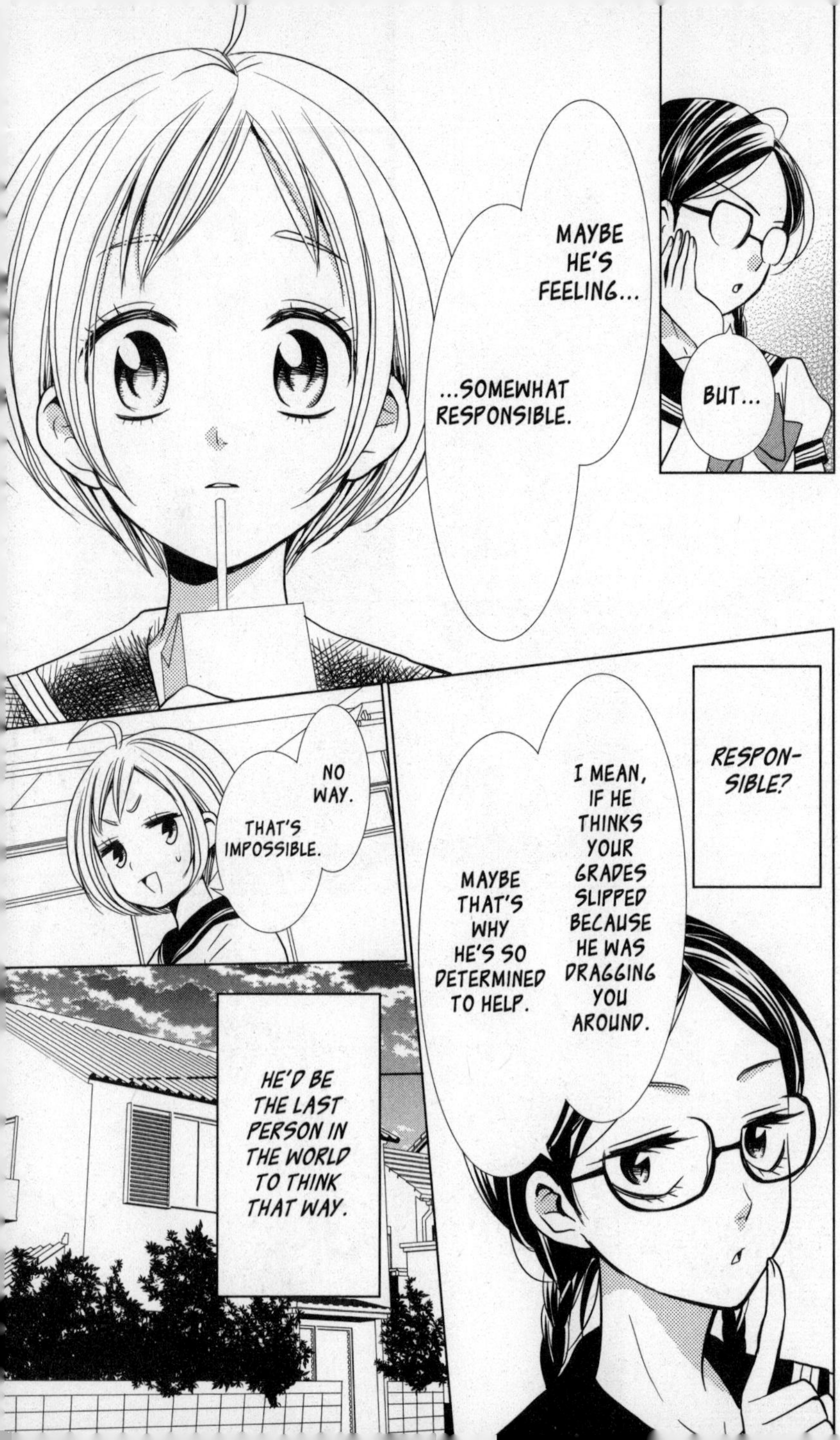
BUT...
MAYBE HE'S FEELING...
...SOMEWHAT RESPONSIBLE.
RESPON-SIBLE?
I MEAN, IF HE THINKS YOUR GRADES SLIPPED BECAUSE HE WAS DRAGGING YOU AROUND.
MAYBE THAT'S WHY HE'S SO DETERMINED TO HELP.
NO WAY.
THAT'S IMPOSSIBLE.
HE'D BE THE LAST PERSON IN THE WORLD TO THINK THAT WAY.

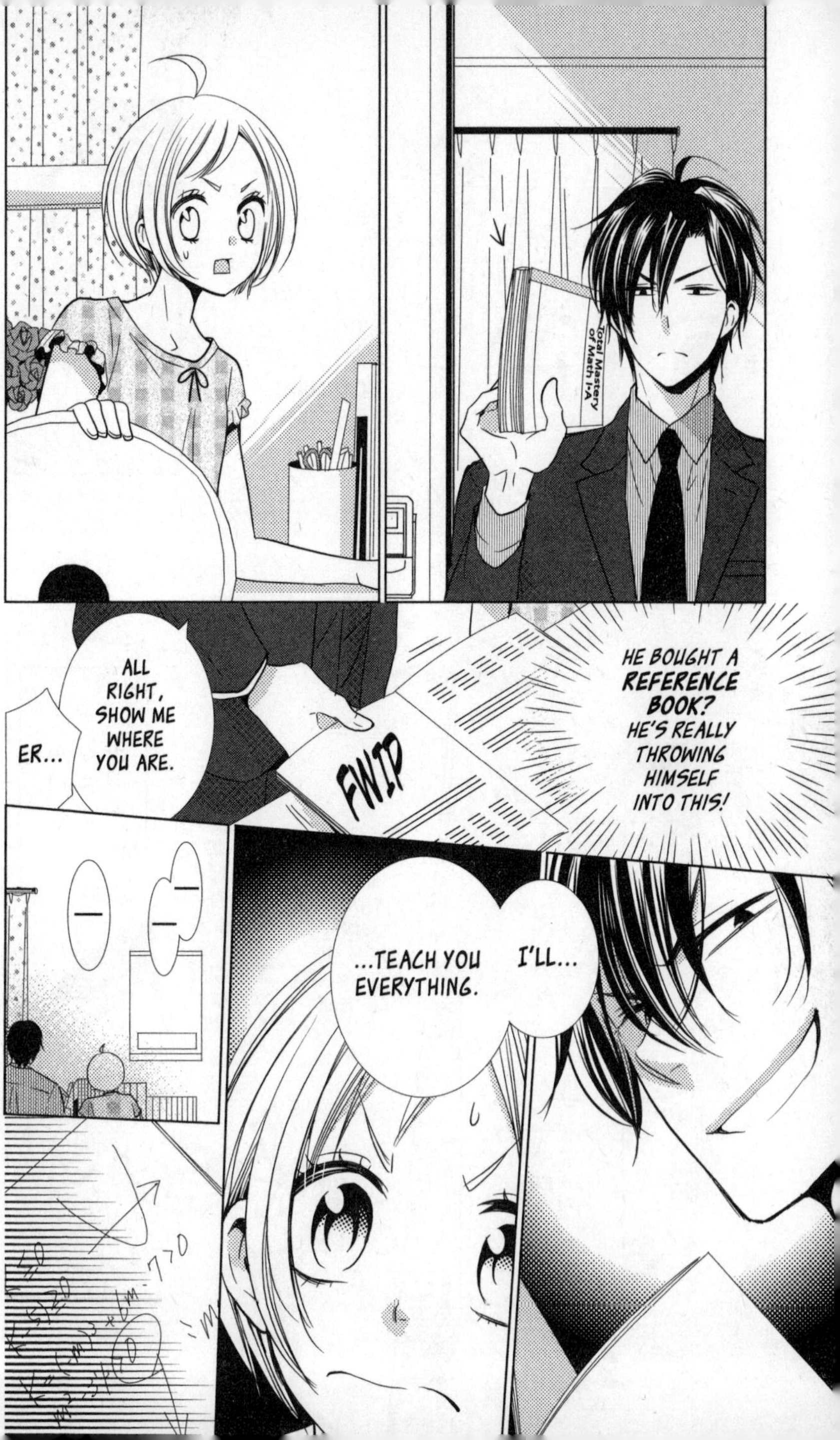
Total Mastery of Math I·A
HE BOUGHT A REFERENCE BOOK? HE'S REALLY THROWING HIMSELF INTO THIS!
FWIP
ALL RIGHT, SHOW ME WHERE YOU ARE.
ER...
I'LL...
...TEACH YOU EVERYTHING.
—
—
—

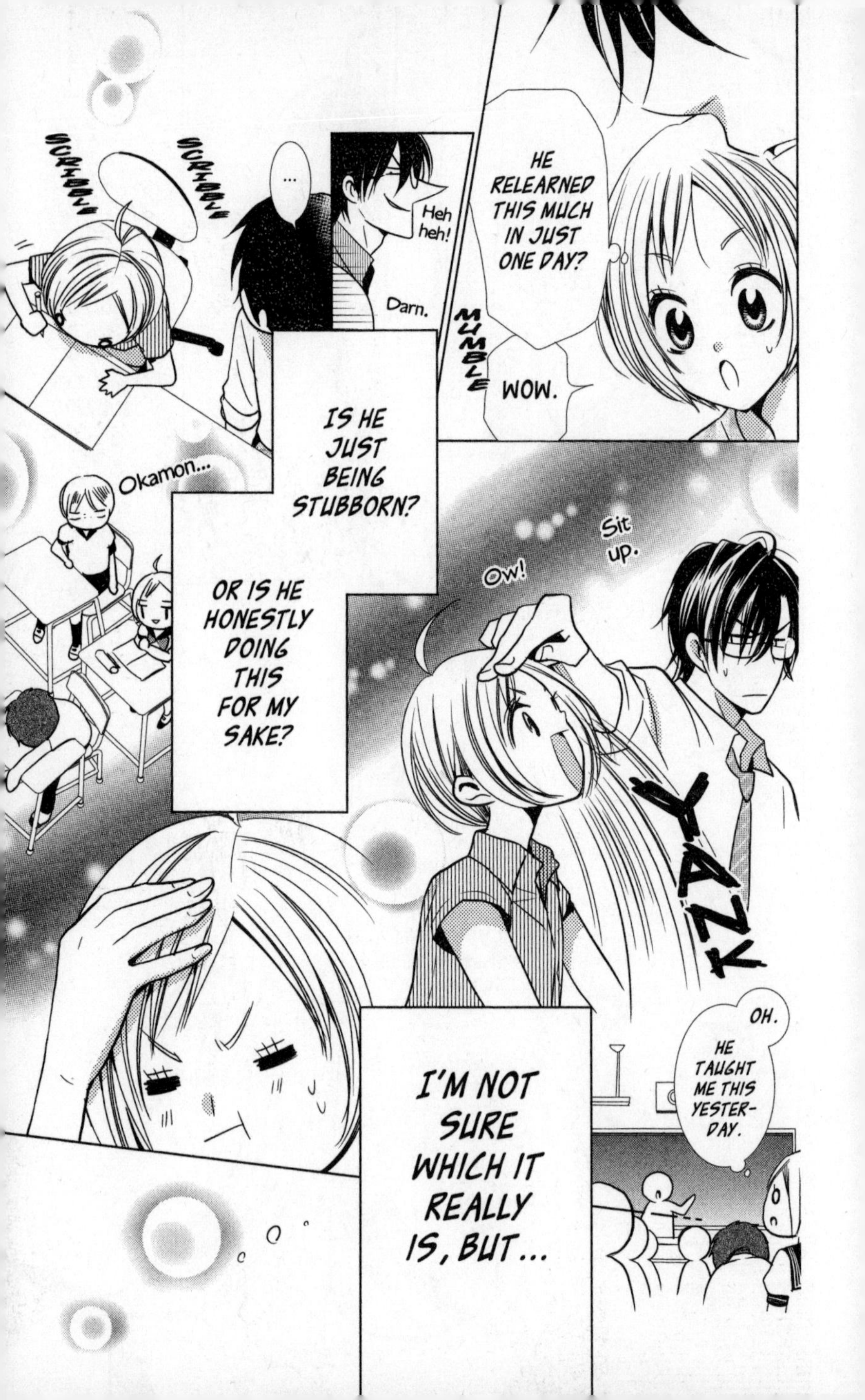
HE RELEARNED THIS MUCH IN JUST ONE DAY?
MUMBLE
WOW.
Heh heh!
...
Darn.
SCRIBBLE
SCRIBBLE
IS HE JUST BEING STUBBORN?
Okamon...
OR IS HE HONESTLY DOING THIS FOR MY SAKE?
Sit up.
Ow!
YANK
OH.
HE TAUGHT ME THIS YESTER-DAY.
I'M NOT SURE WHICH IT REALLY IS, BUT...

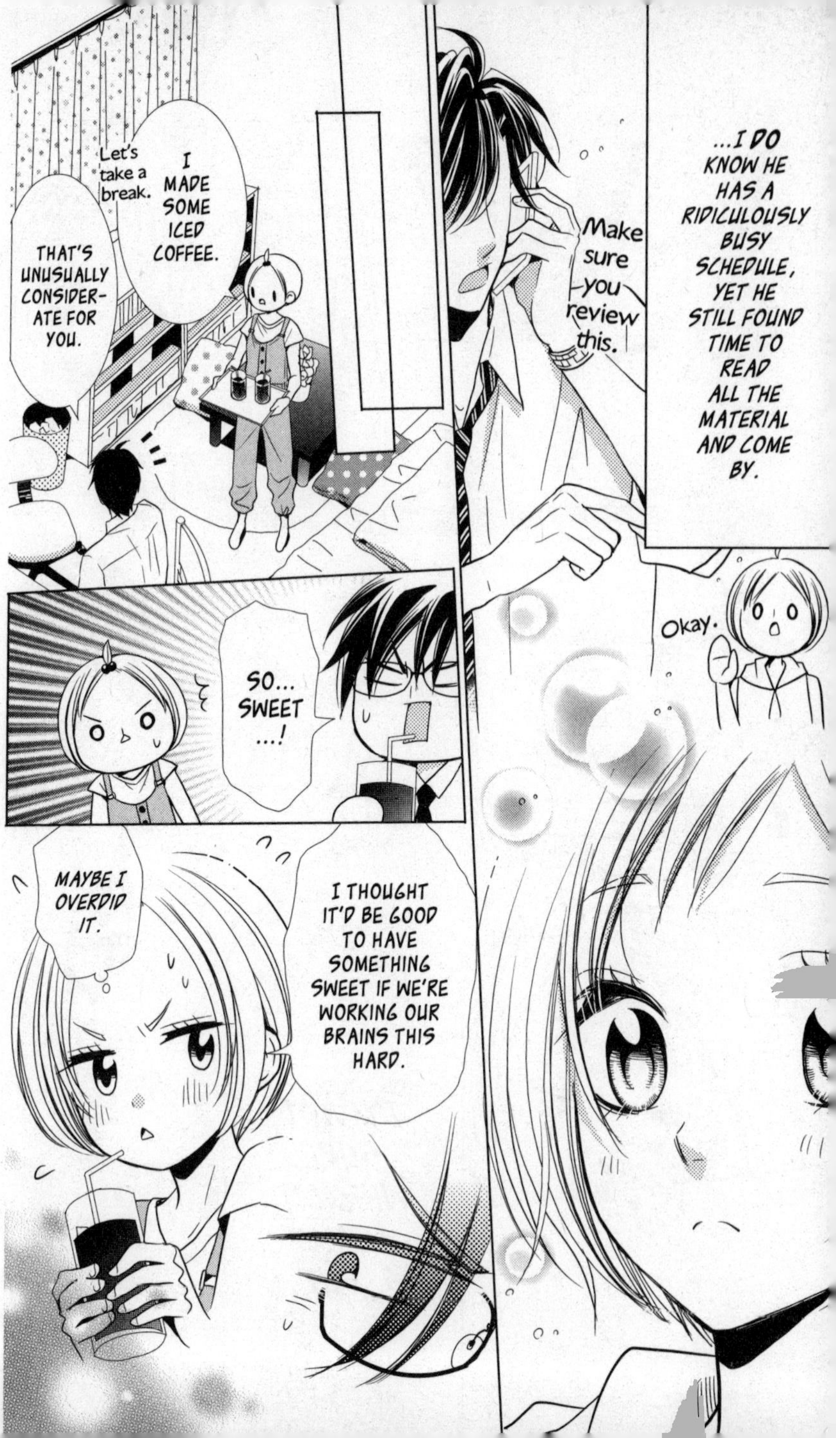
...I DO KNOW HE HAS A RIDICULOUSLY BUSY SCHEDULE, YET HE STILL FOUND TIME TO READ ALL THE MATERIAL AND COME BY.
Make sure you review this.
Okay.
Let's take a break.
I MADE SOME ICED COFFEE.
THAT'S UNUSUALLY CONSIDER-ATE FOR YOU.
SO... SWEET ...!
I THOUGHT IT'D BE GOOD TO HAVE SOMETHING SWEET IF WE'RE WORKING OUR BRAINS THIS HARD.
MAYBE I OVERDID IT.

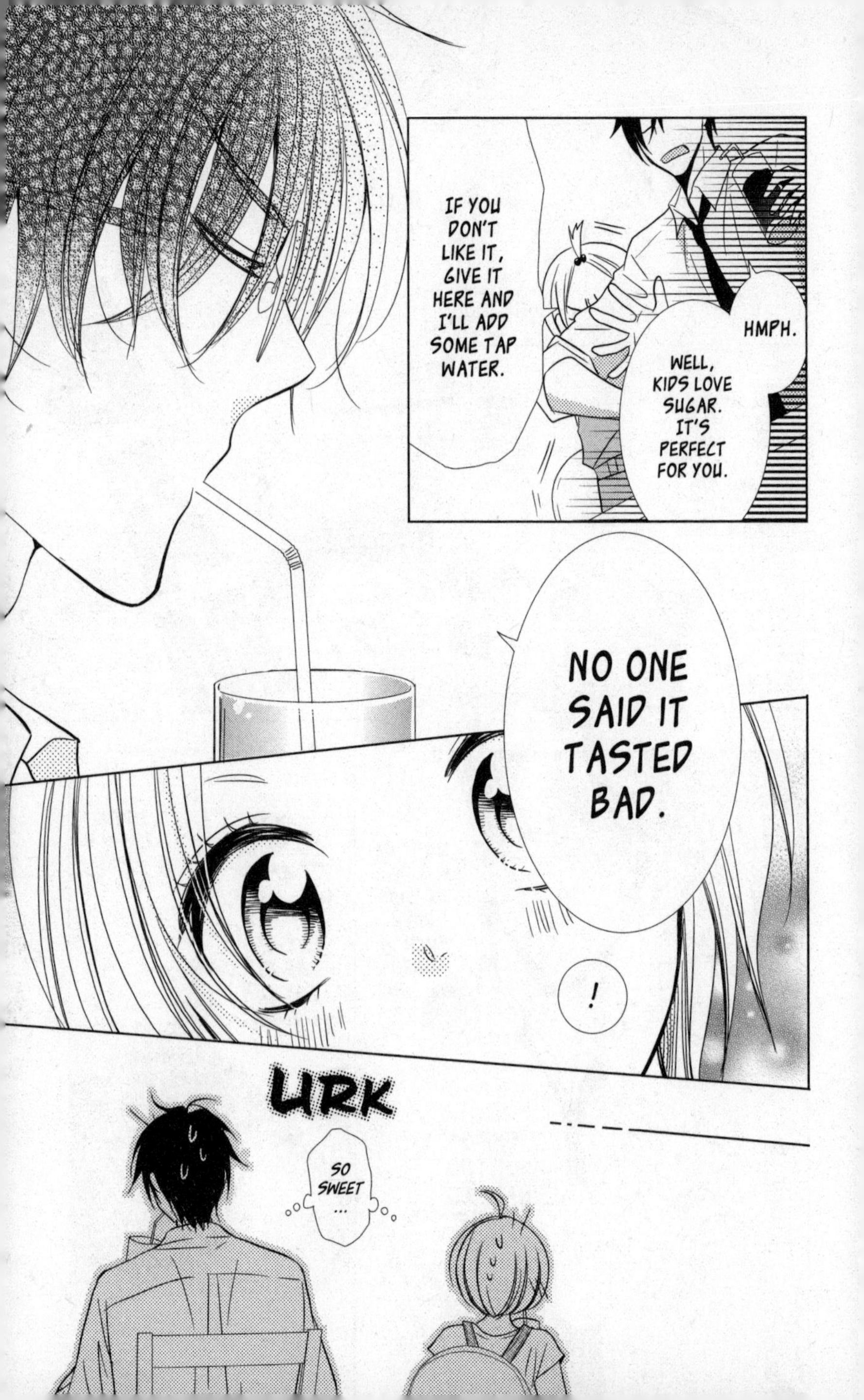
HMPH.
WELL, KIDS LOVE SUGAR. IT'S PERFECT FOR YOU.
IF YOU DON'T LIKE IT, GIVE IT HERE AND I'LL ADD SOME TAP WATER.
NO ONE SAID IT TASTED BAD.
!
URK
SO SWEET...

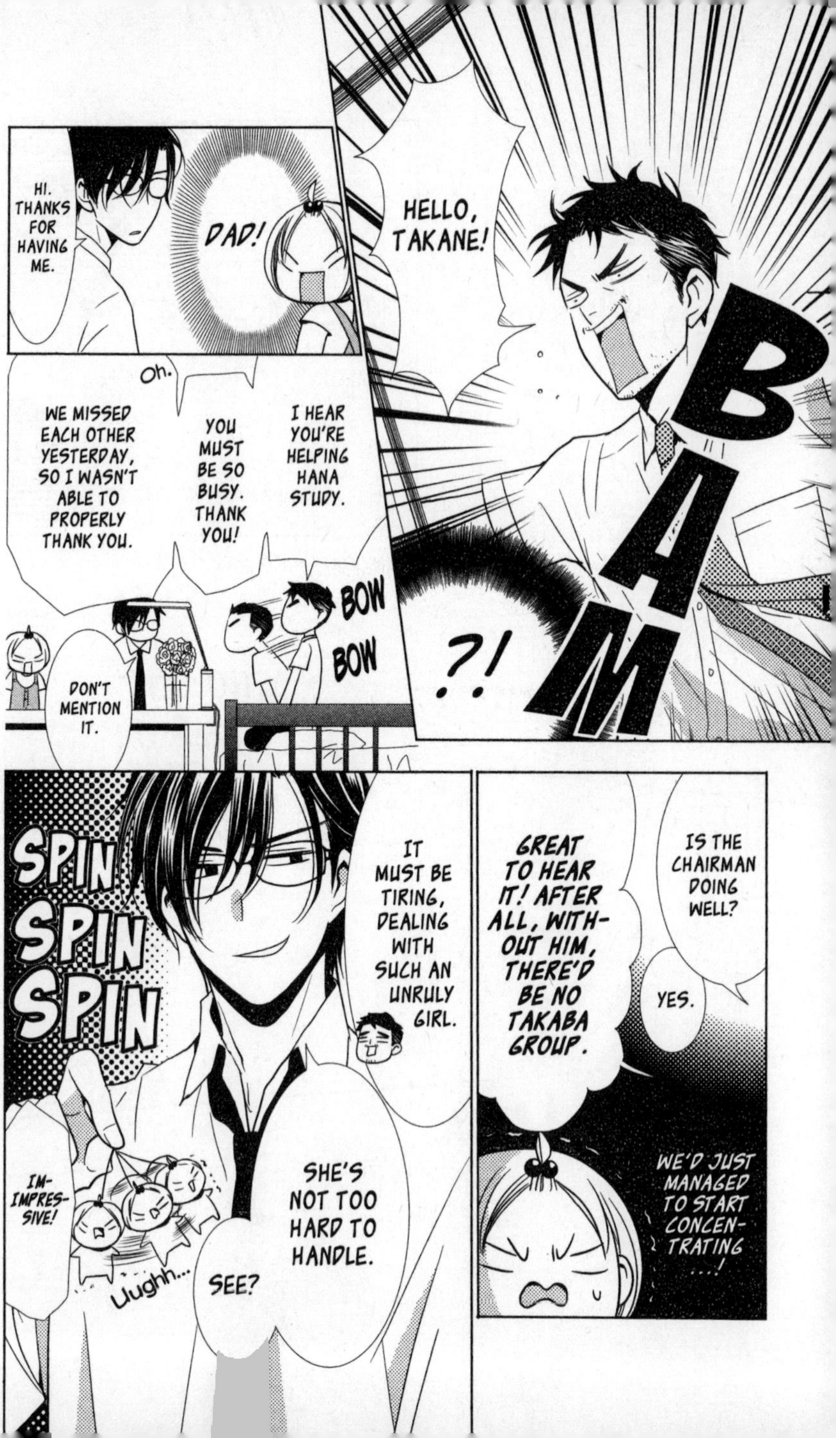
HELLO, TAKANE!
BAM
?!
DAD!
HI. THANKS FOR HAVING ME.
Oh.
I HEAR YOU'RE HELPING HANA STUDY.
YOU MUST BE SO BUSY. THANK YOU!
WE MISSED EACH OTHER YESTERDAY, SO I WASN'T ABLE TO PROPERLY THANK YOU.
BOW BOW
DON'T MENTION IT.
IS THE CHAIRMAN DOING WELL?
YES.
GREAT TO HEAR IT! AFTER ALL, WITH-OUT HIM, THERE'D BE NO TAKABA GROUP.
WE'D JUST MANAGED TO START CONCEN-TRATING...!
IT MUST BE TIRING, DEALING WITH SUCH AN UNRULY GIRL.
SHE'S NOT TOO HARD TO HANDLE.
SEE?
SPIN SPIN SPIN
IM-IMPRES-SIVE!
Uughh...

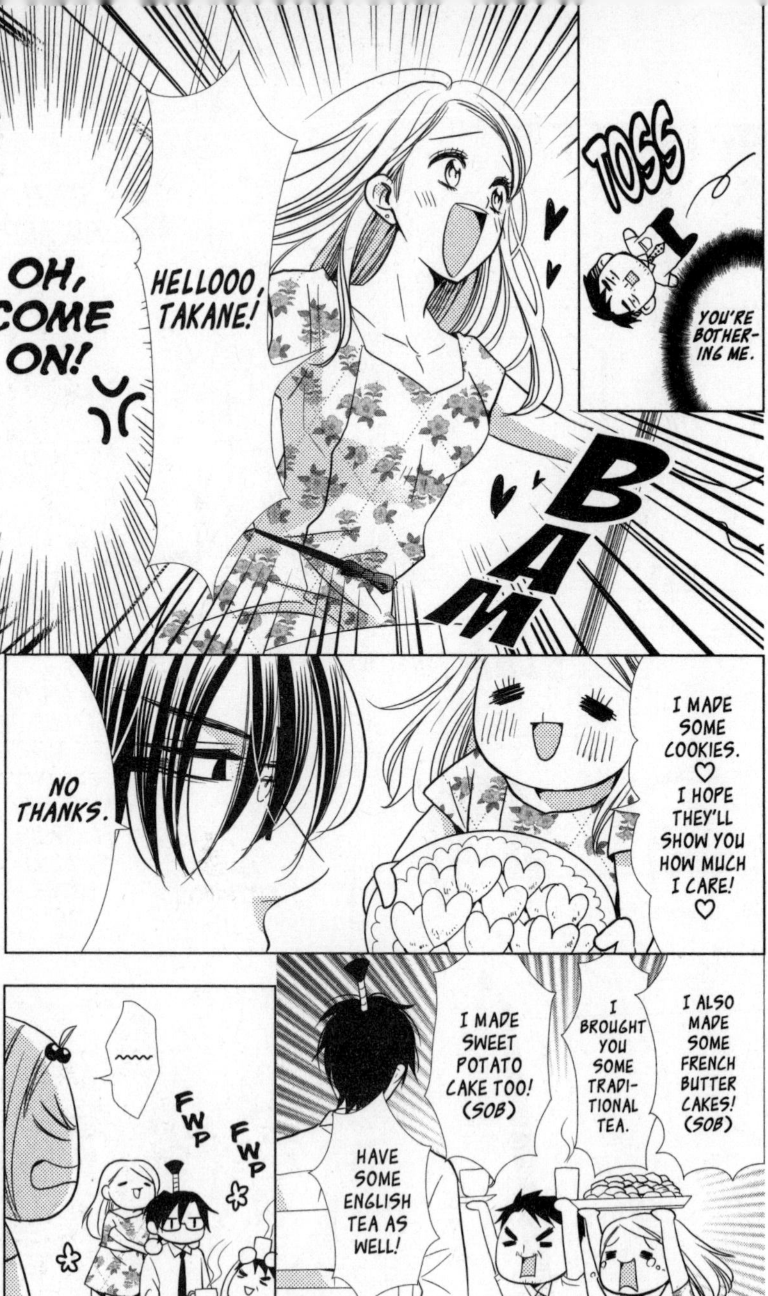
TOSS
YOU'RE BOTHER-ING ME.
BAM
HELLOOO, TAKANE!
OH, COME ON!
I MADE SOME COOKIES. ♡ I HOPE THEY'LL SHOW YOU HOW MUCH I CARE! ♡
NO THANKS.
I ALSO MADE SOME FRENCH BUTTER CAKES! (SOB)
I BROUGHT YOU SOME TRADI-TIONAL TEA.
I MADE SWEET POTATO CAKE TOO! (SOB)
HAVE SOME ENGLISH TEA AS WELL!
~~~
FWP
FWP
~~~

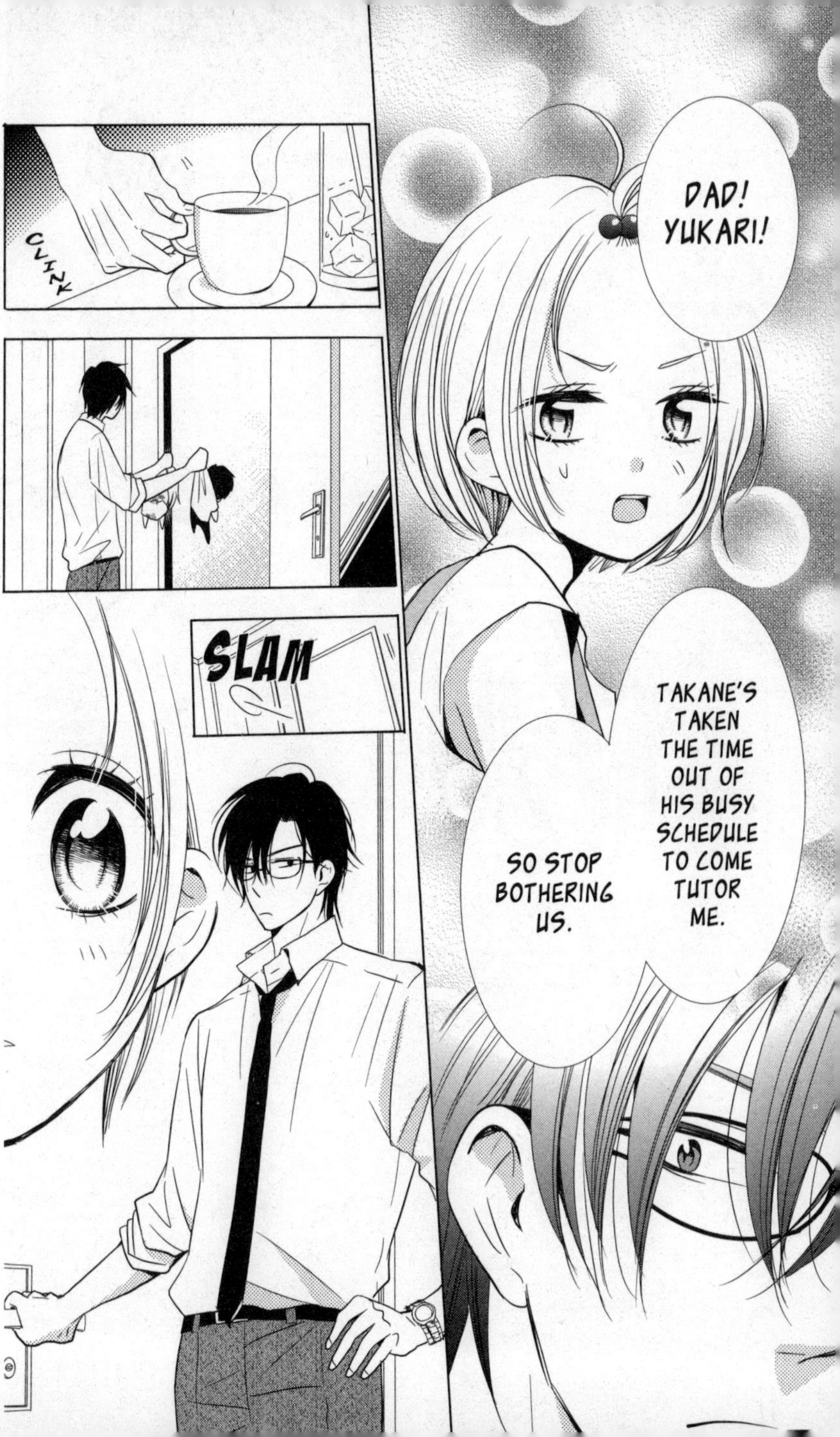
DAD! YUKARI!
TAKANE'S TAKEN THE TIME OUT OF HIS BUSY SCHEDULE TO COME TUTOR ME.
SO STOP BOTHERING US.
CLINK
SLAM

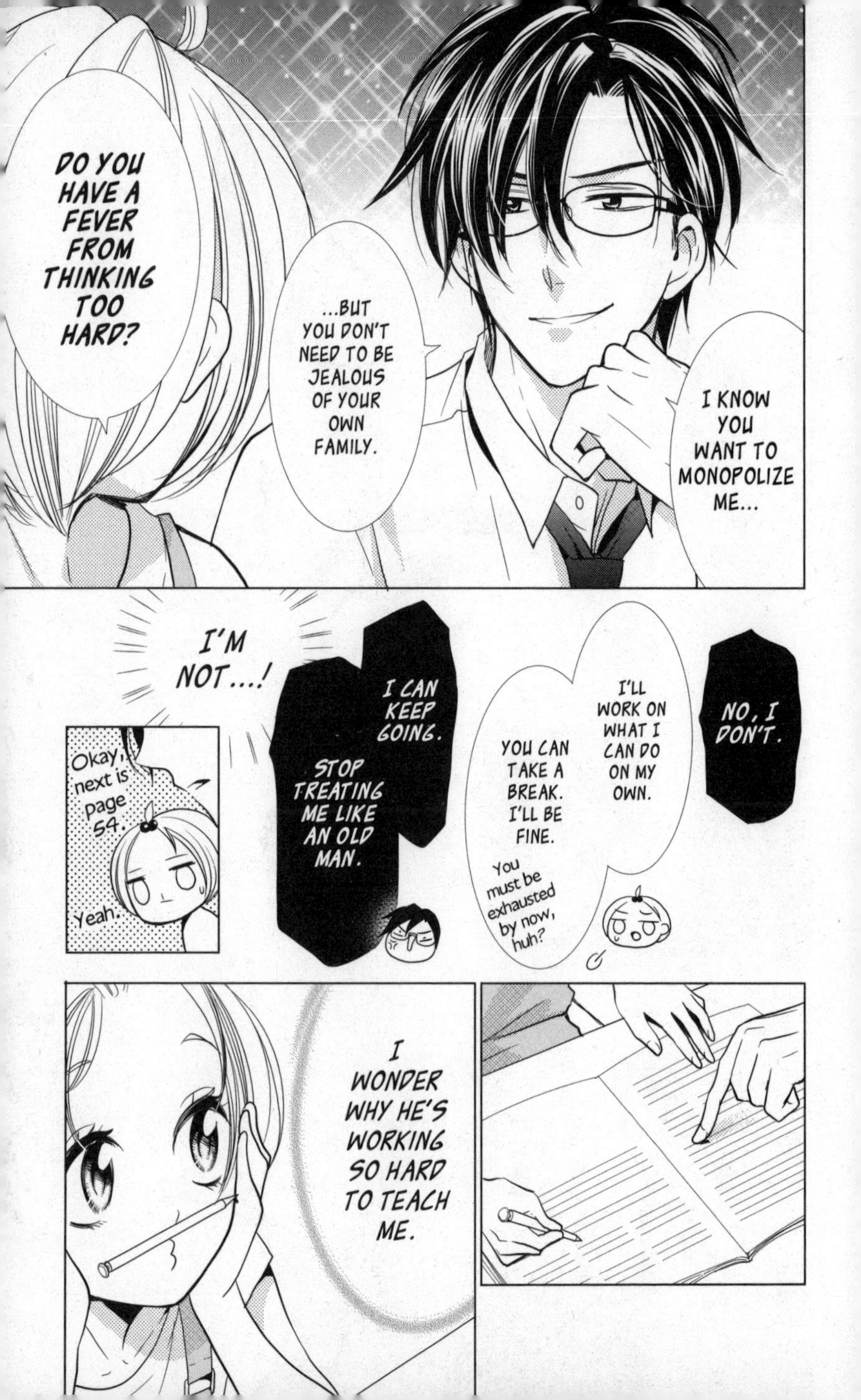
I KNOW YOU WANT TO MONOPOLIZE ME...
...BUT YOU DON'T NEED TO BE JEALOUS OF YOUR OWN FAMILY.
DO YOU HAVE A FEVER FROM THINKING TOO HARD?
NO, I DON'T.
I'LL WORK ON WHAT I CAN DO ON MY OWN.
YOU CAN TAKE A BREAK. I'LL BE FINE.
You must be exhausted by now, huh?
I CAN KEEP GOING.
STOP TREATING ME LIKE AN OLD MAN.
I'M NOT...!
Okay, next is page 54.
Yeah.
I WONDER WHY HE'S WORKING SO HARD TO TEACH ME.

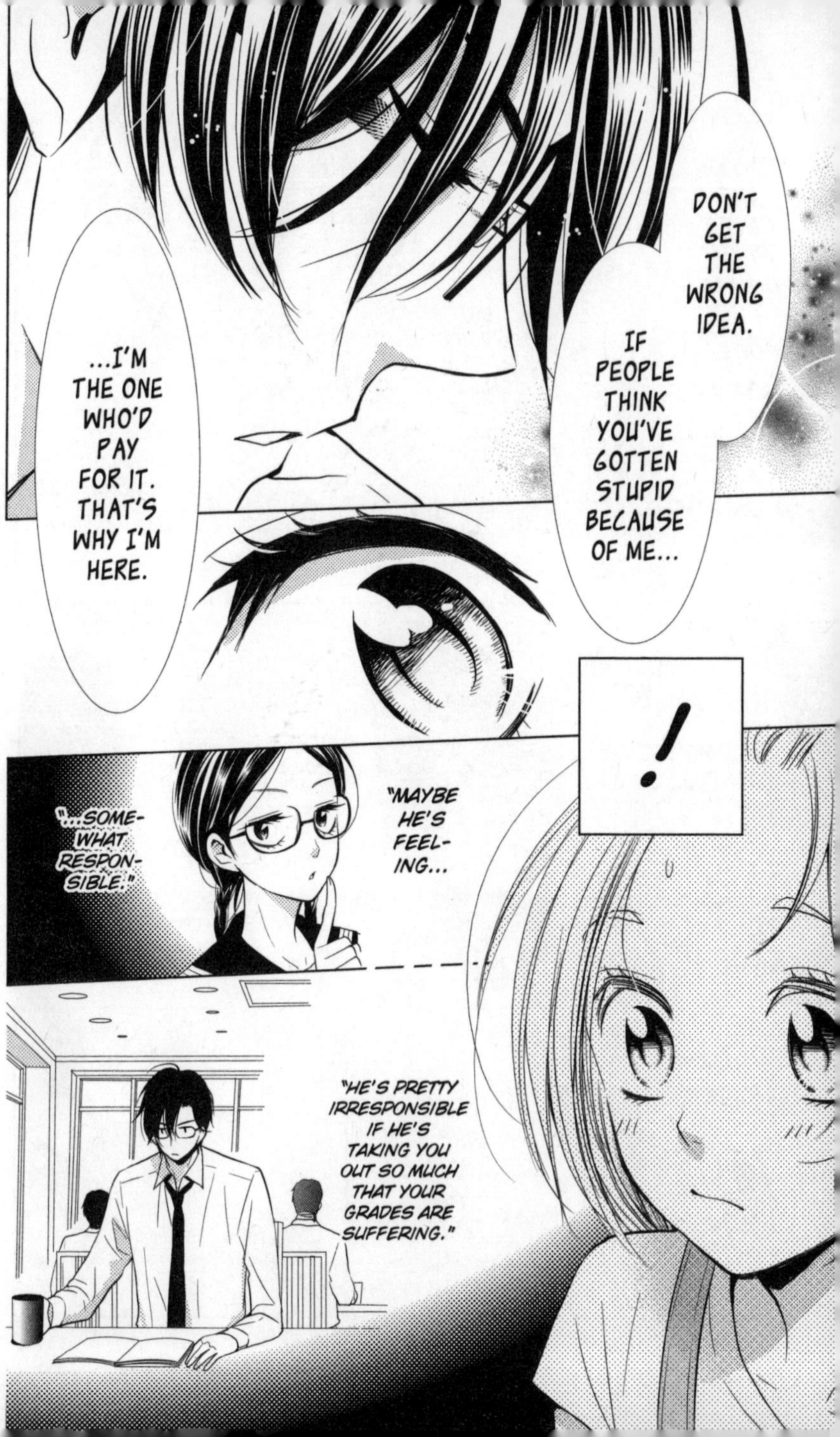
DON'T GET THE WRONG IDEA.
IF PEOPLE THINK YOU'VE GOTTEN STUPID BECAUSE OF ME...
...I'M THE ONE WHO'D PAY FOR IT. THAT'S WHY I'M HERE.
!
"MAYBE HE'S FEEL-ING...
"...SOME-WHAT RESPON-SIBLE."
"HE'S PRETTY IRRESPONSIBLE IF HE'S TAKING YOU OUT SO MUCH THAT YOUR GRADES ARE SUFFERING."

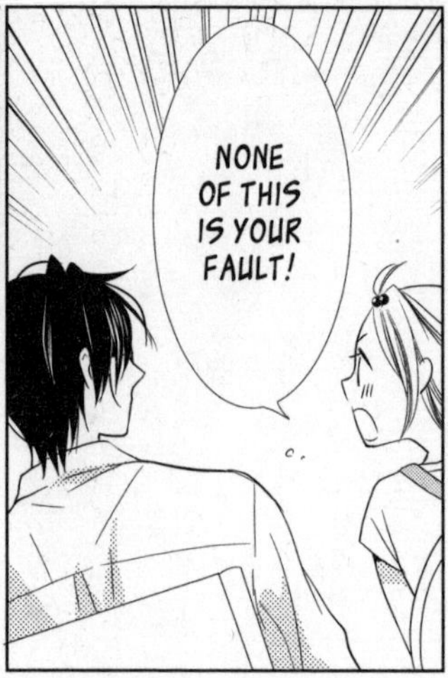
NONE OF THIS IS YOUR FAULT!
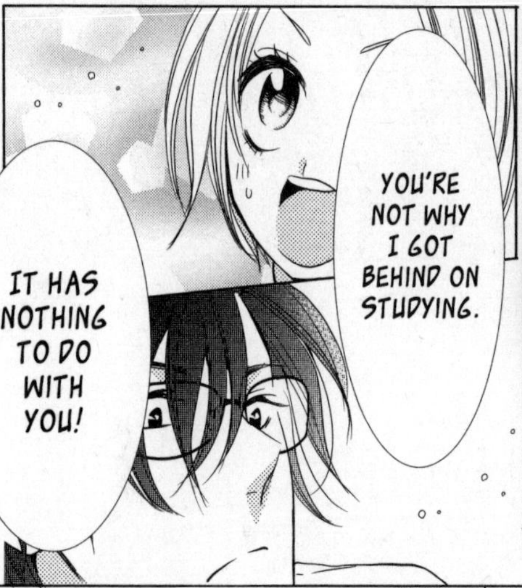
YOU'RE NOT WHY I GOT BEHIND ON STUDYING.
IT HAS NOTHING TO DO WITH YOU!
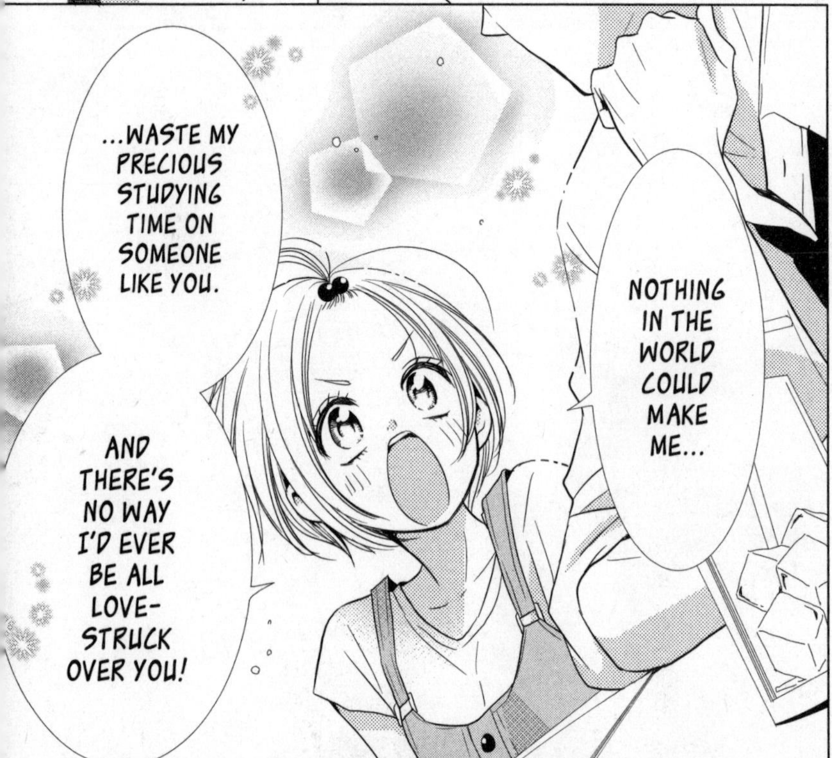
NOTHING IN THE WORLD COULD MAKE ME...
...WASTE MY PRECIOUS STUDYING TIME ON SOMEONE LIKE YOU.
AND THERE'S NO WAY I'D EVER BE ALL LOVE-STRUCK OVER YOU!

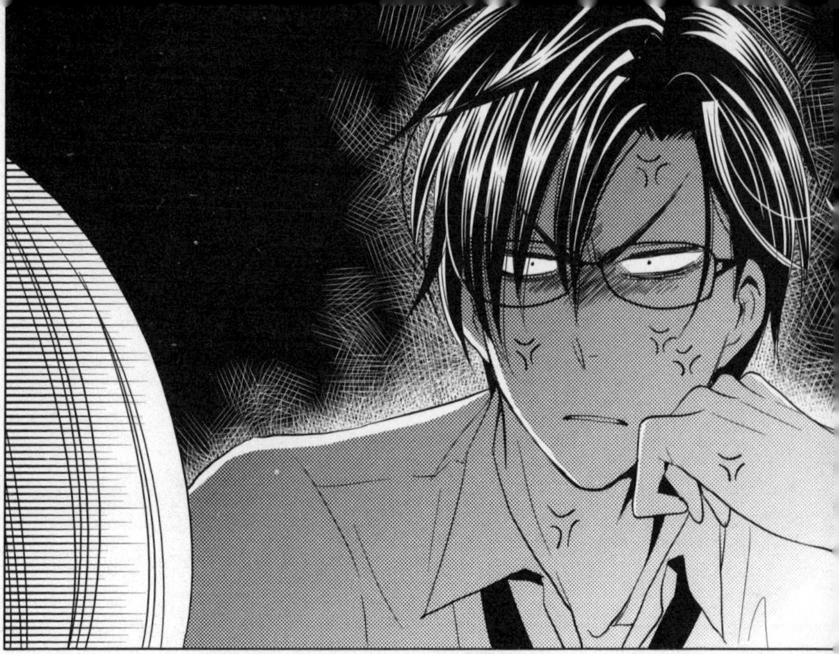

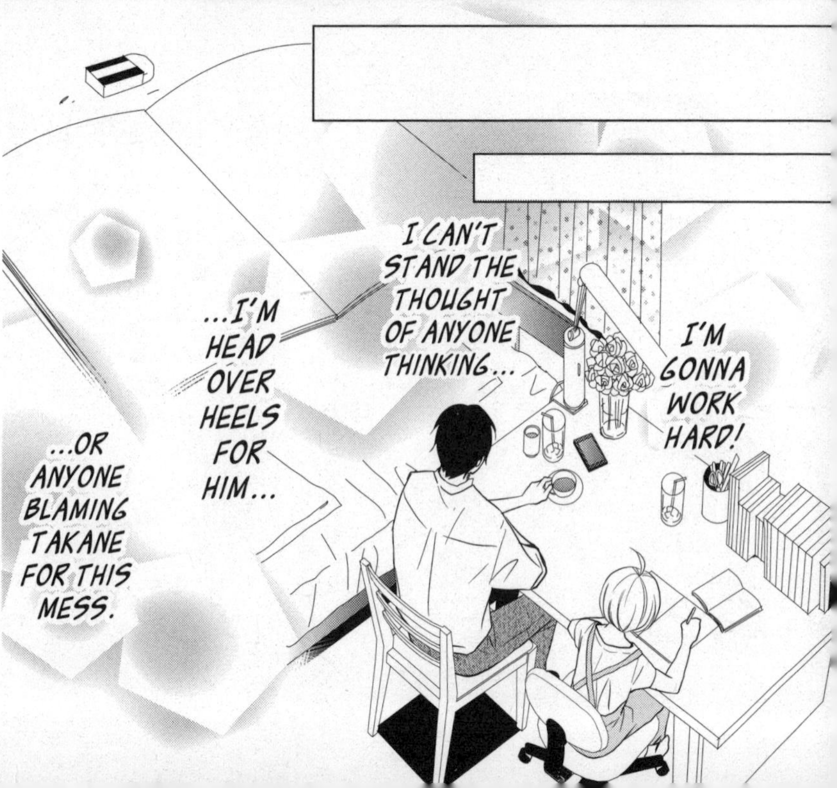
I'M GONNA WORK HARD!
I CAN'T STAND THE THOUGHT OF ANYONE THINKING...
...I'M HEAD OVER HEELS FOR HIM...
...OR ANYONE BLAMING TAKANE FOR THIS MESS.

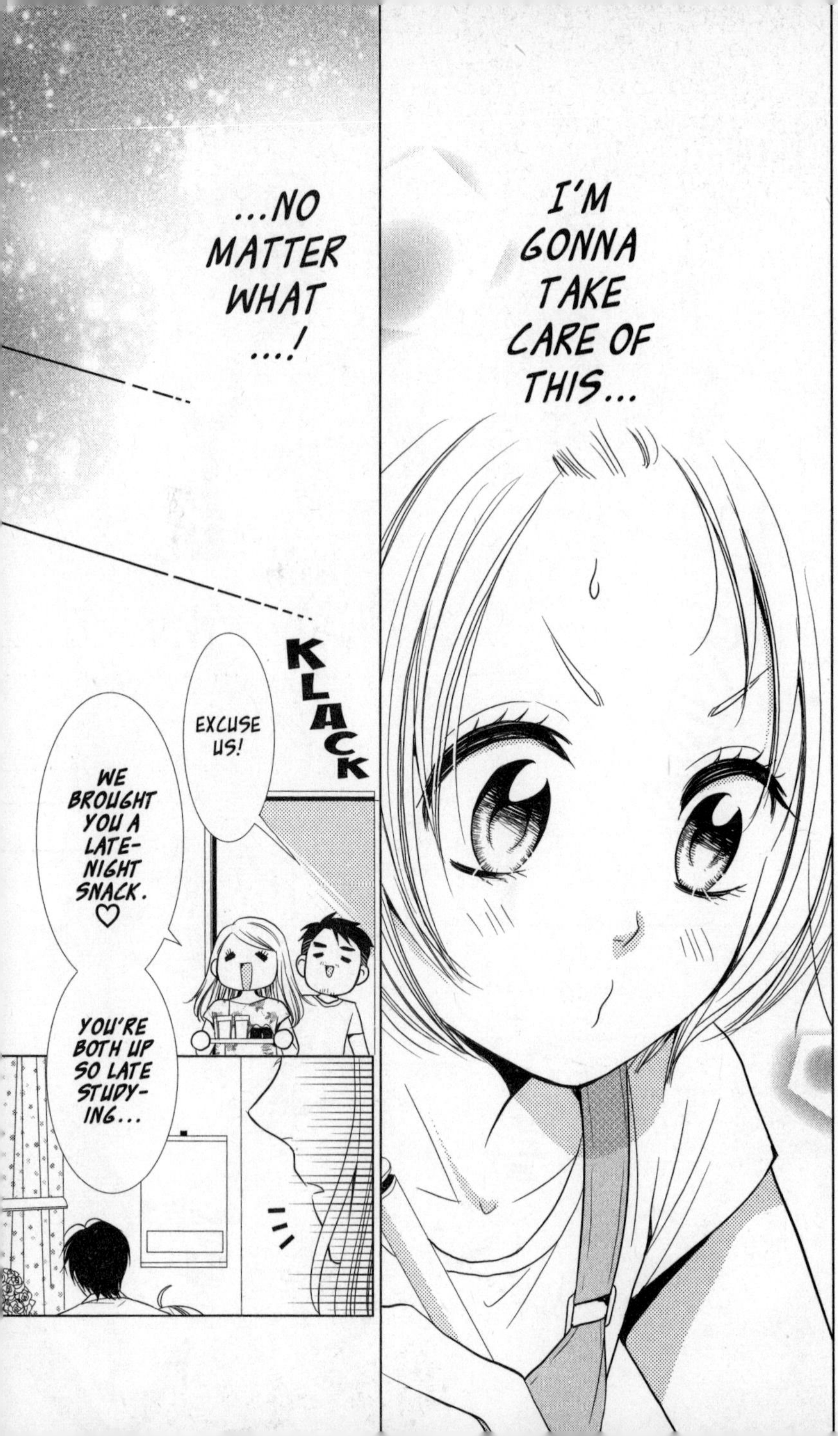
I'M GONNA TAKE CARE OF THIS...
...NO MATTER WHAT ...!
KLACK
EXCUSE US!
WE BROUGHT YOU A LATE-NIGHT SNACK. ♡
YOU'RE BOTH UP SO LATE STUDY-ING...

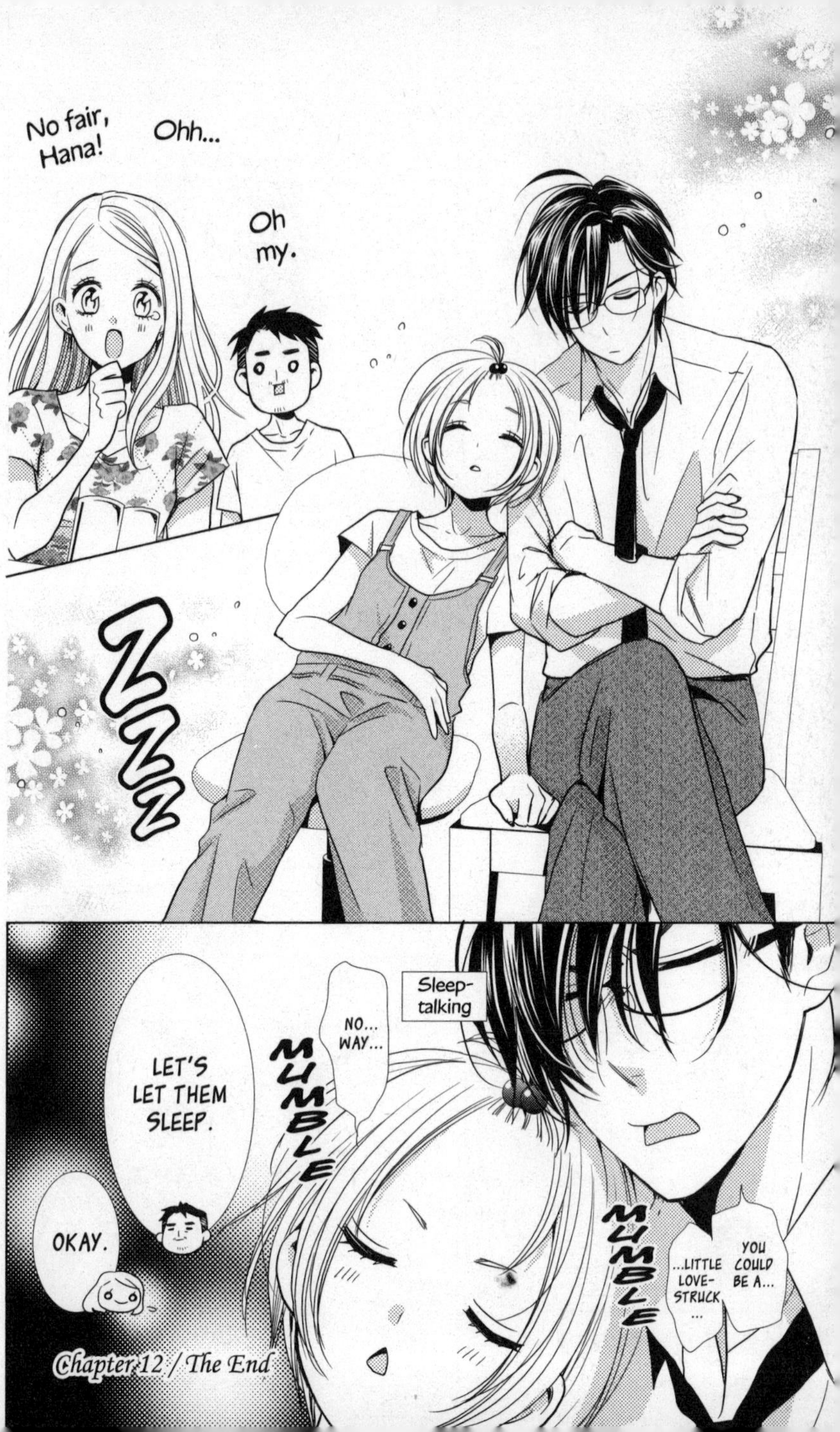
Ohh...
No fair, Hana!
Oh my.
ZZZ
Sleep-talking
NO... WAY...
MUMBLE
LET'S LET THEM SLEEP.
OKAY.
YOU COULD BE A...
MUMBLE
...LITTLE LOVE-STRUCK...
Chapter 12 / The End

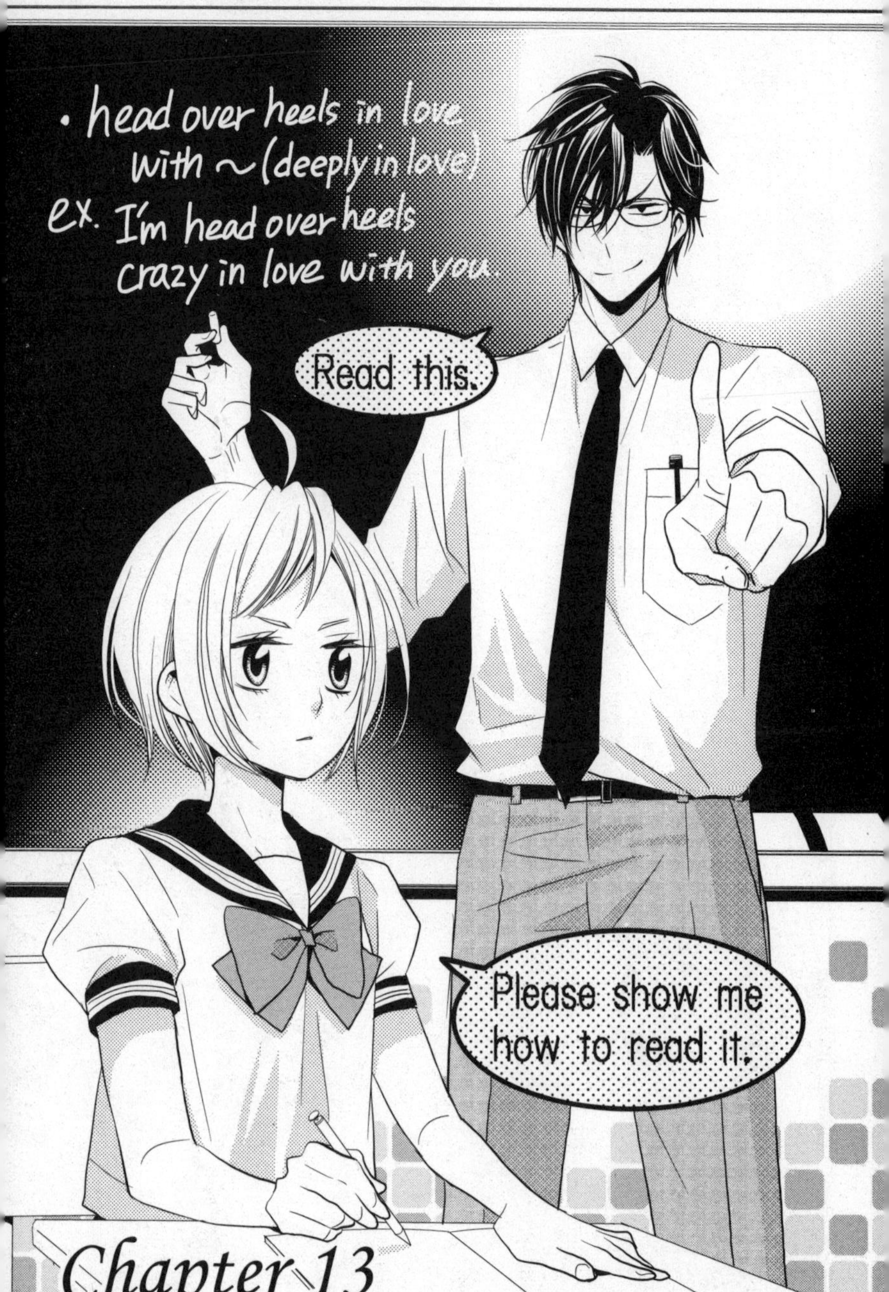
• head over heels in love with ~ (deeply in love)
ex. I'm head over heels crazy in love with you.
Read this.
Please show me how to read it.
Chapter 13

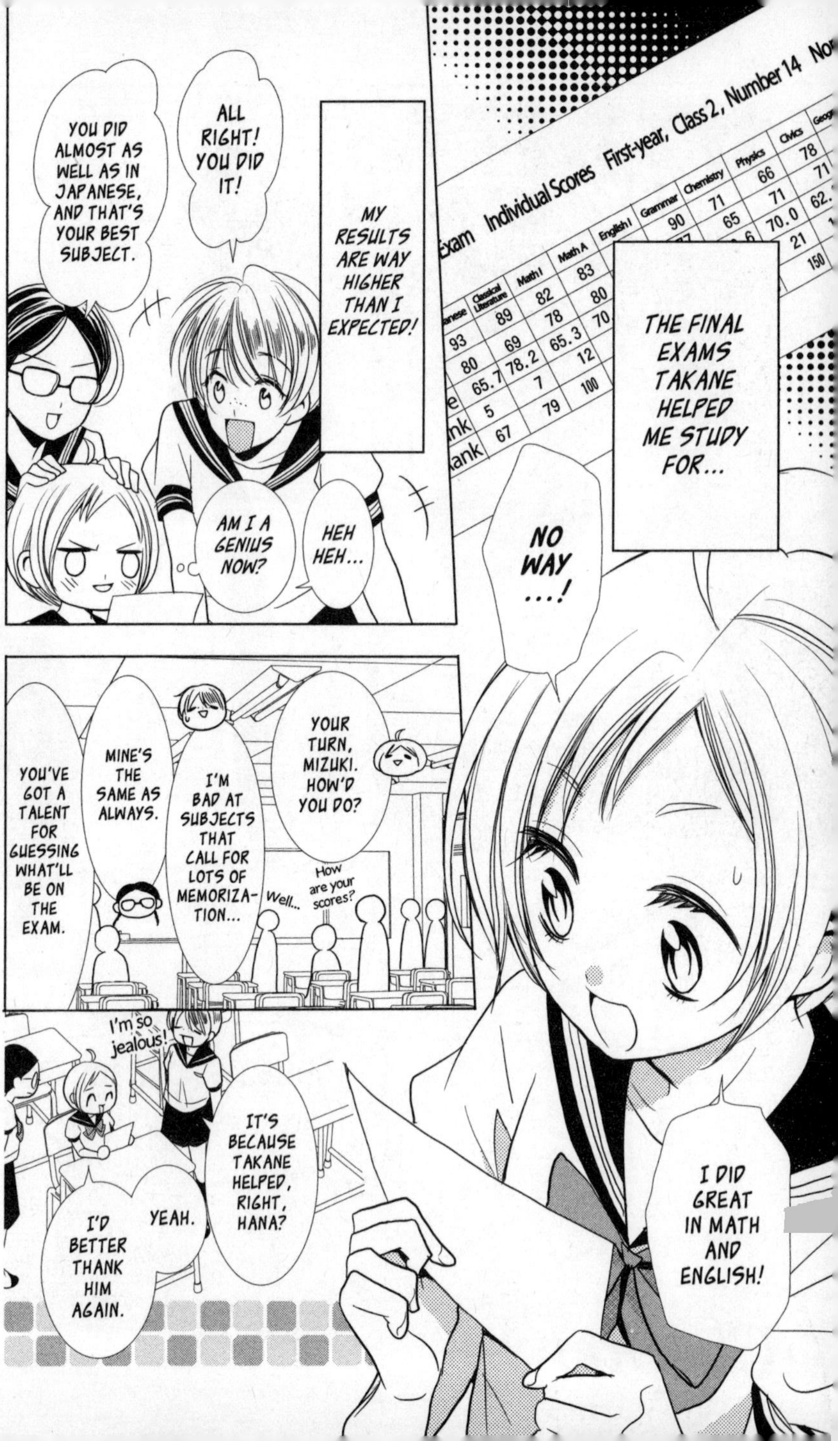
First-year, Class 2, Number 14
Individual Scores
THE FINAL EXAMS TAKANE HELPED ME STUDY FOR...
NO WAY ...!
I DID GREAT IN MATH AND ENGLISH!
MY RESULTS ARE WAY HIGHER THAN I EXPECTED!
ALL RIGHT! YOU DID IT!
YOU DID ALMOST AS WELL AS IN JAPANESE, AND THAT'S YOUR BEST SUBJECT.
AM I A GENIUS NOW?
HEH HEH...
YOUR TURN, MIZUKI. HOW'D YOU DO?
How are your scores?
I'M BAD AT SUBJECTS THAT CALL FOR LOTS OF MEMORIZATION...
Well...
MINE'S THE SAME AS ALWAYS.
YOU'VE GOT A TALENT FOR GUESSING WHAT'LL BE ON THE EXAM.
I'm so jealous!
IT'S BECAUSE TAKANE HELPED, RIGHT, HANA?
YEAH.
I'D BETTER THANK HIM AGAIN.

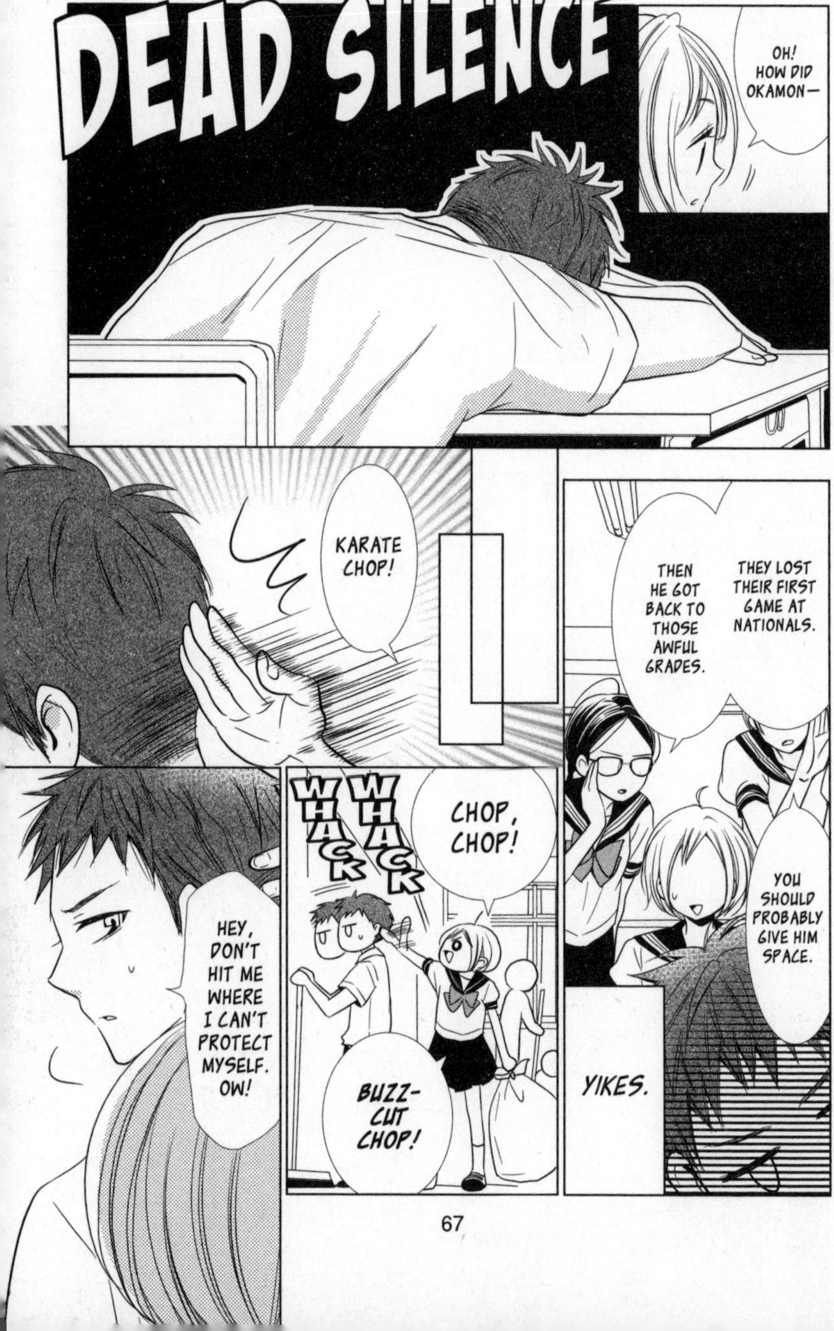
OH! HOW DID OKAMON—
DEAD SILENCE
THEY LOST THEIR FIRST GAME AT NATIONALS.
THEN HE GOT BACK TO THOSE AWFUL GRADES.
YOU SHOULD PROBABLY GIVE HIM SPACE.
YIKES.
KARATE CHOP!
CHOP, CHOP!
WHACK
WHACK
BUZZ-CUT CHOP!
HEY, DON'T HIT ME WHERE I CAN'T PROTECT MYSELF. OW!

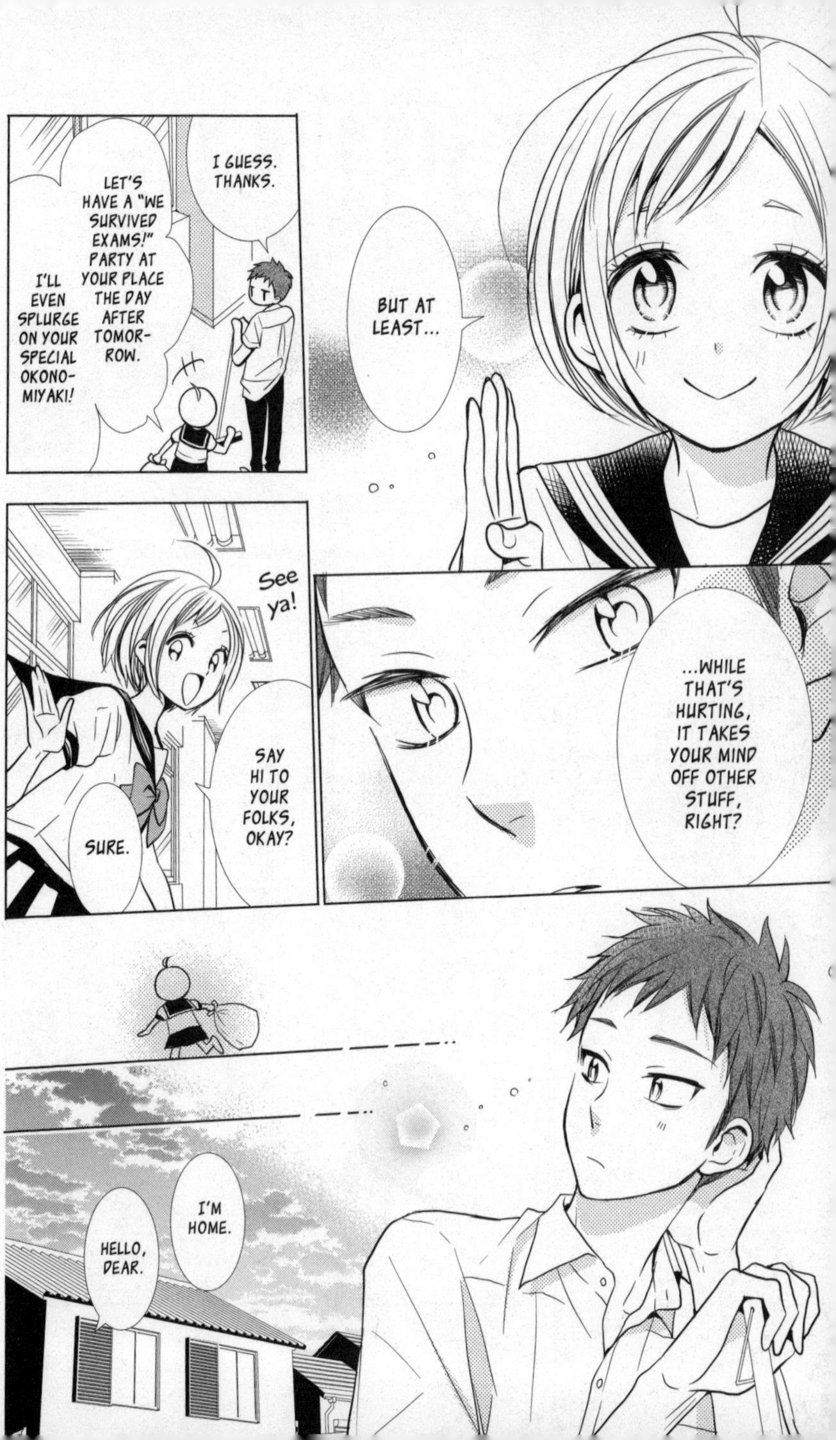
LET'S HAVE A "WE SURVIVED EXAMS!" PARTY AT YOUR PLACE THE DAY AFTER TOMOR-ROW.
I'LL EVEN SPLURGE ON YOUR SPECIAL OKONO-MIYAKI!
I GUESS. THANKS.
BUT AT LEAST...
...WHILE THAT'S HURTING, IT TAKES YOUR MIND OFF OTHER STUFF, RIGHT?
See ya!
SAY HI TO YOUR FOLKS, OKAY?
SURE.
I'M HOME.
HELLO, DEAR.

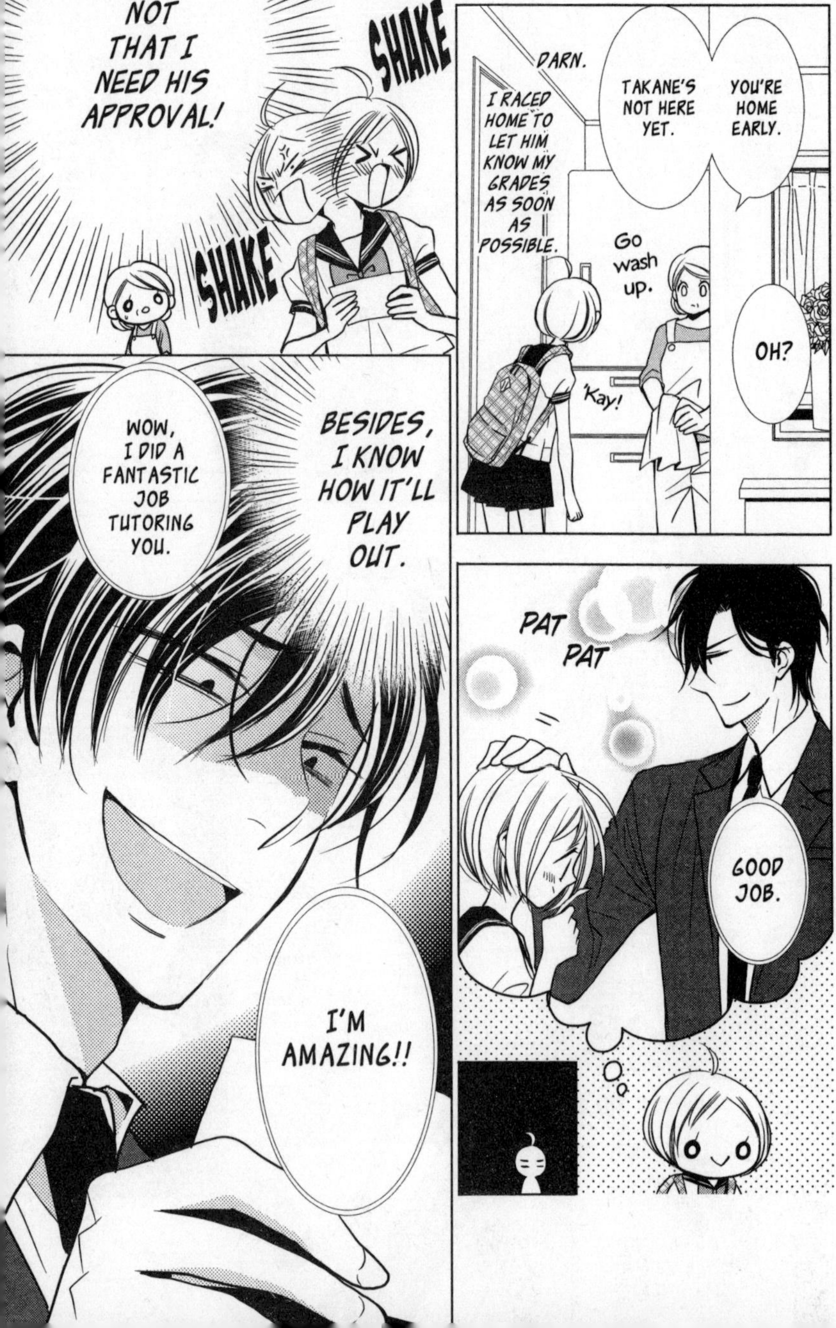
YOU'RE HOME EARLY.
TAKANE'S NOT HERE YET.
OH?
Go wash up.
DARN.
I RACED HOME TO LET HIM KNOW MY GRADES AS SOON AS POSSIBLE.
'Kay!
SHAKE
SHAKE
NOT THAT I NEED HIS APPROVAL!
PAT PAT
GOOD JOB.
BESIDES, I KNOW HOW IT'LL PLAY OUT.
WOW, I DID A FANTASTIC JOB TUTORING YOU.
I'M AMAZING!!

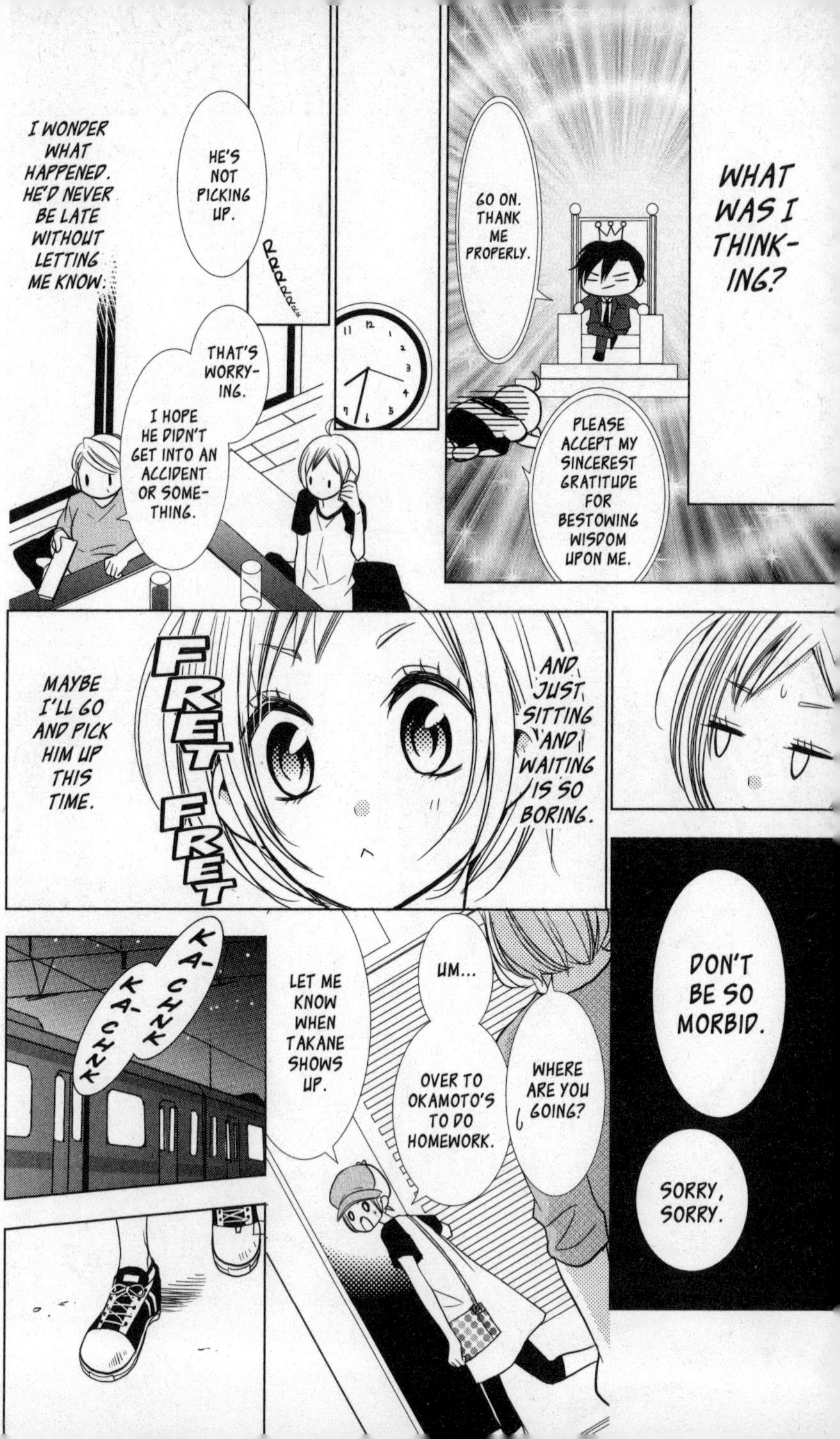
WHAT WAS I THINKING?
GO ON. THANK ME PROPERLY.
PLEASE ACCEPT MY SINCEREST GRATITUDE FOR BESTOWING WISDOM UPON ME.
RRRRRRRR
HE'S NOT PICKING UP.
I WONDER WHAT HAPPENED. HE'D NEVER BE LATE WITHOUT LETTING ME KNOW.
THAT'S WORRYING.
I HOPE HE DIDN'T GET INTO AN ACCIDENT OR SOMETHING.
AND JUST SITTING AND WAITING IS SO BORING.
FRET FRET
MAYBE I'LL GO AND PICK HIM UP THIS TIME.
DON'T BE SO MORBID.
SORRY, SORRY.
WHERE ARE YOU GOING?
OVER TO OKAMOTO'S TO DO HOMEWORK.
UM...
LET ME KNOW WHEN TAKANE SHOWS UP.
KA-CHNK
KA-CHNK

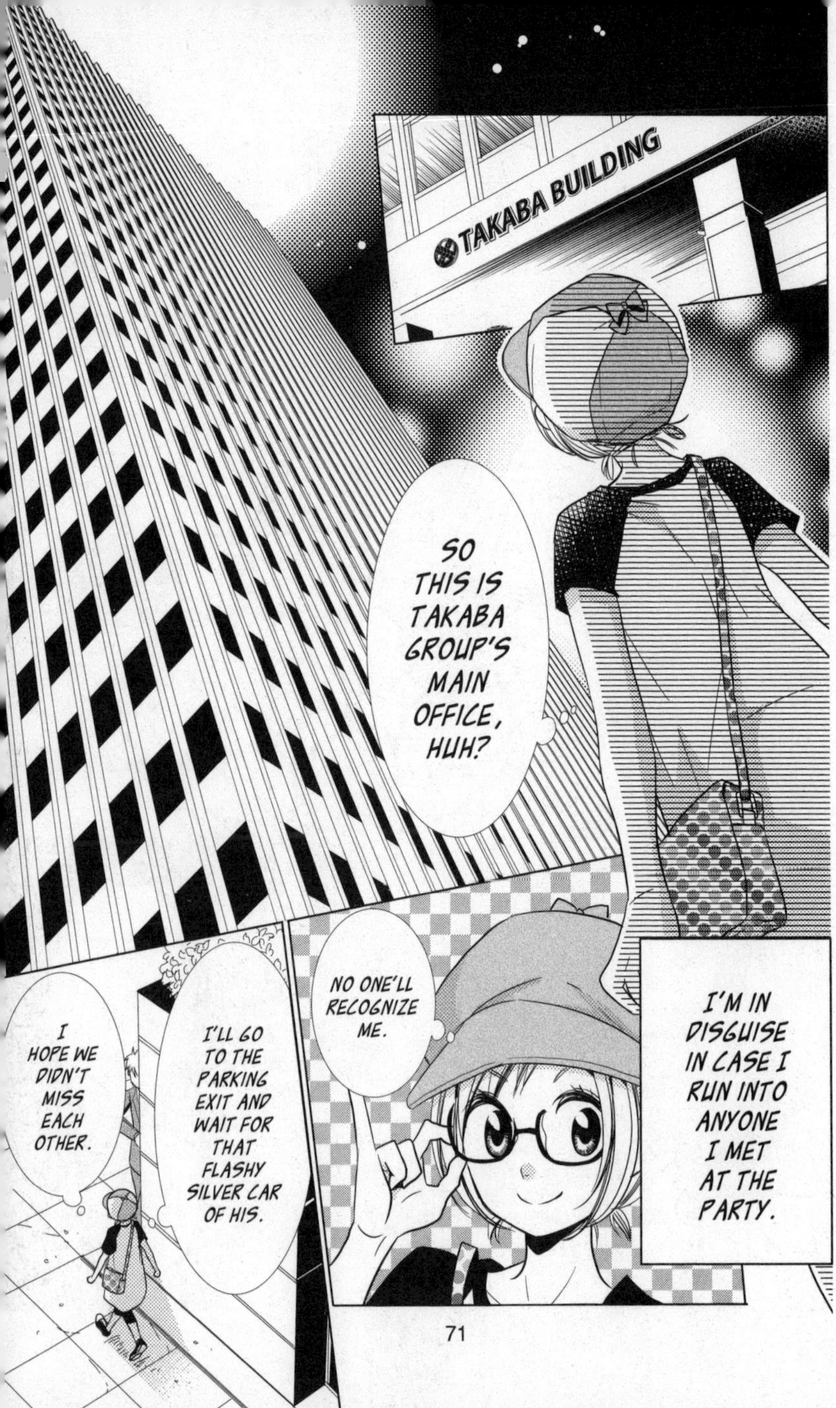
TAKABA BUILDING
SO THIS IS TAKABA GROUP'S MAIN OFFICE, HUH?
I'M IN DISGUISE IN CASE I RUN INTO ANYONE I MET AT THE PARTY.
NO ONE'LL RECOGNIZE ME.
I'LL GO TO THE PARKING EXIT AND WAIT FOR THAT FLASHY SILVER CAR OF HIS.
I HOPE WE DIDN'T MISS EACH OTHER.

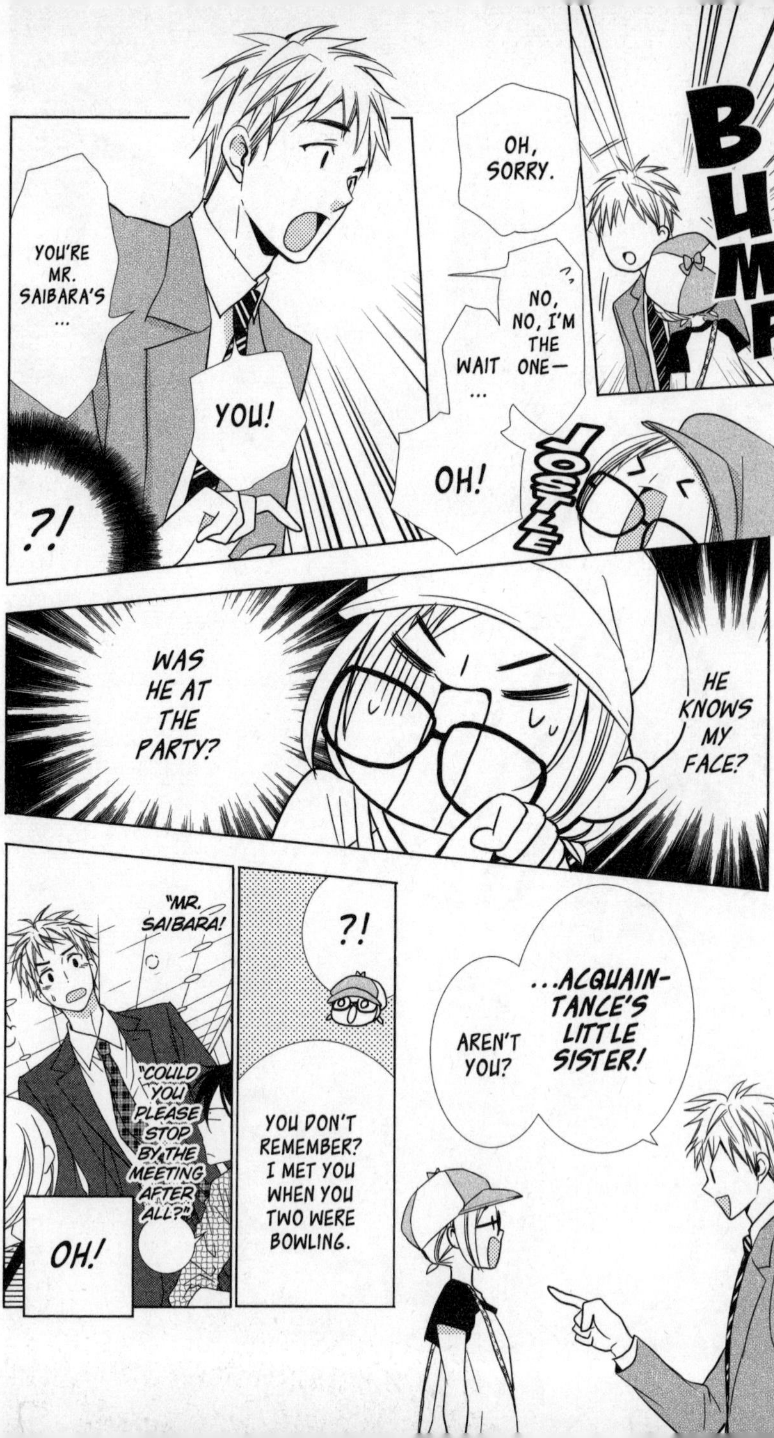
BUMP
OH, SORRY.
NO, NO, I'M THE ONE—
WAIT ...
JOSTLE
OH!
YOU!
YOU'RE MR. SAIBARA'S ...
?!
HE KNOWS MY FACE?
WAS HE AT THE PARTY?
...ACQUAINTANCE'S LITTLE SISTER!
AREN'T YOU?
?!
YOU DON'T REMEMBER? I MET YOU WHEN YOU TWO WERE BOWLING.
"MR. SAIBARA!
"COULD YOU PLEASE STOP BY THE MEETING AFTER ALL?"
OH!

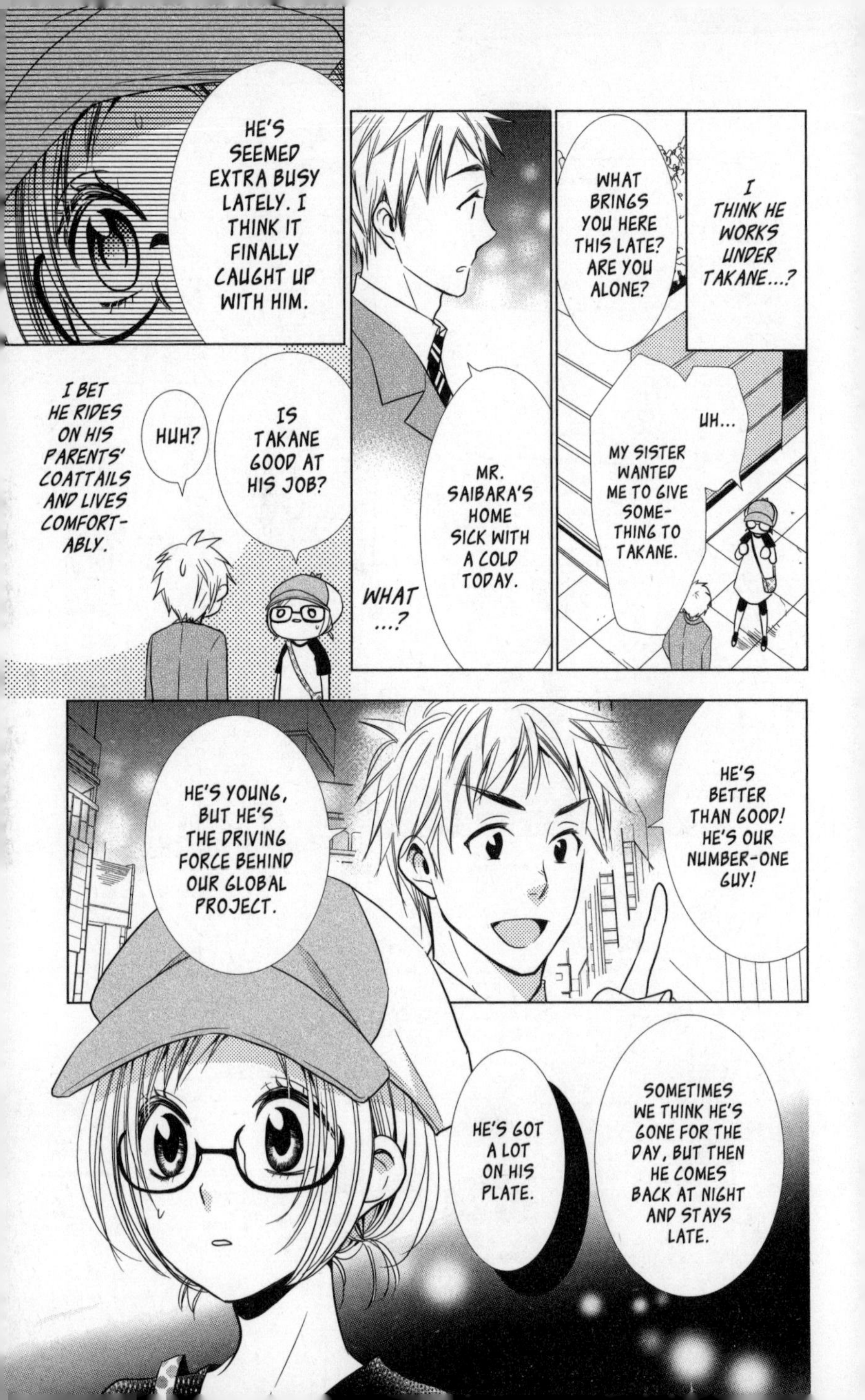
I THINK HE WORKS UNDER TAKANE...?
WHAT BRINGS YOU HERE THIS LATE? ARE YOU ALONE?
UH...
MY SISTER WANTED ME TO GIVE SOME-THING TO TAKANE.
MR. SAIBARA'S HOME SICK WITH A COLD TODAY.
WHAT ...?
HE'S SEEMED EXTRA BUSY LATELY. I THINK IT FINALLY CAUGHT UP WITH HIM.
IS TAKANE GOOD AT HIS JOB?
HUH?
I BET HE RIDES ON HIS PARENTS' COATTAILS AND LIVES COMFORT-ABLY.
HE'S BETTER THAN GOOD! HE'S OUR NUMBER-ONE GUY!
HE'S YOUNG, BUT HE'S THE DRIVING FORCE BEHIND OUR GLOBAL PROJECT.
SOMETIMES WE THINK HE'S GONE FOR THE DAY, BUT THEN HE COMES BACK AT NIGHT AND STAYS LATE.
HE'S GOT A LOT ON HIS PLATE.

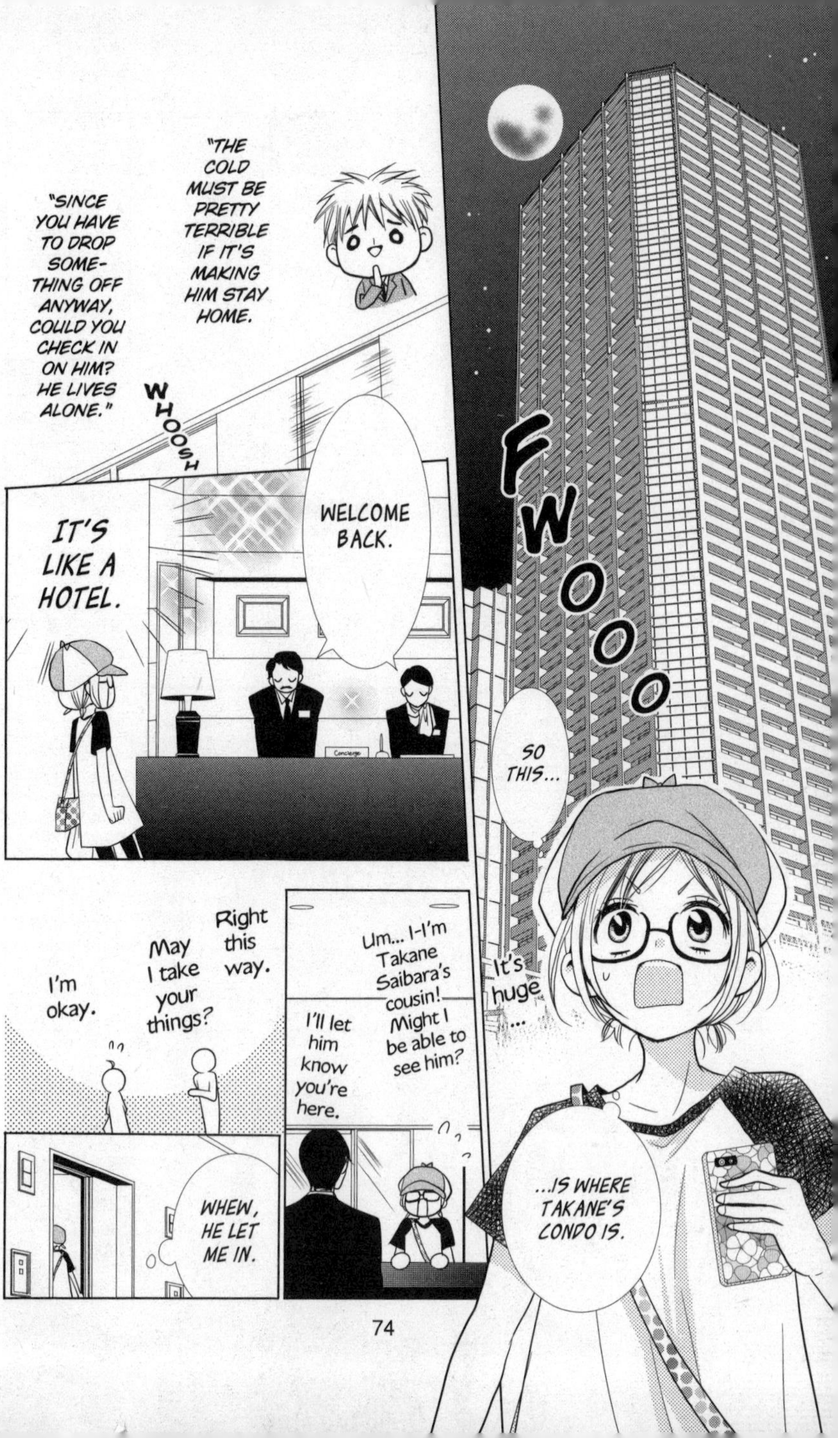
FWOOOO
SO THIS...
It's huge...
...IS WHERE TAKANE'S CONDO IS.
"THE COLD MUST BE PRETTY TERRIBLE IF IT'S MAKING HIM STAY HOME.
"SINCE YOU HAVE TO DROP SOME-THING OFF ANYWAY, COULD YOU CHECK IN ON HIM? HE LIVES ALONE."
WHOOSH
WELCOME BACK.
IT'S LIKE A HOTEL.
Um... I-I'm Takane Saibara's cousin! Might I be able to see him?
I'll let him know you're here.
Right this way.
May I take your things?
I'm okay.
WHEW, HE LET ME IN.

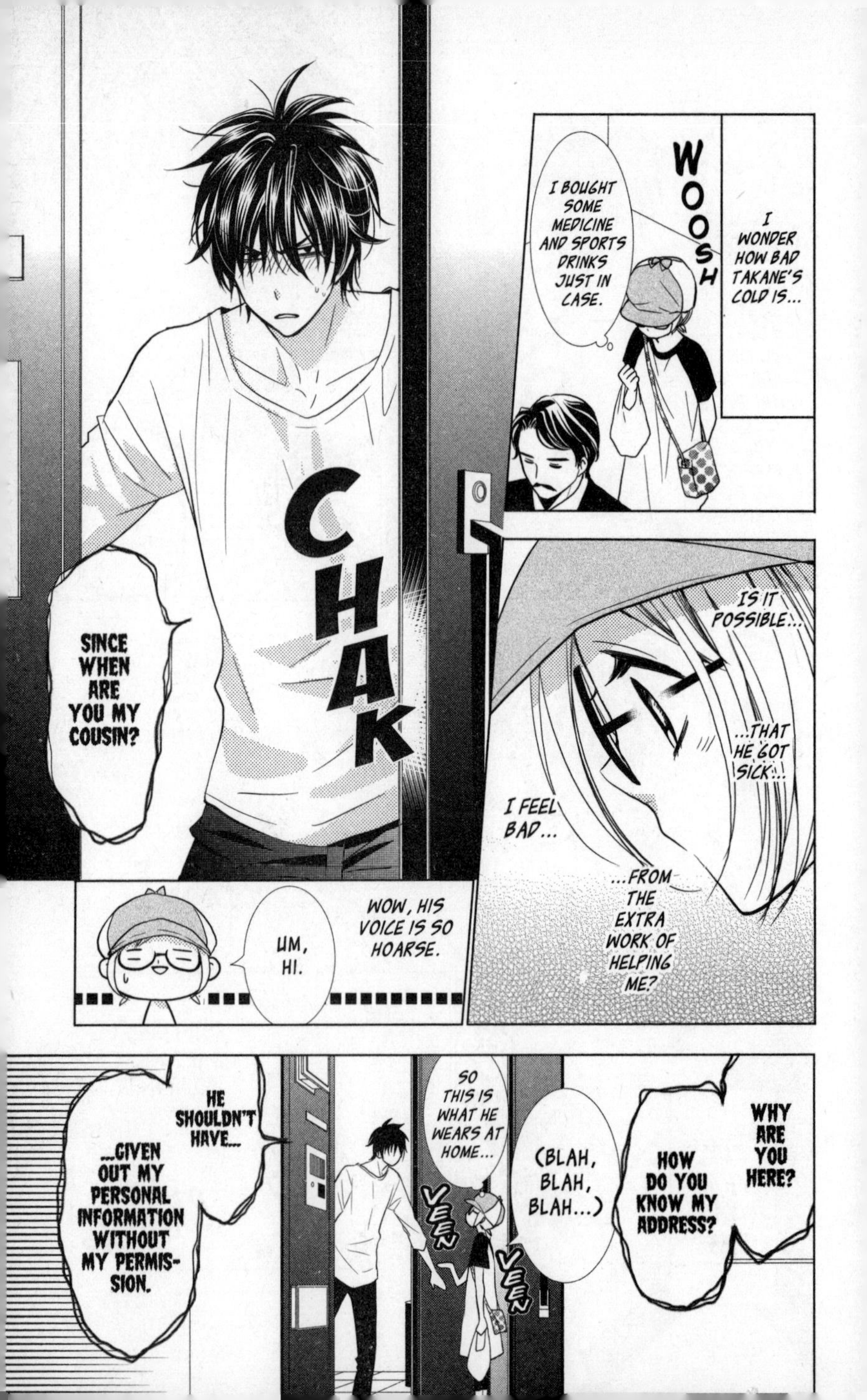
I WONDER HOW BAD TAKANE'S COLD IS...
WOOSH
I BOUGHT SOME MEDICINE AND SPORTS DRINKS JUST IN CASE.
IS IT POSSIBLE...
...THAT HE GOT SICK...
I FEEL BAD...
...FROM THE EXTRA WORK OF HELPING ME?
CHAK
SINCE WHEN ARE YOU MY COUSIN?
WOW, HIS VOICE IS SO HOARSE.
UM, HI.
WHY ARE YOU HERE?
HOW DO YOU KNOW MY ADDRESS?
(BLAH, BLAH, BLAH...)
VEEN
VEEN
SO THIS IS WHAT HE WEARS AT HOME...
HE SHOULDN'T HAVE...
...GIVEN OUT MY PERSONAL INFORMATION WITHOUT MY PERMIS-SION.

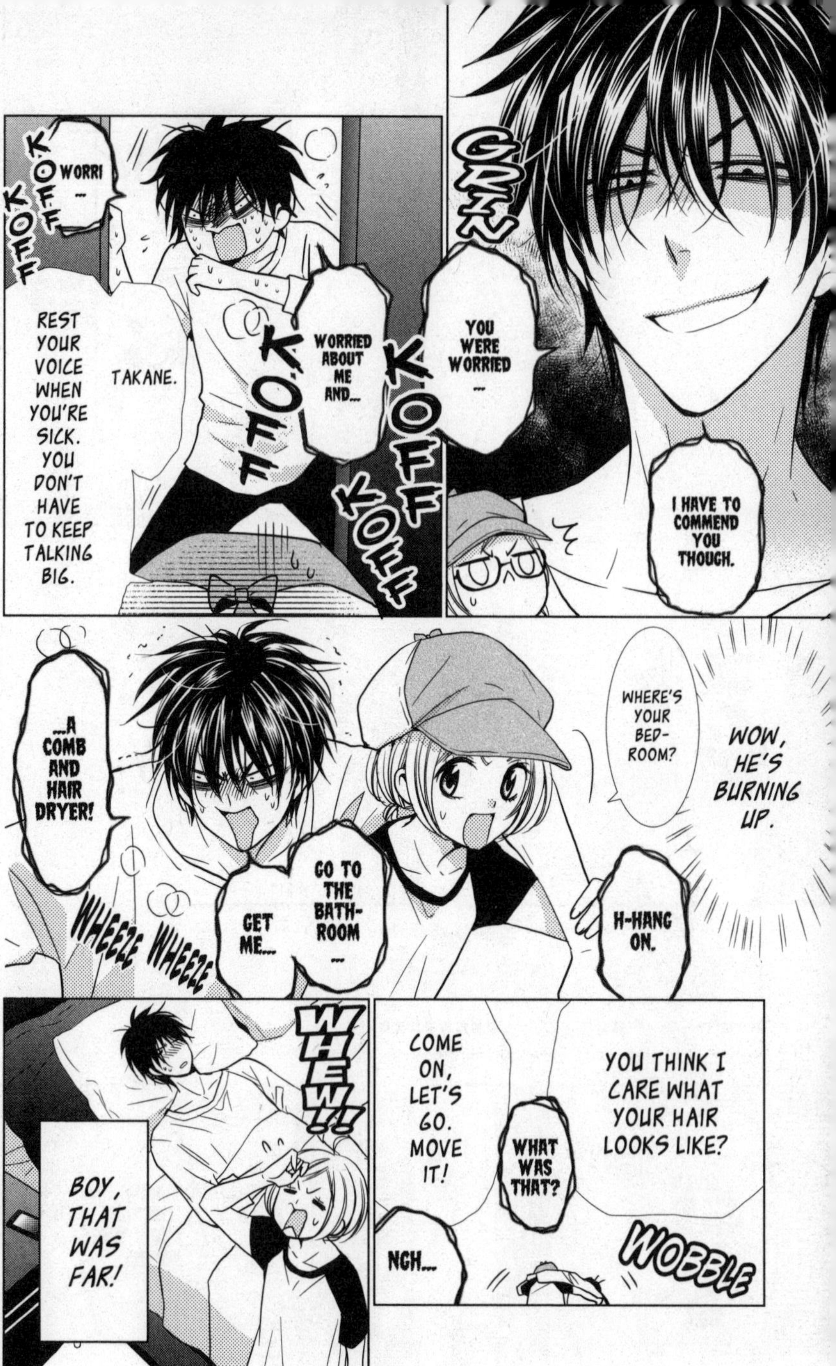
I HAVE TO COMMEND YOU THOUGH.
GRIN
YOU WERE WORRIED...
KOFF KOFF
WORRIED ABOUT ME AND...
KOFF
WORRI...
KOFF KOFF
TAKANE.
REST YOUR VOICE WHEN YOU'RE SICK. YOU DON'T HAVE TO KEEP TALKING BIG.
WOW, HE'S BURNING UP.
WHERE'S YOUR BED-ROOM?
H-HANG ON.
GO TO THE BATH-ROOM... GET ME...
...A COMB AND HAIR DRYER!
WHEEZE WHEEZE
YOU THINK I CARE WHAT YOUR HAIR LOOKS LIKE?
WHAT WAS THAT?
COME ON, LET'S GO. MOVE IT!
WOBBLE
NGH...
WHEW!!
BOY, THAT WAS FAR!

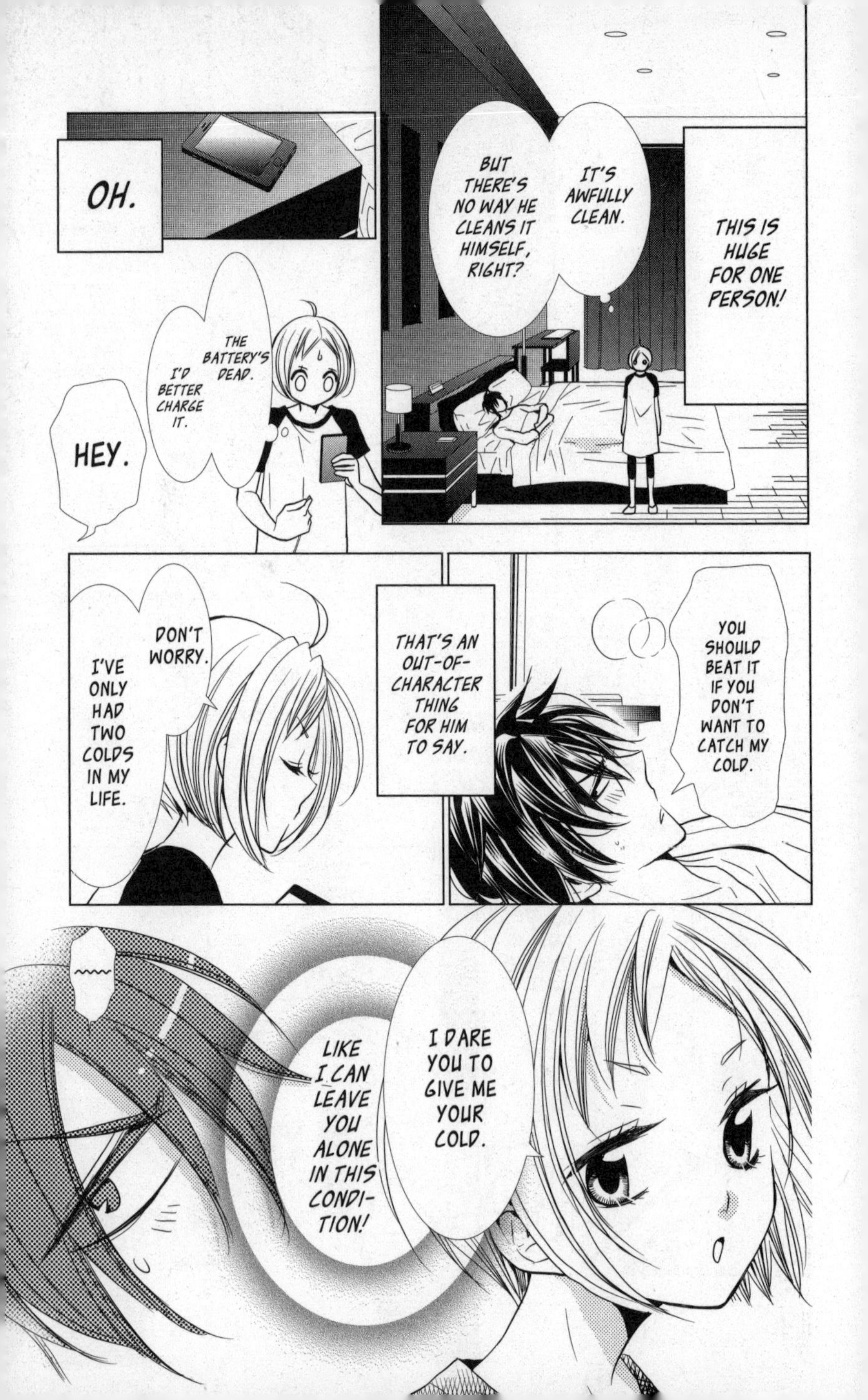
THIS IS HUGE FOR ONE PERSON!
IT'S AWFULLY CLEAN.
BUT THERE'S NO WAY HE CLEANS IT HIMSELF, RIGHT?
OH.
THE BATTERY'S DEAD.
I'D BETTER CHARGE IT.
HEY.
YOU SHOULD BEAT IT IF YOU DON'T WANT TO CATCH MY COLD.
THAT'S AN OUT-OF-CHARACTER THING FOR HIM TO SAY.
DON'T WORRY.
I'VE ONLY HAD TWO COLDS IN MY LIFE.
I DARE YOU TO GIVE ME YOUR COLD.
LIKE I CAN LEAVE YOU ALONE IN THIS CONDITION!
~~~
~~~

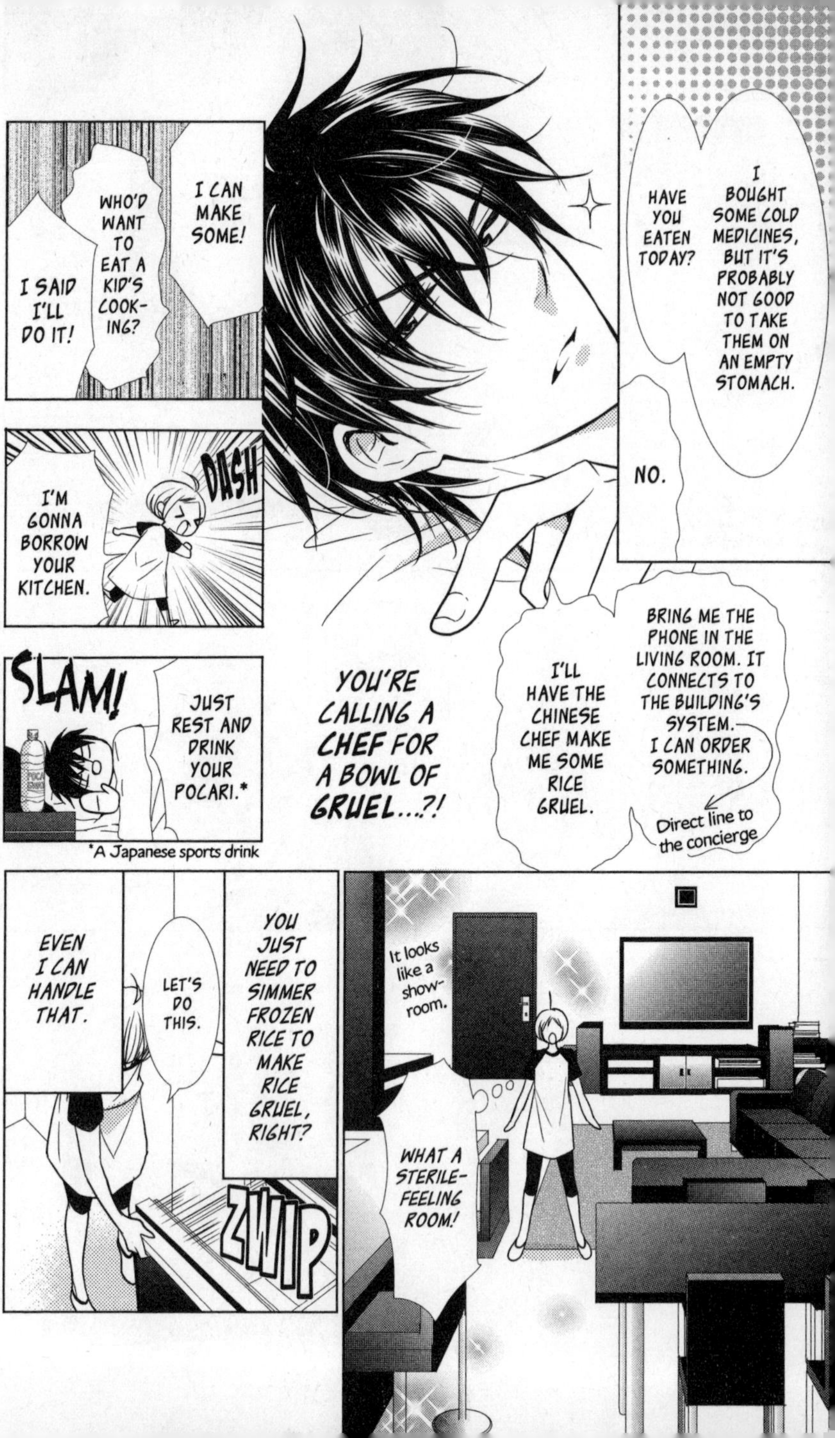
I BOUGHT SOME COLD MEDICINES, BUT IT'S PROBABLY NOT GOOD TO TAKE THEM ON AN EMPTY STOMACH.
HAVE YOU EATEN TODAY?
NO.
BRING ME THE PHONE IN THE LIVING ROOM. IT CONNECTS TO THE BUILDING'S SYSTEM. I CAN ORDER SOMETHING.
Direct line to the concierge
I'LL HAVE THE CHINESE CHEF MAKE ME SOME RICE GRUEL.
YOU'RE CALLING A CHEF FOR A BOWL OF GRUEL...?!
I CAN MAKE SOME!
WHO'D WANT TO EAT A KID'S COOKING?
I SAID I'LL DO IT!
I'M GONNA BORROW YOUR KITCHEN.
DASH
SLAM!
JUST REST AND DRINK YOUR POCARI.*
It looks like a showroom.
WHAT A STERILE-FEELING ROOM!
YOU JUST NEED TO SIMMER FROZEN RICE TO MAKE RICE GRUEL, RIGHT?
LET'S DO THIS.
EVEN I CAN HANDLE THAT.
ZWIP
*A Japanese sports drink

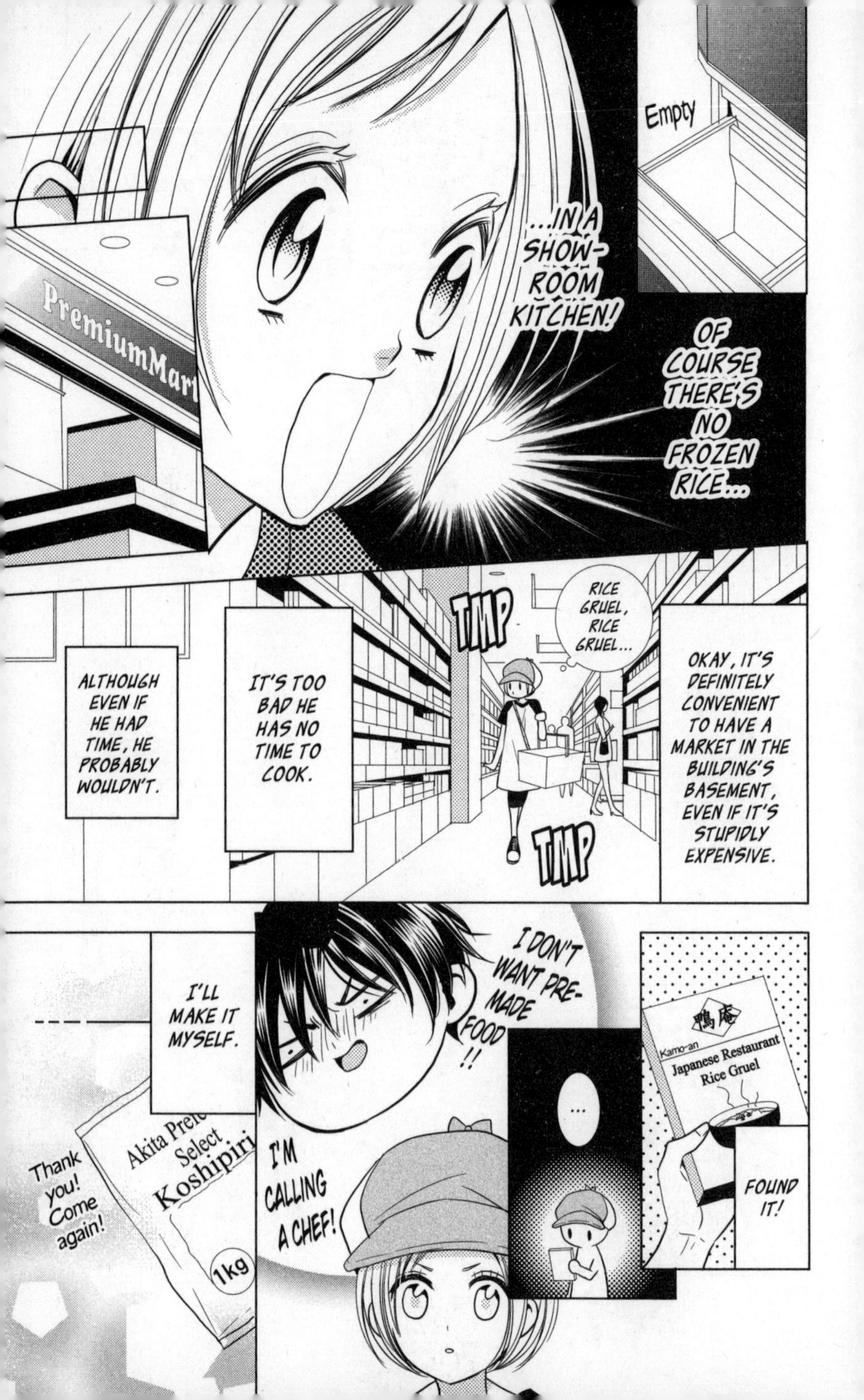
Empty
...IN A SHOW-ROOM KITCHEN!
OF COURSE THERE'S NO FROZEN RICE...
PremiumMart
OKAY, IT'S DEFINITELY CONVENIENT TO HAVE A MARKET IN THE BUILDING'S BASEMENT, EVEN IF IT'S STUPIDLY EXPENSIVE.
RICE GRUEL, RICE GRUEL...
TMP
TMP
IT'S TOO BAD HE HAS NO TIME TO COOK.
ALTHOUGH EVEN IF HE HAD TIME, HE PROBABLY WOULDN'T.
鴨庵
Kamo-an
Japanese Restaurant
Rice Gruel
FOUND IT!
...
I DON'T WANT PRE-MADE FOOD!!
I'M CALLING A CHEF!
I'LL MAKE IT MYSELF.
Akita Prefe
Select
Koshipiri
1kg
Thank you! Come again!

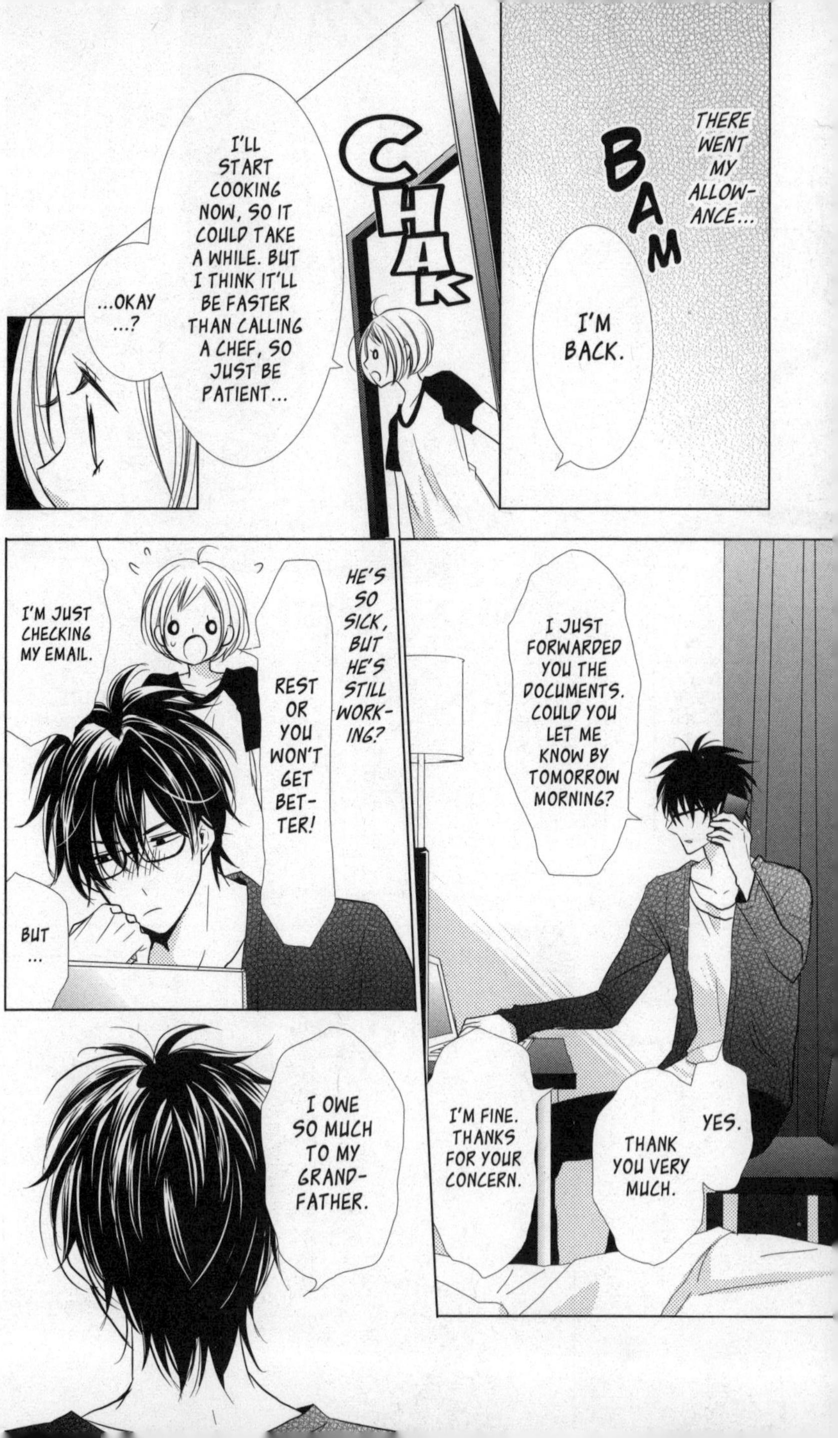
THERE WENT MY ALLOW-ANCE...
BAM
I'M BACK.
CHAK
I'LL START COOKING NOW, SO IT COULD TAKE A WHILE. BUT I THINK IT'LL BE FASTER THAN CALLING A CHEF, SO JUST BE PATIENT...
...OKAY ...?
I JUST FORWARDED YOU THE DOCUMENTS. COULD YOU LET ME KNOW BY TOMORROW MORNING?
YES.
THANK YOU VERY MUCH.
I'M FINE. THANKS FOR YOUR CONCERN.
HE'S SO SICK, BUT HE'S STILL WORK-ING?
REST OR YOU WON'T GET BET-TER!
I'M JUST CHECKING MY EMAIL.
BUT ...
I OWE SO MUCH TO MY GRAND-FATHER.

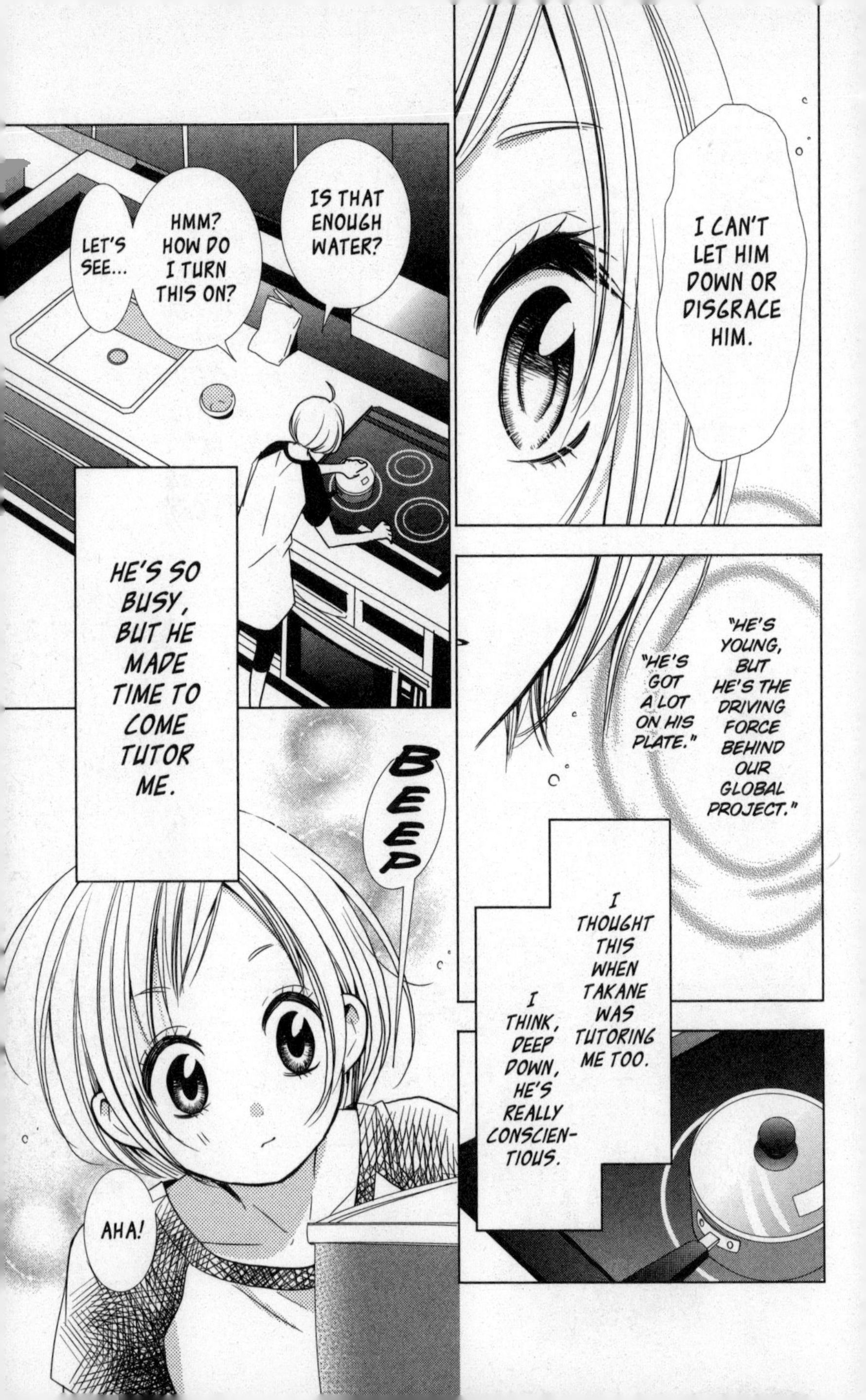
I CAN'T LET HIM DOWN OR DISGRACE HIM.
"HE'S YOUNG, BUT HE'S THE DRIVING FORCE BEHIND OUR GLOBAL PROJECT."
"HE'S GOT A LOT ON HIS PLATE."
I THOUGHT THIS WHEN TAKANE WAS TUTORING ME TOO.
I THINK, DEEP DOWN, HE'S REALLY CONSCIEN-TIOUS.
IS THAT ENOUGH WATER?
HMM? HOW DO I TURN THIS ON?
LET'S SEE...
HE'S SO BUSY, BUT HE MADE TIME TO COME TUTOR ME.
BEEP
AHA!

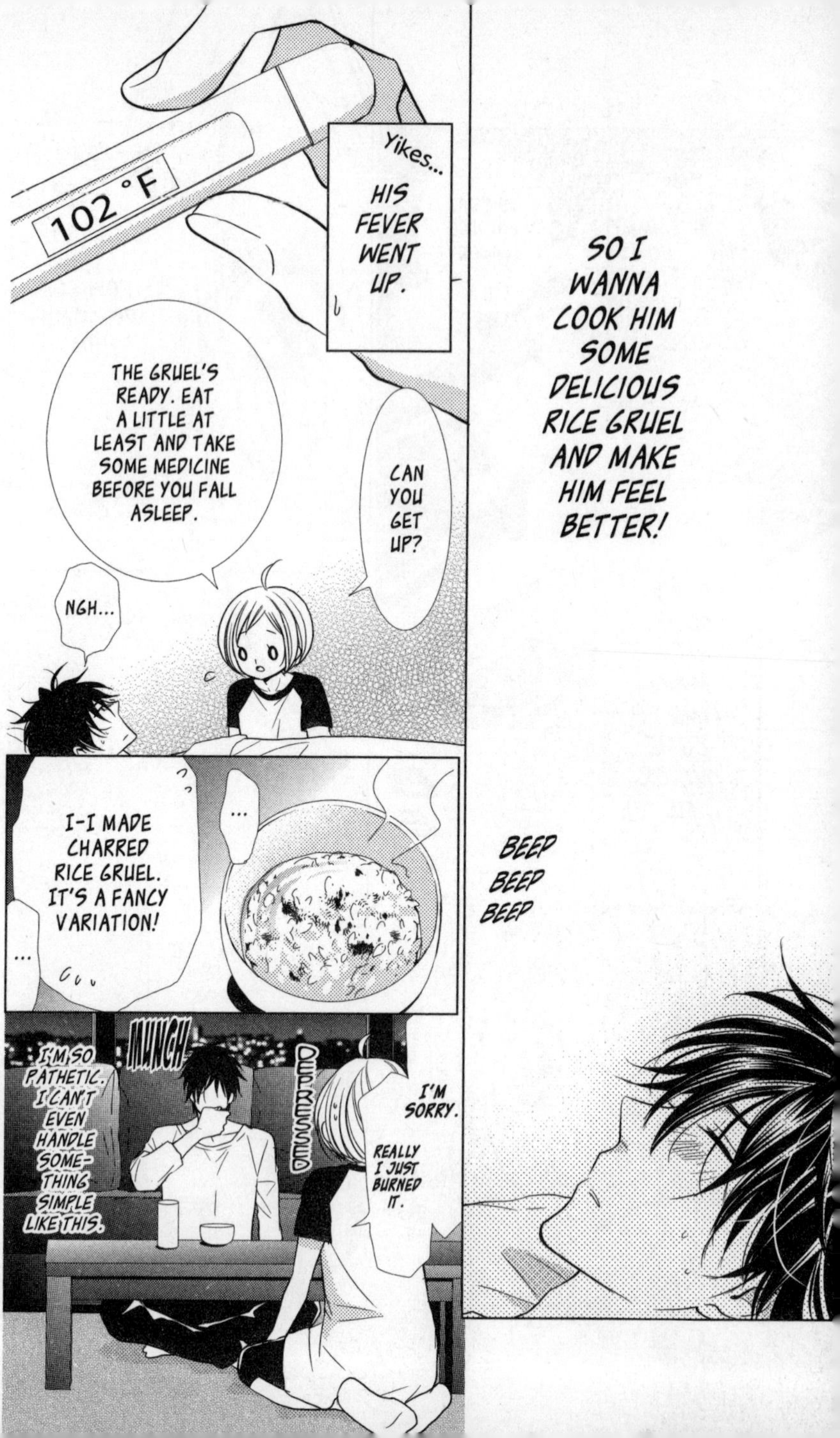
SO I WANNA COOK HIM SOME DELICIOUS RICE GRUEL AND MAKE HIM FEEL BETTER!
BEEP BEEP BEEP
102 °F
Yikes...
HIS FEVER WENT UP.
CAN YOU GET UP?
THE GRUEL'S READY. EAT A LITTLE AT LEAST AND TAKE SOME MEDICINE BEFORE YOU FALL ASLEEP.
NGH...
...
I-I MADE CHARRED RICE GRUEL. IT'S A FANCY VARIATION!
...
I'M SORRY.
REALLY I JUST BURNED IT.
DEPRESSED
MUNCH
I'M SO PATHETIC. I CAN'T EVEN HANDLE SOME-THING SIMPLE LIKE THIS.

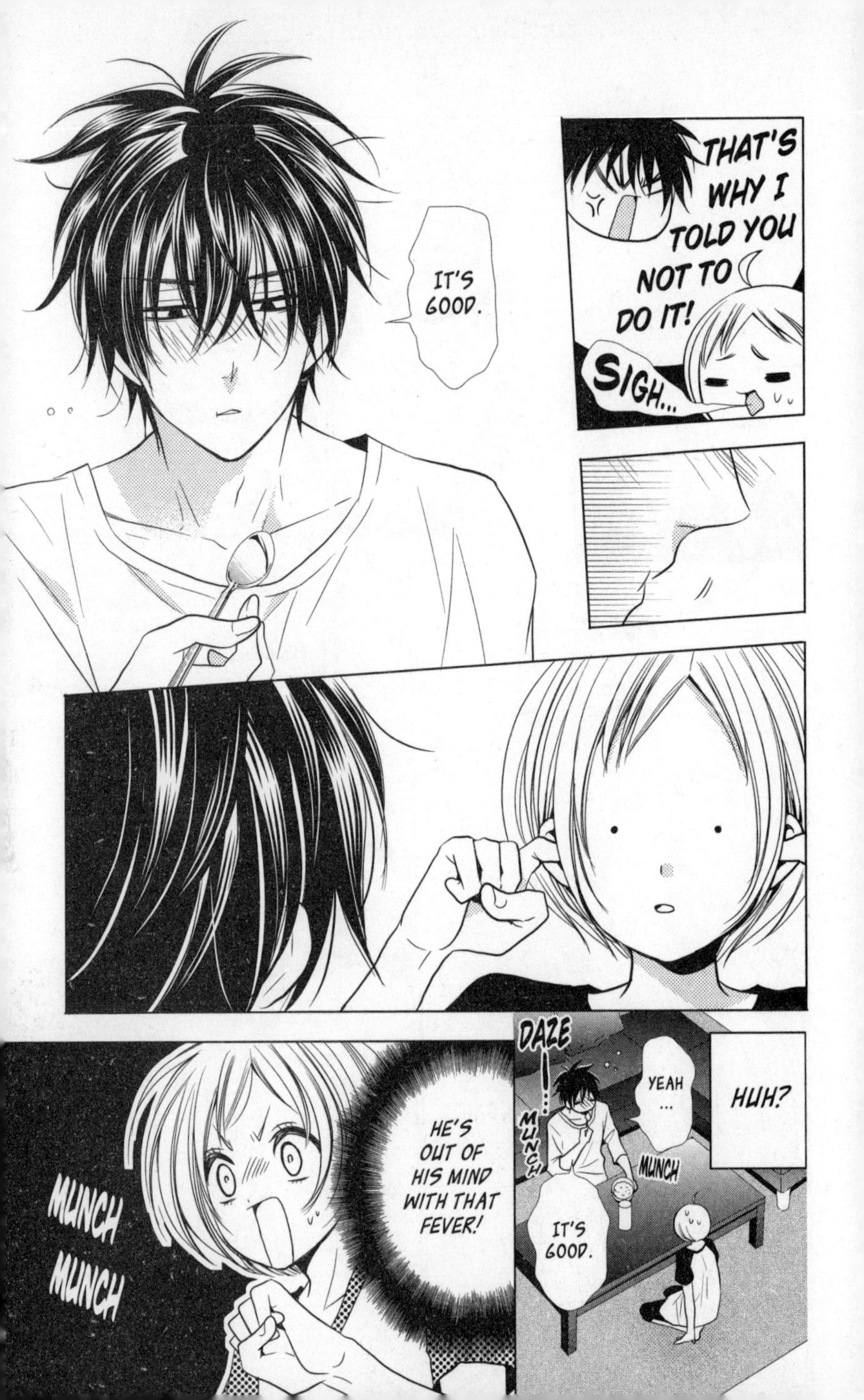
THAT'S WHY I TOLD YOU NOT TO DO IT!
SIGH...
IT'S GOOD.
HUH?
YEAH ...
DAZE
MUNCH
MUNCH
IT'S GOOD.
HE'S OUT OF HIS MIND WITH THAT FEVER!
MUNCH MUNCH

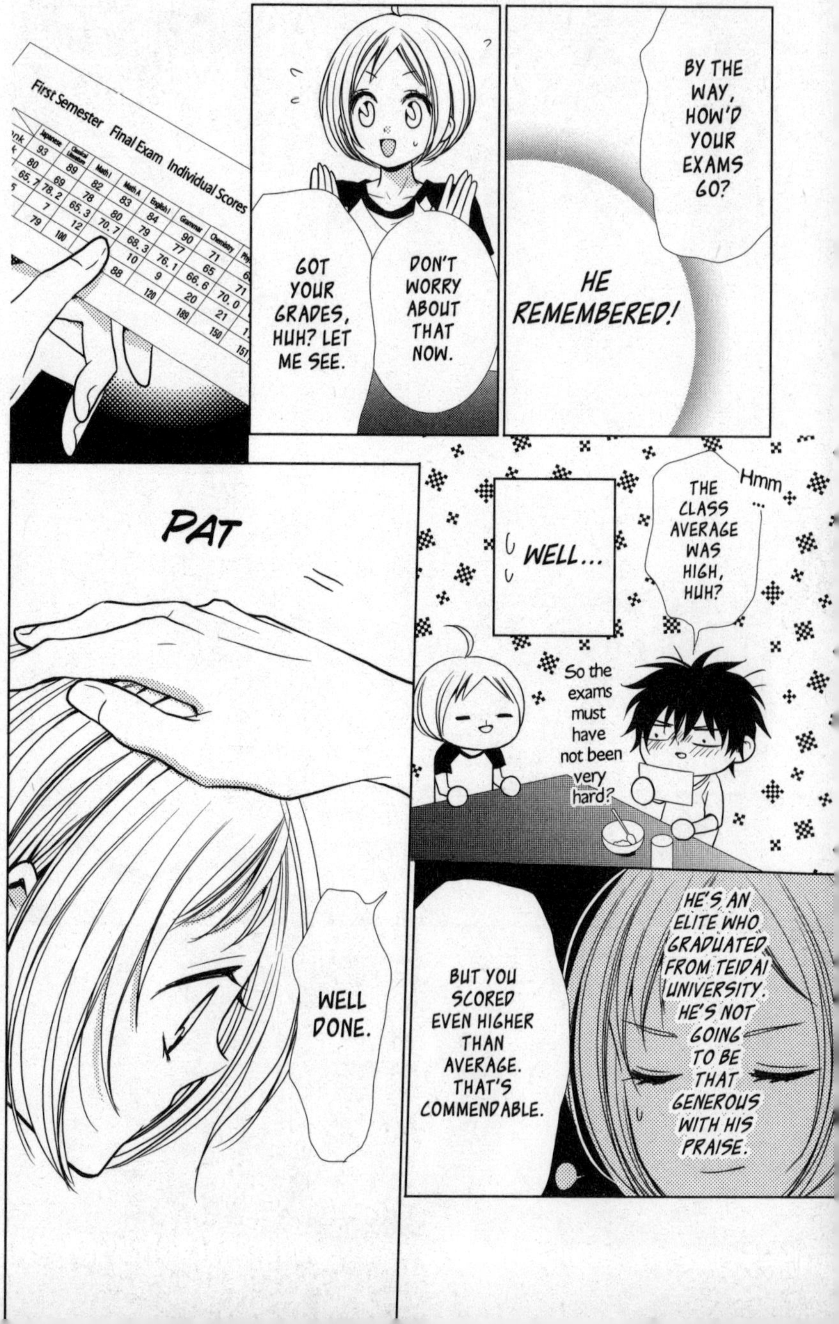
BY THE WAY, HOW'D YOUR EXAMS GO?
HE REMEMBERED!
DON'T WORRY ABOUT THAT NOW.
GOT YOUR GRADES, HUH? LET ME SEE.
First Semester Final Exam Individual Scores
Japanese
Classical Literature
Math I
Math A
English I
Grammar
Chemistry
Hmm...
THE CLASS AVERAGE WAS HIGH, HUH?
WELL...
So the exams must have not been very hard?
HE'S AN ELITE WHO GRADUATED FROM TEIDAI UNIVERSITY. HE'S NOT GOING TO BE THAT GENEROUS WITH HIS PRAISE.
BUT YOU SCORED EVEN HIGHER THAN AVERAGE. THAT'S COMMENDABLE.
PAT
WELL DONE.

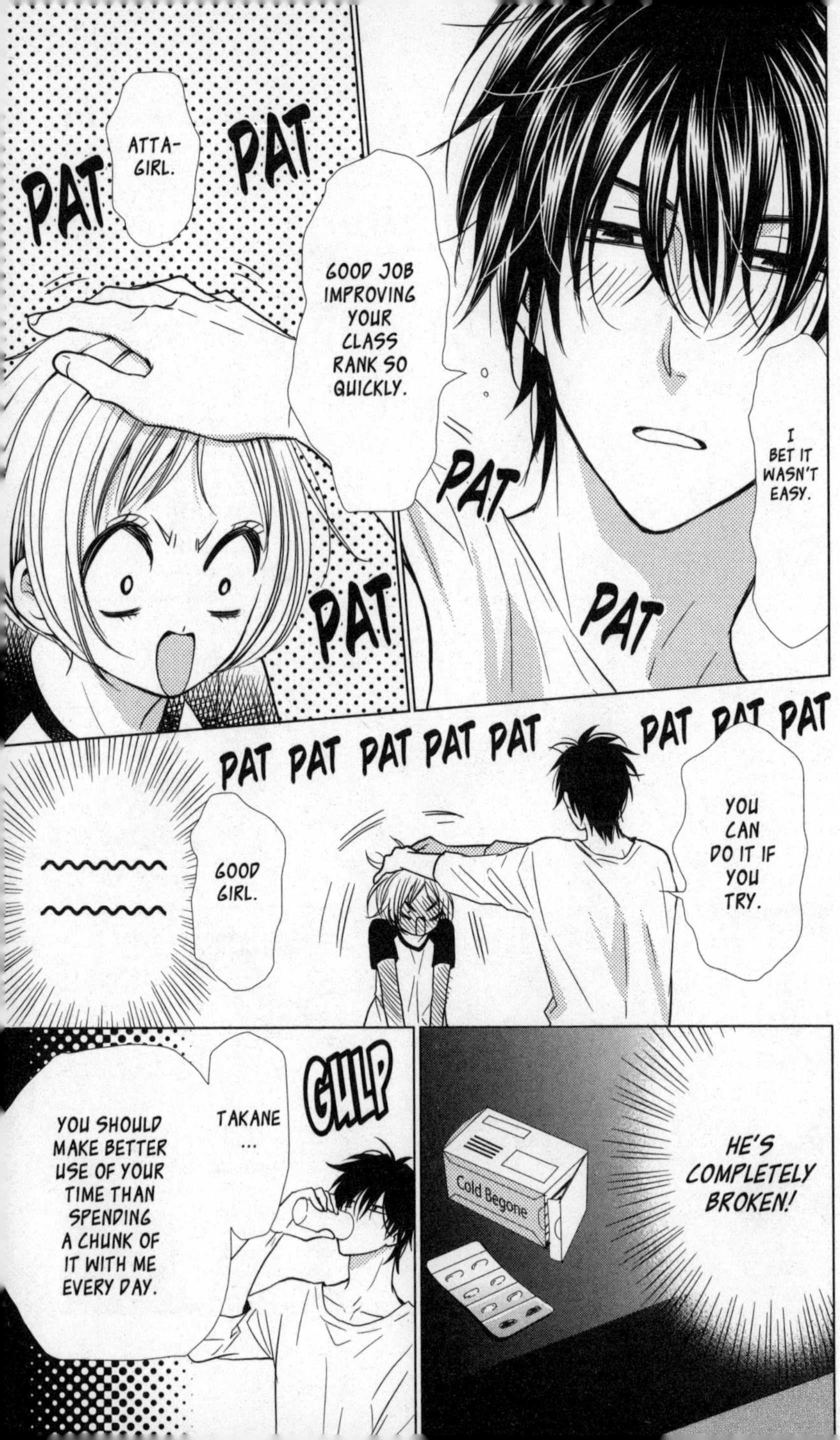
I BET IT WASN'T EASY.
PAT
PAT
GOOD JOB IMPROVING YOUR CLASS RANK SO QUICKLY.
PAT
PAT
PAT
ATTA-GIRL.
PAT PAT PAT
YOU CAN DO IT IF YOU TRY.
PAT PAT PAT PAT PAT
GOOD GIRL.
~~~~~~
HE'S COMPLETELY BROKEN!
Cold Begone
GULP
TAKANE ...
YOU SHOULD MAKE BETTER USE OF YOUR TIME THAN SPENDING A CHUNK OF IT WITH ME EVERY DAY.
~~~~~~

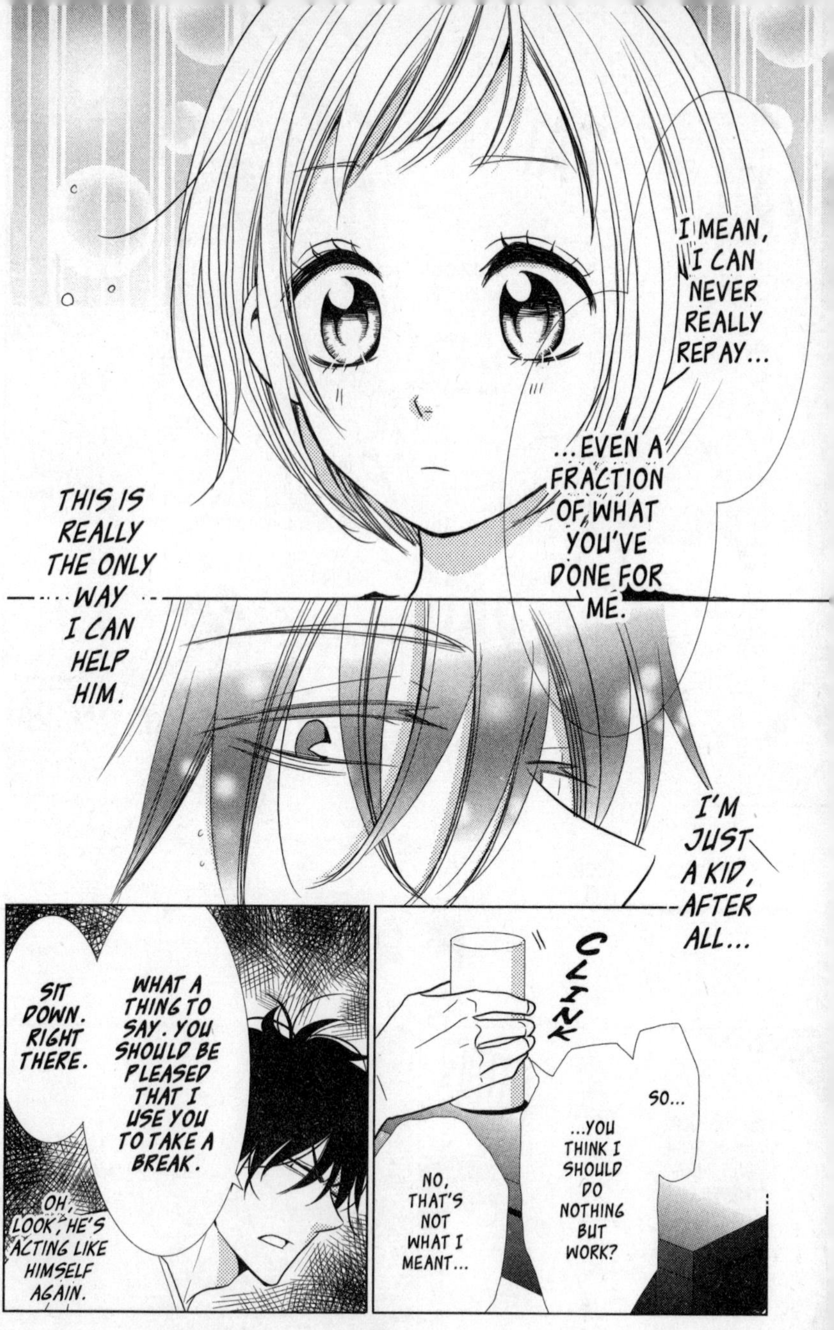
I MEAN, I CAN NEVER REALLY REPAY...
...EVEN A FRACTION OF WHAT YOU'VE DONE FOR ME.
THIS IS REALLY THE ONLY ...WAY I CAN HELP HIM.
I'M JUST A KID, AFTER ALL...
CLINK
SO...
...YOU THINK I SHOULD DO NOTHING BUT WORK?
NO, THAT'S NOT WHAT I MEANT...
WHAT A THING TO SAY. YOU SHOULD BE PLEASED THAT I USE YOU TO TAKE A BREAK.
SIT DOWN. RIGHT THERE.
OH, LOOK, HE'S ACTING LIKE HIMSELF AGAIN.

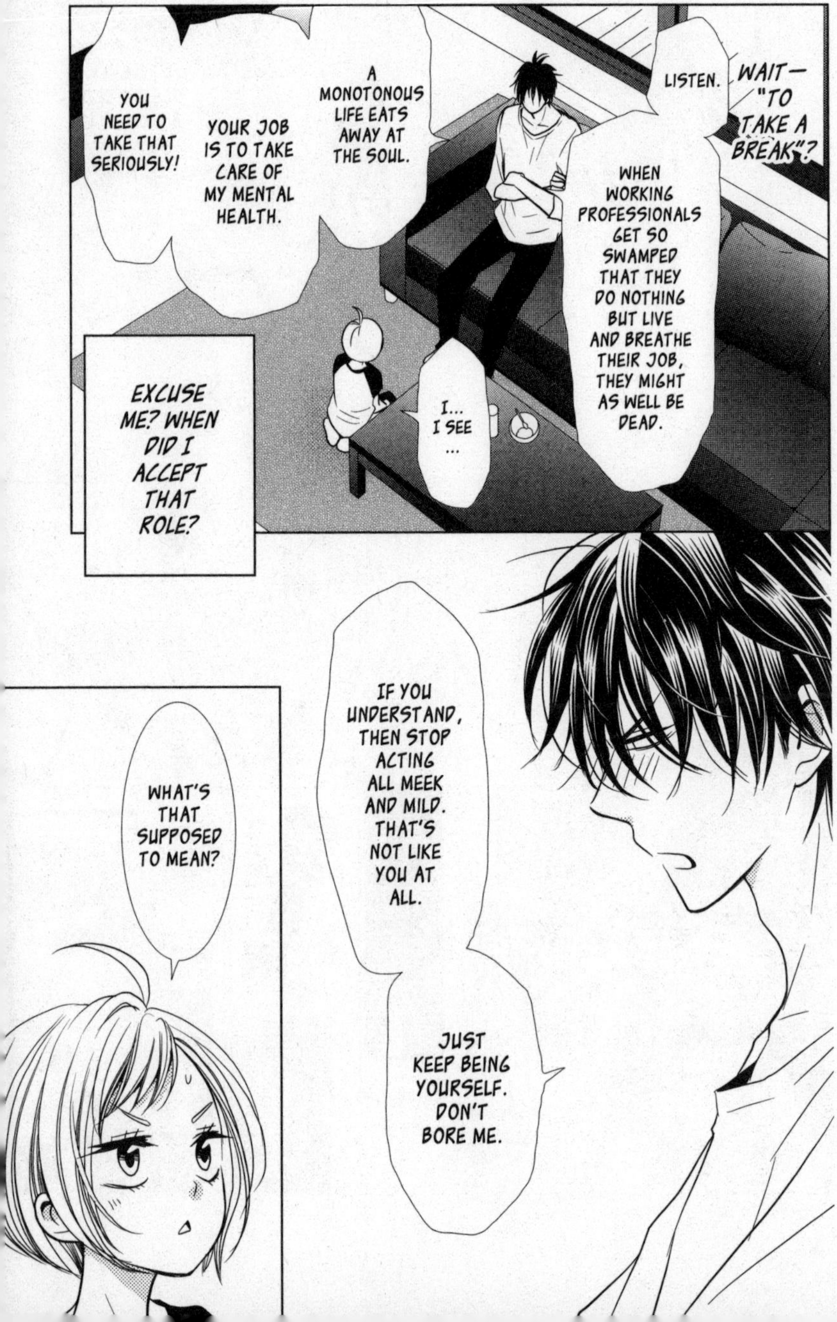
WAIT— "TO TAKE A BREAK"?
LISTEN.
WHEN WORKING PROFESSIONALS GET SO SWAMPED THAT THEY DO NOTHING BUT LIVE AND BREATHE THEIR JOB, THEY MIGHT AS WELL BE DEAD.
A MONOTONOUS LIFE EATS AWAY AT THE SOUL.
I... I SEE ...
YOUR JOB IS TO TAKE CARE OF MY MENTAL HEALTH.
YOU NEED TO TAKE THAT SERIOUSLY!
EXCUSE ME? WHEN DID I ACCEPT THAT ROLE?
IF YOU UNDERSTAND, THEN STOP ACTING ALL MEEK AND MILD. THAT'S NOT LIKE YOU AT ALL.
JUST KEEP BEING YOURSELF. DON'T BORE ME.
WHAT'S THAT SUPPOSED TO MEAN?

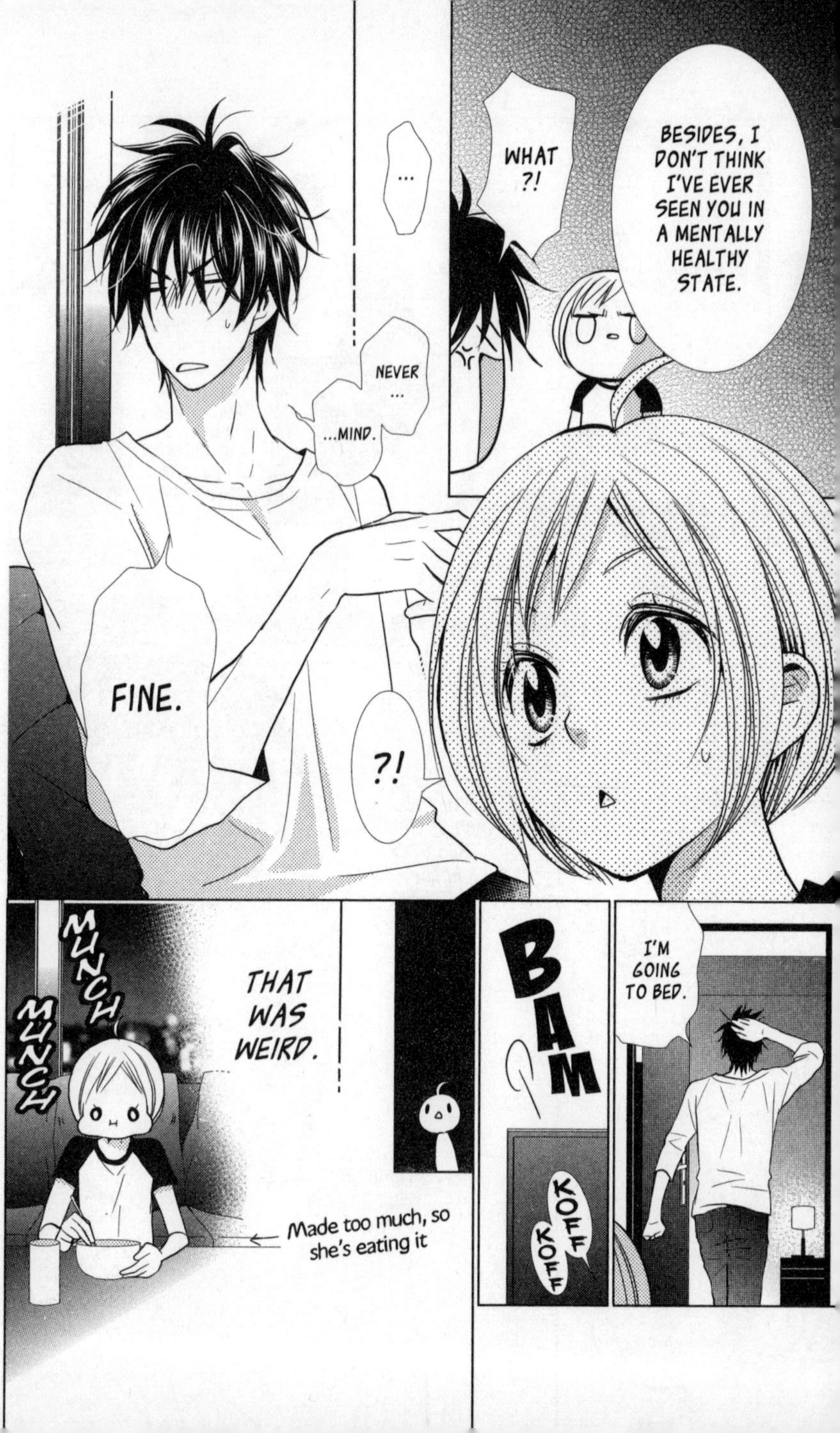
BESIDES, I DON'T THINK I'VE EVER SEEN YOU IN A MENTALLY HEALTHY STATE.
WHAT ?!
...
NEVER ...
...MIND.
FINE.
?!
I'M GOING TO BED.
BAM
KOFF KOFF
THAT WAS WEIRD.
MUNCH MUNCH
Made too much, so she's eating it

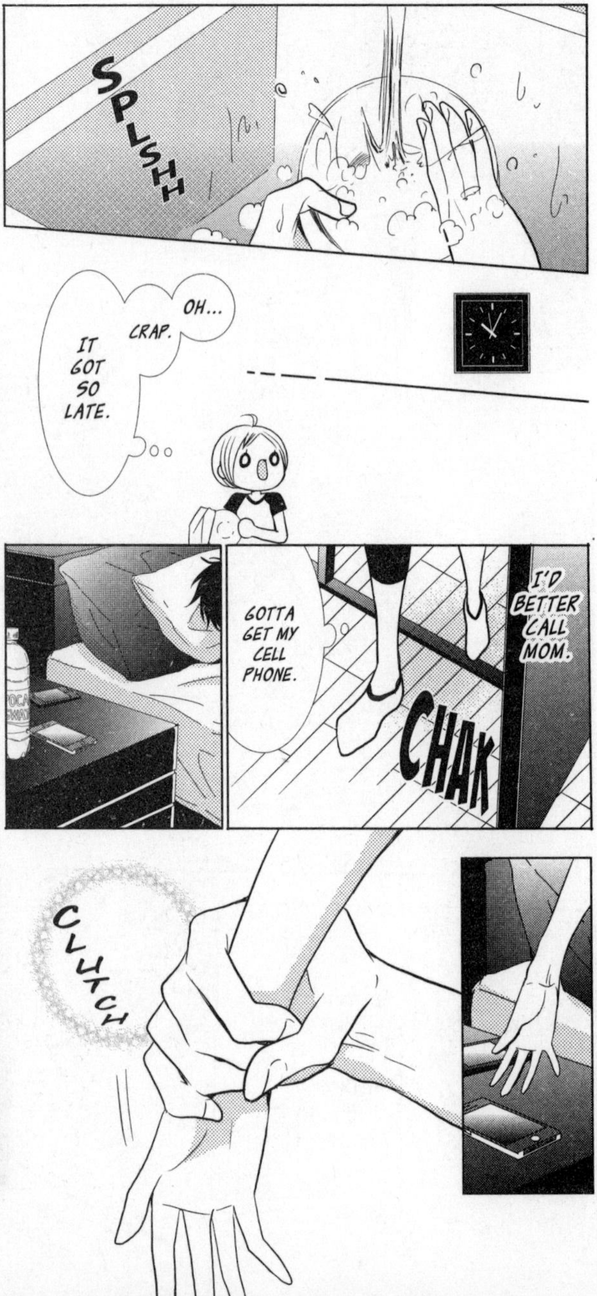
SPLSHH
OH...
CRAP.
IT GOT SO LATE.
I'D BETTER CALL MOM.
CHAK
GOTTA GET MY CELL PHONE.
CLUTCH

•Nameless Supporting Roles•

Mizuki and Hikaruko are prime examples of this, but I drew in a few background extras without really thinking much about them. Then they turned out to be great, so I kept them in the story.

• Takane's Coworker •

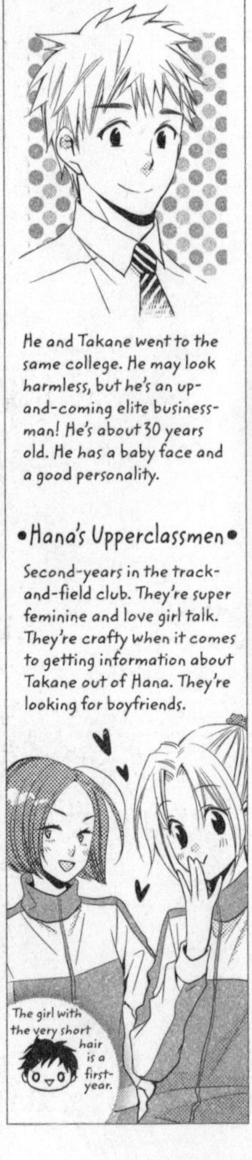
The girl with the very short hair is a first-year.

He and Takane went to the same college. He may look harmless, but he's an up-and-coming elite businessman! He's about 30 years old. He has a baby face and a good personality.

•Hana's Upperclassmen•

Second-years in the track-and-field club. They're super feminine and love girl talk. They're crafty when it comes to getting information about Takane out of Hana. They're looking for boyfriends.

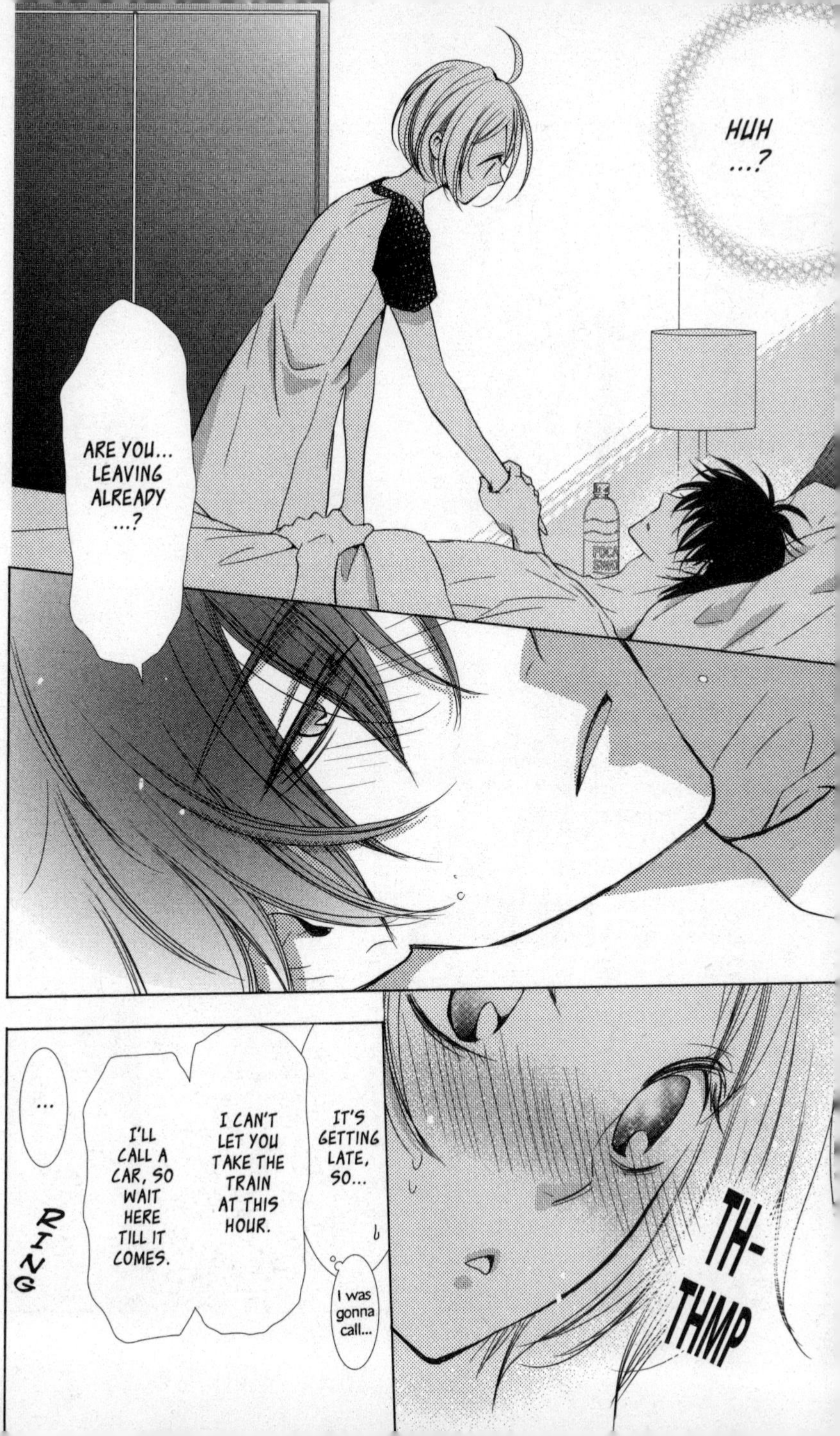
HUH ...?
ARE YOU... LEAVING ALREADY ...?
TH-THMP
I was gonna call...
IT'S GETTING LATE, SO...
I CAN'T LET YOU TAKE THE TRAIN AT THIS HOUR.
I'LL CALL A CAR, SO WAIT HERE TILL IT COMES.
...
RING

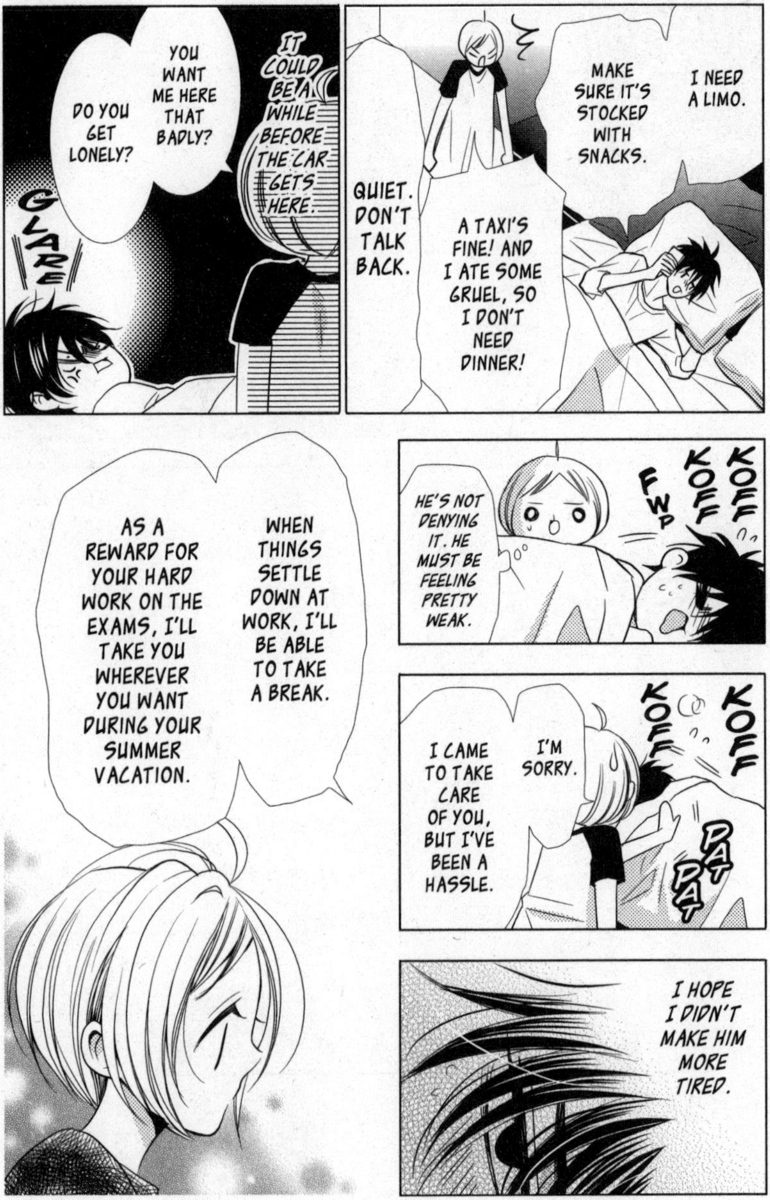
I NEED A LIMO.
MAKE SURE IT'S STOCKED WITH SNACKS.
A TAXI'S FINE! AND I ATE SOME GRUEL, SO I DON'T NEED DINNER!
QUIET. DON'T TALK BACK.
IT COULD BE A WHILE BEFORE THE CAR GETS HERE.
YOU WANT ME HERE THAT BADLY?
DO YOU GET LONELY?
GLARE
KOFF KOFF
FWP
HE'S NOT DENYING IT. HE MUST BE FEELING PRETTY WEAK.
KOFF KOFF
I'M SORRY.
I CAME TO TAKE CARE OF YOU, BUT I'VE BEEN A HASSLE.
PAT PAT
I HOPE I DIDN'T MAKE HIM MORE TIRED.
WHEN THINGS SETTLE DOWN AT WORK, I'LL BE ABLE TO TAKE A BREAK.
AS A REWARD FOR YOUR HARD WORK ON THE EXAMS, I'LL TAKE YOU WHEREVER YOU WANT DURING YOUR SUMMER VACATION.

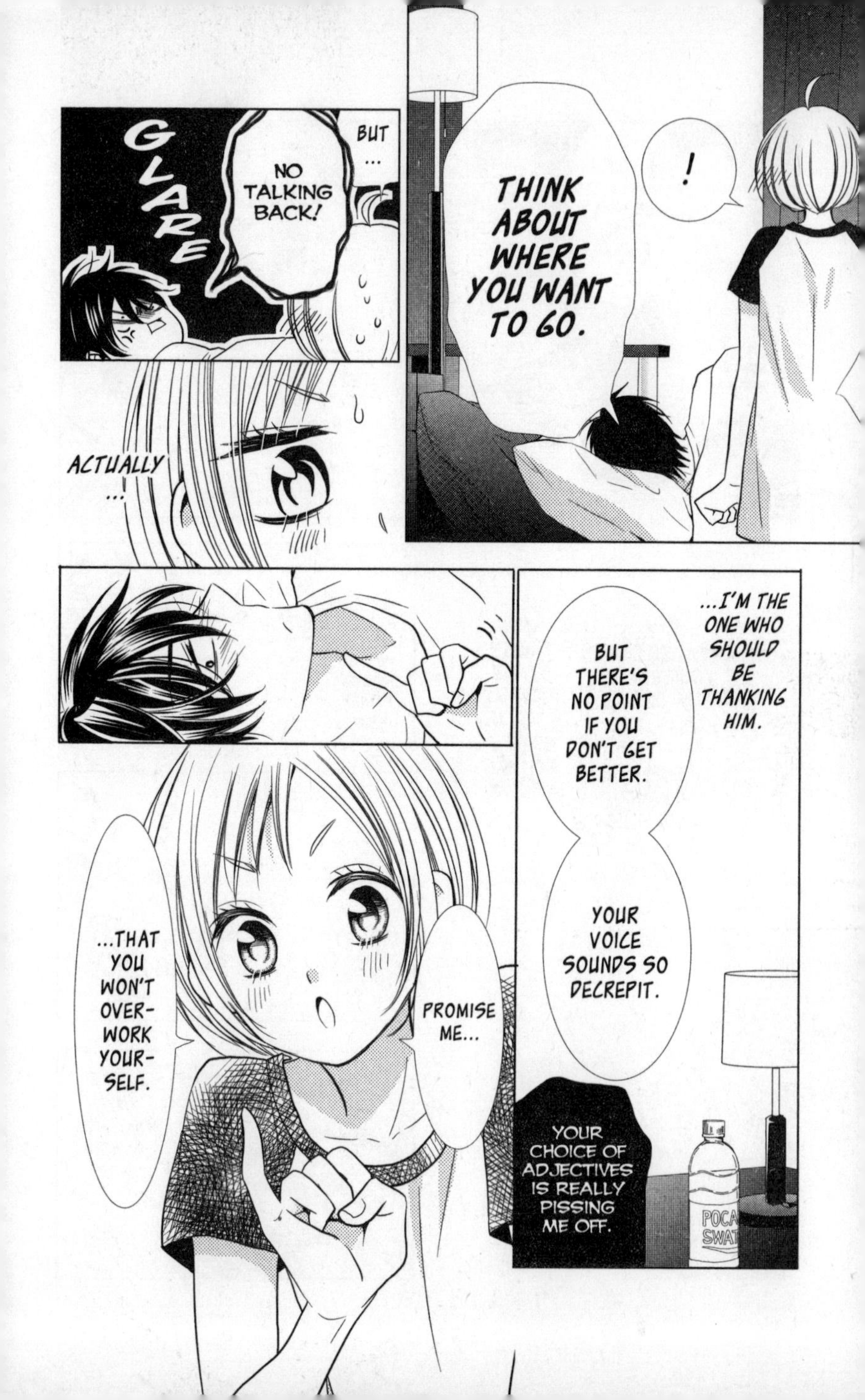
!
THINK ABOUT WHERE YOU WANT TO GO.
BUT ...
NO TALKING BACK!
GLARE
ACTUALLY ...
...I'M THE ONE WHO SHOULD BE THANKING HIM.
BUT THERE'S NO POINT IF YOU DON'T GET BETTER.
YOUR VOICE SOUNDS SO DECREPIT.
YOUR CHOICE OF ADJECTIVES IS REALLY PISSING ME OFF.
PROMISE ME...
...THAT YOU WON'T OVER-WORK YOUR-SELF.

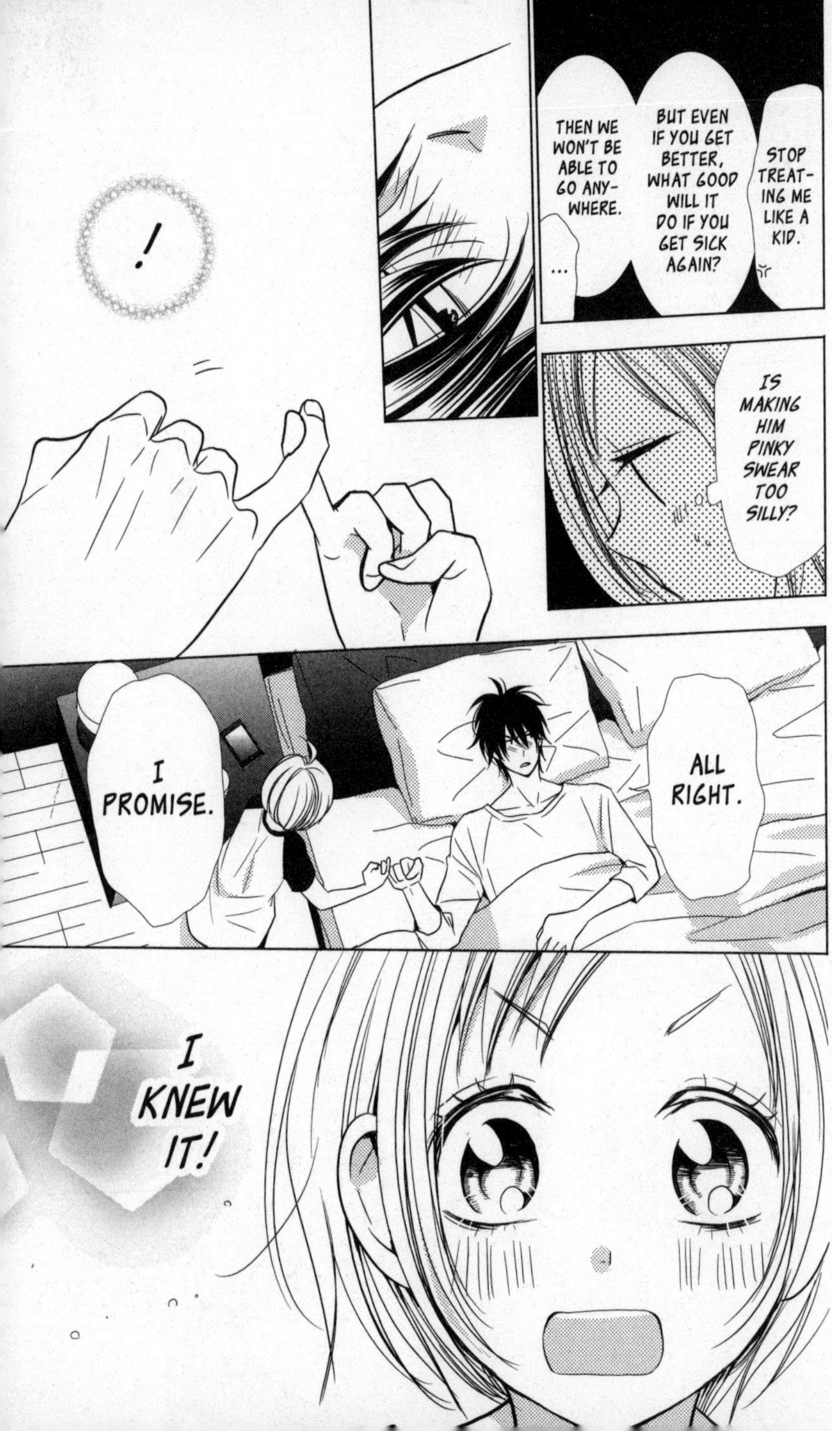
STOP TREAT-ING ME LIKE A KID.
BUT EVEN IF YOU GET BETTER, WHAT GOOD WILL IT DO IF YOU GET SICK AGAIN?
THEN WE WON'T BE ABLE TO GO ANY-WHERE.
...
IS MAKING HIM PINKY SWEAR TOO SILLY?
!
ALL RIGHT.
I PROMISE.
I KNEW IT!

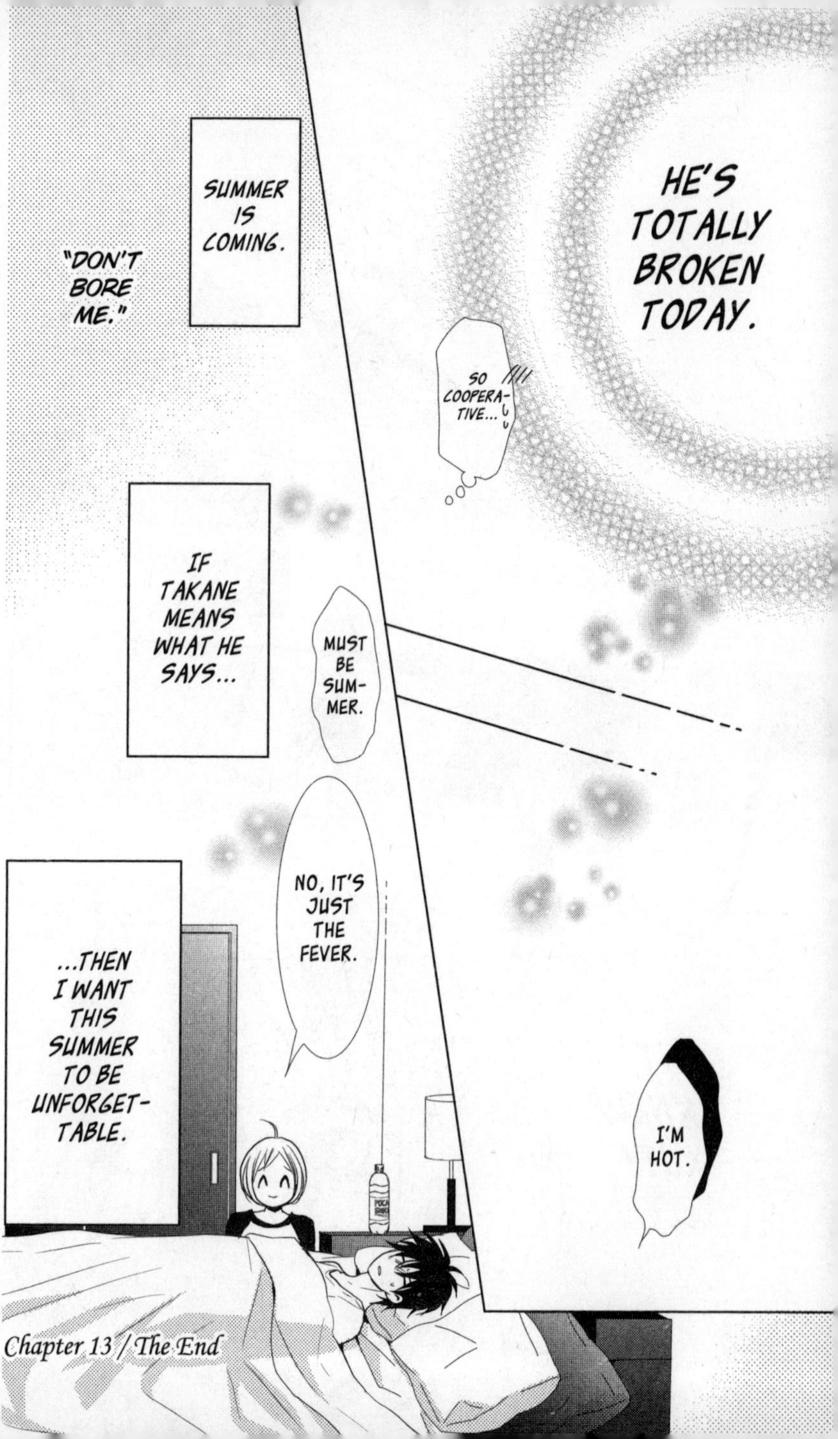
HE'S TOTALLY BROKEN TODAY.
SO COOPERATIVE...
I'M HOT.
SUMMER IS COMING.
"DON'T BORE ME."
MUST BE SUMMER.
IF TAKANE MEANS WHAT HE SAYS...
NO, IT'S JUST THE FEVER.
...THEN I WANT THIS SUMMER TO BE UNFORGETTABLE.
Chapter 13 / The End

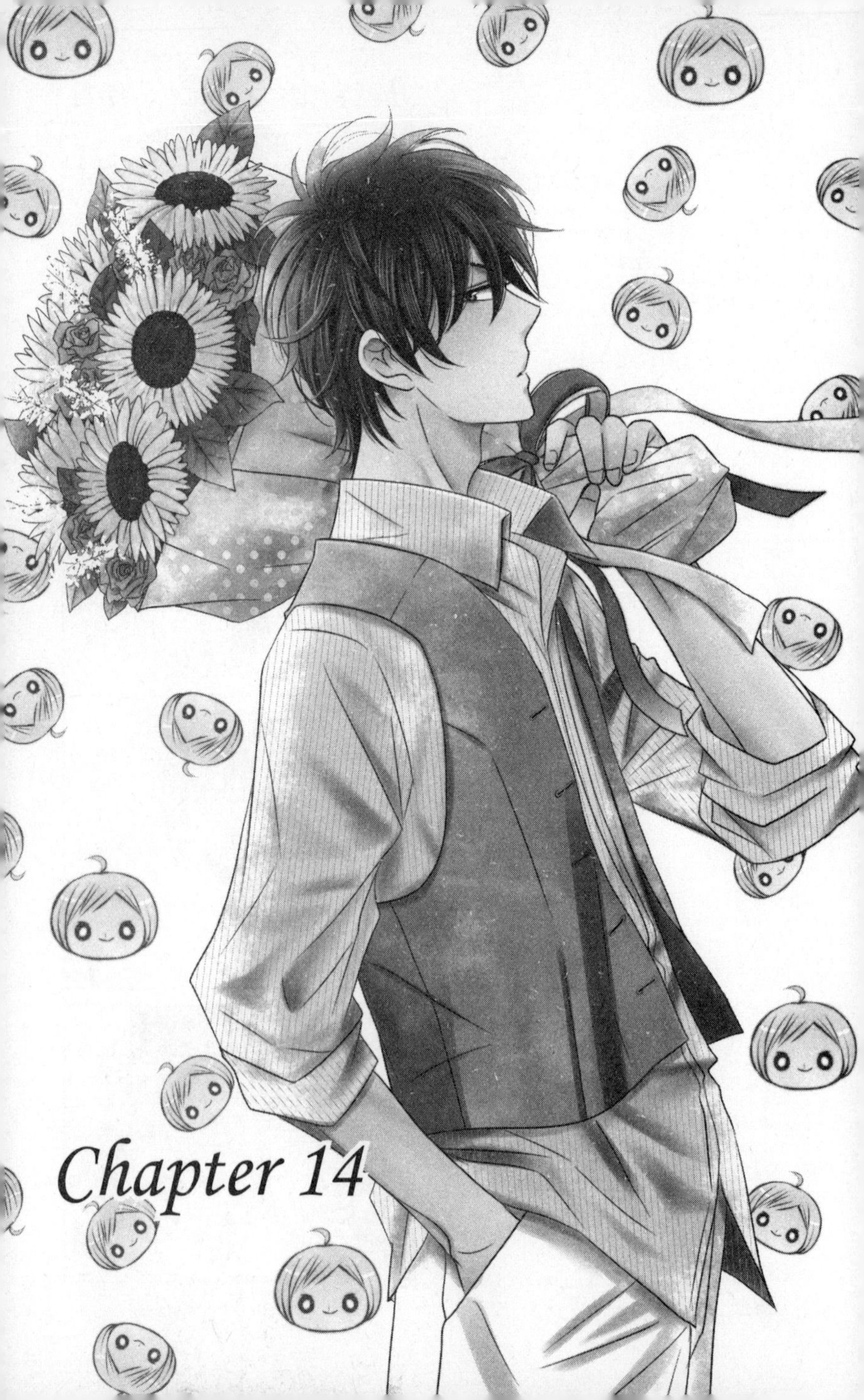
Chapter 14

Fever and Rice Gruel

IT'S EDIBLE, BUT IT'S JUST RICE GRUEL. DON'T LET IT GO TO YOUR HEAD.

98.6 °F

MUNCH

IT'S SO-SO.

100.4 °F

MUNCH MUNCH

...

DELI-CIOUS...

102.2 °F

DAZE

IT'S GOOD.

YES, IT'S EDIBLE, BUT ALL YOU DID WAS GRILL SOME DRIED CUTTLE-FISH. DON'T LET IT GO TO YOUR HEAD.

104 °F

CHOMP CHOMP CHOMP CHOMP CHOMP

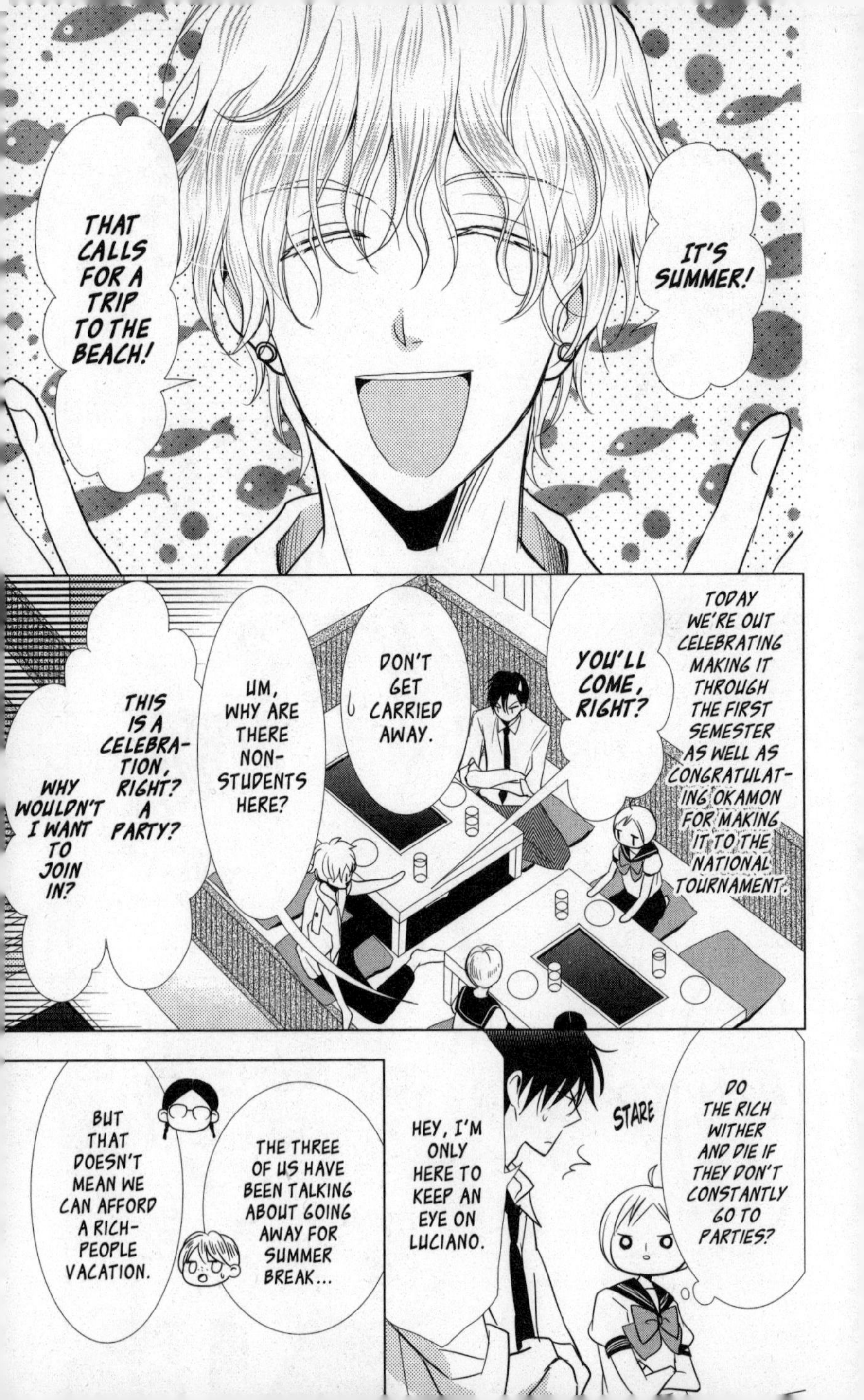
IT'S SUMMER!
THAT CALLS FOR A TRIP TO THE BEACH!
TODAY WE'RE OUT CELEBRATING MAKING IT THROUGH THE FIRST SEMESTER AS WELL AS CONGRATULAT-ING OKAMON FOR MAKING IT TO THE NATIONAL TOURNAMENT.
YOU'LL COME, RIGHT?
DON'T GET CARRIED AWAY.
UM, WHY ARE THERE NON-STUDENTS HERE?
THIS IS A CELEBRA-TION, RIGHT? A PARTY?
WHY WOULDN'T I WANT TO JOIN IN?
DO THE RICH WITHER AND DIE IF THEY DON'T CONSTANTLY GO TO PARTIES?
STARE
HEY, I'M ONLY HERE TO KEEP AN EYE ON LUCIANO.
THE THREE OF US HAVE BEEN TALKING ABOUT GOING AWAY FOR SUMMER BREAK...
BUT THAT DOESN'T MEAN WE CAN AFFORD A RICH-PEOPLE VACATION.

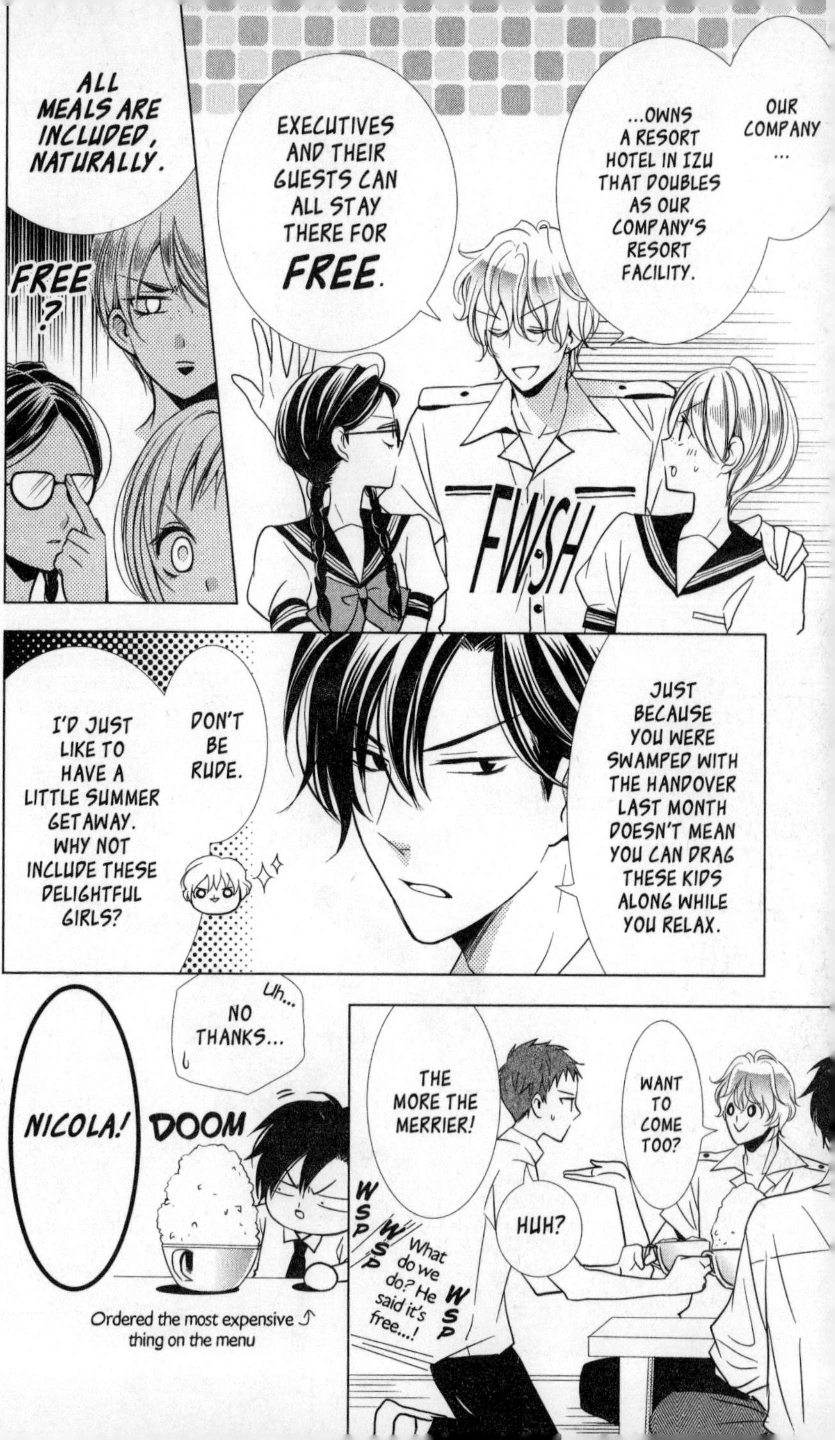
OUR COMPANY...
...OWNS A RESORT HOTEL IN IZU THAT DOUBLES AS OUR COMPANY'S RESORT FACILITY.
EXECUTIVES AND THEIR GUESTS CAN ALL STAY THERE FOR FREE.
FWSH
ALL MEALS ARE INCLUDED, NATURALLY.
FREE?
JUST BECAUSE YOU WERE SWAMPED WITH THE HANDOVER LAST MONTH DOESN'T MEAN YOU CAN DRAG THESE KIDS ALONG WHILE YOU RELAX.
DON'T BE RUDE.
I'D JUST LIKE TO HAVE A LITTLE SUMMER GETAWAY. WHY NOT INCLUDE THESE DELIGHTFUL GIRLS?
WANT TO COME TOO?
THE MORE THE MERRIER!
HUH?
WSP WSP
What do we do? He said it's free...!
WSP
Uh... NO THANKS...
DOOM
NICOLA!
Ordered the most expensive thing on the menu

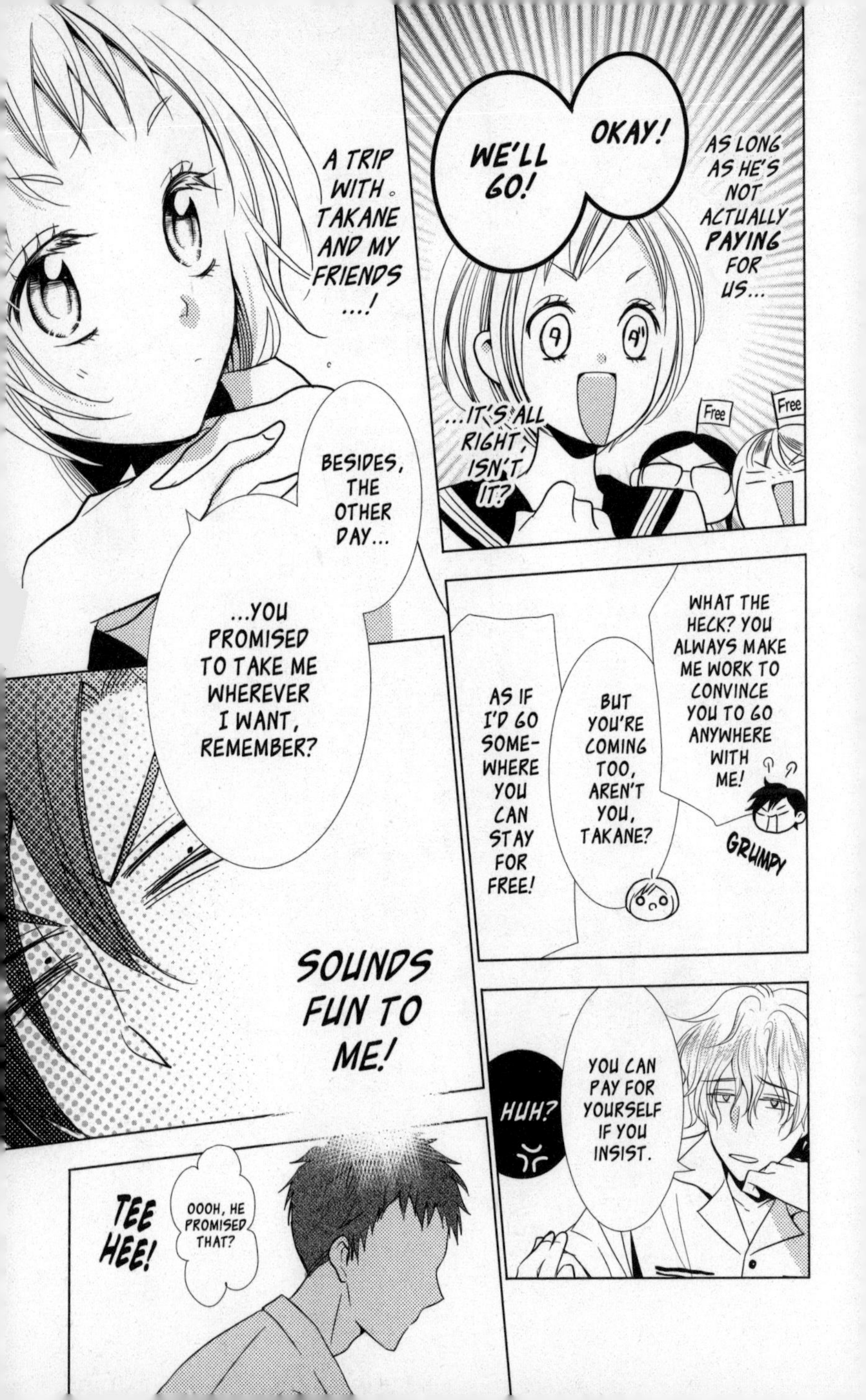
AS LONG AS HE'S NOT ACTUALLY PAYING FOR US...
OKAY!
WE'LL GO!
...IT'S ALL RIGHT, ISN'T IT?
Free
Free
WHAT THE HECK? YOU ALWAYS MAKE ME WORK TO CONVINCE YOU TO GO ANYWHERE WITH ME!
GRUMPY
BUT YOU'RE COMING TOO, AREN'T YOU, TAKANE?
AS IF I'D GO SOME-WHERE YOU CAN STAY FOR FREE!
YOU CAN PAY FOR YOURSELF IF YOU INSIST.
HUH?
A TRIP WITH TAKANE AND MY FRIENDS ...!
BESIDES, THE OTHER DAY...
...YOU PROMISED TO TAKE ME WHEREVER I WANT, REMEMBER?
SOUNDS FUN TO ME!
OOOH, HE PROMISED THAT?
TEE HEE!

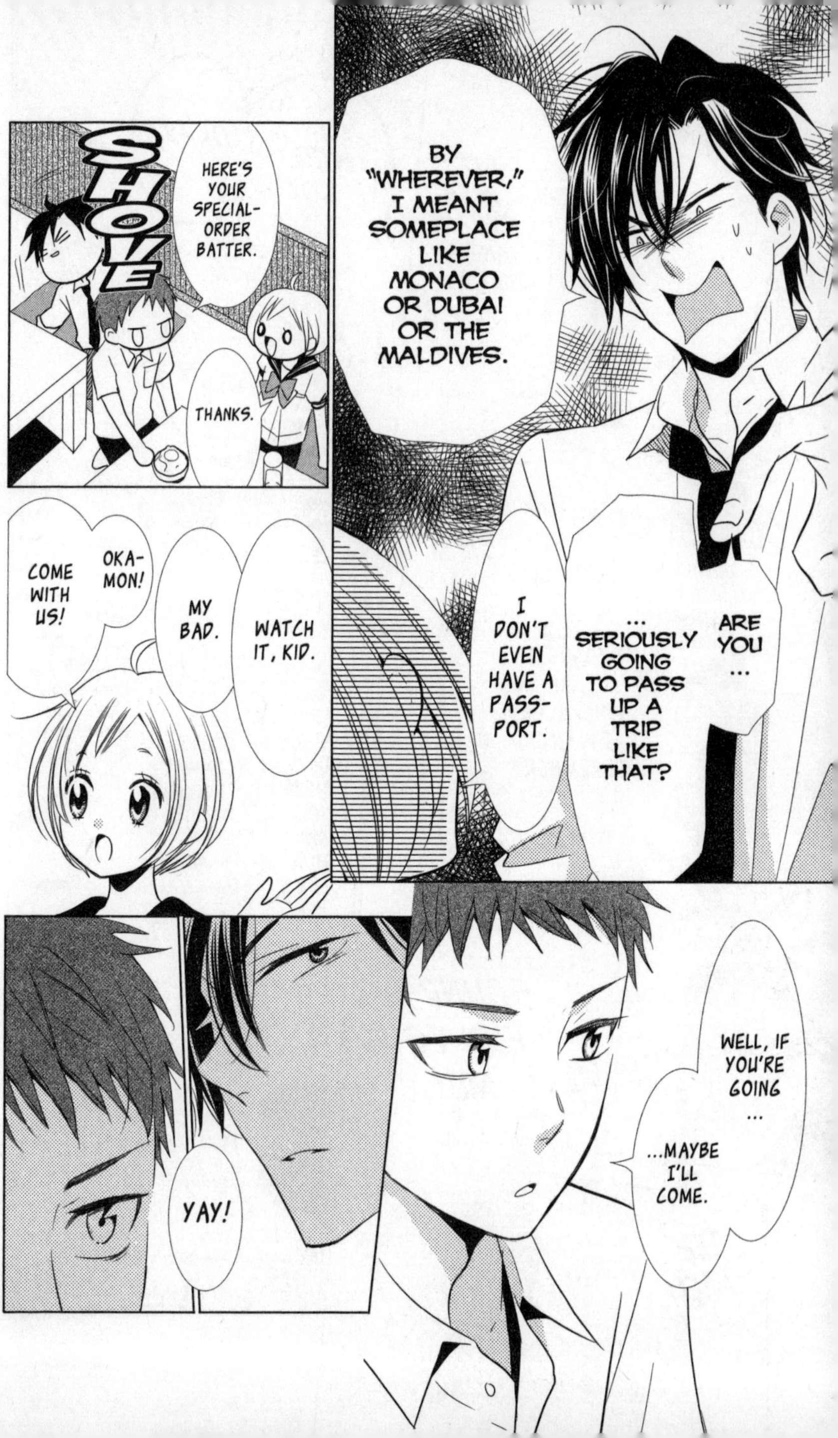
BY "WHEREVER," I MEANT SOMEPLACE LIKE MONACO OR DUBAI OR THE MALDIVES.
ARE YOU ...
... SERIOUSLY GOING TO PASS UP A TRIP LIKE THAT?
I DON'T EVEN HAVE A PASS-PORT.
SHOVE
HERE'S YOUR SPECIAL-ORDER BATTER.
THANKS.
WATCH IT, KID.
MY BAD.
OKA-MON!
COME WITH US!
WELL, IF YOU'RE GOING ...
...MAYBE I'LL COME.
YAY!

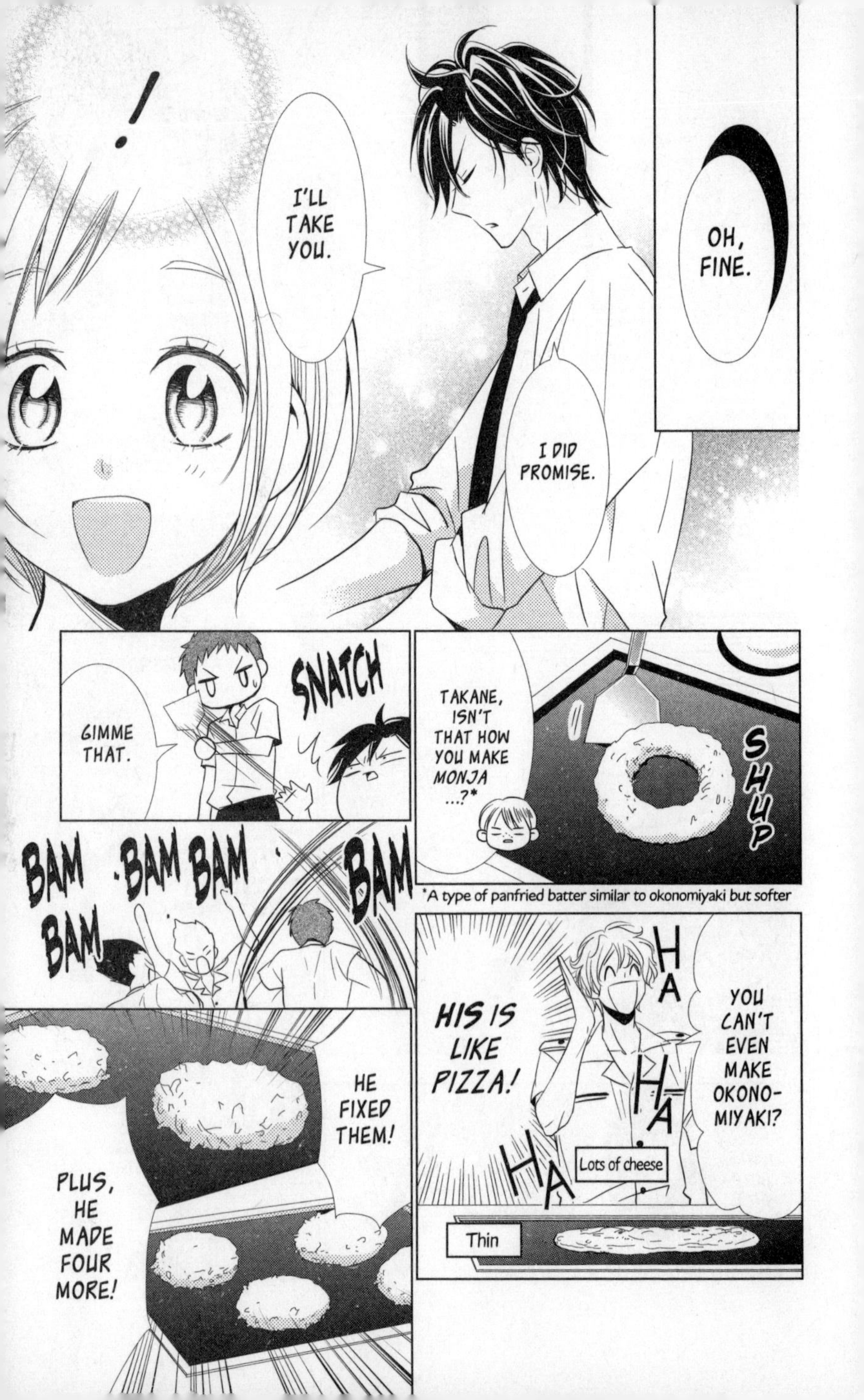
OH, FINE.
I DID PROMISE.
I'LL TAKE YOU.
!
SHUP
TAKANE, ISN'T THAT HOW YOU MAKE MONJA ...?*
SNATCH
GIMME THAT.
BAM
BAM BAM
BAM
BAM BAM
YOU CAN'T EVEN MAKE OKONOMIYAKI?
HA HA HA
HIS IS LIKE PIZZA!
Lots of cheese
Thin
HE FIXED THEM!
PLUS, HE MADE FOUR MORE!
*A type of panfried batter similar to okonomiyaki but softer

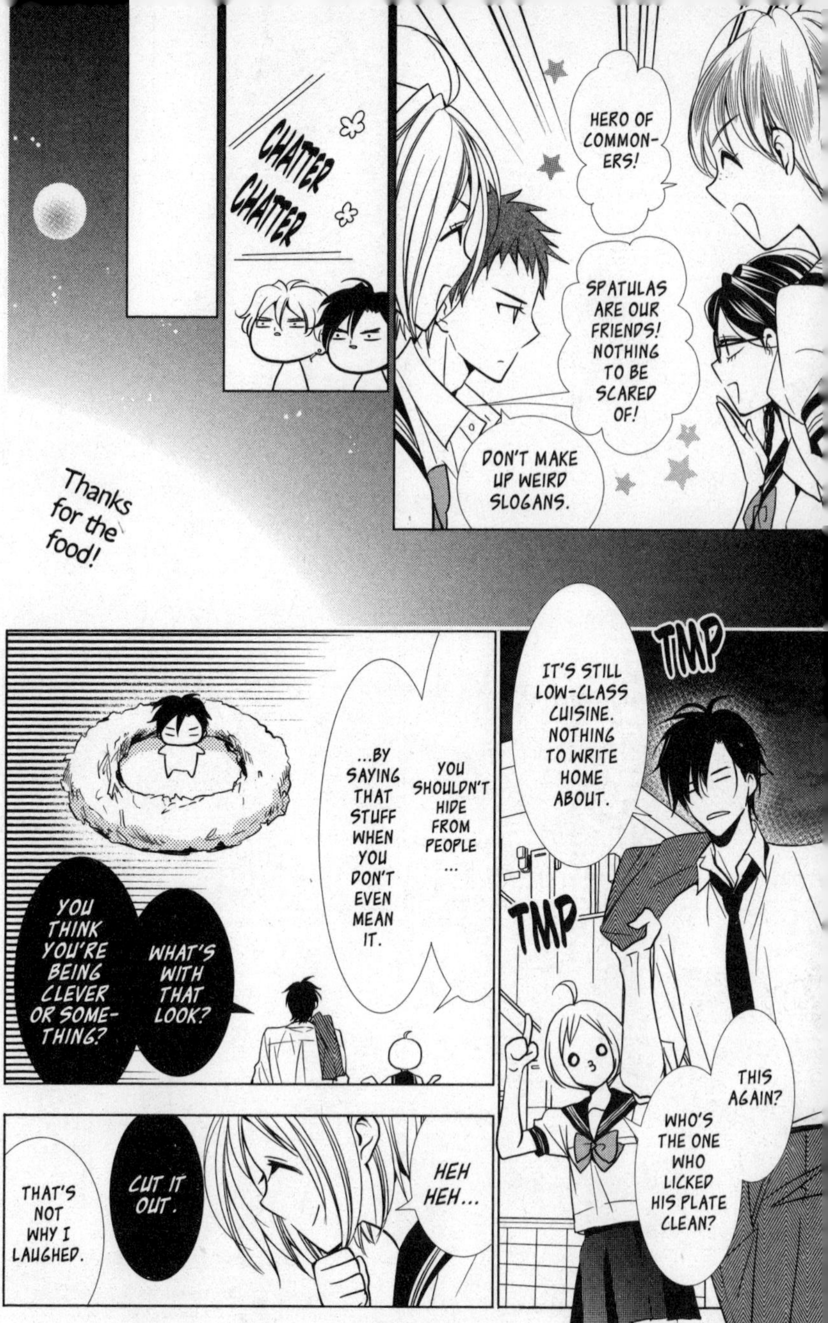
HERO OF COMMONERS!
SPATULAS ARE OUR FRIENDS! NOTHING TO BE SCARED OF!
DON'T MAKE UP WEIRD SLOGANS.
CHATTER CHATTER
Thanks for the food!
TMP
IT'S STILL LOW-CLASS CUISINE. NOTHING TO WRITE HOME ABOUT.
TMP
THIS AGAIN?
WHO'S THE ONE WHO LICKED HIS PLATE CLEAN?
YOU SHOULDN'T HIDE FROM PEOPLE...
...BY SAYING THAT STUFF WHEN YOU DON'T EVEN MEAN IT.
WHAT'S WITH THAT LOOK?
YOU THINK YOU'RE BEING CLEVER OR SOMETHING?
HEH HEH...
CUT IT OUT.
THAT'S NOT WHY I LAUGHED.

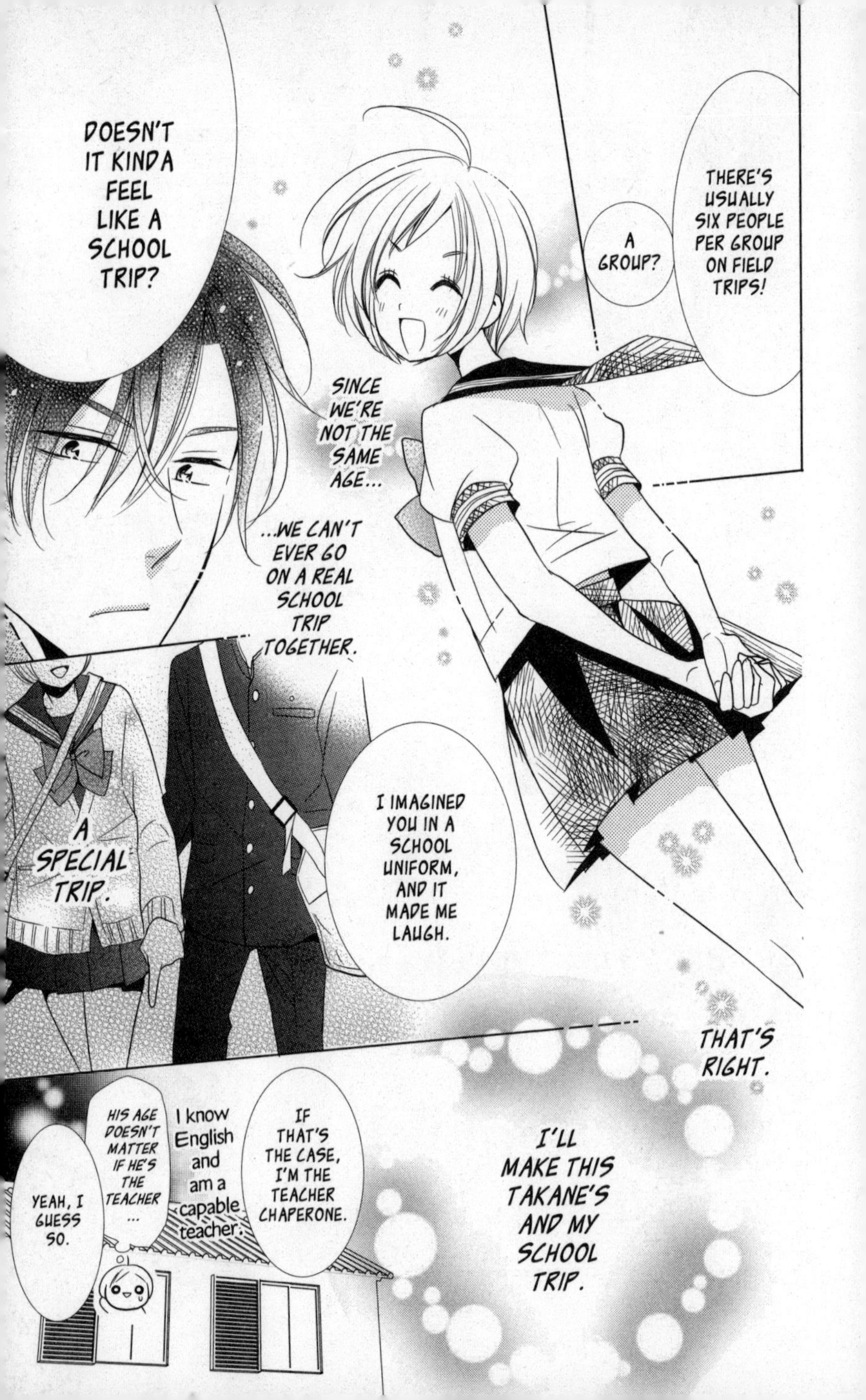
THERE'S USUALLY SIX PEOPLE PER GROUP ON FIELD TRIPS!
A GROUP?
DOESN'T IT KINDA FEEL LIKE A SCHOOL TRIP?
SINCE WE'RE NOT THE SAME AGE...
...WE CAN'T EVER GO ON A REAL SCHOOL TRIP TOGETHER.
I IMAGINED YOU IN A SCHOOL UNIFORM, AND IT MADE ME LAUGH.
A SPECIAL TRIP.
THAT'S RIGHT.
I'LL MAKE THIS TAKANE'S AND MY SCHOOL TRIP.
IF THAT'S THE CASE, I'M THE TEACHER CHAPERONE.
I know English and am a capable teacher.
HIS AGE DOESN'T MATTER IF HE'S THE TEACHER ...
YEAH, I GUESS SO.

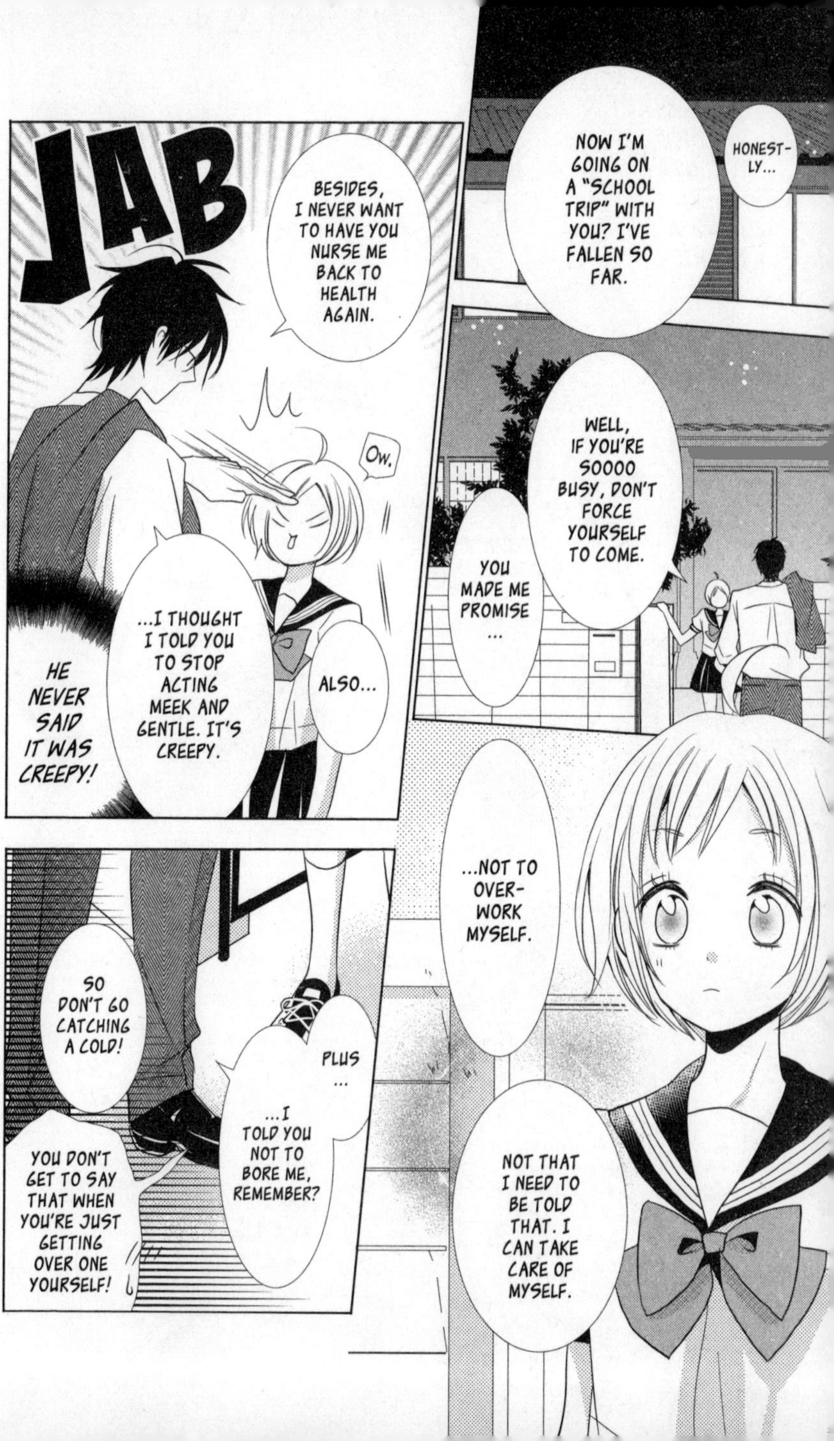
HONEST-LY...
NOW I'M GOING ON A "SCHOOL TRIP" WITH YOU? I'VE FALLEN SO FAR.
WELL, IF YOU'RE SOOOO BUSY, DON'T FORCE YOURSELF TO COME.
YOU MADE ME PROMISE ...
...NOT TO OVER-WORK MYSELF.
NOT THAT I NEED TO BE TOLD THAT. I CAN TAKE CARE OF MYSELF.
BESIDES, I NEVER WANT TO HAVE YOU NURSE ME BACK TO HEALTH AGAIN.
JAB
OW.
...I THOUGHT I TOLD YOU TO STOP ACTING MEEK AND GENTLE. IT'S CREEPY.
ALSO...
HE NEVER SAID IT WAS CREEPY!
PLUS ...
...I TOLD YOU NOT TO BORE ME, REMEMBER?
SO DON'T GO CATCHING A COLD!
YOU DON'T GET TO SAY THAT WHEN YOU'RE JUST GETTING OVER ONE YOURSELF!

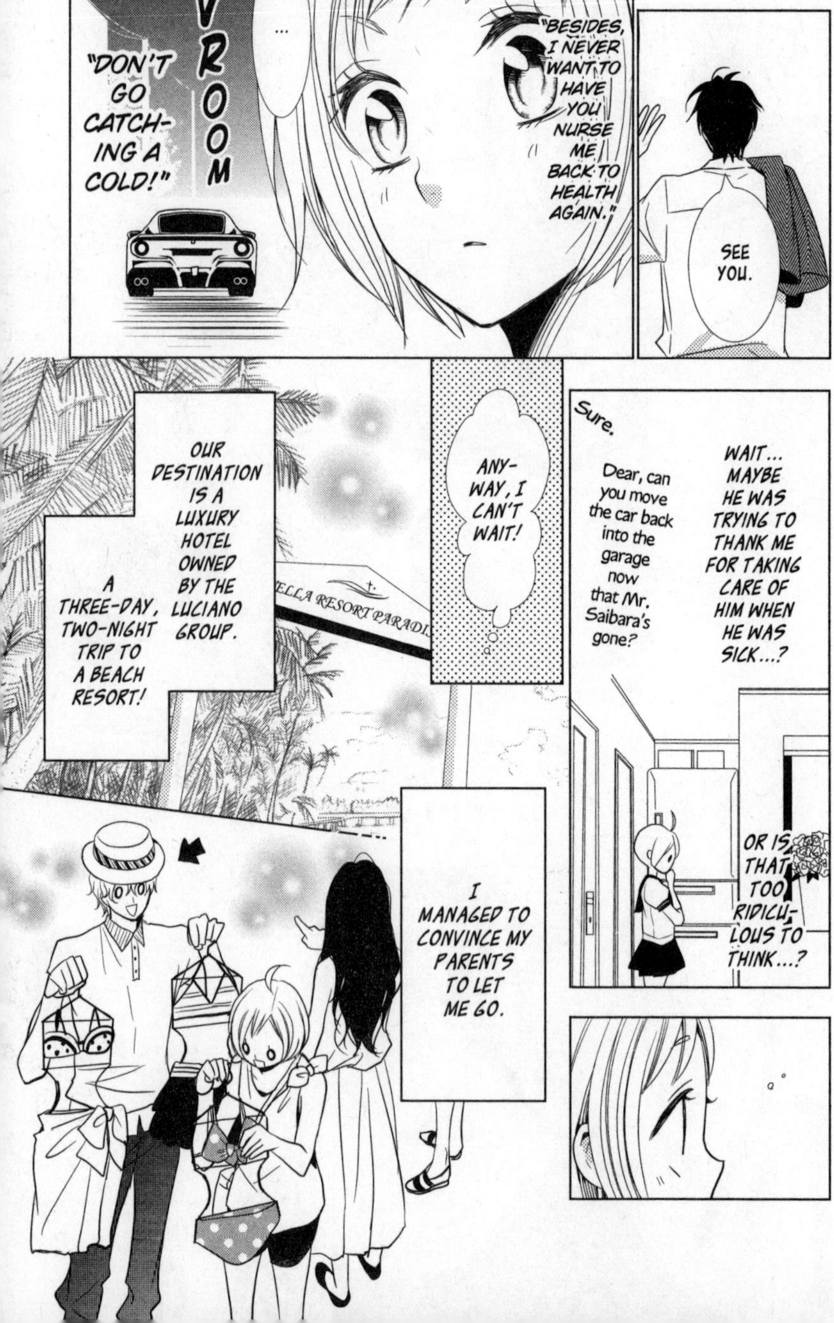
SEE YOU.
"BESIDES, I NEVER WANT TO HAVE YOU NURSE ME BACK TO HEALTH AGAIN."
...
VROOM
"DON'T GO CATCHING A COLD!"
WAIT... MAYBE HE WAS TRYING TO THANK ME FOR TAKING CARE OF HIM WHEN HE WAS SICK...?
Dear, can you move the car back into the garage now that Mr. Saibara's gone?
Sure.
OR IS THAT TOO RIDICULOUS TO THINK...?
ANYWAY, I CAN'T WAIT!
OUR DESTINATION IS A LUXURY HOTEL OWNED BY THE LUCIANO GROUP.
A THREE-DAY, TWO-NIGHT TRIP TO A BEACH RESORT!
I MANAGED TO CONVINCE MY PARENTS TO LET ME GO.

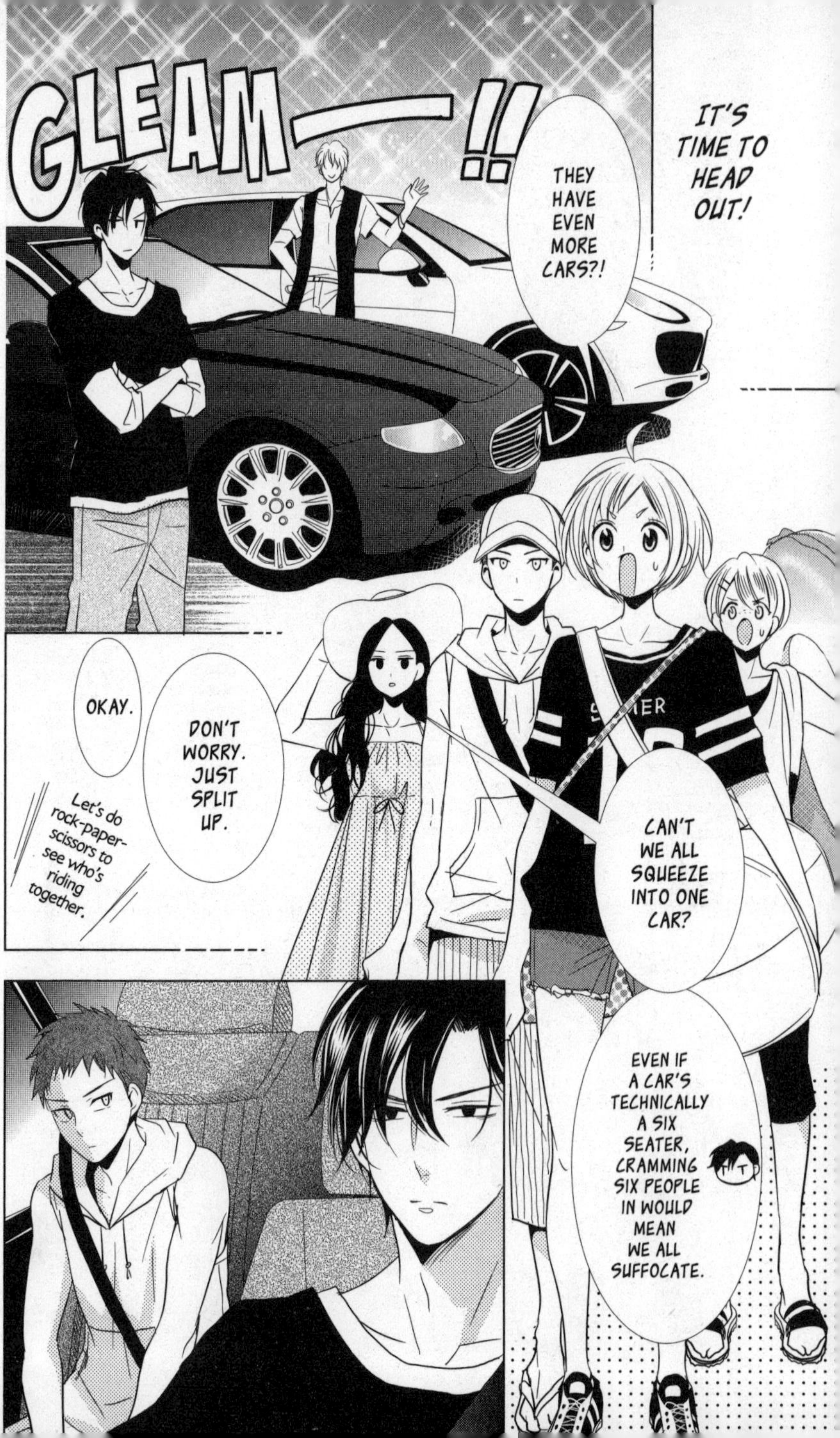
IT'S TIME TO HEAD OUT!
THEY HAVE EVEN MORE CARS?!
GLEAM—!!
CAN'T WE ALL SQUEEZE INTO ONE CAR?
EVEN IF A CAR'S TECHNICALLY A SIX SEATER, CRAMMING SIX PEOPLE IN WOULD MEAN WE ALL SUFFOCATE.
DON'T WORRY. JUST SPLIT UP.
OKAY.
Let's do rock-paper-scissors to see who's riding together.

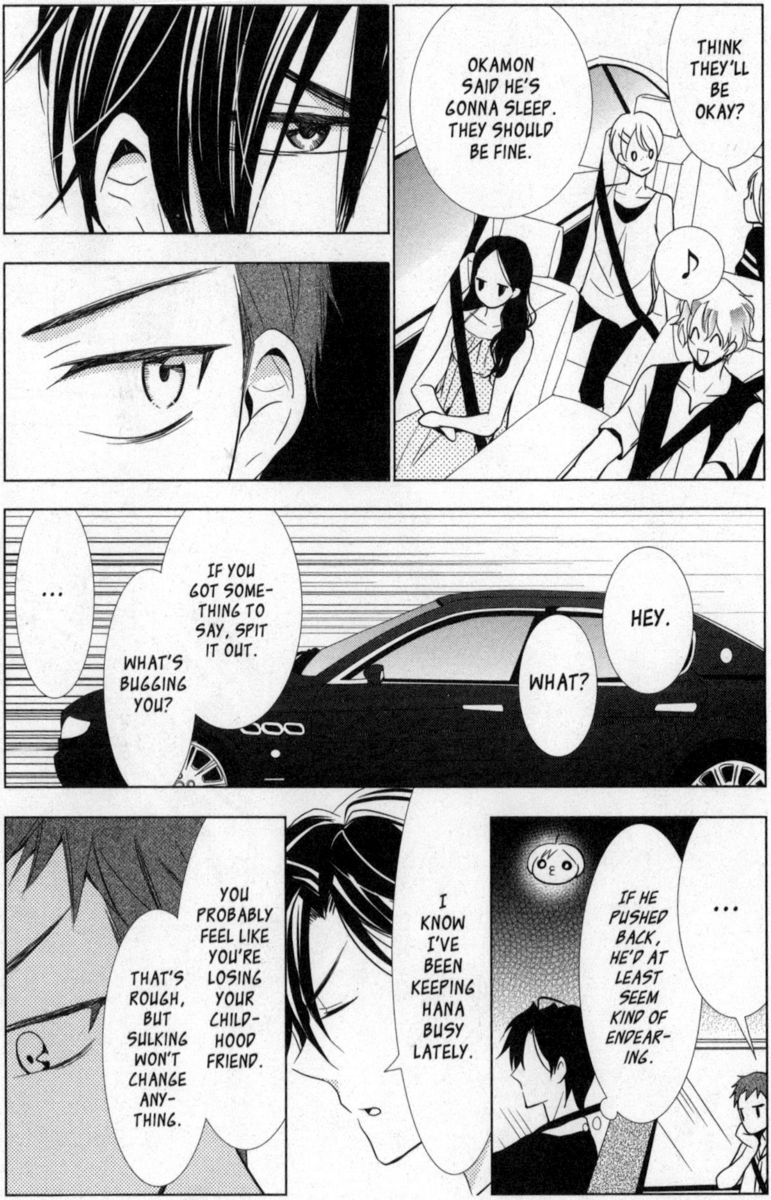
THINK THEY'LL BE OKAY?
OKAMON SAID HE'S GONNA SLEEP. THEY SHOULD BE FINE.
♪
HEY.
WHAT?
IF YOU GOT SOME-THING TO SAY, SPIT IT OUT.
WHAT'S BUGGING YOU?
...
...
IF HE PUSHED BACK, HE'D AT LEAST SEEM KIND OF ENDEAR-ING.
I KNOW I'VE BEEN KEEPING HANA BUSY LATELY.
YOU PROBABLY FEEL LIKE YOU'RE LOSING YOUR CHILD-HOOD FRIEND.
THAT'S ROUGH, BUT SULKING WON'T CHANGE ANY-THING.

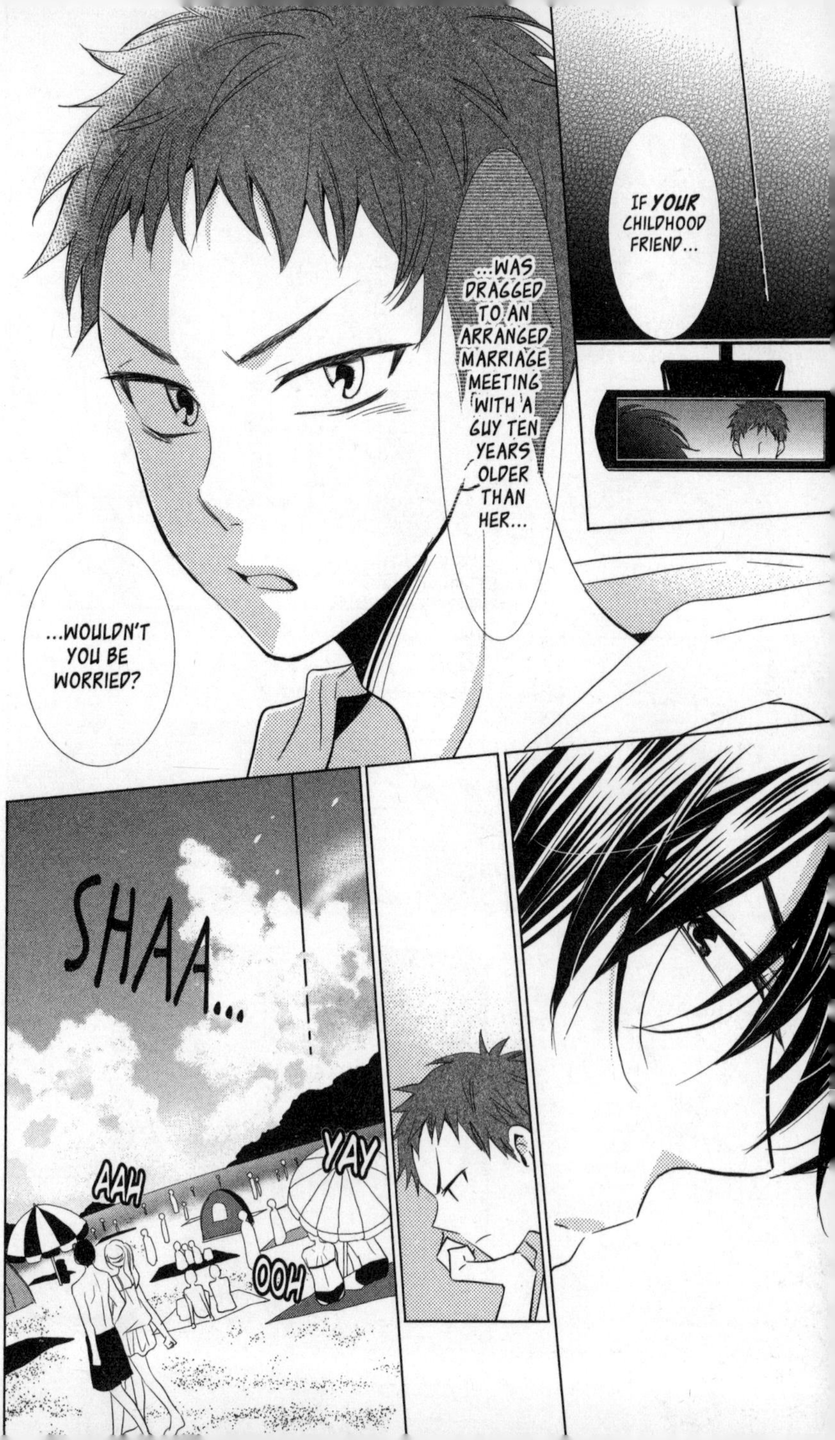
IF *YOUR* CHILDHOOD FRIEND...
...WAS DRAGGED TO AN ARRANGED MARRIAGE MEETING WITH A GUY TEN YEARS OLDER THAN HER...
...WOULDN'T YOU BE WORRIED?
SHAA...
YAY
AAH
OOH

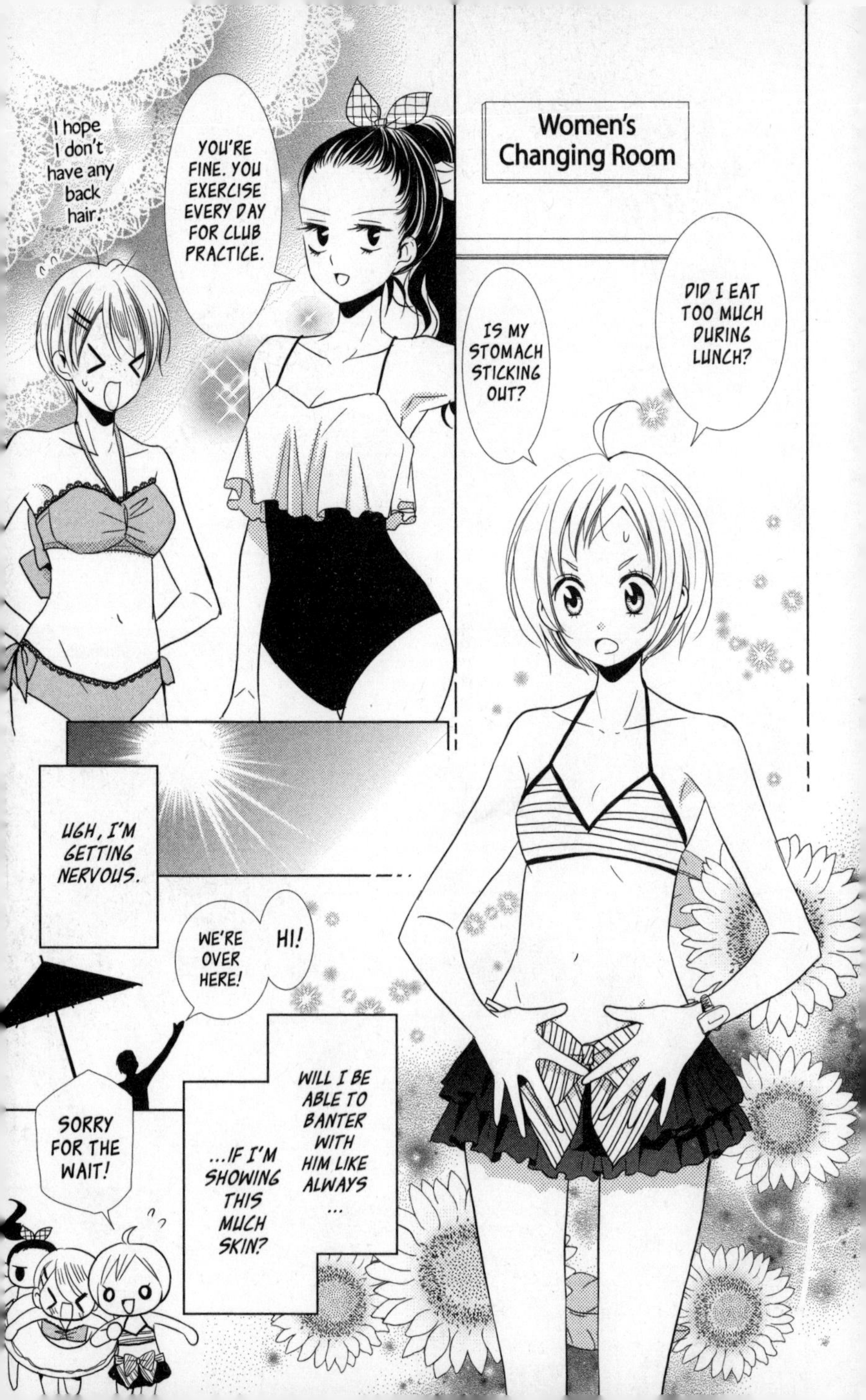
Women's Changing Room
DID I EAT TOO MUCH DURING LUNCH?
IS MY STOMACH STICKING OUT?
YOU'RE FINE. YOU EXERCISE EVERY DAY FOR CLUB PRACTICE.
I hope I don't have any back hair.
UGH, I'M GETTING NERVOUS.
HI!
WE'RE OVER HERE!
WILL I BE ABLE TO BANTER WITH HIM LIKE ALWAYS...
...IF I'M SHOWING THIS MUCH SKIN?
SORRY FOR THE WAIT!

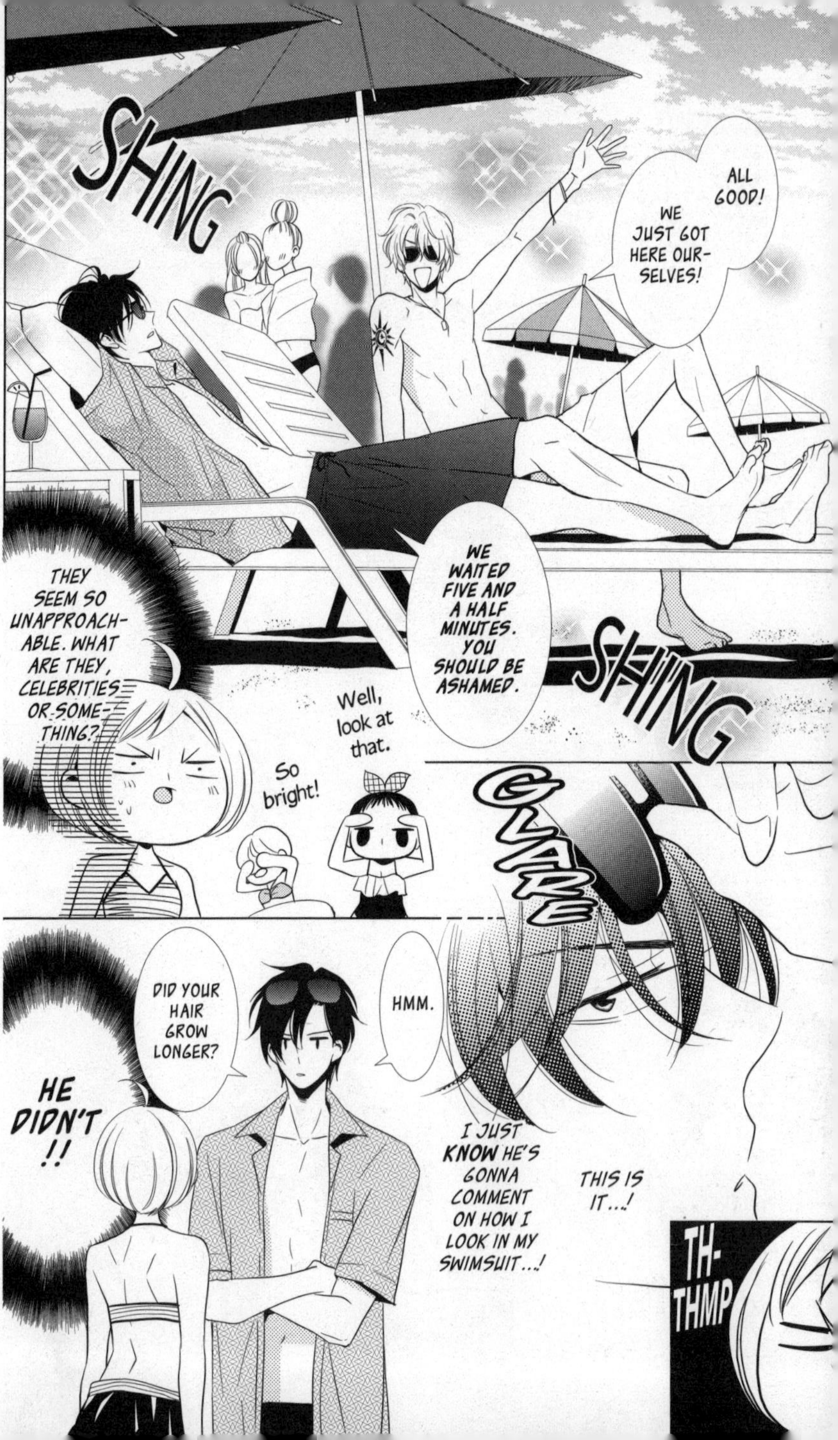
ALL GOOD!
WE JUST GOT HERE OURSELVES!
SHING
WE WAITED FIVE AND A HALF MINUTES. YOU SHOULD BE ASHAMED.
SHING
THEY SEEM SO UNAPPROACHABLE. WHAT ARE THEY, CELEBRITIES-OR-SOMETHING?
Well, look at that.
So bright!
GLARE
HMM.
DID YOUR HAIR GROW LONGER?
HE DIDN'T !!
TH-THMP
THIS IS IT...!
I JUST KNOW HE'S GONNA COMMENT ON HOW I LOOK IN MY SWIMSUIT...!

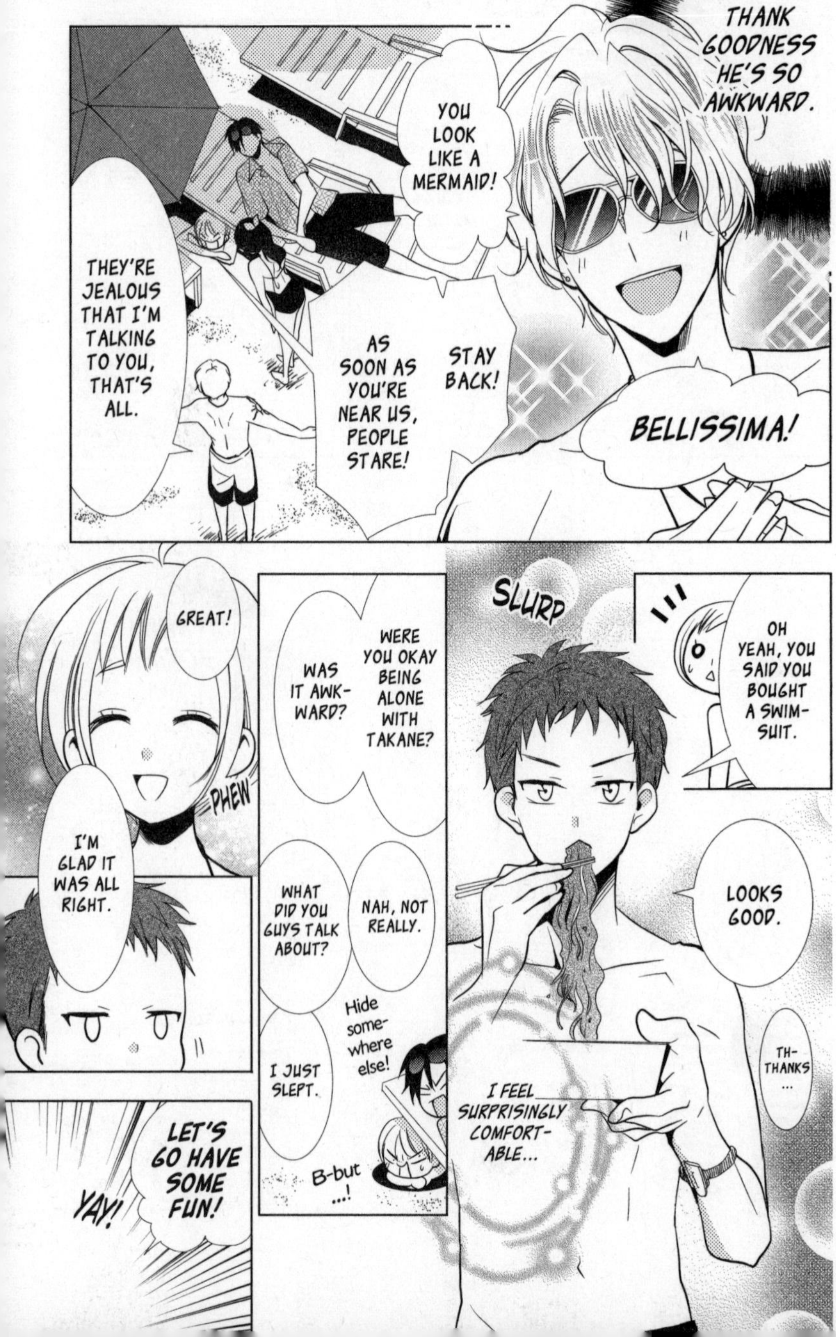
THANK GOODNESS HE'S SO AWKWARD.
YOU LOOK LIKE A MERMAID!
BELLISSIMA!
STAY BACK!
AS SOON AS YOU'RE NEAR US, PEOPLE STARE!
THEY'RE JEALOUS THAT I'M TALKING TO YOU, THAT'S ALL.
OH YEAH, YOU SAID YOU BOUGHT A SWIM-SUIT.
SLURP
LOOKS GOOD.
TH-THANKS...
I FEEL SURPRISINGLY COMFORT-ABLE...
WERE YOU OKAY BEING ALONE WITH TAKANE?
WAS IT AWK-WARD?
NAH, NOT REALLY.
WHAT DID YOU GUYS TALK ABOUT?
Hide some-where else!
I JUST SLEPT.
B-but...!
GREAT!
PHEW
I'M GLAD IT WAS ALL RIGHT.
LET'S GO HAVE SOME FUN!
YAY!

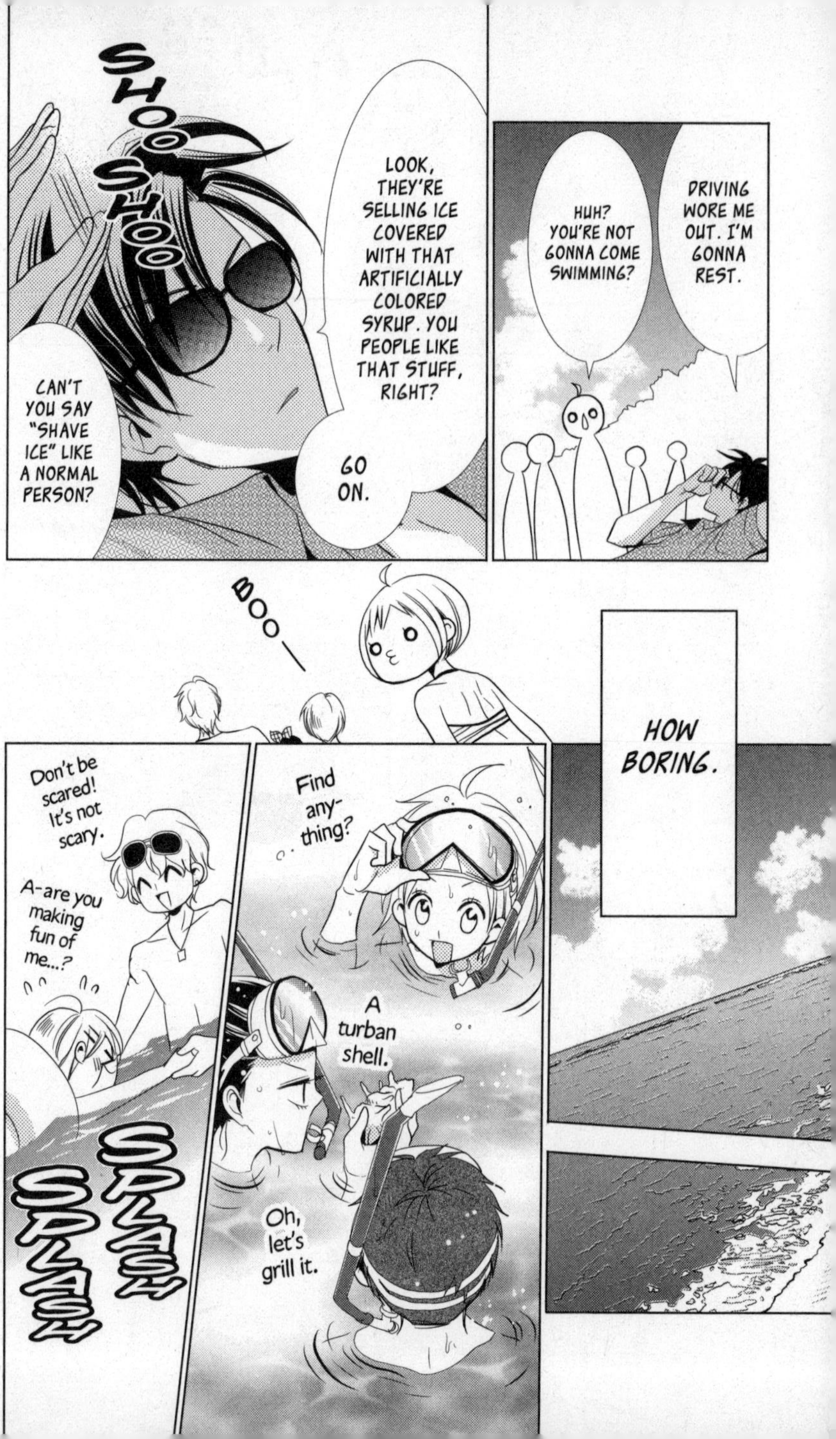
DRIVING WORE ME OUT. I'M GONNA REST.
HUH? YOU'RE NOT GONNA COME SWIMMING?
LOOK, THEY'RE SELLING ICE COVERED WITH THAT ARTIFICIALLY COLORED SYRUP. YOU PEOPLE LIKE THAT STUFF, RIGHT?
GO ON.
SHOO SHOO
CAN'T YOU SAY "SHAVE ICE" LIKE A NORMAL PERSON?
HOW BORING.
BOO—
Find anything?
A turban shell.
Oh, let's grill it.
Don't be scared! It's not scary.
A-are you making fun of me...?
SPLASH SPLASH

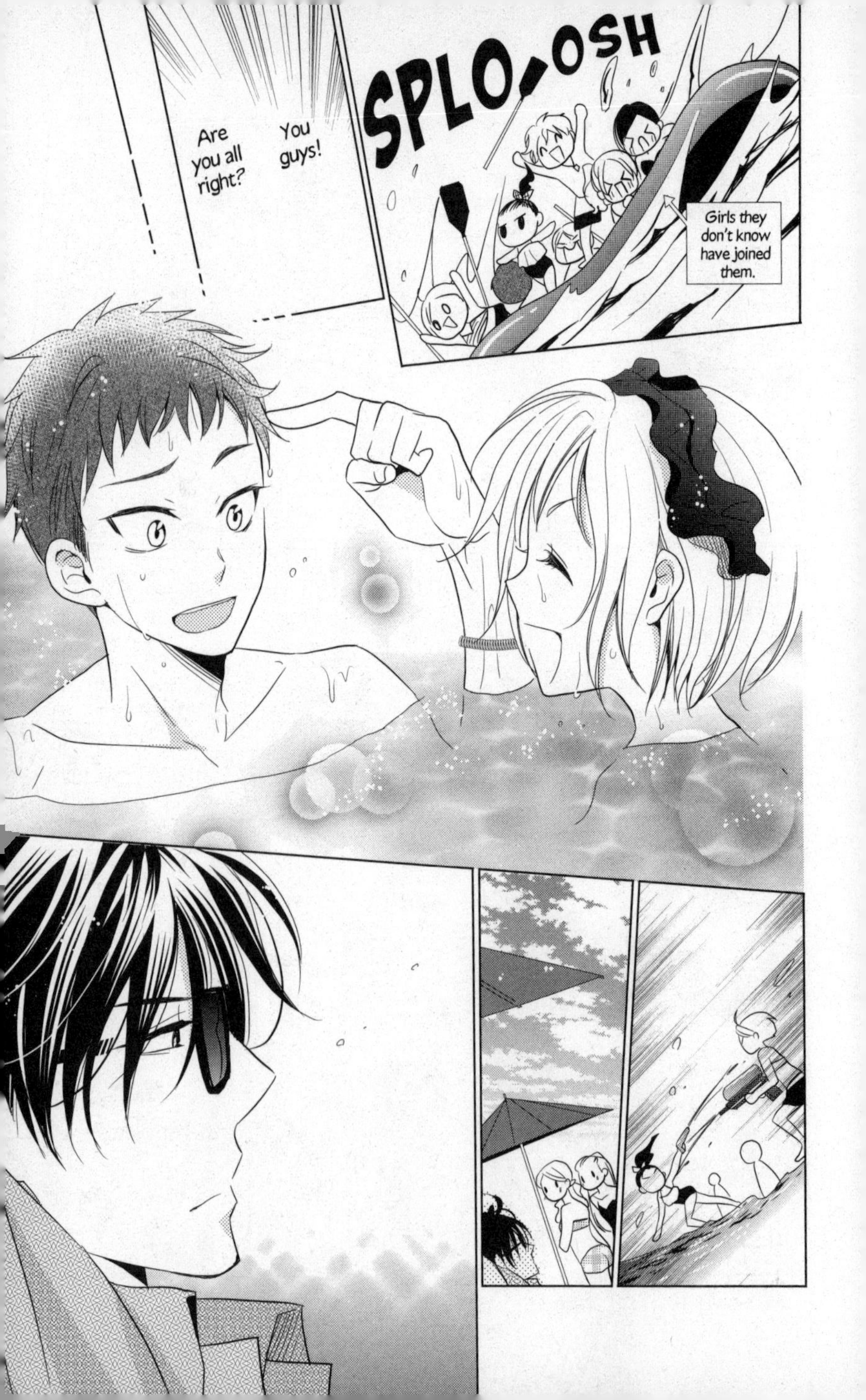
SPLOOSH
Girls they don't know have joined them.
You guys!
Are you all right?

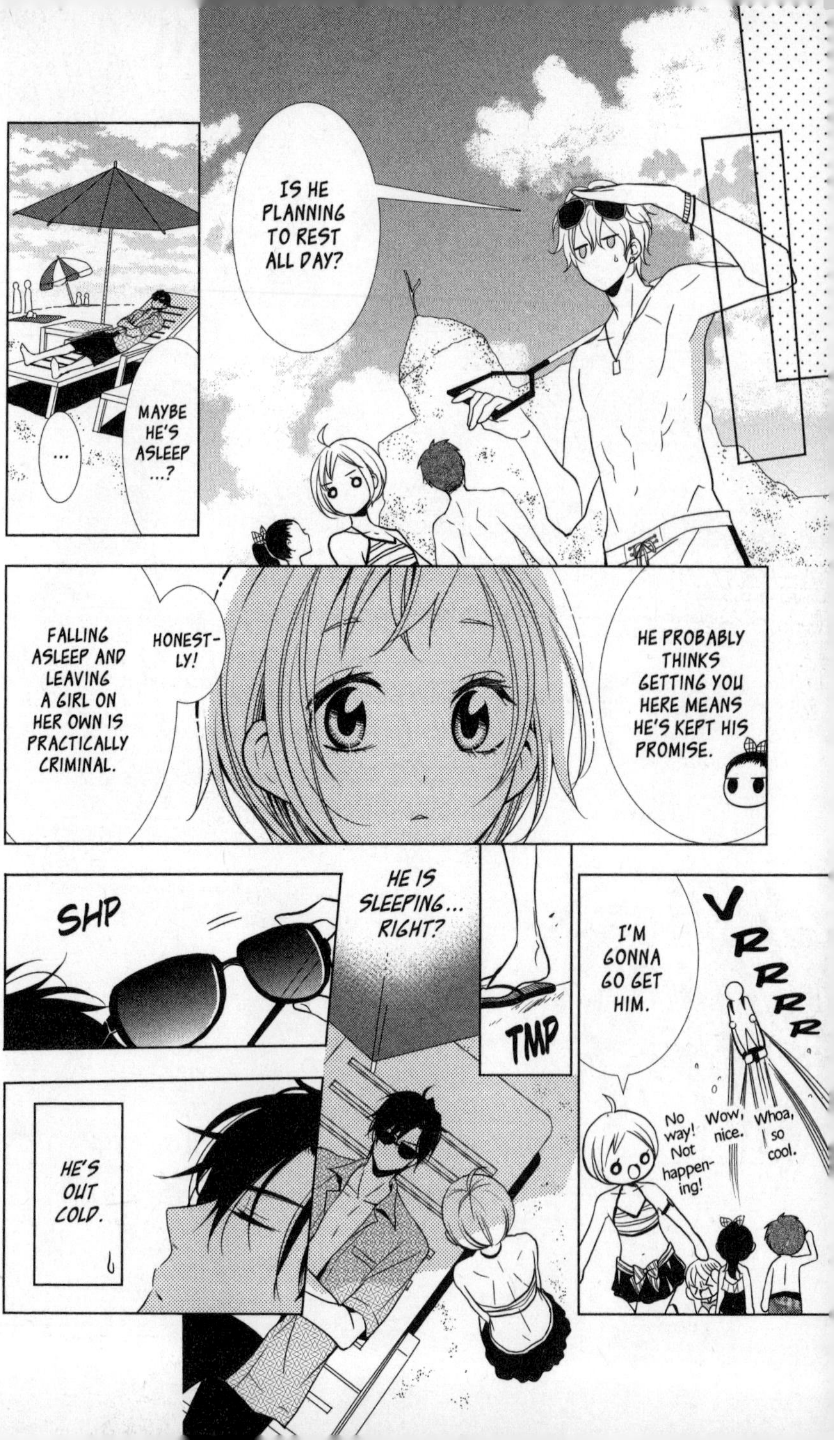
IS HE PLANNING TO REST ALL DAY?
MAYBE HE'S ASLEEP ...?
...
HE PROBABLY THINKS GETTING YOU HERE MEANS HE'S KEPT HIS PROMISE.
HONEST-LY!
FALLING ASLEEP AND LEAVING A GIRL ON HER OWN IS PRACTICALLY CRIMINAL.
VRRRR
I'M GONNA GO GET HIM.
Whoa, so cool.
Wow, nice.
No way! Not happen-ing!
TMP
HE IS SLEEPING... RIGHT?
SHP
HE'S OUT COLD.

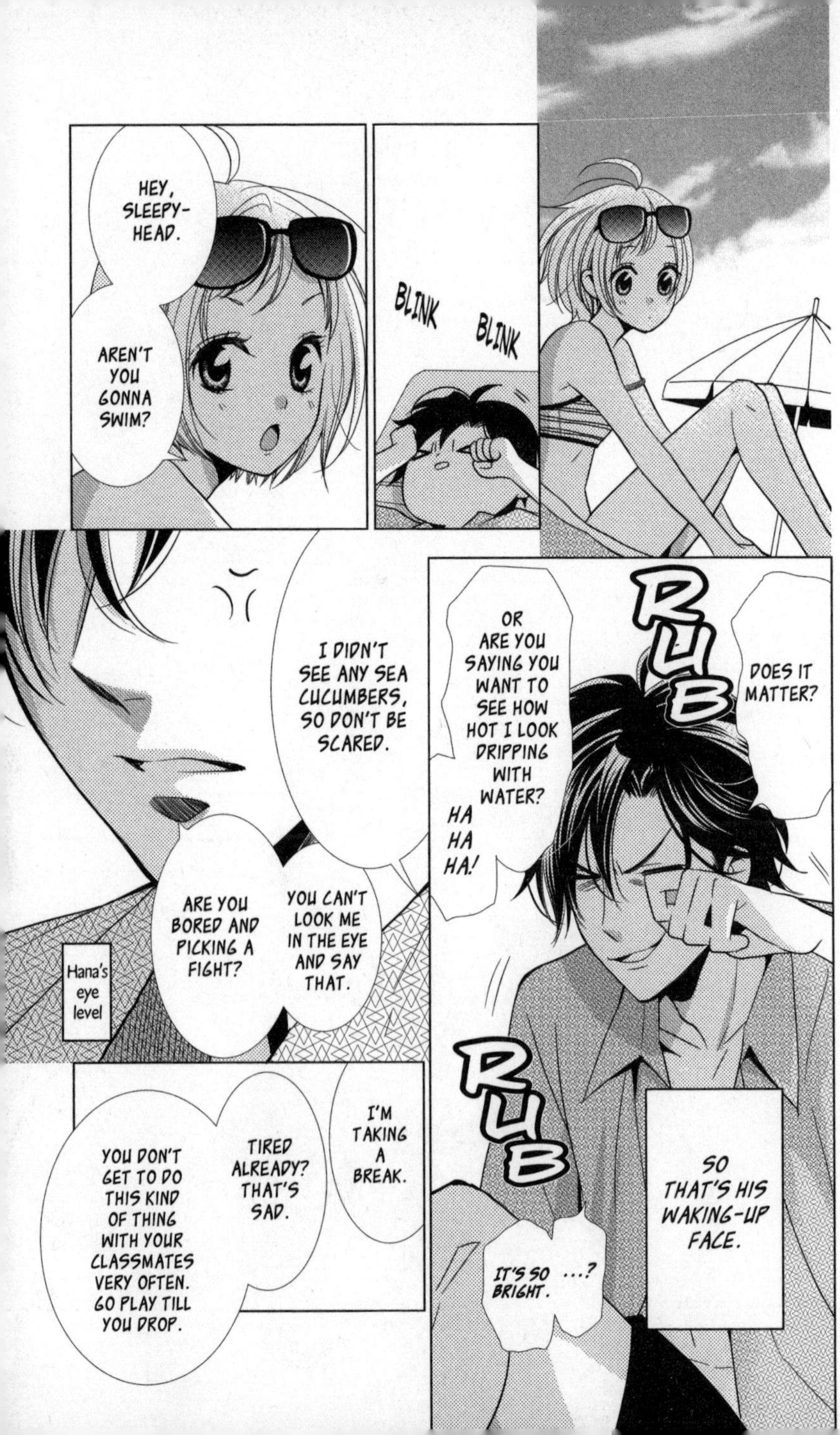
BLINK
BLINK
HEY, SLEEPY-HEAD.
AREN'T YOU GONNA SWIM?
RUB
DOES IT MATTER?
OR ARE YOU SAYING YOU WANT TO SEE HOW HOT I LOOK DRIPPING WITH WATER?
HA HA HA!
RUB
SO THAT'S HIS WAKING-UP FACE.
...?
IT'S SO BRIGHT.
I DIDN'T SEE ANY SEA CUCUMBERS, SO DON'T BE SCARED.
YOU CAN'T LOOK ME IN THE EYE AND SAY THAT.
ARE YOU BORED AND PICKING A FIGHT?
Hana's eye level
I'M TAKING A BREAK.
TIRED ALREADY? THAT'S SAD.
YOU DON'T GET TO DO THIS KIND OF THING WITH YOUR CLASSMATES VERY OFTEN. GO PLAY TILL YOU DROP.

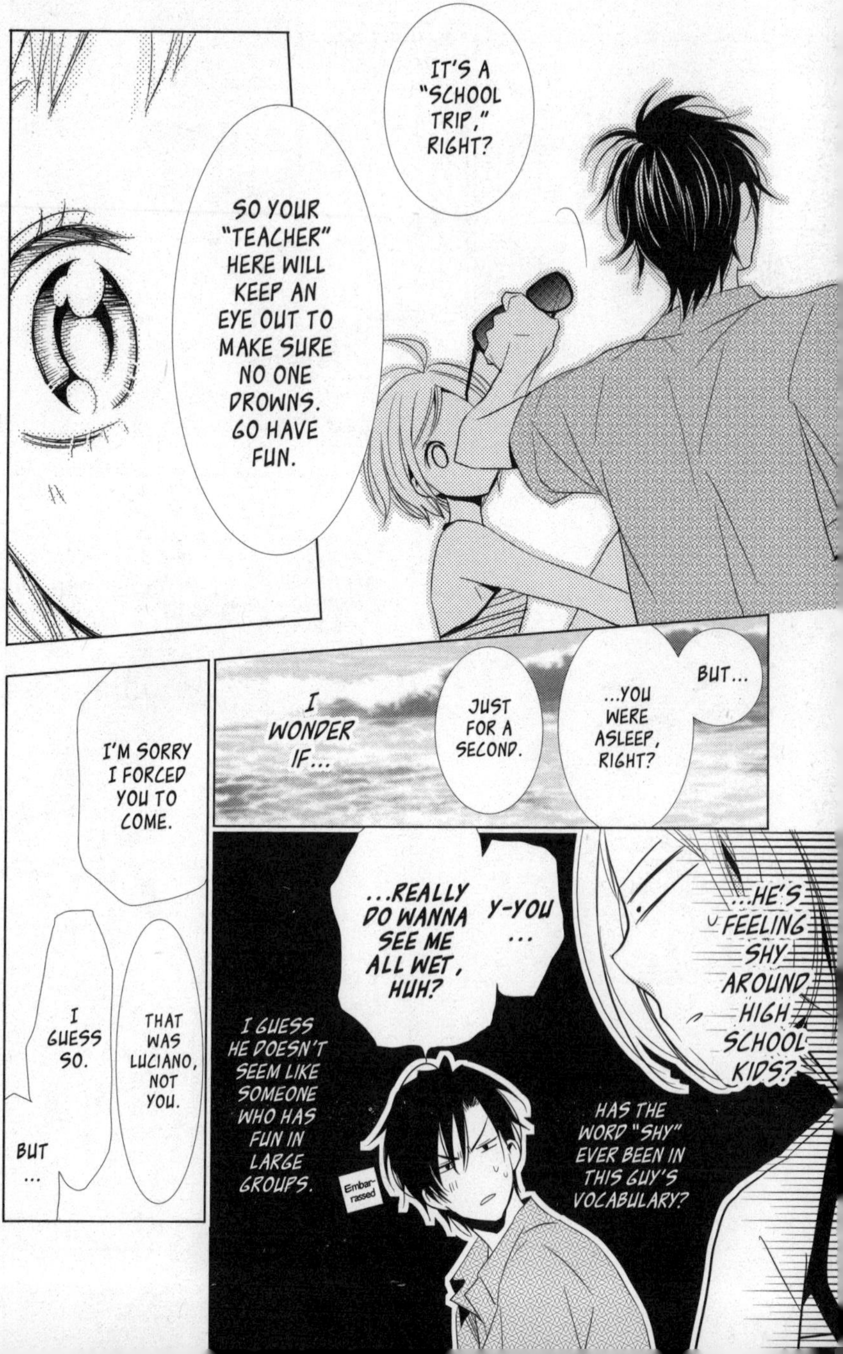
IT'S A "SCHOOL TRIP," RIGHT?
SO YOUR "TEACHER" HERE WILL KEEP AN EYE OUT TO MAKE SURE NO ONE DROWNS. GO HAVE FUN.
BUT...
...YOU WERE ASLEEP, RIGHT?
JUST FOR A SECOND.
I WONDER IF...
I'M SORRY I FORCED YOU TO COME.
THAT WAS LUCIANO, NOT YOU.
I GUESS SO.
BUT ...
...HE'S FEELING SHY AROUND HIGH SCHOOL KIDS?
Y-YOU ...
...REALLY DO WANNA SEE ME ALL WET, HUH?
HAS THE WORD "SHY" EVER BEEN IN THIS GUY'S VOCABULARY?
Embarrassed
I GUESS HE DOESN'T SEEM LIKE SOMEONE WHO HAS FUN IN LARGE GROUPS.

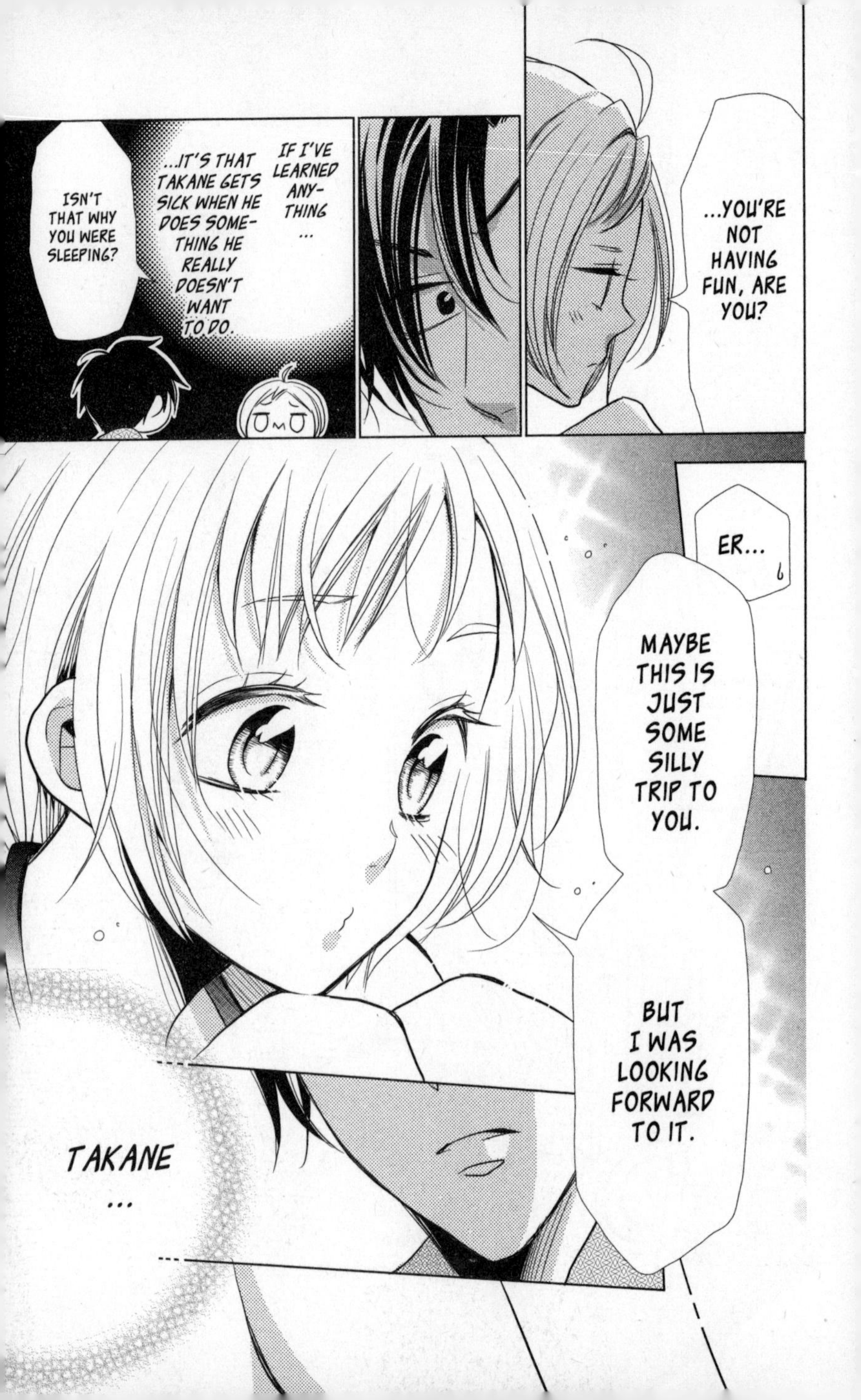
...YOU'RE NOT HAVING FUN, ARE YOU?
IF I'VE LEARNED ANYTHING ...
...IT'S THAT TAKANE GETS SICK WHEN HE DOES SOMETHING HE REALLY DOESN'T WANT TO DO.
ISN'T THAT WHY YOU WERE SLEEPING?
ER...
MAYBE THIS IS JUST SOME SILLY TRIP TO YOU.
BUT I WAS LOOKING FORWARD TO IT.
TAKANE ...

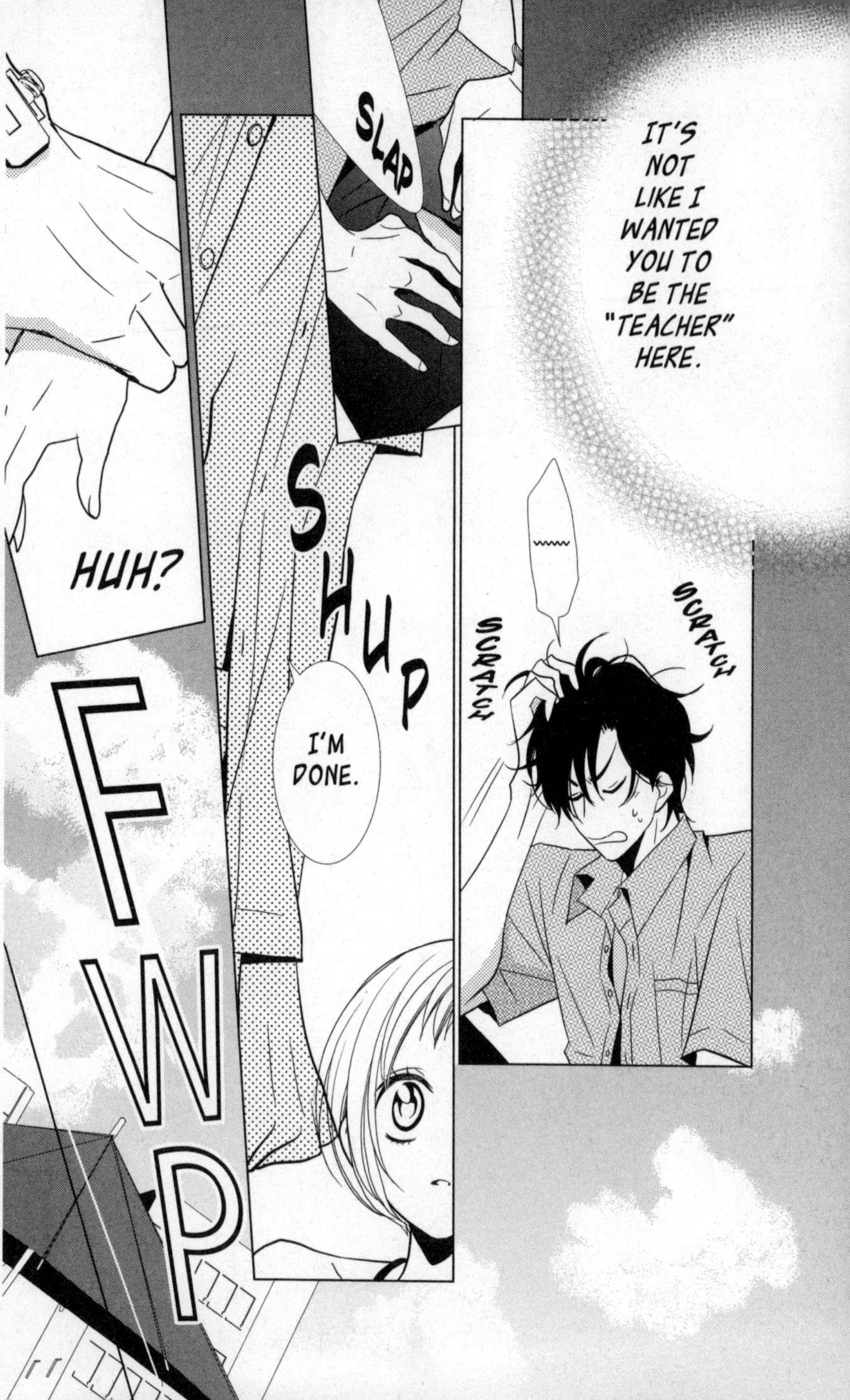
IT'S NOT LIKE I WANTED YOU TO BE THE "TEACHER" HERE.
SCRATCH
SCRATCH
~~~
SLAP
SHUP
I'M DONE.
HUH?
FWP
~~~

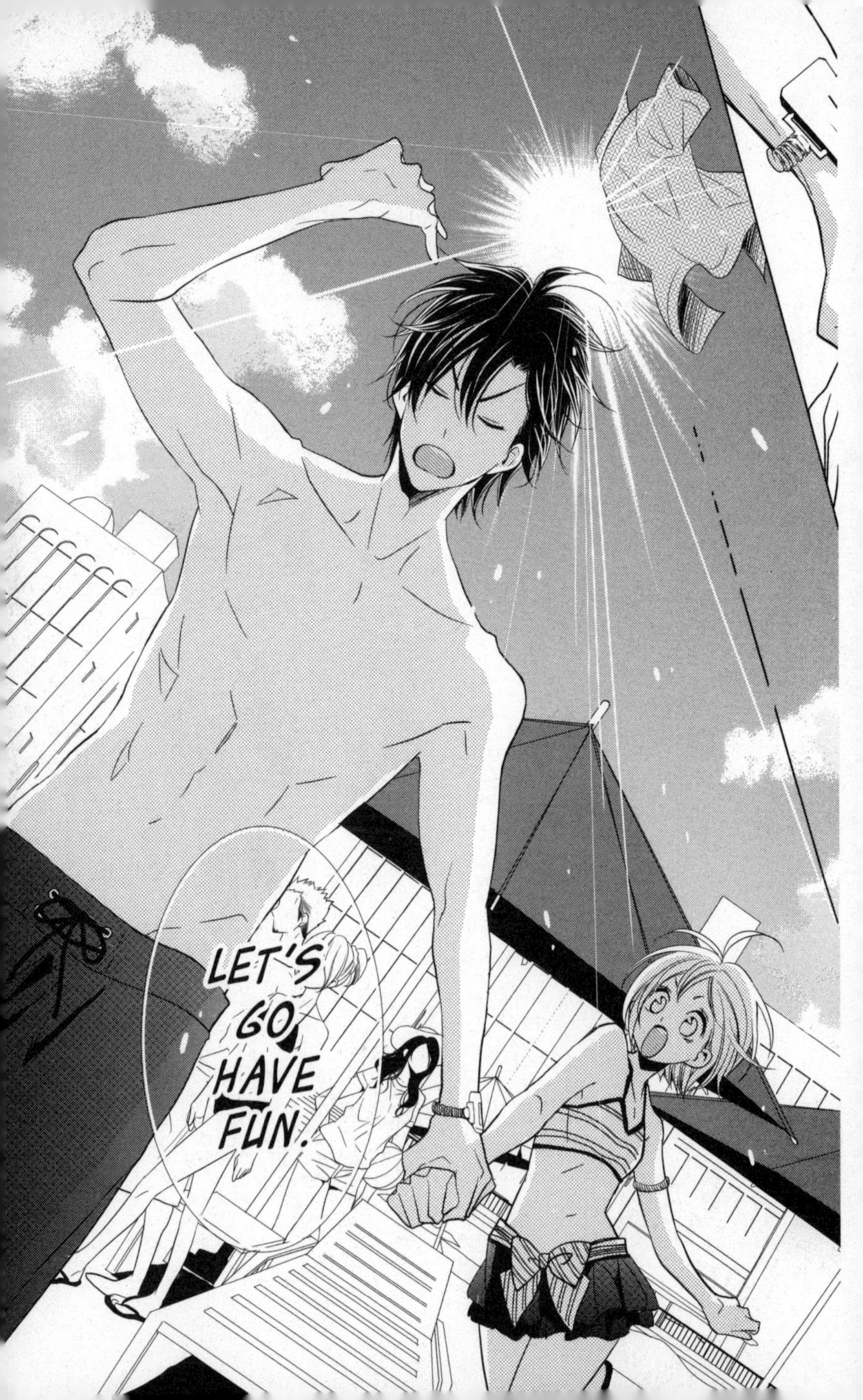
LET'S GO. HAVE FUN.

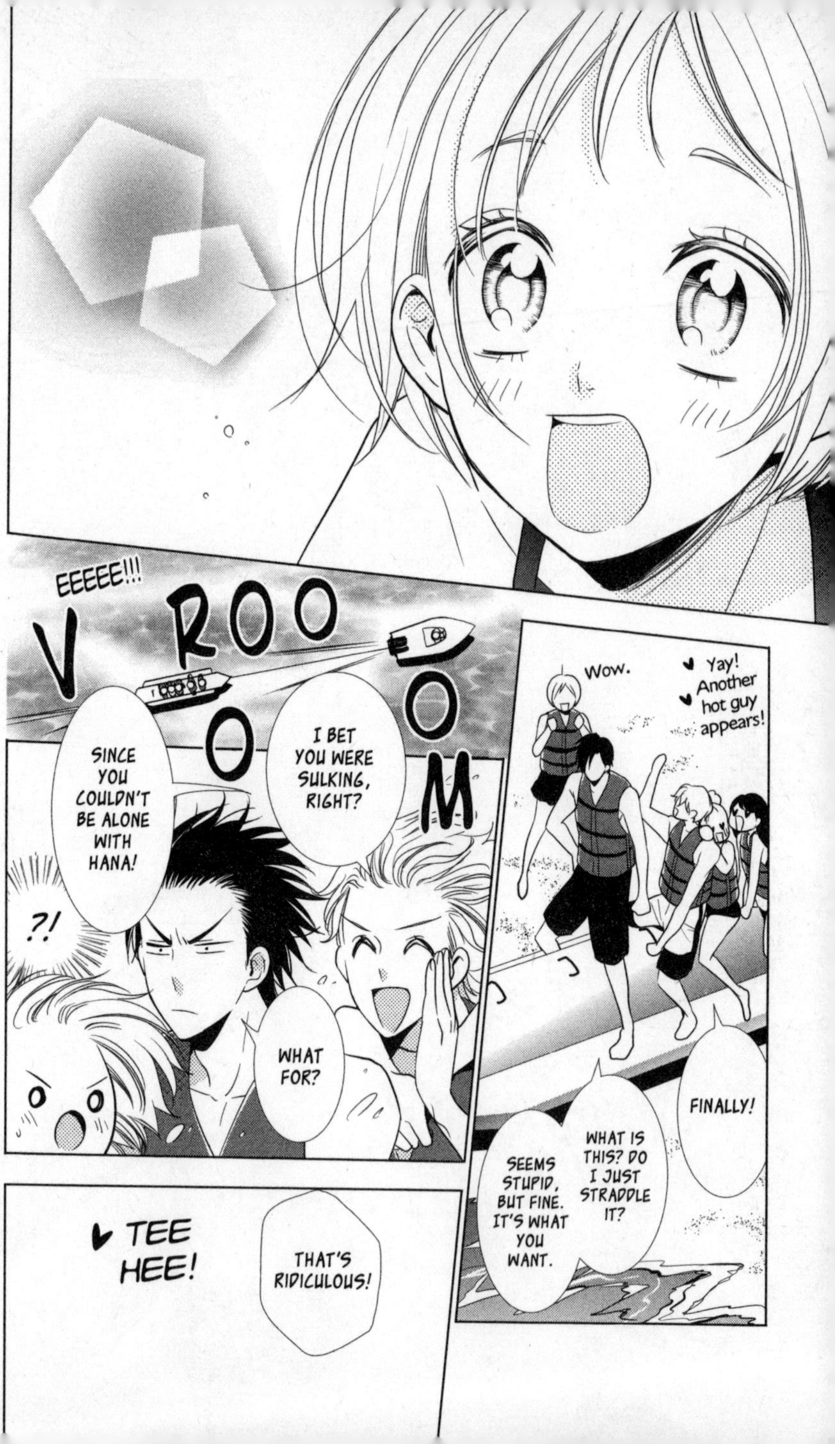
♥ Yay! ♥ Another hot guy appears!
Wow.
FINALLY!
WHAT IS THIS? DO I JUST STRADDLE IT?
SEEMS STUPID, BUT FINE. IT'S WHAT YOU WANT.
EEEEE!!!
VROOOOM
I BET YOU WERE SULKING, RIGHT?
SINCE YOU COULDN'T BE ALONE WITH HANA!
?!
WHAT FOR?
♥ TEE HEE!
THAT'S RIDICULOUS!

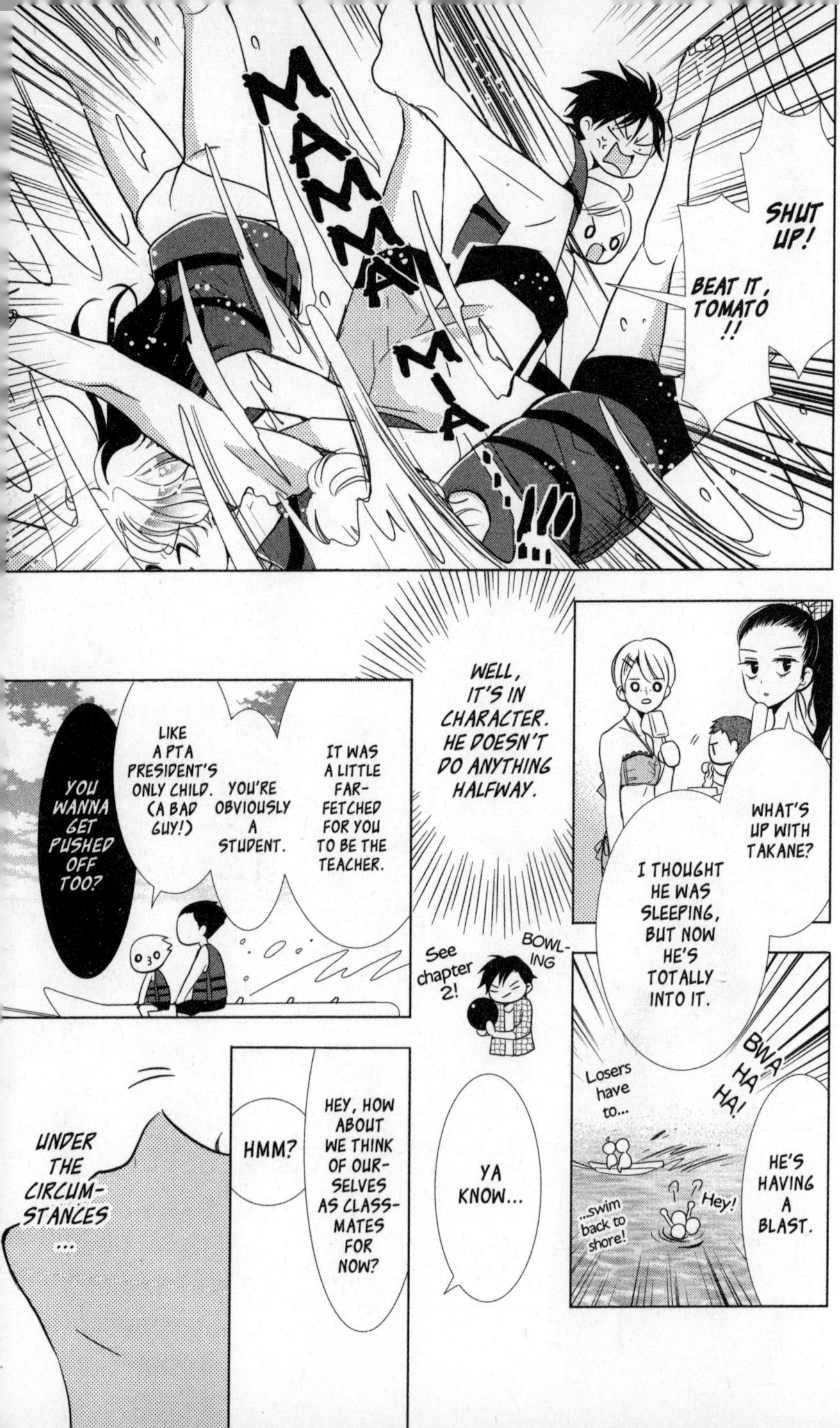
SHUT UP!
BEAT IT, TOMATO!!
MAMMA MIA...!!!
WHAT'S UP WITH TAKANE?
I THOUGHT HE WAS SLEEPING, BUT NOW HE'S TOTALLY INTO IT.
BWA HA HA!
Losers have to...
...swim back to shore!
Hey!
HE'S HAVING A BLAST.
WELL, IT'S IN CHARACTER. HE DOESN'T DO ANYTHING HALFWAY.
BOWL-ING
See chapter 2!
IT WAS A LITTLE FAR-FETCHED FOR YOU TO BE THE TEACHER.
YOU'RE OBVIOUSLY A STUDENT.
LIKE A PTA PRESIDENT'S ONLY CHILD. (A BAD GUY!)
YOU WANNA GET PUSHED OFF TOO?
YA KNOW...
HEY, HOW ABOUT WE THINK OF OUR-SELVES AS CLASS-MATES FOR NOW?
HMM?
UNDER THE CIRCUM-STANCES...

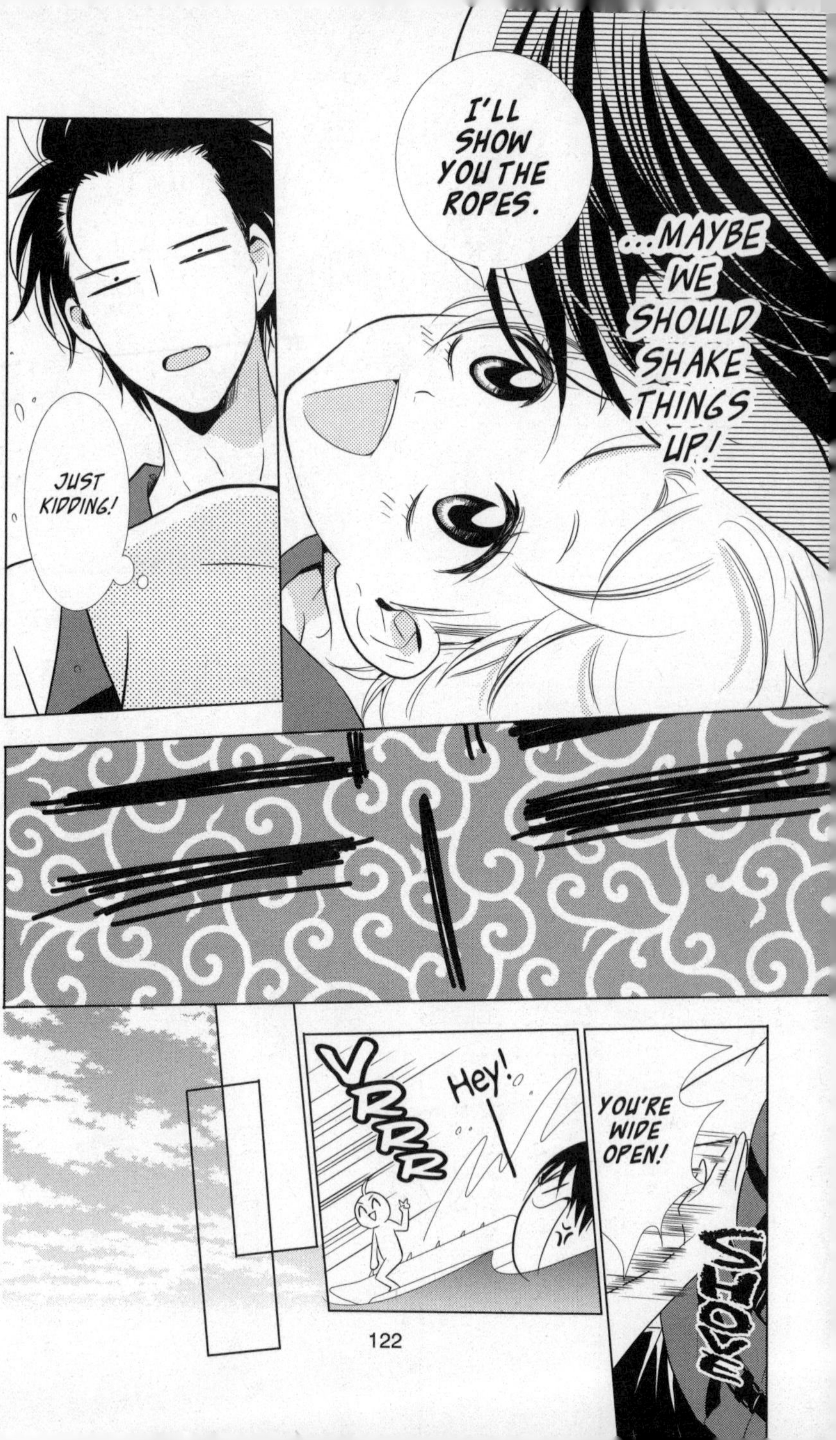
...MAYBE WE SHOULD SHAKE THINGS UP!
I'LL SHOW YOU THE ROPES.
JUST KIDDING!
WHOOSH
YOU'RE WIDE OPEN!
VRRR
Hey!

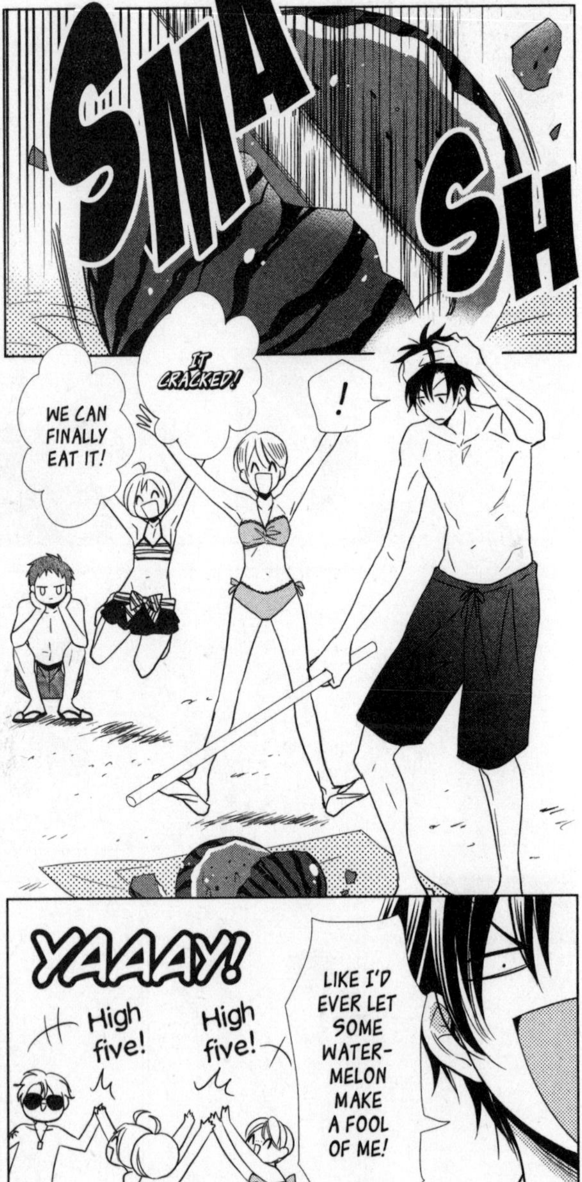
SMASH
!
IT CRACKED!
WE CAN FINALLY EAT IT!
LIKE I'D EVER LET SOME WATER-MELON MAKE A FOOL OF ME!
YAAAY!
High five!
High five!

• Bonus Info •

A drawing error

In volume 1, on a certain page, I drew six fingers on Hana's hand. I fixed it! Newer printings should only have five fingers now.

Phrasing

In the original volume 1, I used the phrase "*oshi mo osarenu elito danshi*" for "an elite with an established reputation," but apparently the correct phrase is "*oshi mo osaremo senu*." My editor did point it out to me, but I felt like it flowed better as is, so I left it alone. Keep that in mind, though, if you're a student who might see it on a test!

Time lapse

When this was initially written as a one-shot, the story took place during the season when it was published. But starting with spring (the flower-viewing chapter), the seasons are now progressing normally.

• Special Thanks •

-Master of a girl's heart, my chief editor, "S"!
-Everyone who handles sales and marketing
-The person in charge of the cover design
-Everyone who had a hand in making this book a reality
-Readers, family and friends

Please Send Me • Your Thoughts • and Impressions!

Yuki Shiwasu
c/o Takane & Hana Editor
VIZ Media
P.O. Box 77010
San Francisco, CA 94107

I'm only able to write back about once a year, but I read every single one of your letters!

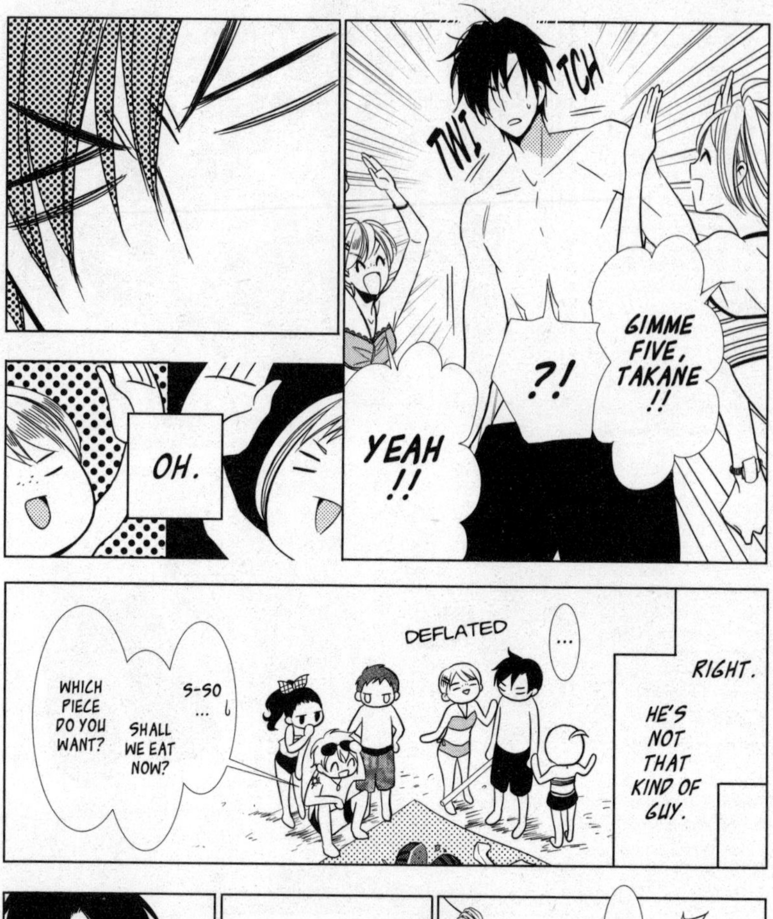
GIMME FIVE, TAKANE !!
?!
YEAH !!
TWITCH
OH.
RIGHT.
HE'S NOT THAT KIND OF GUY.
...
DEFLATED
S-SO ...
SHALL WE EAT NOW?
WHICH PIECE DO YOU WANT?
This one.
THWAK
I'll...
LIKE THAT, RIGHT?

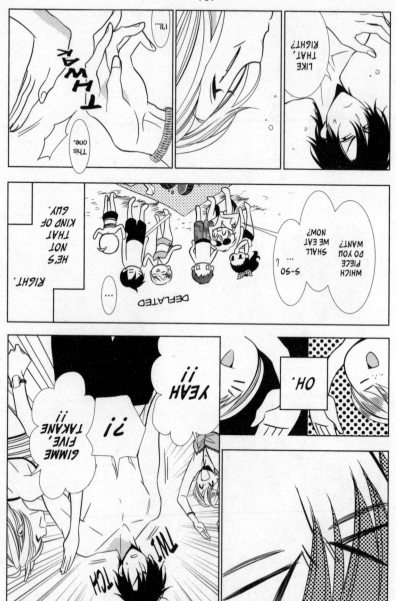

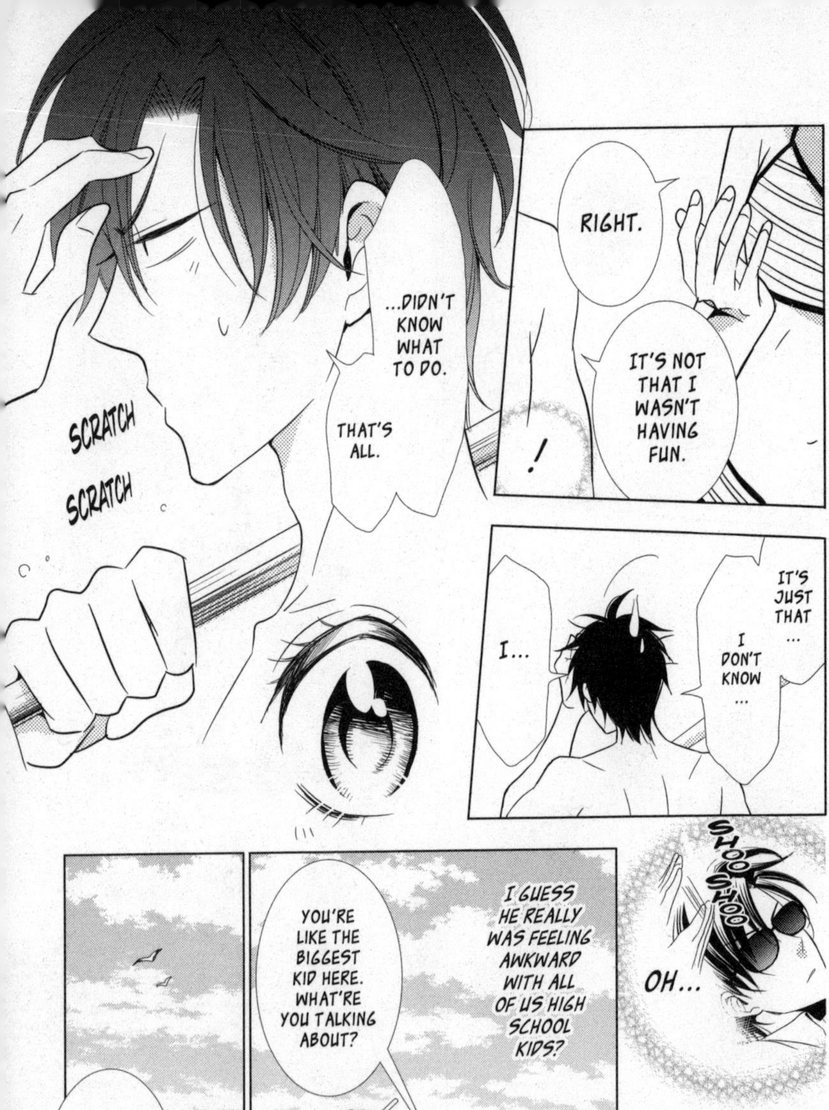
RIGHT.
IT'S NOT THAT I WASN'T HAVING FUN.
!
...DIDN'T KNOW WHAT TO DO.
THAT'S ALL.
SCRATCH
SCRATCH
IT'S JUST THAT ...
I DON'T KNOW ...
I...
SHOO SHOO
OH...
I GUESS HE REALLY WAS FEELING AWKWARD WITH ALL OF US HIGH SCHOOL KIDS?
YOU'RE LIKE THE BIGGEST KID HERE. WHAT'RE YOU TALKING ABOUT?
HEE!
EXCUSE ME?
BUT...

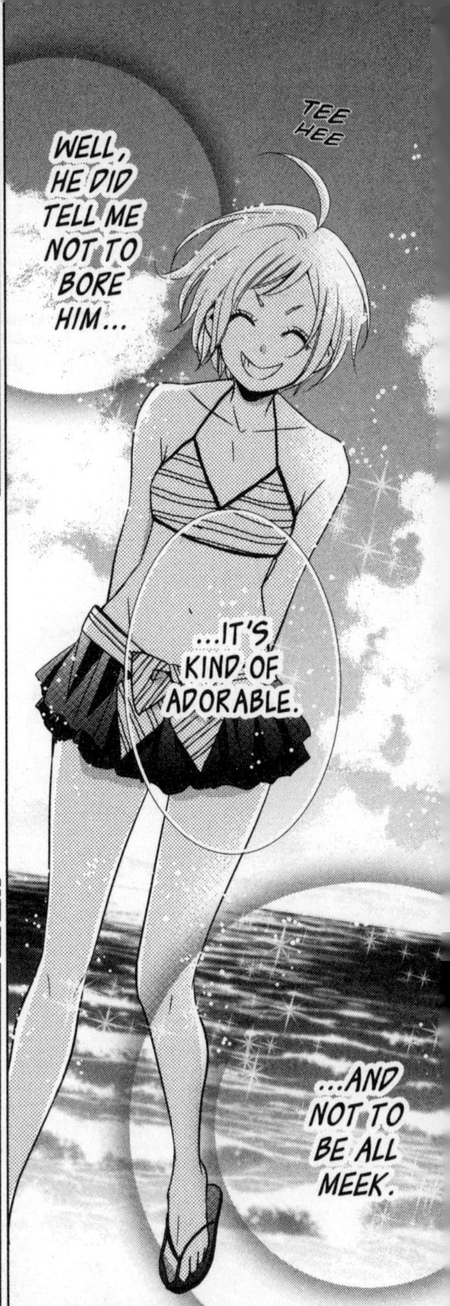
TEE HEE
WELL, HE DID TELL ME NOT TO BORE HIM...
...IT'S KIND OF ADORABLE.
...AND NOT TO BE ALL MEEK.

Chapter 14 / The End

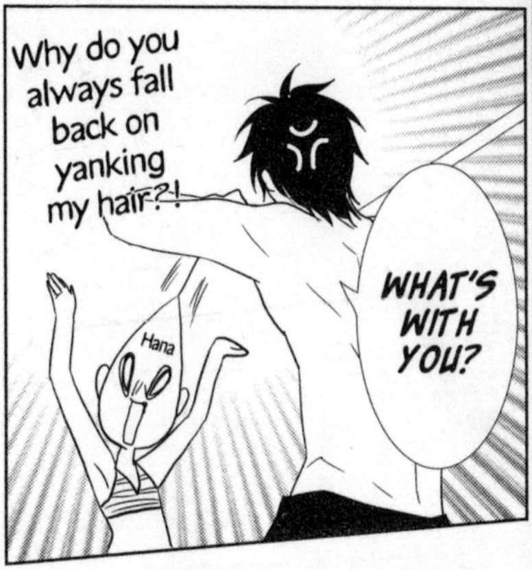
WHAT'S WITH YOU?
Why do you always fall back on yanking my hair?!
Hana

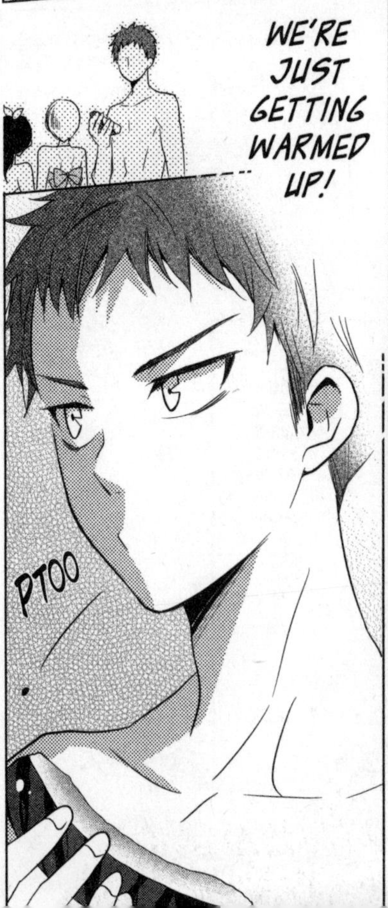
WE'RE JUST GETTING WARMED UP!
PTOO

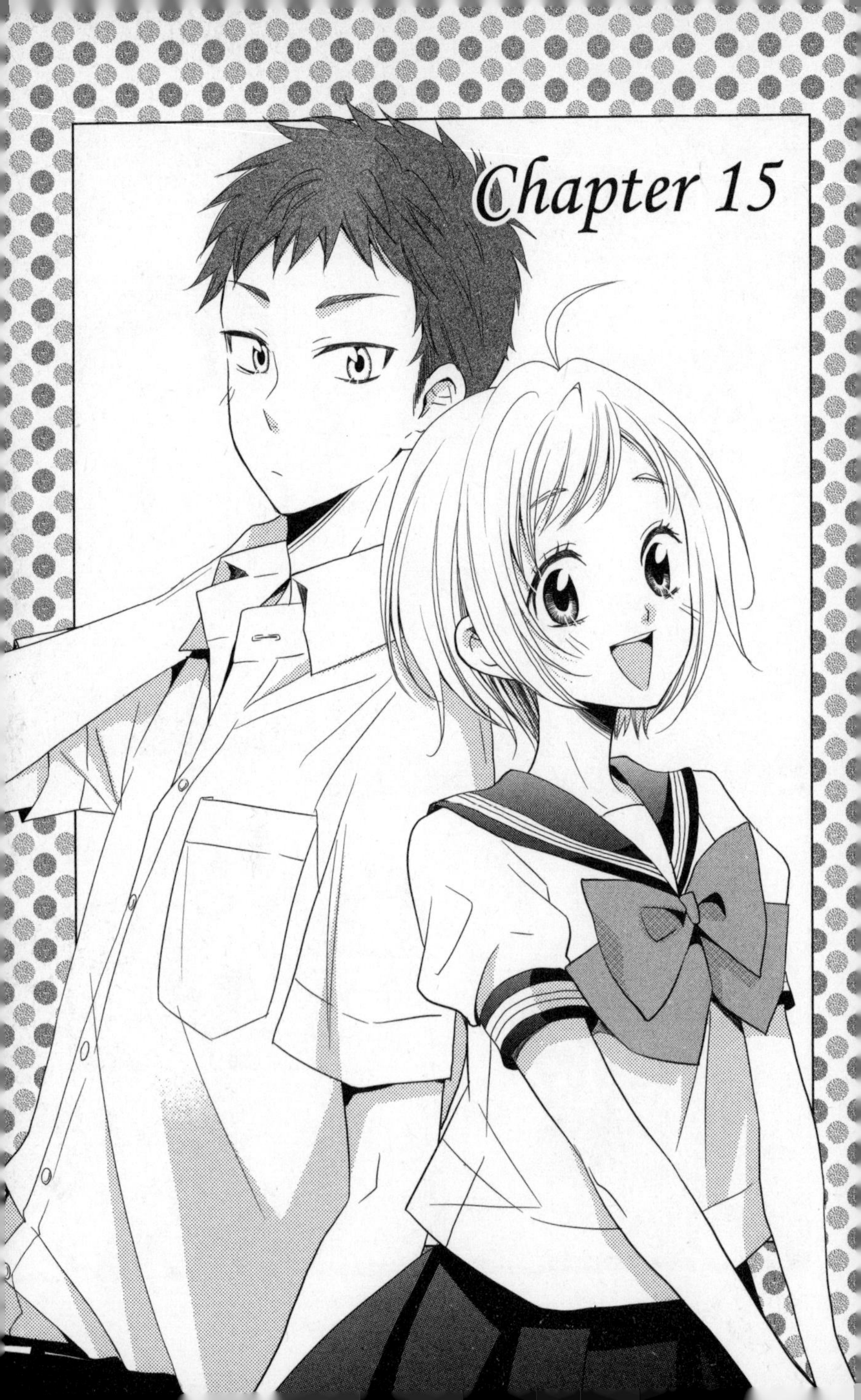
Chapter 15

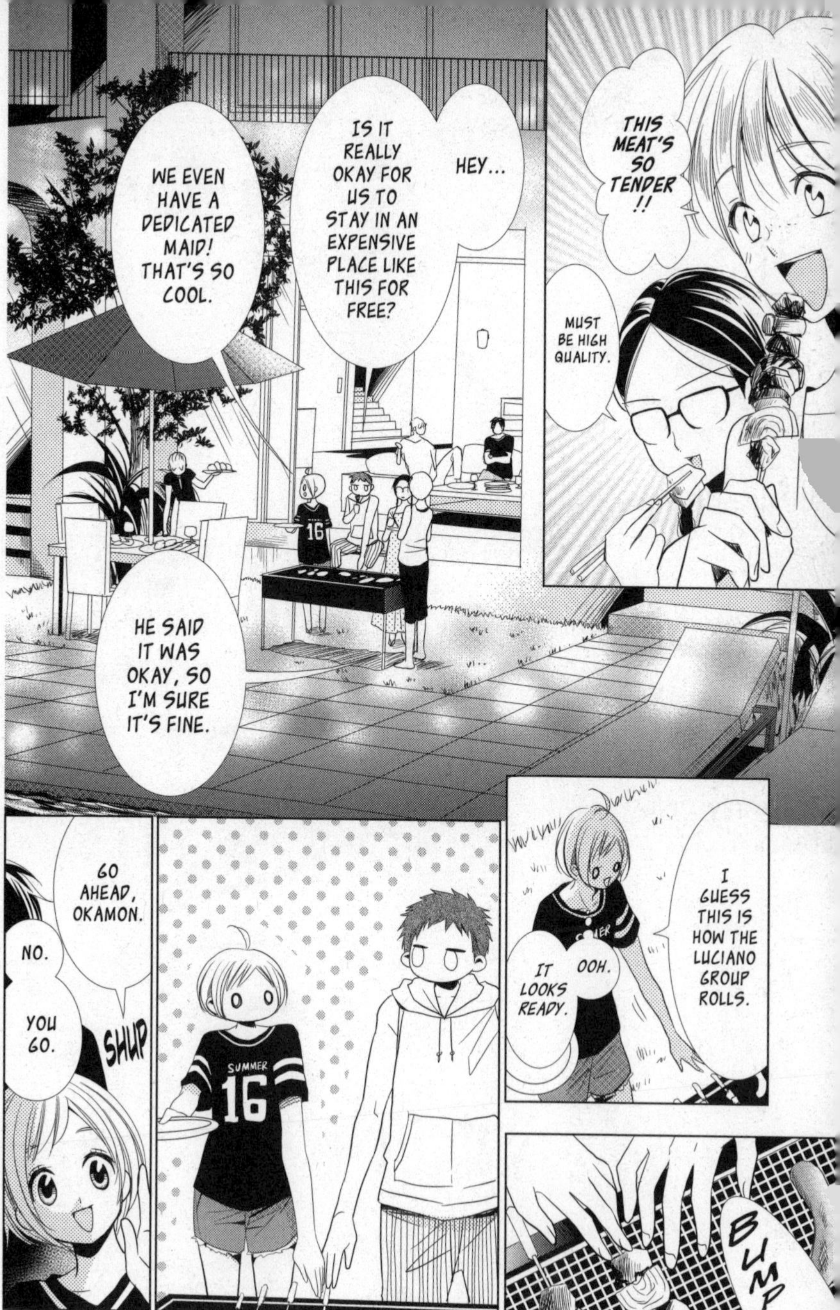
THIS MEAT'S SO TENDER!!
MUST BE HIGH QUALITY.
HEY...
IS IT REALLY OKAY FOR US TO STAY IN AN EXPENSIVE PLACE LIKE THIS FOR FREE?
WE EVEN HAVE A DEDICATED MAID! THAT'S SO COOL.
HE SAID IT WAS OKAY, SO I'M SURE IT'S FINE.
I GUESS THIS IS HOW THE LUCIANO GROUP ROLLS.
OOH.
IT LOOKS READY.
BUMP
SUMMER 16
GO AHEAD, OKAMON.
NO.
YOU GO.
SHUP

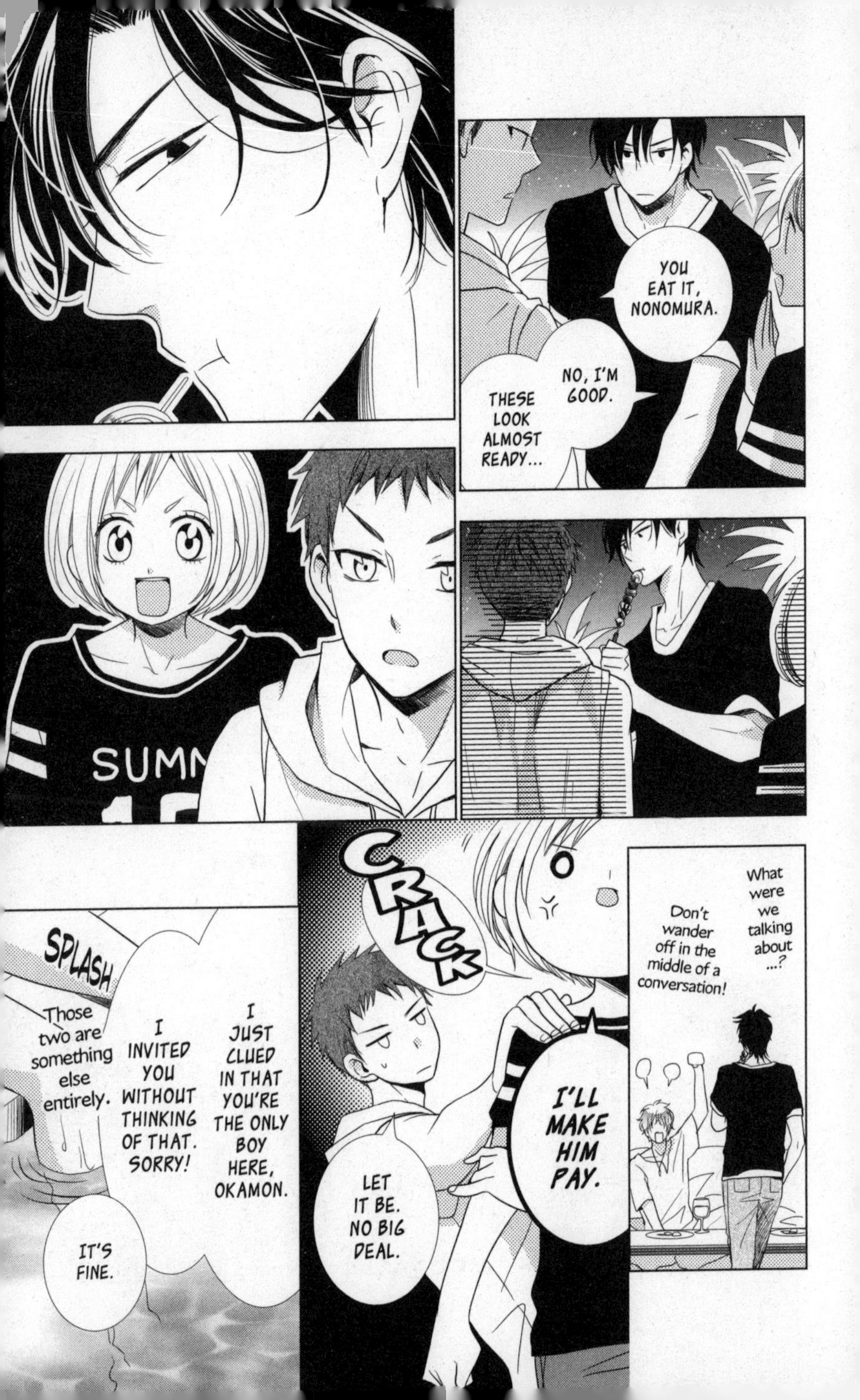
YOU EAT IT, NONOMURA.
NO, I'M GOOD.
THESE LOOK ALMOST READY...
SUMM
What were we talking about ...?
Don't wander off in the middle of a conversation!
CRACK
I'LL MAKE HIM PAY.
LET IT BE. NO BIG DEAL.
I JUST CLUED IN THAT YOU'RE THE ONLY BOY HERE, OKAMON.
I INVITED YOU WITHOUT THINKING OF THAT. SORRY!
IT'S FINE.
SPLASH
Those two are something else entirely.

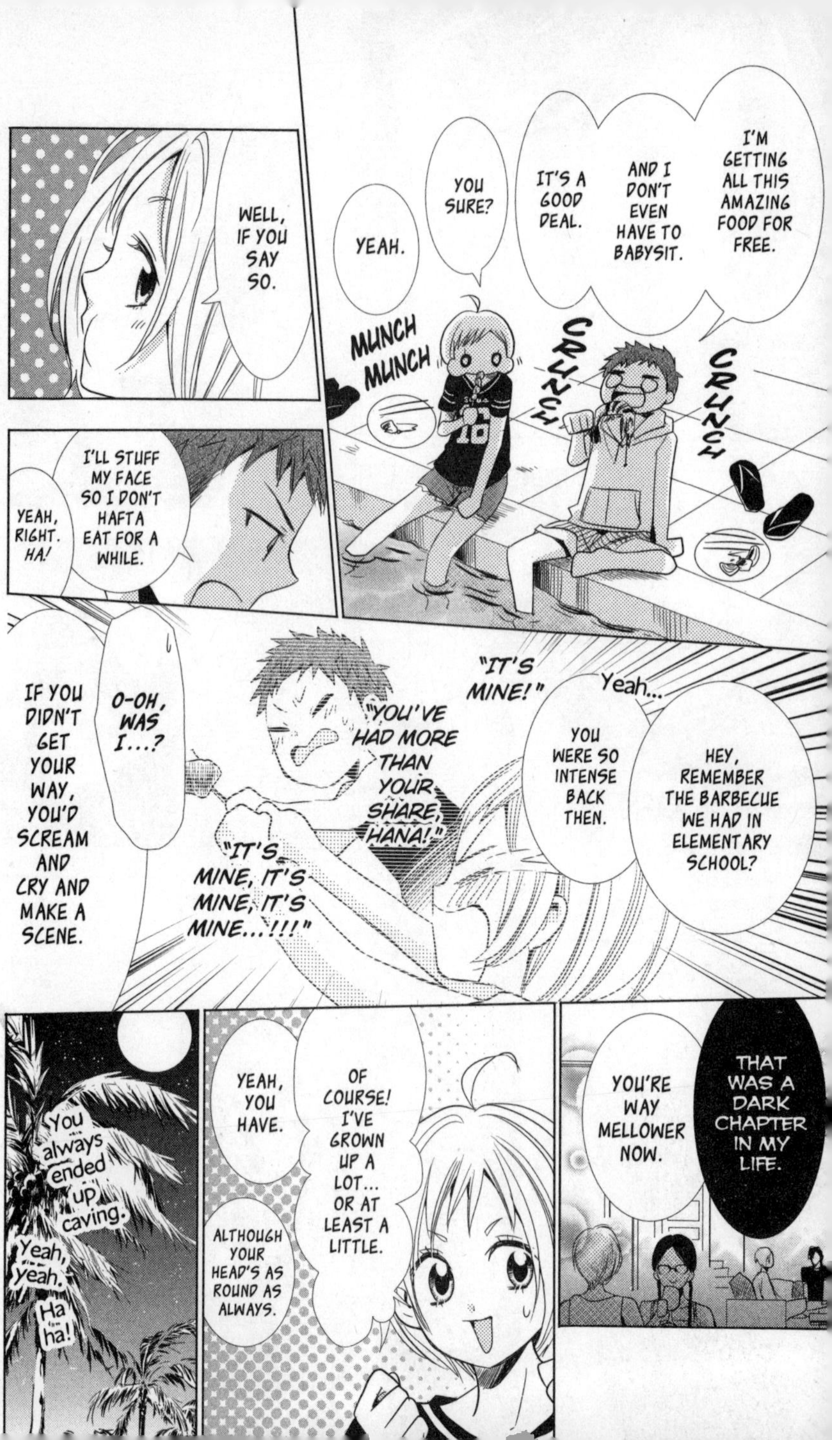
I'M GETTING ALL THIS AMAZING FOOD FOR FREE.
AND I DON'T EVEN HAVE TO BABYSIT.
IT'S A GOOD DEAL.
CRUNCH
CRUNCH
YOU SURE?
YEAH.
MUNCH MUNCH
WELL, IF YOU SAY SO.
I'LL STUFF MY FACE SO I DON'T HAFTA EAT FOR A WHILE.
YEAH, RIGHT. HA!
HEY, REMEMBER THE BARBECUE WE HAD IN ELEMENTARY SCHOOL?
YOU WERE SO INTENSE BACK THEN.
Yeah...
"IT'S MINE!"
"YOU'VE HAD MORE THAN YOUR SHARE, HANA!"
"IT'S MINE, IT'S MINE, IT'S MINE...!!!"
O-OH, WAS I...?
IF YOU DIDN'T GET YOUR WAY, YOU'D SCREAM AND CRY AND MAKE A SCENE.
THAT WAS A DARK CHAPTER IN MY LIFE.
YOU'RE WAY MELLOWER NOW.
OF COURSE! I'VE GROWN UP A LOT... OR AT LEAST A LITTLE.
YEAH, YOU HAVE.
ALTHOUGH YOUR HEAD'S AS ROUND AS ALWAYS.
You always ended up caving.
Yeah, yeah.
Ha ha!

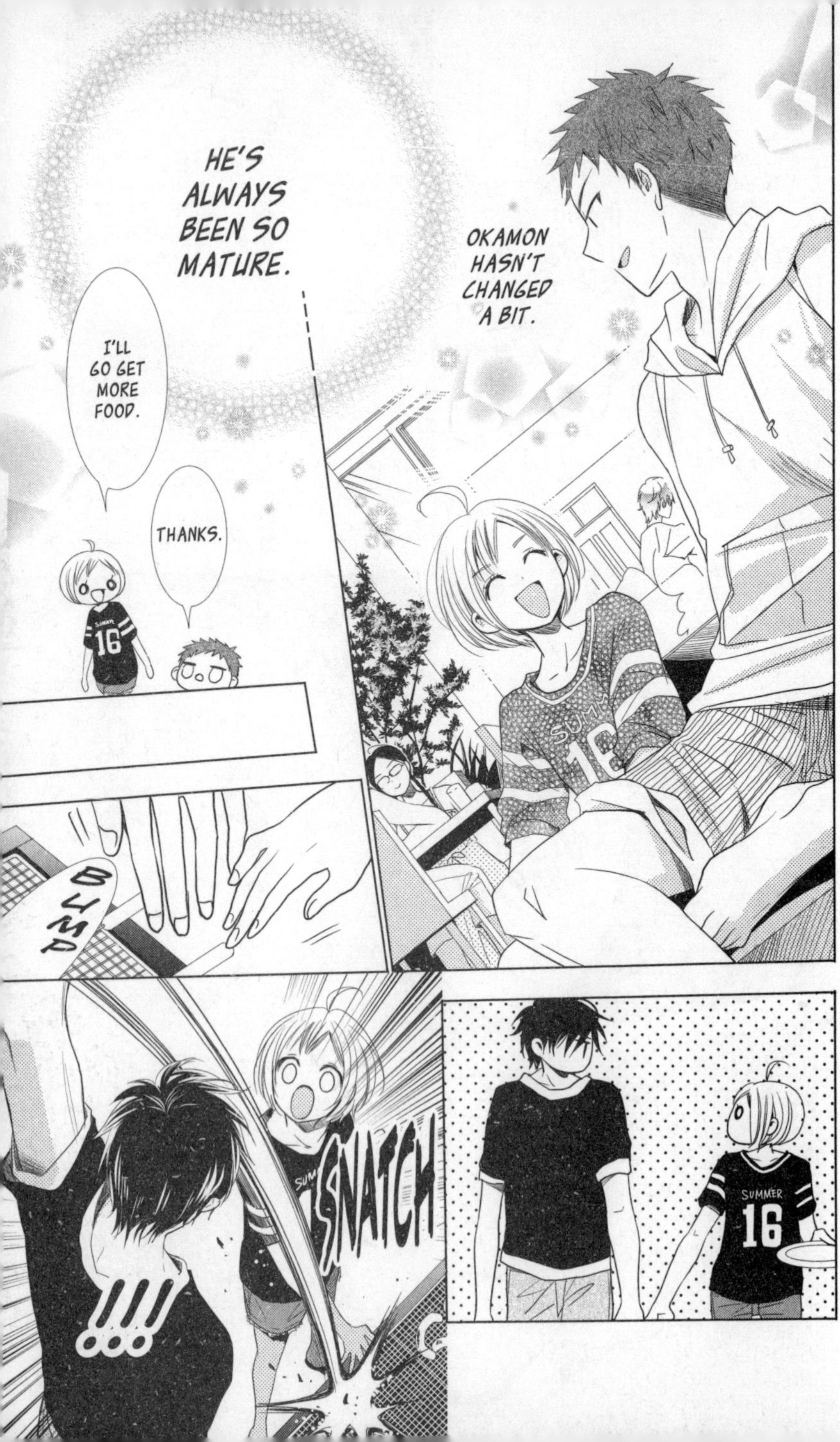
OKAMON HASN'T CHANGED A BIT.
HE'S ALWAYS BEEN SO MATURE.
I'LL GO GET MORE FOOD.
THANKS.
BUMP
SNATCH
!!!

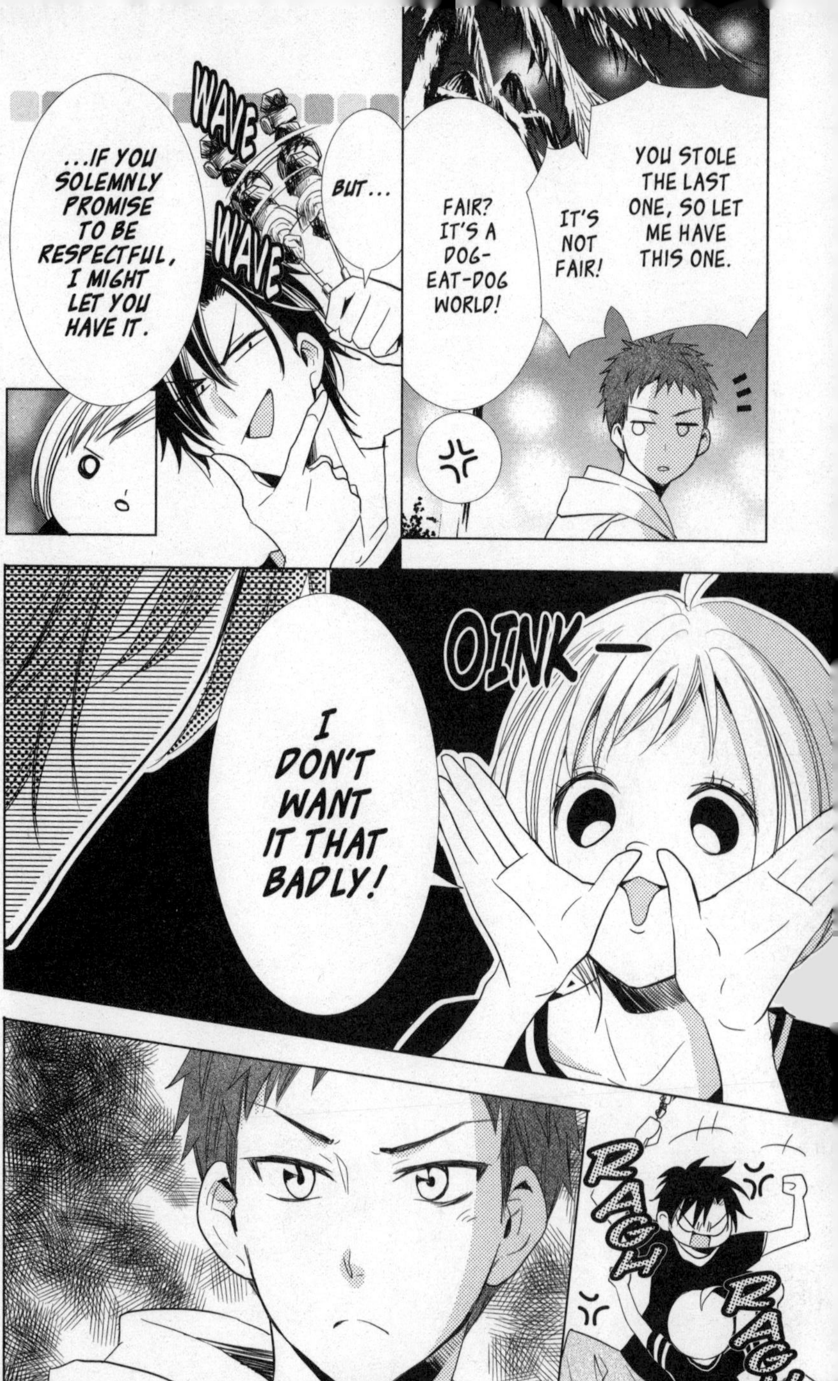
YOU STOLE THE LAST ONE, SO LET ME HAVE THIS ONE.
IT'S NOT FAIR!
FAIR? IT'S A DOG-EAT-DOG WORLD!
BUT...
WAVE
WAVE
...IF YOU SOLEMNLY PROMISE TO BE RESPECTFUL, I MIGHT LET YOU HAVE IT.
OINK—
I DON'T WANT IT THAT BADLY!
RAGH
RAGH

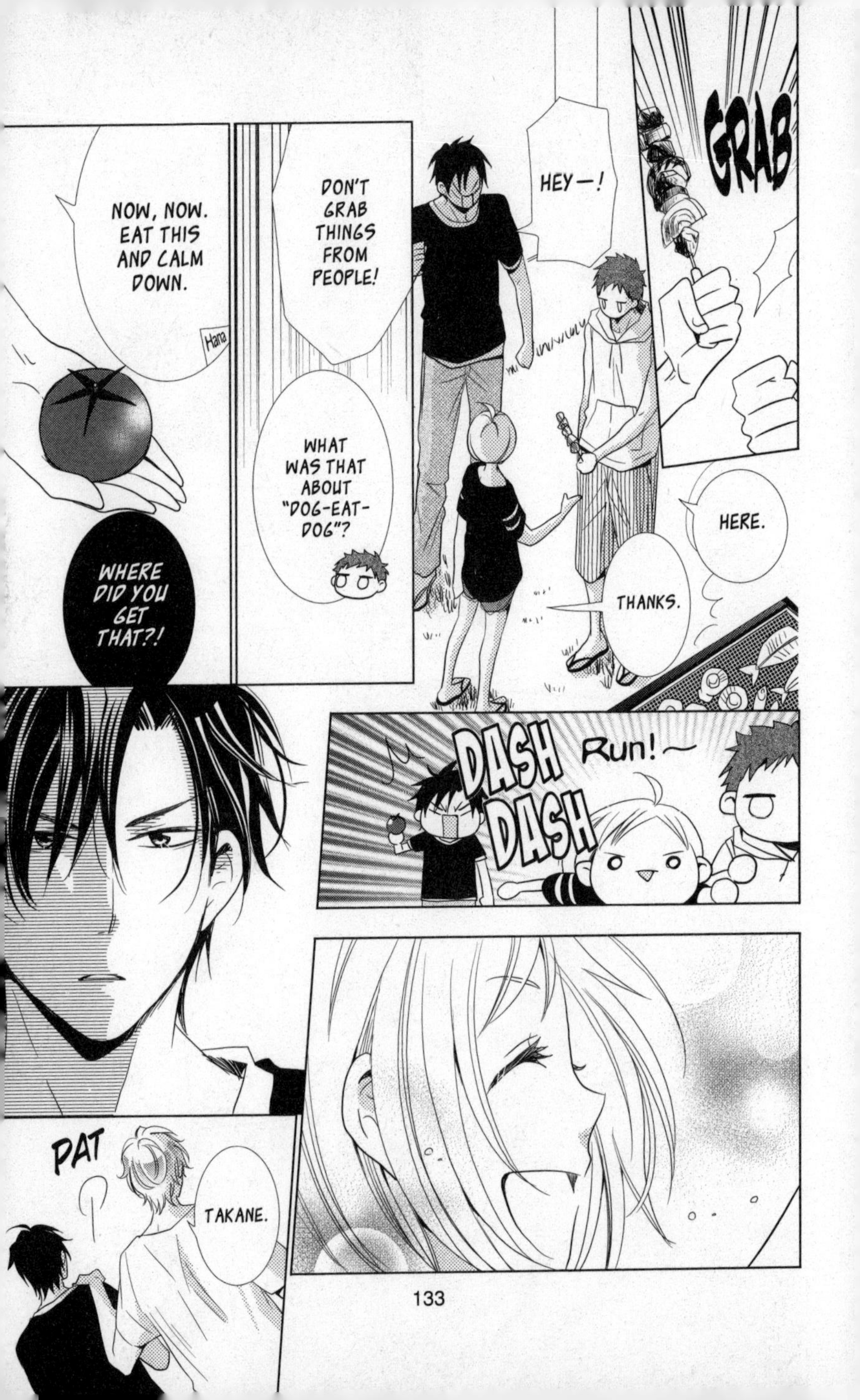
GRAB
HEY—!
HERE.
THANKS.
DON'T GRAB THINGS FROM PEOPLE!
WHAT WAS THAT ABOUT "DOG-EAT-DOG"?
NOW, NOW. EAT THIS AND CALM DOWN.
Hana
WHERE DID YOU GET THAT?!
DASH DASH
Run!~
PAT
TAKANE.

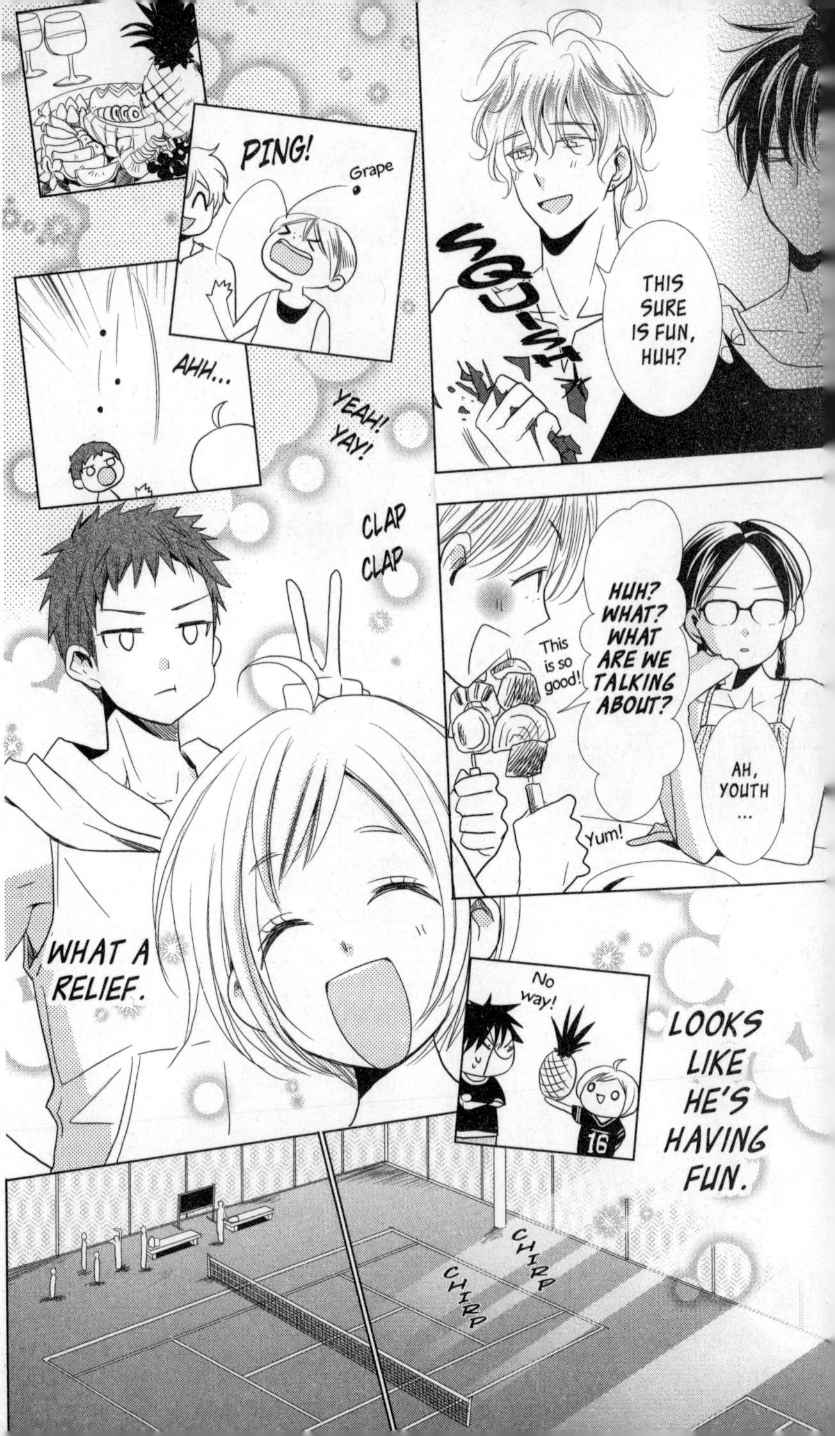
THIS SURE IS FUN, HUH?
GOJI-!!
PING!
Grape
AHH...
YEAH! YAY!
HUH? WHAT? WHAT ARE WE TALKING ABOUT?
This is so good!
Yum!
AH, YOUTH ...
CLAP CLAP
WHAT A RELIEF.
No way!
LOOKS LIKE HE'S HAVING FUN.
CHIRP
CHIRP

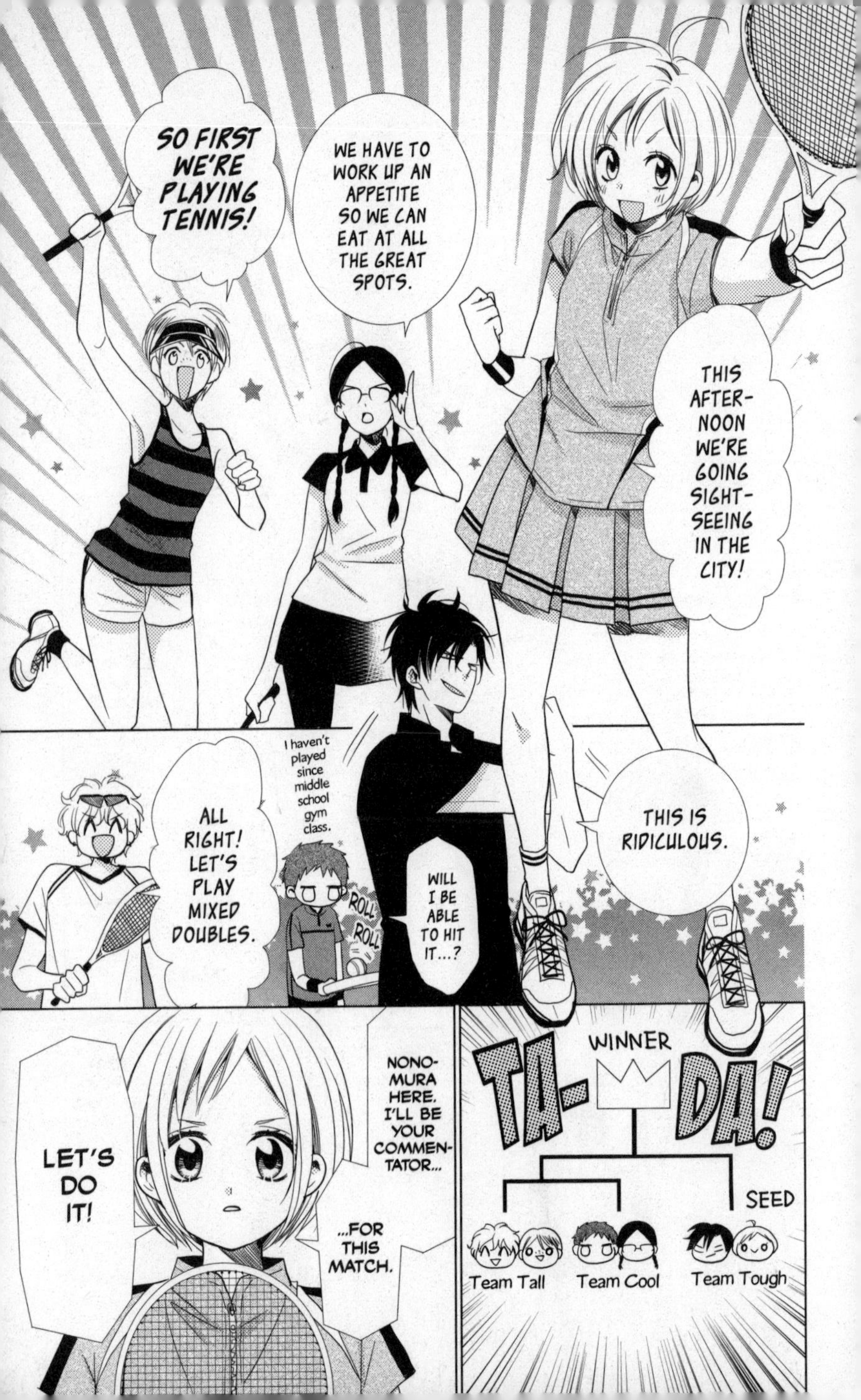
THIS AFTER-NOON WE'RE GOING SIGHT-SEEING IN THE CITY!
WE HAVE TO WORK UP AN APPETITE SO WE CAN EAT AT ALL THE GREAT SPOTS.
SO FIRST WE'RE PLAYING TENNIS!
THIS IS RIDICULOUS.
WILL I BE ABLE TO HIT IT...?
I haven't played since middle school gym class.
ROLL ROLL
ALL RIGHT! LET'S PLAY MIXED DOUBLES.
TA-DA!
WINNER
SEED
Team Tall
Team Cool
Team Tough
NONO-MURA HERE. I'LL BE YOUR COMMEN-TATOR...
...FOR THIS MATCH.
LET'S DO IT!

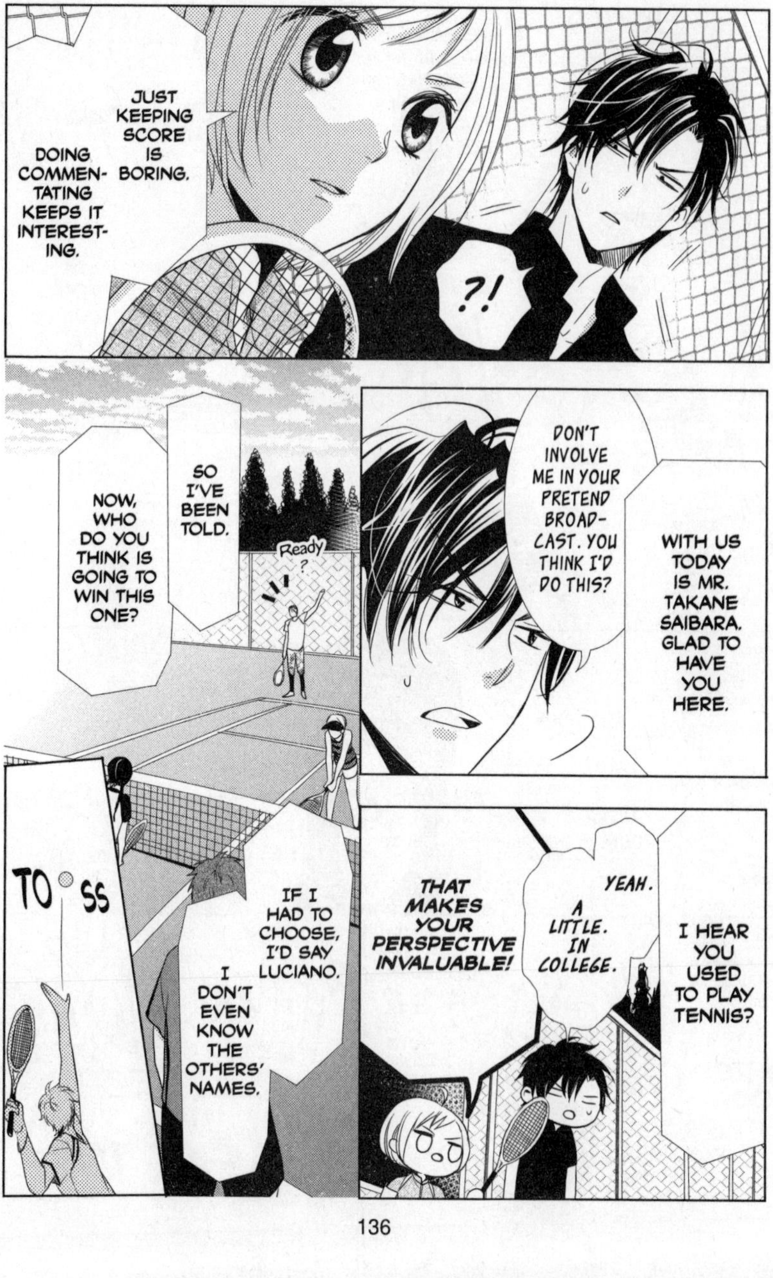
JUST KEEPING SCORE IS BORING.
DOING COMMENTATING KEEPS IT INTERESTING.
?!
WITH US TODAY IS MR. TAKANE SAIBARA. GLAD TO HAVE YOU HERE.
DON'T INVOLVE ME IN YOUR PRETEND BROADCAST. YOU THINK I'D DO THIS?
NOW, WHO DO YOU THINK IS GOING TO WIN THIS ONE?
SO I'VE BEEN TOLD.
Ready?
I HEAR YOU USED TO PLAY TENNIS?
YEAH.
A LITTLE. IN COLLEGE.
THAT MAKES YOUR PERSPECTIVE INVALUABLE!
IF I HAD TO CHOOSE, I'D SAY LUCIANO.
I DON'T EVEN KNOW THE OTHERS' NAMES.
TO SS

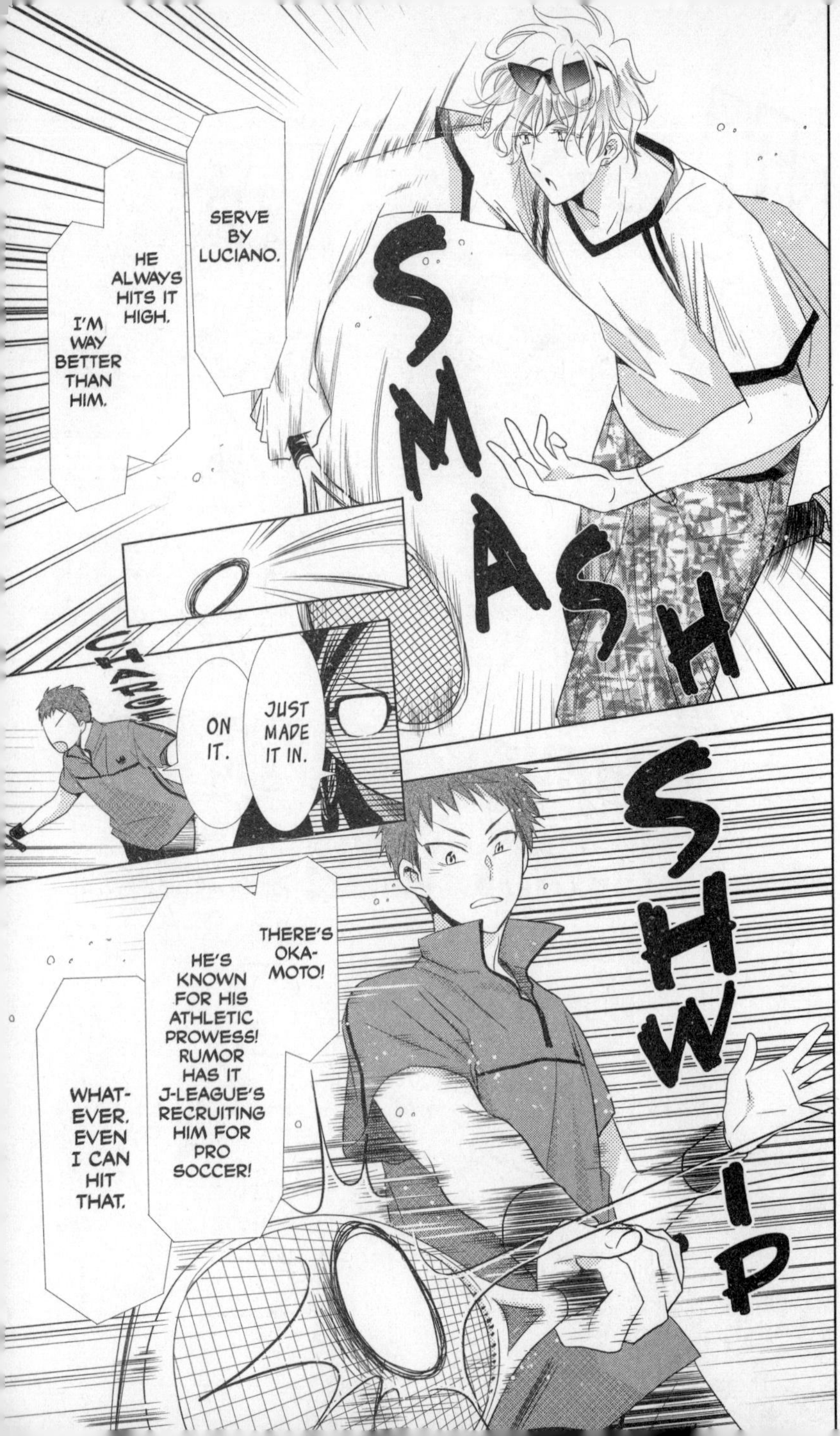
SERVE BY LUCIANO.
HE ALWAYS HITS IT HIGH.
I'M WAY BETTER THAN HIM.
SMASH
JUST MADE IT IN.
ON IT.
SHWIP
THERE'S OKA-MOTO!
HE'S KNOWN FOR HIS ATHLETIC PROWESS! RUMOR HAS IT J-LEAGUE'S RECRUITING HIM FOR PRO SOCCER!
WHAT-EVER. EVEN I CAN HIT THAT.

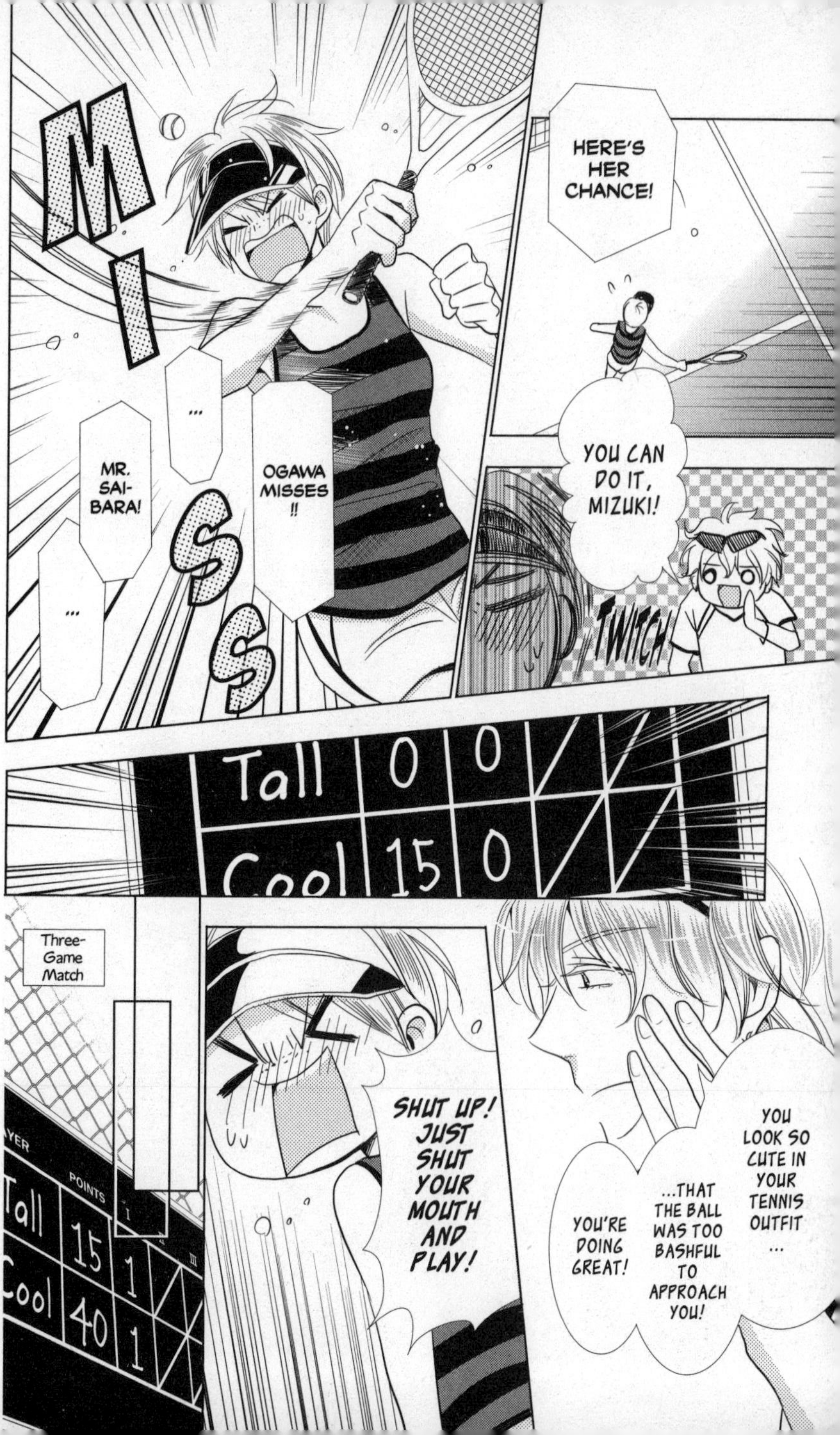
HERE'S HER CHANCE!
YOU CAN DO IT, MIZUKI!
TWITCH
OGAWA MISSES !!
...
MR. SAI-BARA!
...
MISS
Tall 0 0
Cool 15 0
YOU LOOK SO CUTE IN YOUR TENNIS OUTFIT ...
...THAT THE BALL WAS TOO BASHFUL TO APPROACH YOU!
YOU'RE DOING GREAT!
SHUT UP! JUST SHUT YOUR MOUTH AND PLAY!
Three-Game Match
POINTS
Tall 15 1
Cool 40 1

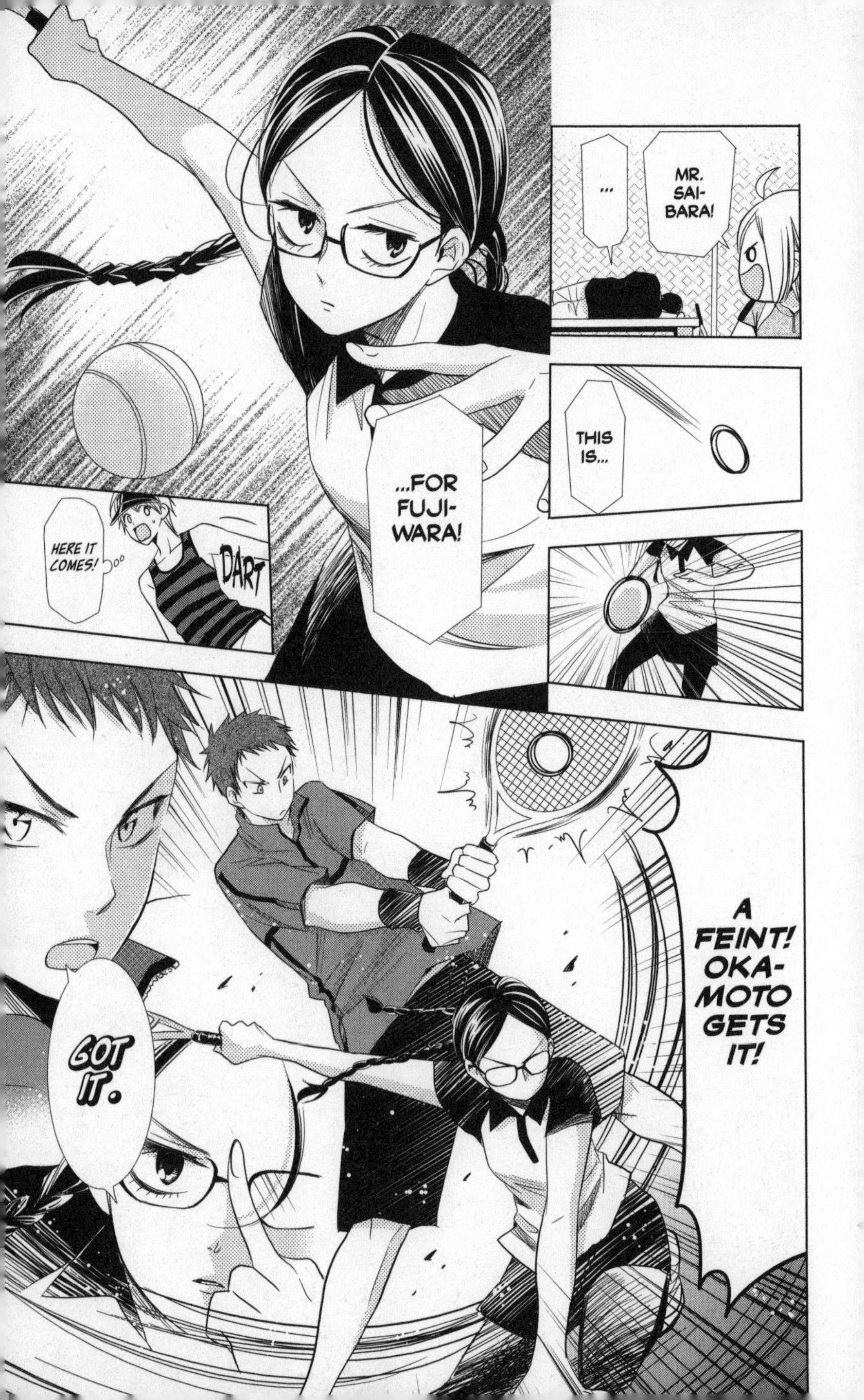
MR. SAI-BARA!
...
THIS IS...
...FOR FUJI-WARA!
HERE IT COMES!
DART
A FEINT! OKA-MOTO GETS IT!
GOT IT.

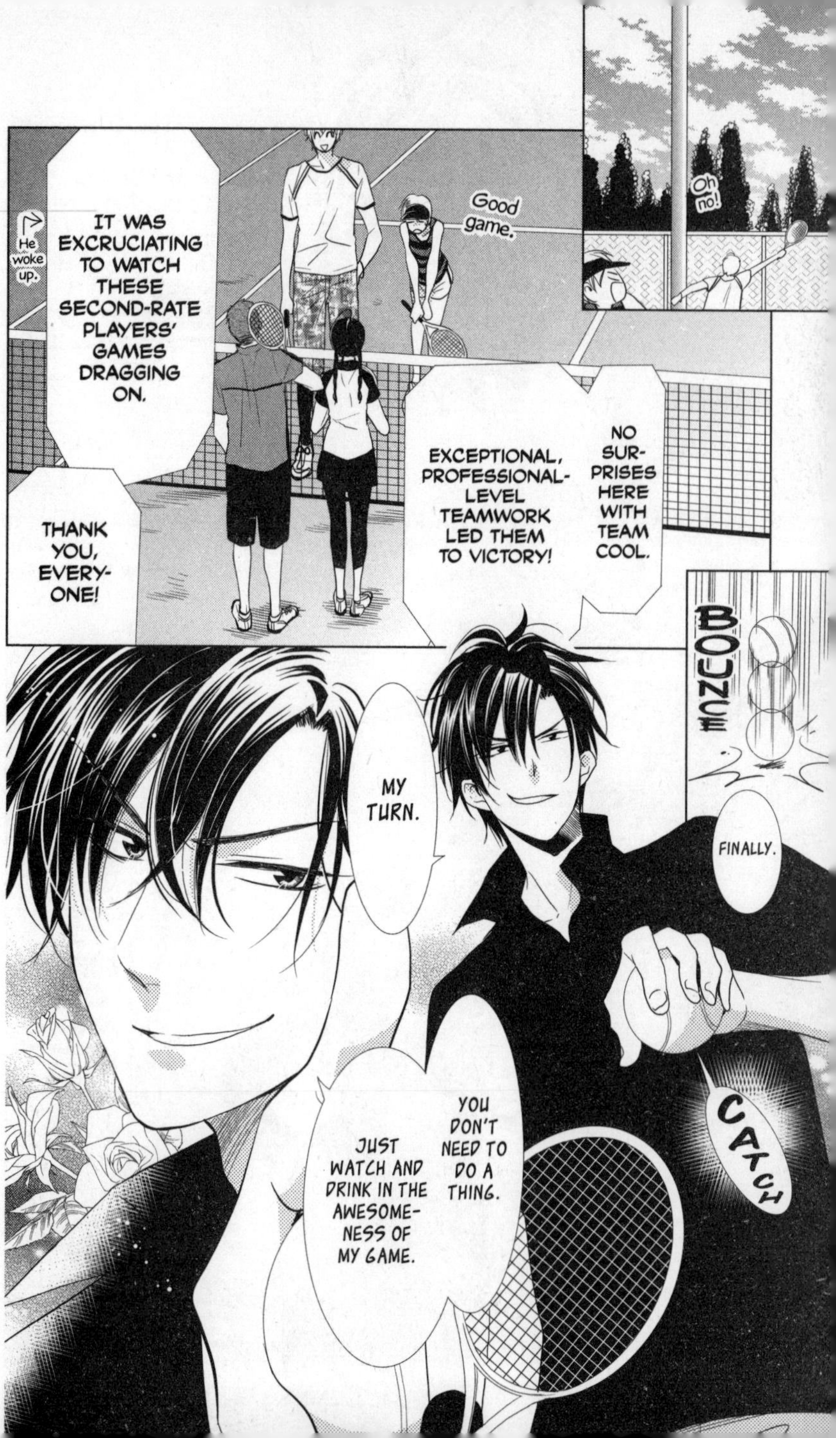
Oh no!
NO SUR-PRISES HERE WITH TEAM COOL.
EXCEPTIONAL, PROFESSIONAL-LEVEL TEAMWORK LED THEM TO VICTORY!
Good game.
IT WAS EXCRUCIATING TO WATCH THESE SECOND-RATE PLAYERS' GAMES DRAGGING ON.
He woke up.
THANK YOU, EVERY-ONE!
BOUNCE
FINALLY.
MY TURN.
CATCH
YOU DON'T NEED TO DO A THING.
JUST WATCH AND DRINK IN THE AWESOME-NESS OF MY GAME.

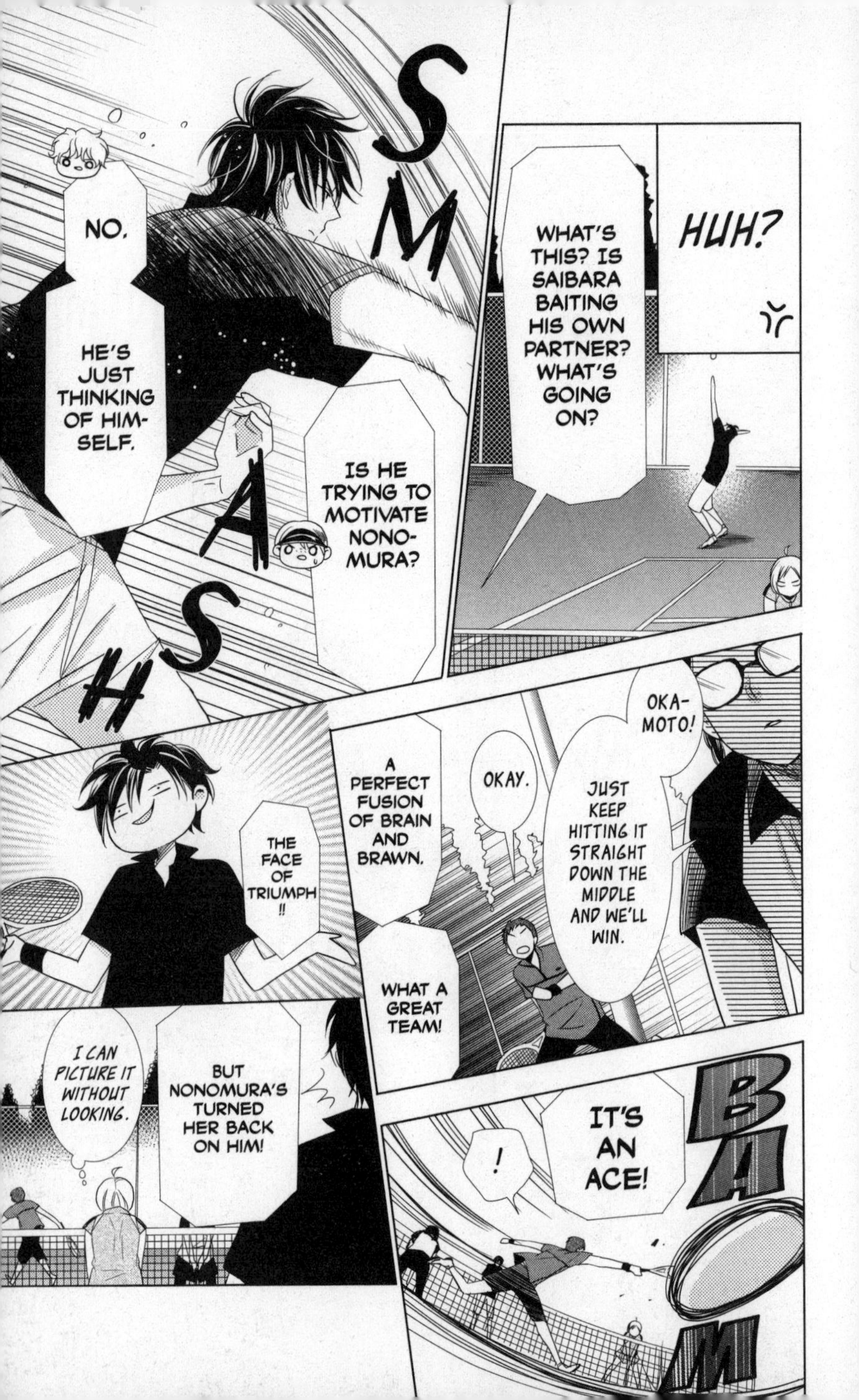
HUH?
WHAT'S THIS? IS SAIBARA BAITING HIS OWN PARTNER? WHAT'S GOING ON?
SMASH
IS HE TRYING TO MOTIVATE NONOMURA?
NO.
HE'S JUST THINKING OF HIMSELF.
OKAMOTO!
JUST KEEP HITTING IT STRAIGHT DOWN THE MIDDLE AND WE'LL WIN.
OKAY.
A PERFECT FUSION OF BRAIN AND BRAWN.
WHAT A GREAT TEAM!
THE FACE OF TRIUMPH!!
BAM
IT'S AN ACE!
!
BUT NONOMURA'S TURNED HER BACK ON HIM!
I CAN PICTURE IT WITHOUT LOOKING.

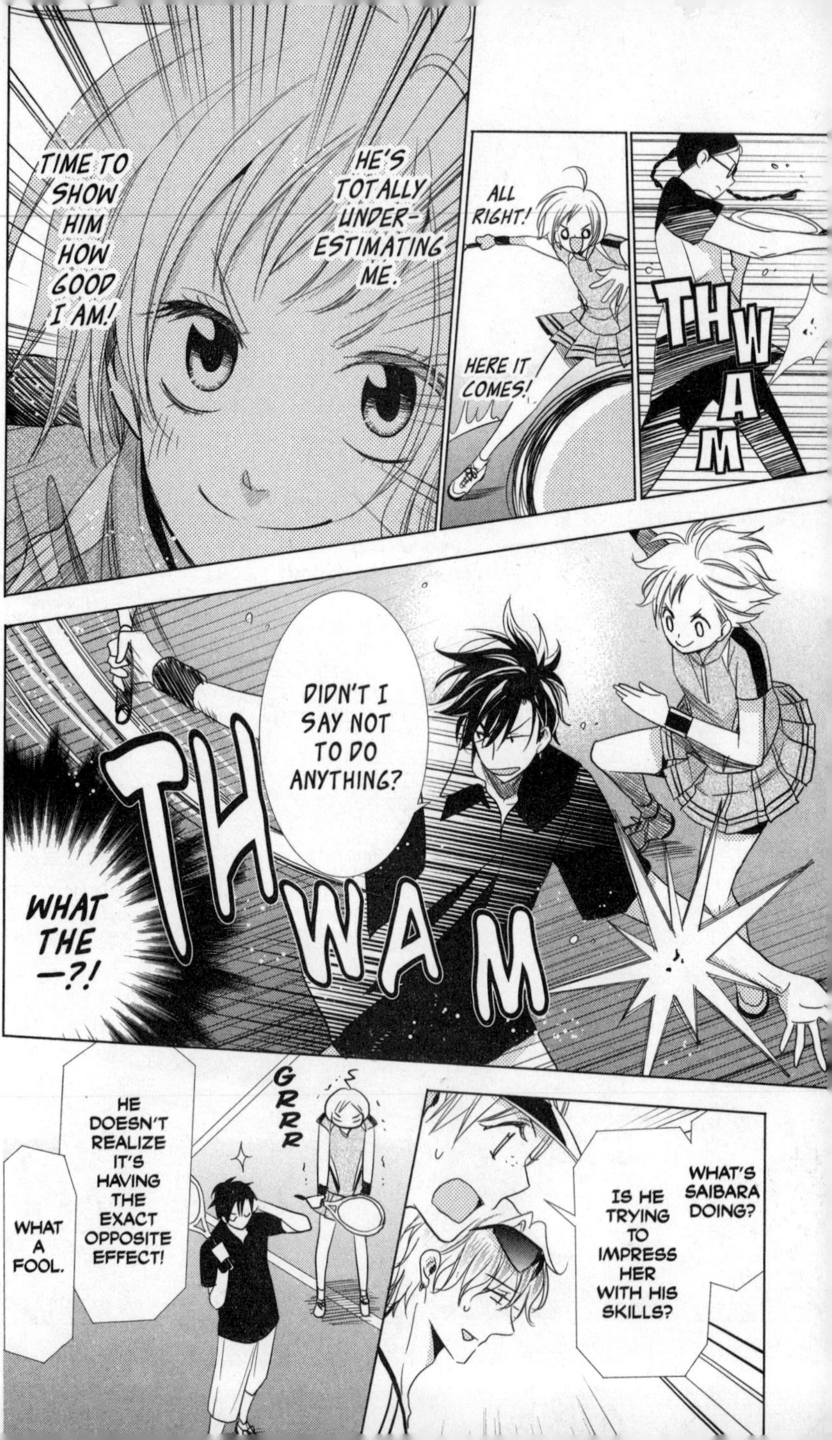
THWAM
ALL RIGHT!
HERE IT COMES!
HE'S TOTALLY UNDER-ESTIMATING ME.
TIME TO SHOW HIM HOW GOOD I AM!
DIDN'T I SAY NOT TO DO ANYTHING?
THWAM
WHAT THE —?!
WHAT'S SAIBARA DOING?
IS HE TRYING TO IMPRESS HER WITH HIS SKILLS?
GRRR
HE DOESN'T REALIZE IT'S HAVING THE EXACT OPPOSITE EFFECT!
WHAT A FOOL.

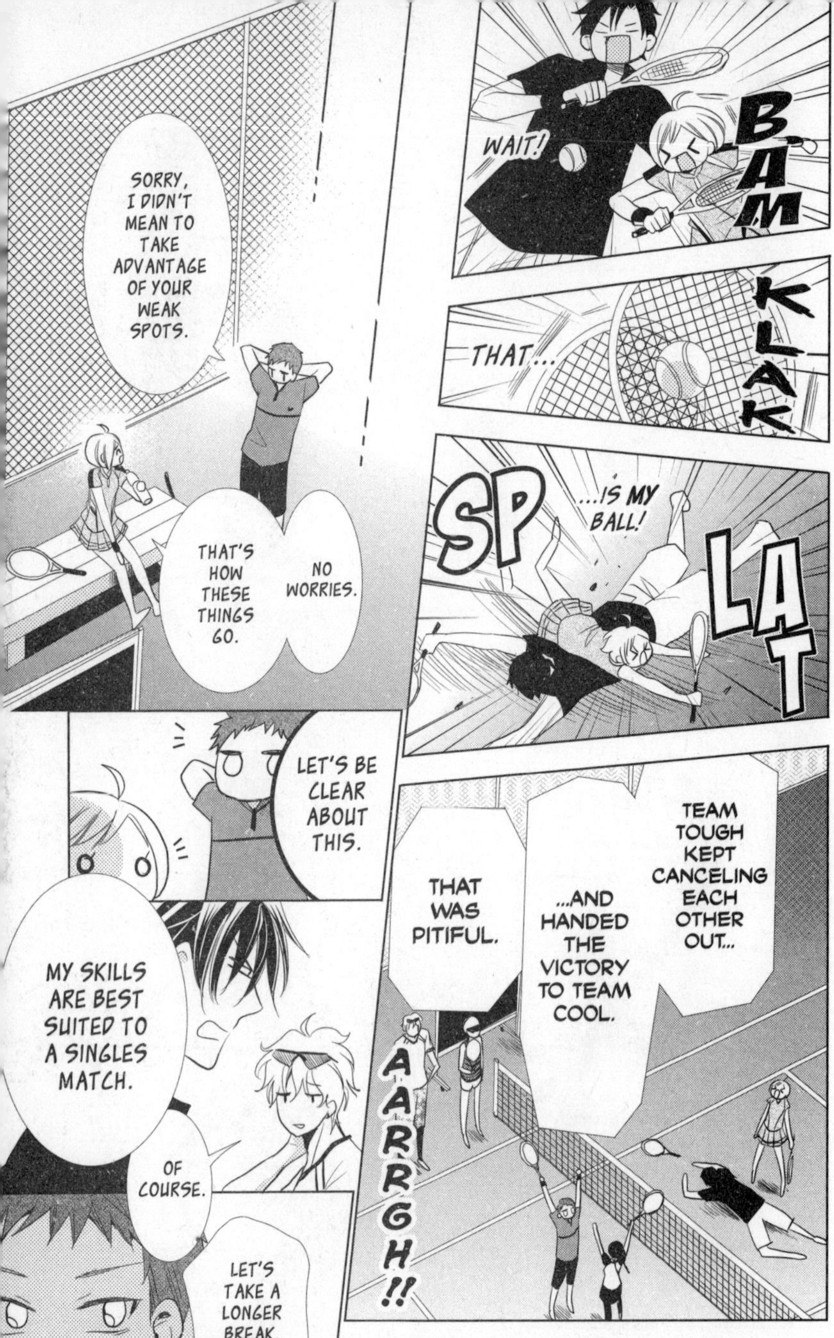
BAM
WAIT!
KLAK
THAT...
SPLAT
...IS MY BALL!
TEAM TOUGH KEPT CANCELING EACH OTHER OUT...
...AND HANDED THE VICTORY TO TEAM COOL.
THAT WAS PITIFUL.
AARRGH!!
SORRY, I DIDN'T MEAN TO TAKE ADVANTAGE OF YOUR WEAK SPOTS.
NO WORRIES.
THAT'S HOW THESE THINGS GO.
LET'S BE CLEAR ABOUT THIS.
MY SKILLS ARE BEST SUITED TO A SINGLES MATCH.
OF COURSE.
LET'S TAKE A LONGER BREAK.

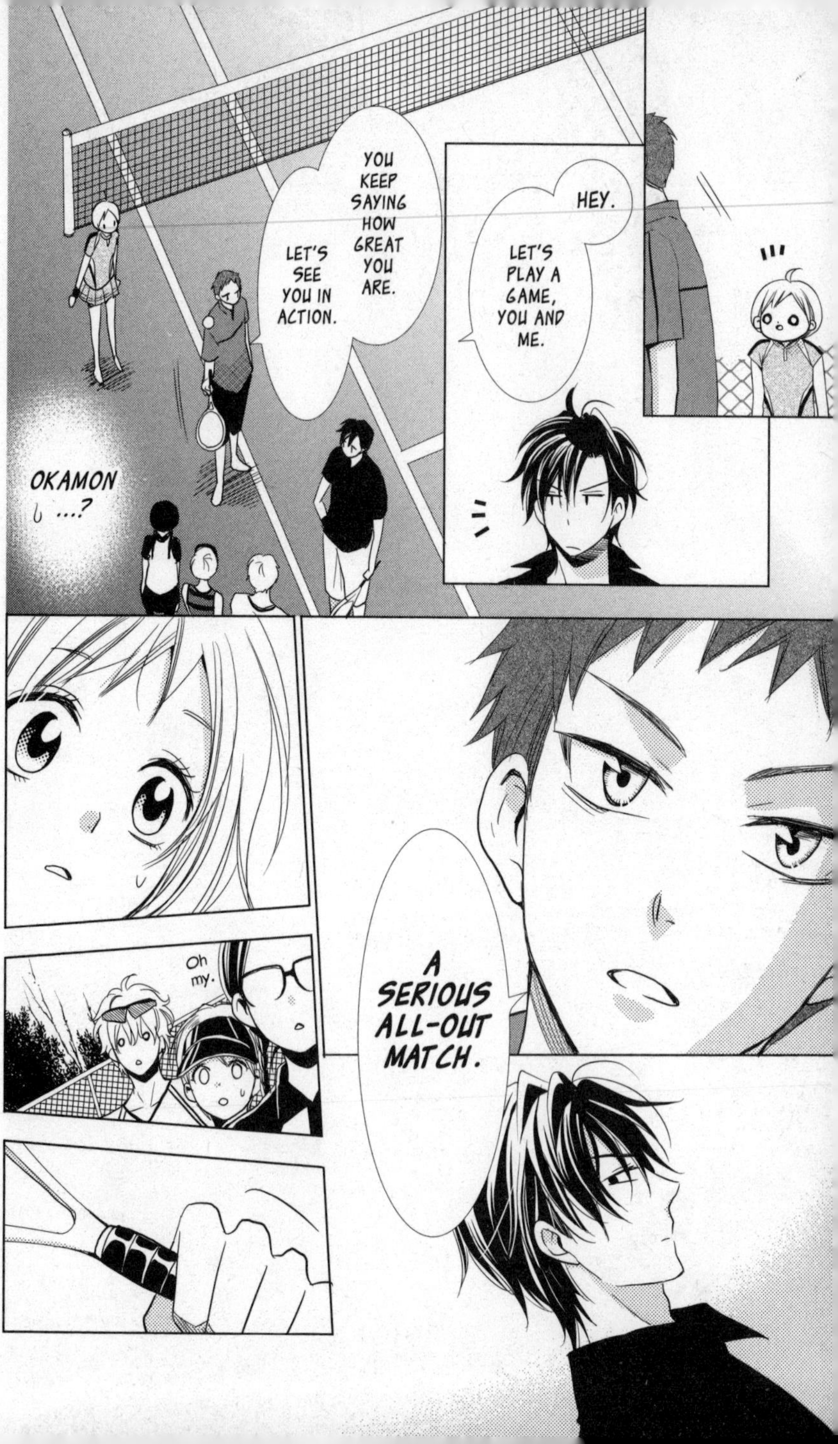
HEY.
LET'S PLAY A GAME, YOU AND ME.
YOU KEEP SAYING HOW GREAT YOU ARE.
LET'S SEE YOU IN ACTION.
OKAMON ...?
A SERIOUS ALL-OUT MATCH.
Oh my.

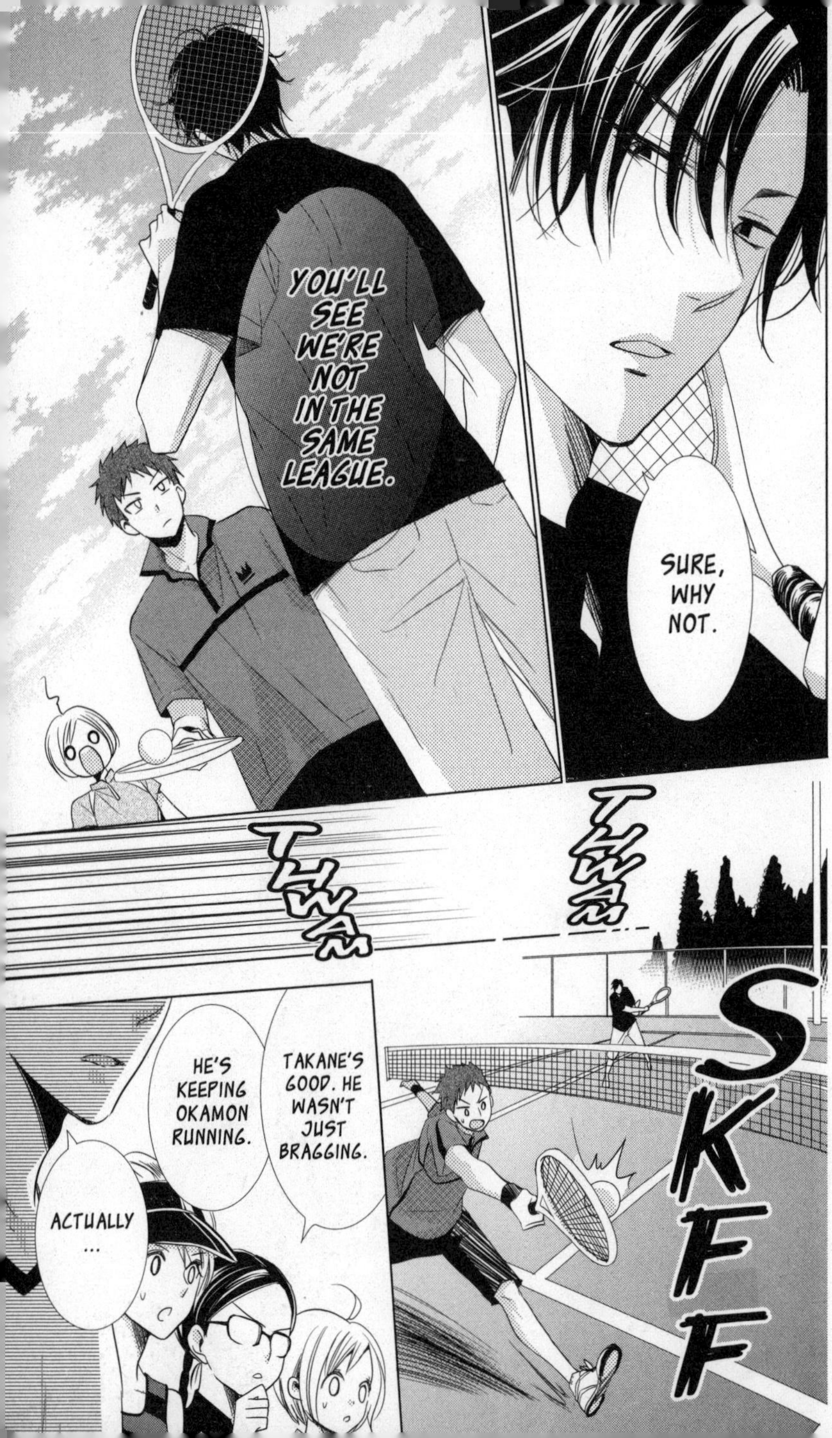
SURE, WHY NOT.
YOU'LL SEE WE'RE NOT IN THE SAME LEAGUE.
THWAM
THWAM
SKFF
TAKANE'S GOOD. HE WASN'T JUST BRAGGING.
HE'S KEEPING OKAMON RUNNING.
ACTUALLY ...

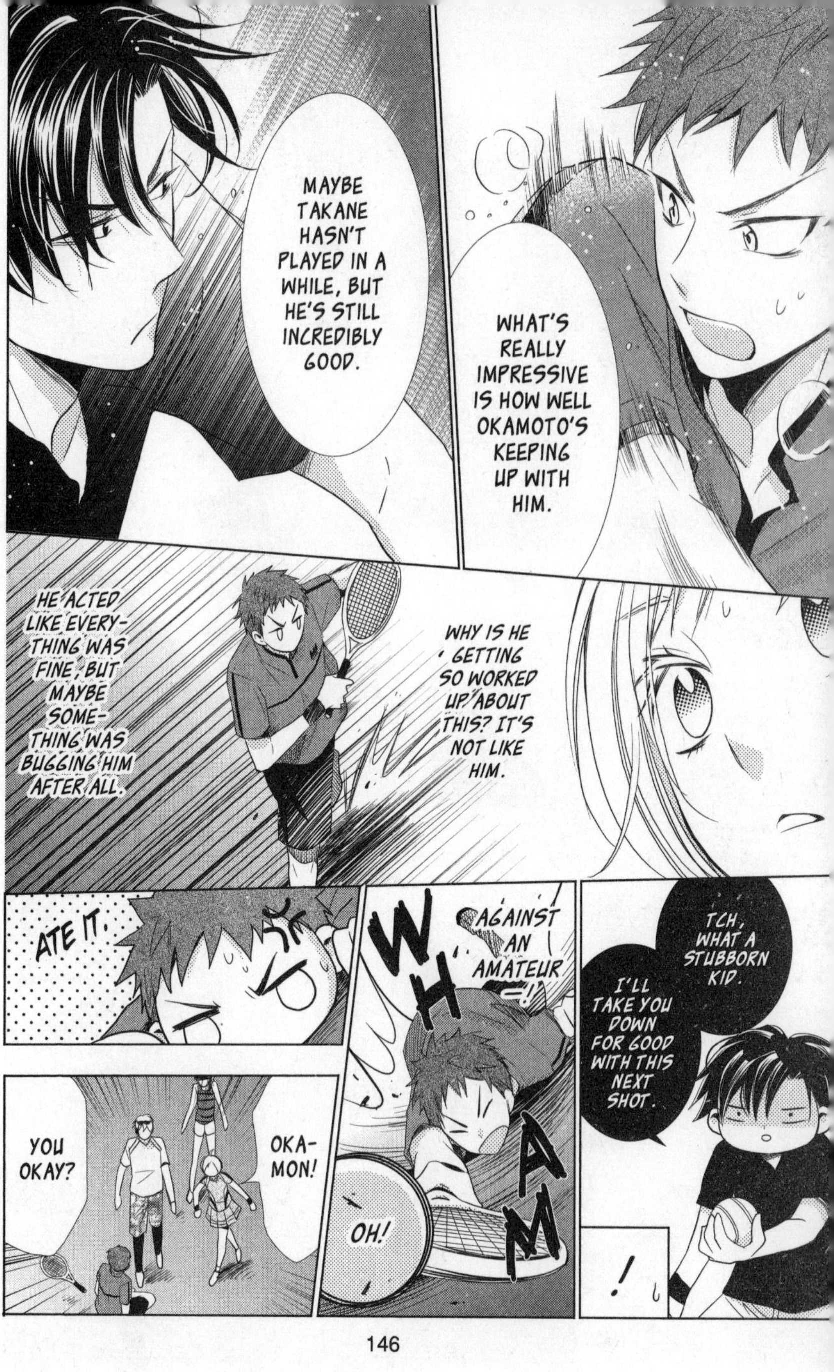
WHAT'S REALLY IMPRESSIVE IS HOW WELL OKAMOTO'S KEEPING UP WITH HIM.
MAYBE TAKANE HASN'T PLAYED IN A WHILE, BUT HE'S STILL INCREDIBLY GOOD.
WHY IS HE GETTING SO WORKED UP ABOUT THIS? IT'S NOT LIKE HIM.
HE ACTED LIKE EVERY-THING WAS FINE, BUT MAYBE SOME-THING WAS BUGGING HIM AFTER ALL.
TCH, WHAT A STUBBORN KID.
I'LL TAKE YOU DOWN FOR GOOD WITH THIS NEXT SHOT.
!
AGAINST AN AMATEUR—!
WHAM
OH!
ATE IT.
OKA-MON!
YOU OKAY?

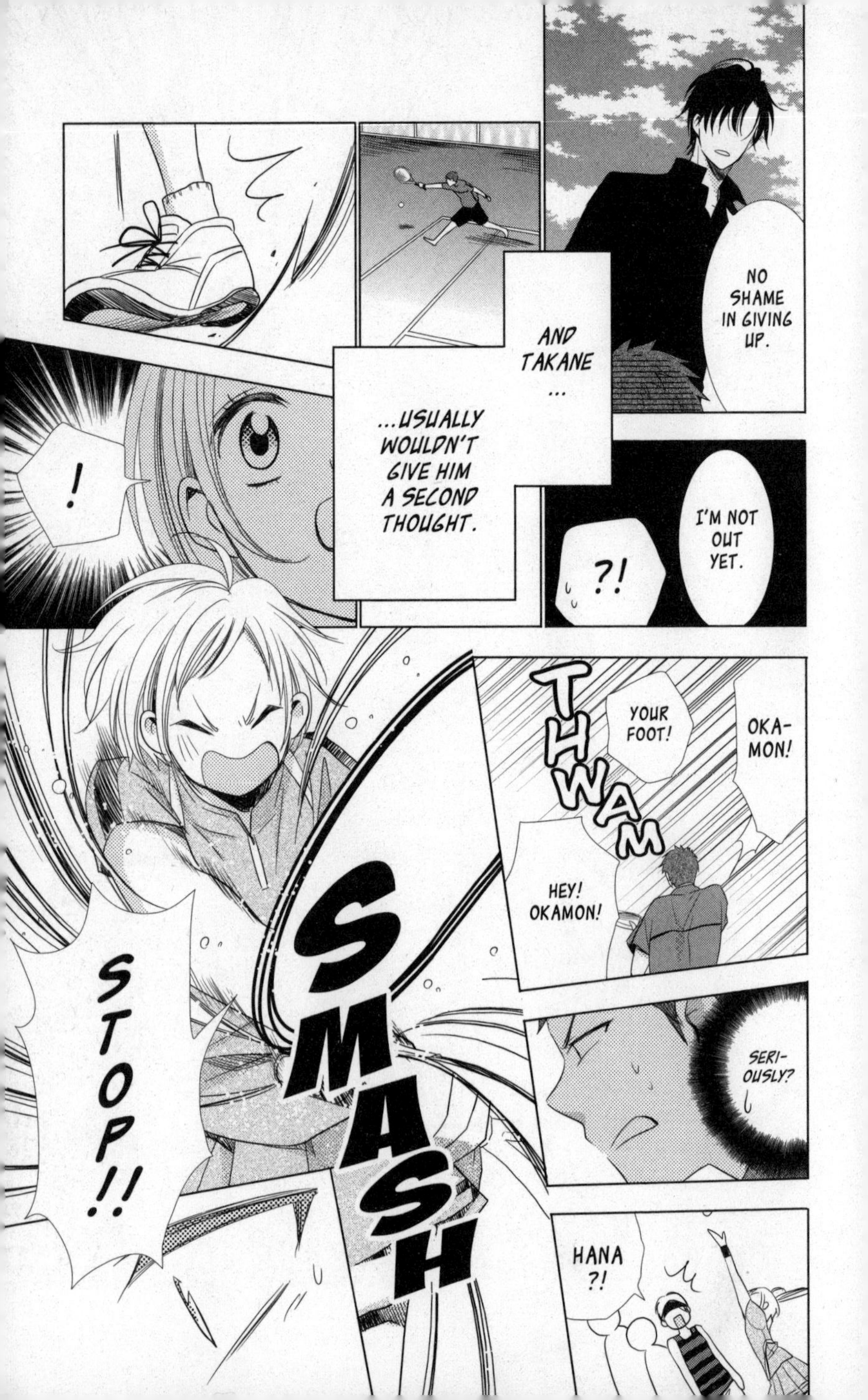
NO SHAME IN GIVING UP.
AND TAKANE ...
...USUALLY WOULDN'T GIVE HIM A SECOND THOUGHT.
I'M NOT OUT YET.
?!
!
OKA-MON!
YOUR FOOT!
THWAM
HEY! OKAMON!
SERI-OUSLY?
HANA ?!
SMASH
STOP!!

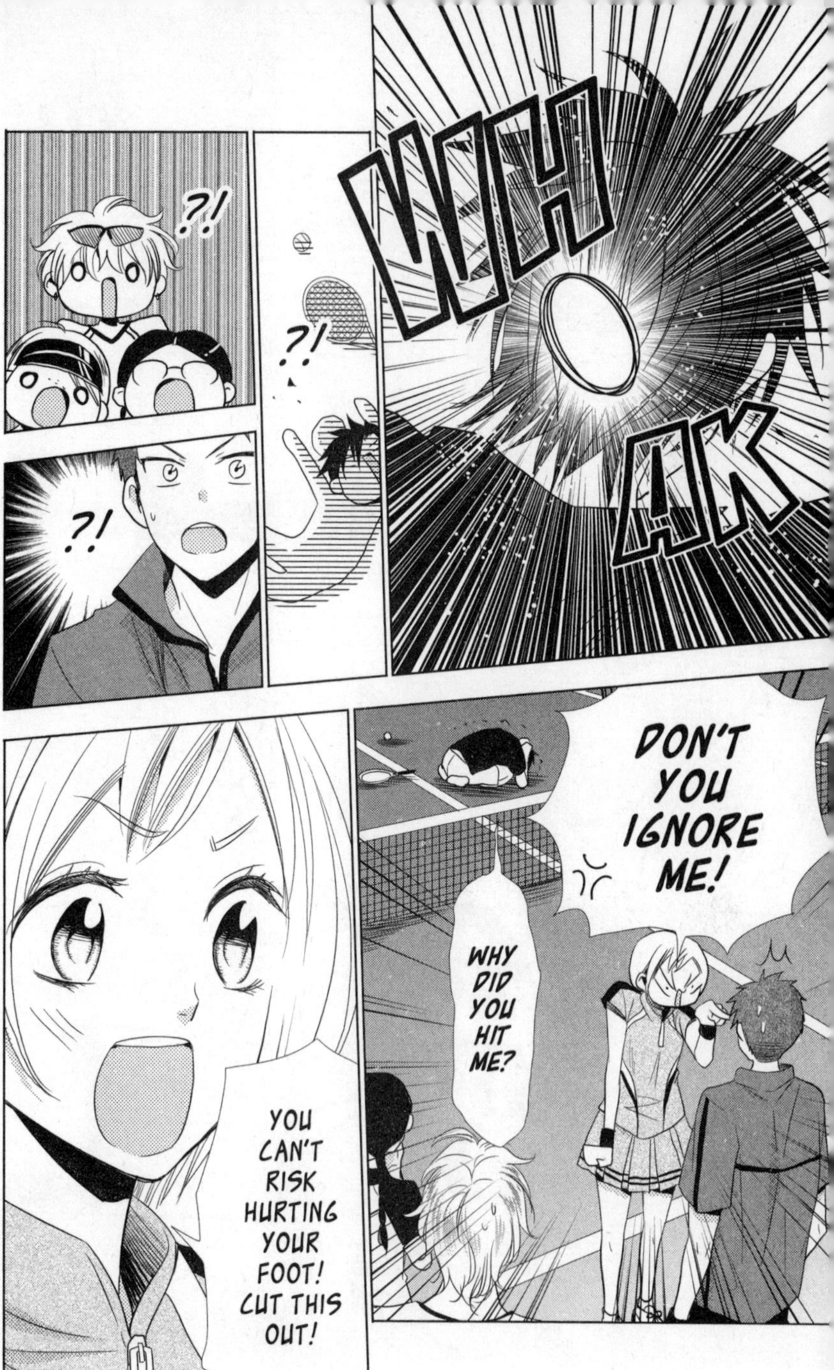
WH
AK
?!
?!
?!
DON'T YOU IGNORE ME!
WHY DID YOU HIT ME?
YOU CAN'T RISK HURTING YOUR FOOT! CUT THIS OUT!

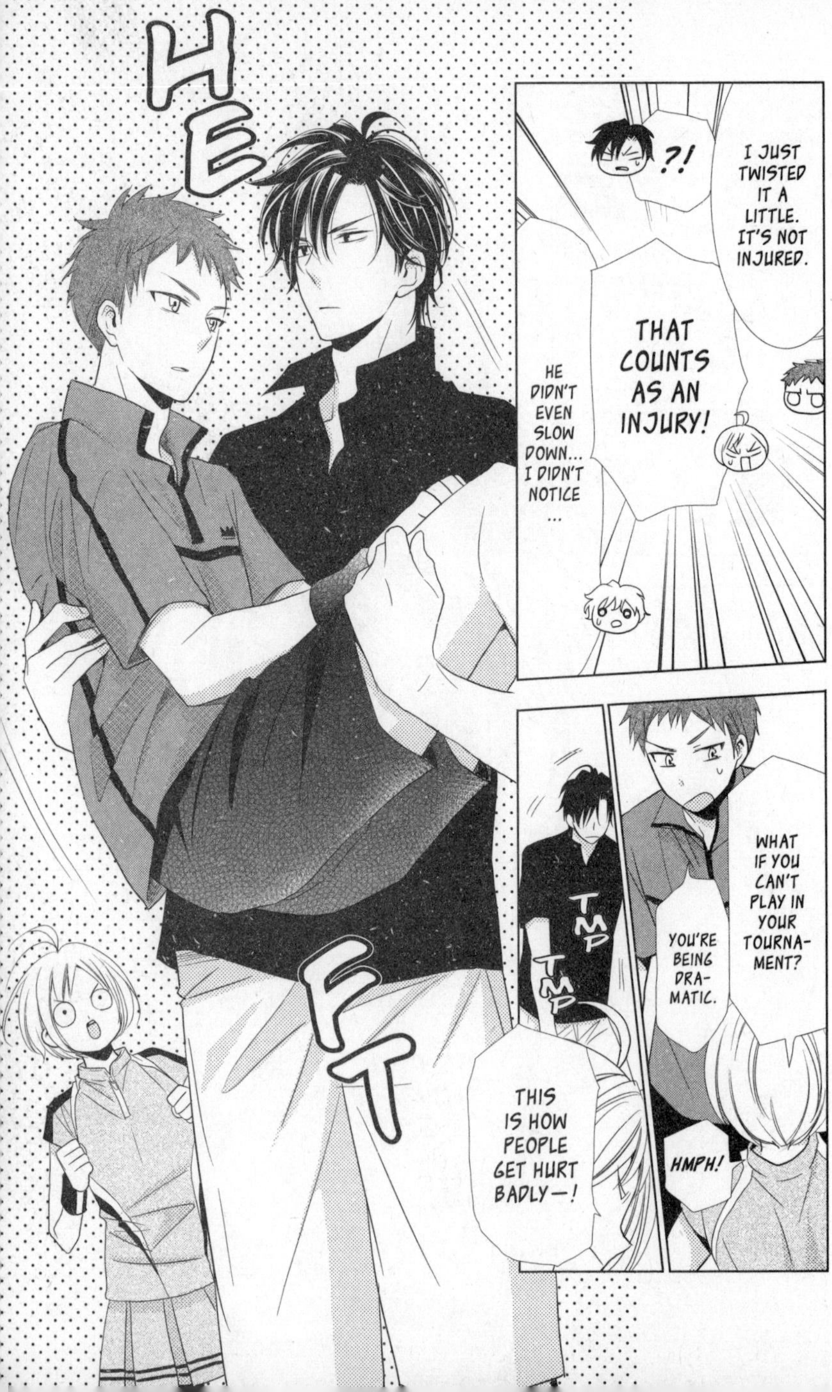
?!
I JUST TWISTED IT A LITTLE. IT'S NOT INJURED.
THAT COUNTS AS AN INJURY!
HE DIDN'T EVEN SLOW DOWN... I DIDN'T NOTICE...
WHAT IF YOU CAN'T PLAY IN YOUR TOURNAMENT?
YOU'RE BEING DRAMATIC.
HMPH!
TMP
TMP
THIS IS HOW PEOPLE GET HURT BADLY—!
HEFT

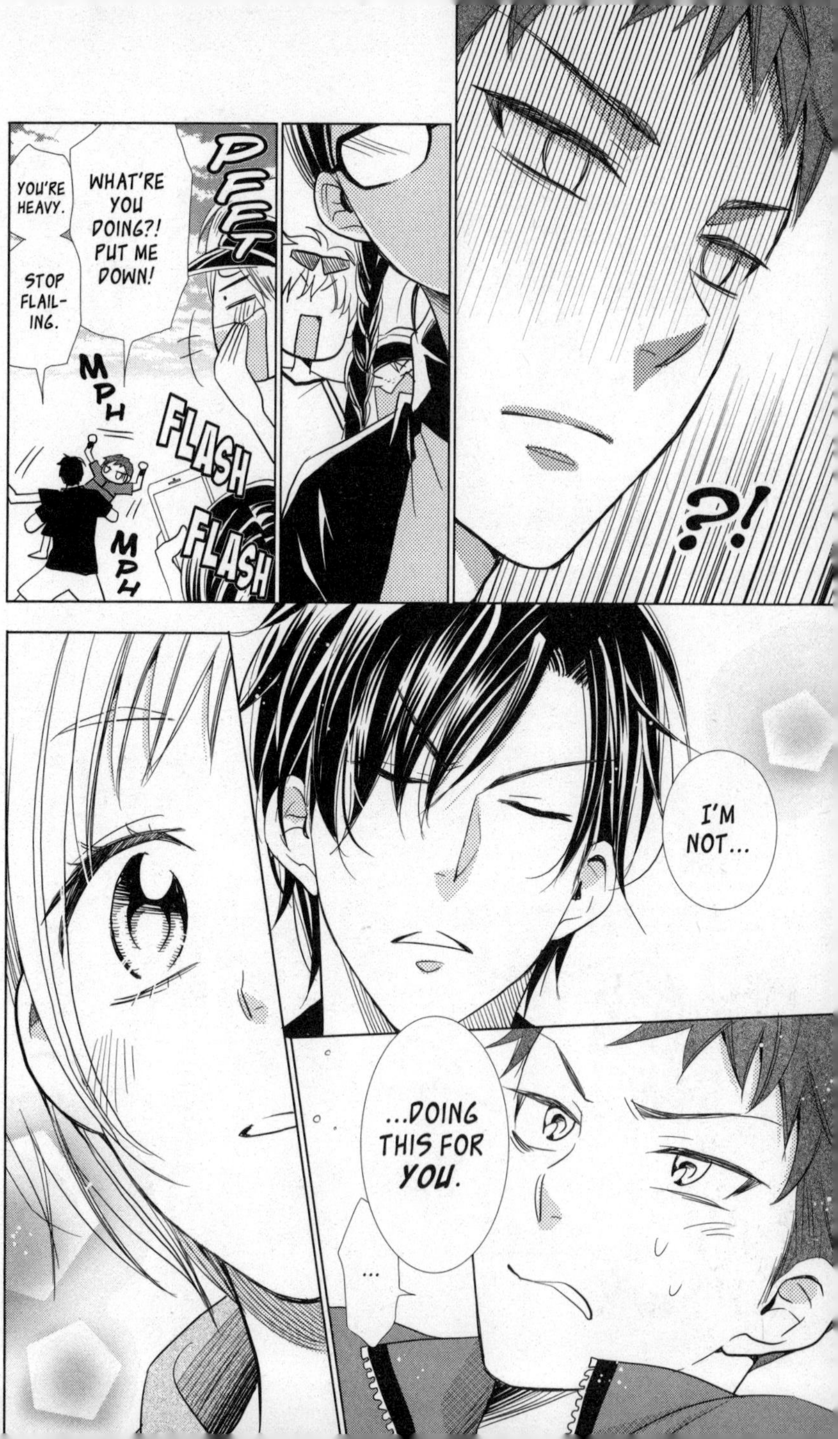
?!
PFFT
WHAT'RE YOU DOING?! PUT ME DOWN!
YOU'RE HEAVY.
STOP FLAIL-ING.
MPH
MPH
FLASH
FLASH
I'M NOT...
...DOING THIS FOR YOU.
...

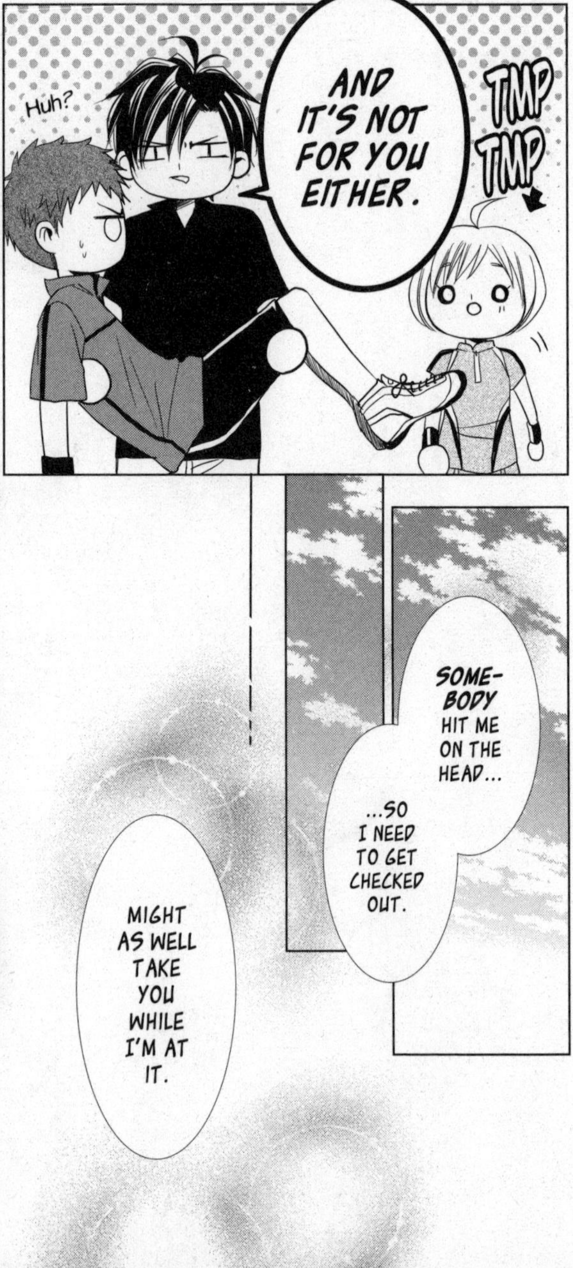
TMP TMP
AND IT'S NOT FOR YOU EITHER.
Huh?
SOME-BODY HIT ME ON THE HEAD...
...SO I NEED TO GET CHECKED OUT.
MIGHT AS WELL TAKE YOU WHILE I'M AT IT.
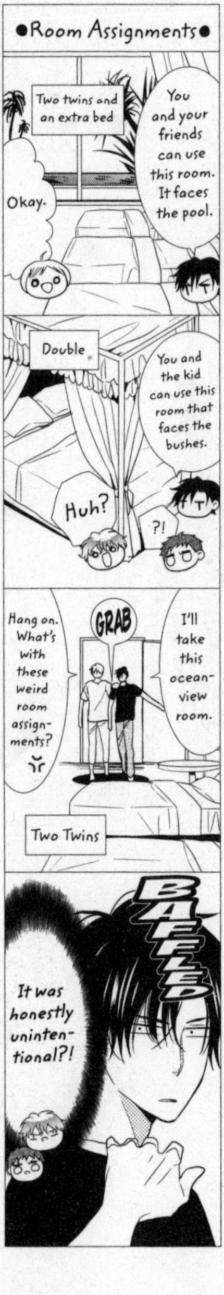
●Room Assignments●
Two twins and an extra bed
You and your friends can use this room. It faces the pool.
Okay.
Double
You and the kid can use this room that faces the bushes.
Huh?
?!
I'll take this ocean-view room.
GRAB
Hang on. What's with these weird room assign-ments?
Two Twins
BAFFLED
It was honestly uninten-tional?!

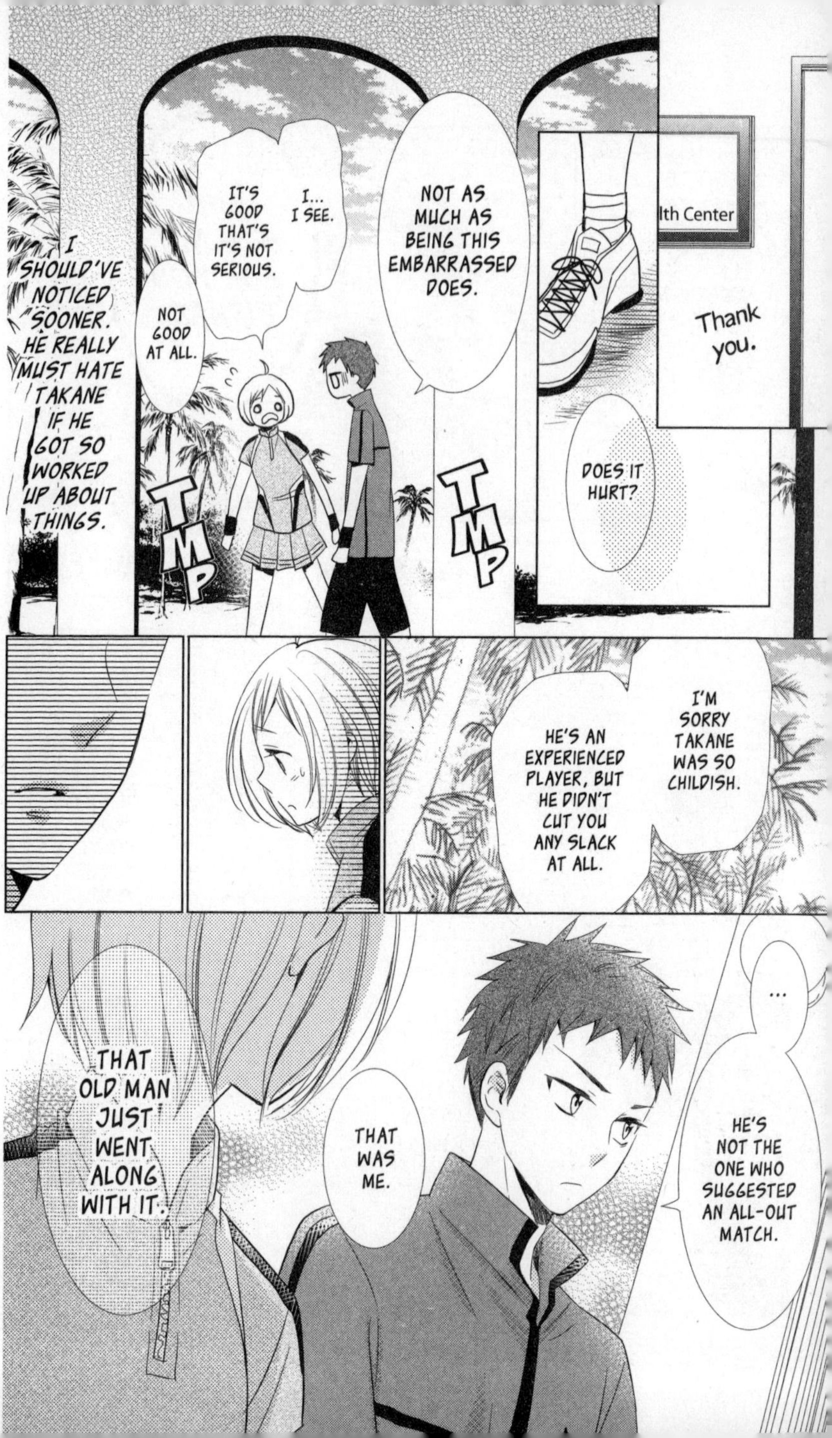
lth Center
Thank you.
DOES IT HURT?
NOT AS MUCH AS BEING THIS EMBARRASSED DOES.
I... I SEE.
IT'S GOOD THAT'S IT'S NOT SERIOUS.
NOT GOOD AT ALL.
TMP
TMP
I SHOULD'VE NOTICED SOONER. HE REALLY MUST HATE TAKANE IF HE GOT SO WORKED UP ABOUT THINGS.
I'M SORRY TAKANE WAS SO CHILDISH.
HE'S AN EXPERIENCED PLAYER, BUT HE DIDN'T CUT YOU ANY SLACK AT ALL.
...
HE'S NOT THE ONE WHO SUGGESTED AN ALL-OUT MATCH.
THAT WAS ME.
THAT OLD MAN JUST WENT ALONG WITH IT.

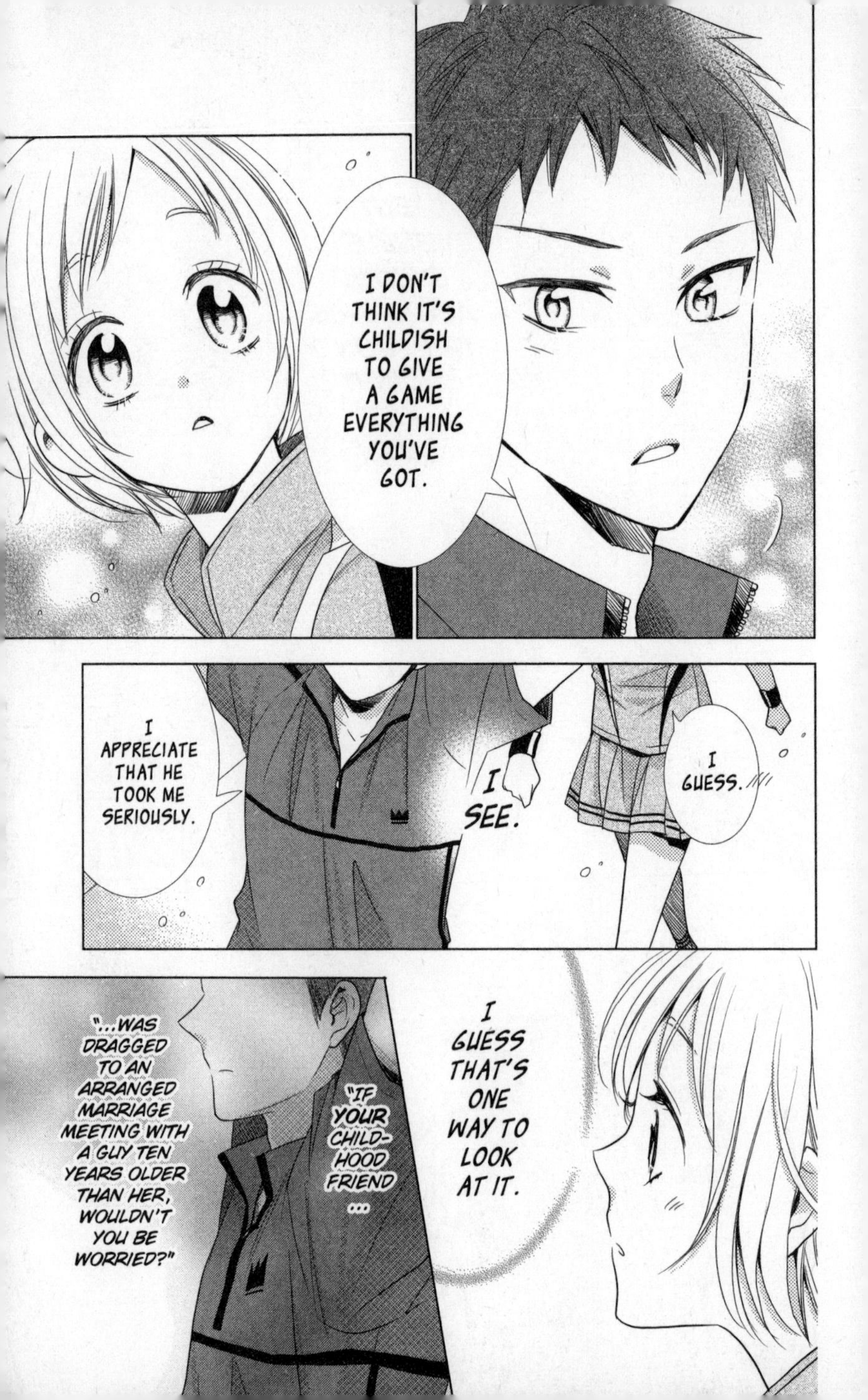
I DON'T THINK IT'S CHILDISH TO GIVE A GAME EVERYTHING YOU'VE GOT.
I GUESS.
I SEE.
I APPRECIATE THAT HE TOOK ME SERIOUSLY.
I GUESS THAT'S ONE WAY TO LOOK AT IT.
"IF YOUR CHILDHOOD FRIEND...
"...WAS DRAGGED TO AN ARRANGED MARRIAGE MEETING WITH A GUY TEN YEARS OLDER THAN HER, WOULDN'T YOU BE WORRIED?"

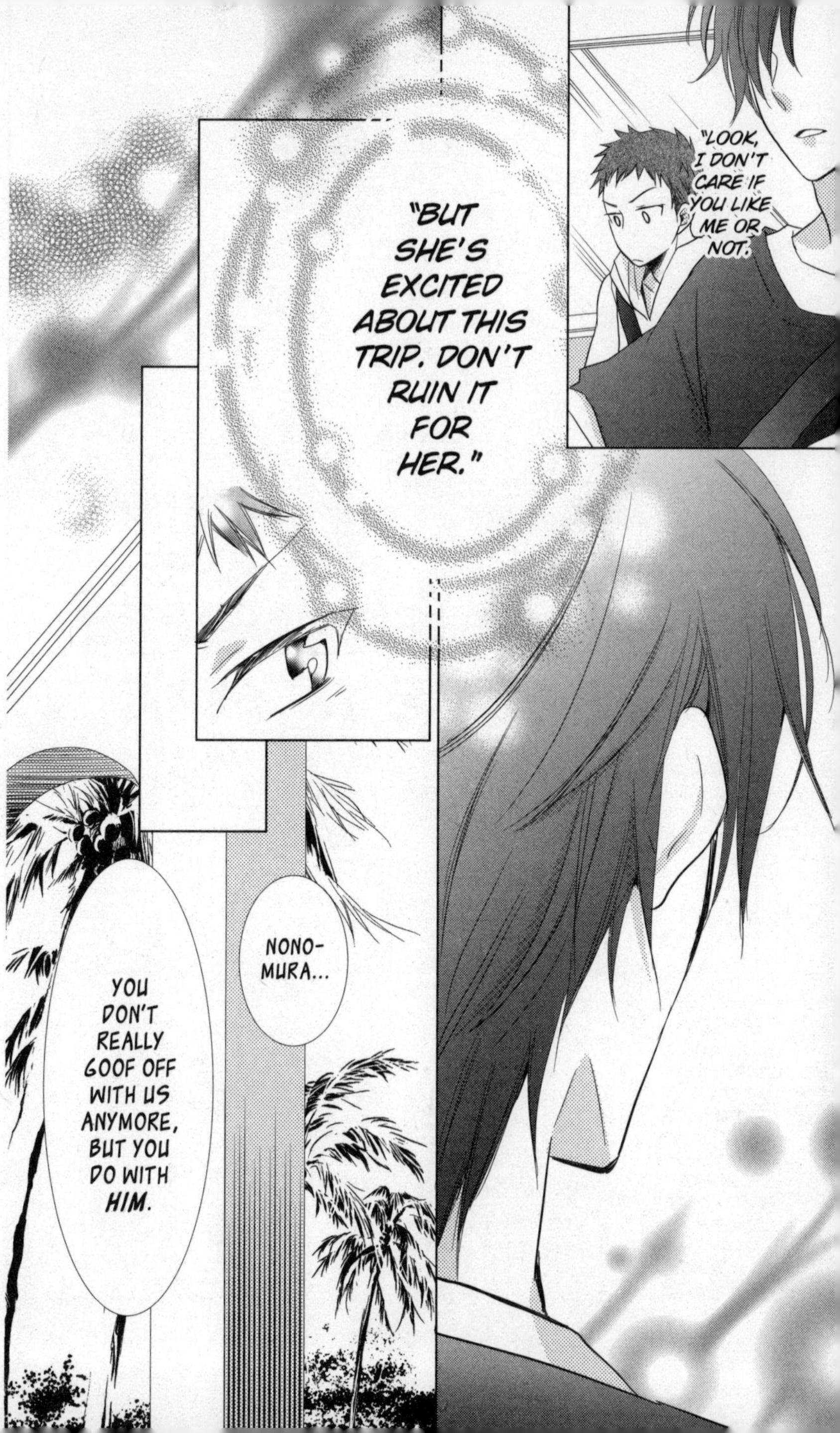
"LOOK, I DON'T CARE IF YOU LIKE ME OR NOT.
"BUT SHE'S EXCITED ABOUT THIS TRIP. DON'T RUIN IT FOR HER."
NONO-MURA...
YOU DON'T REALLY GOOF OFF WITH US ANYMORE, BUT YOU DO WITH HIM.

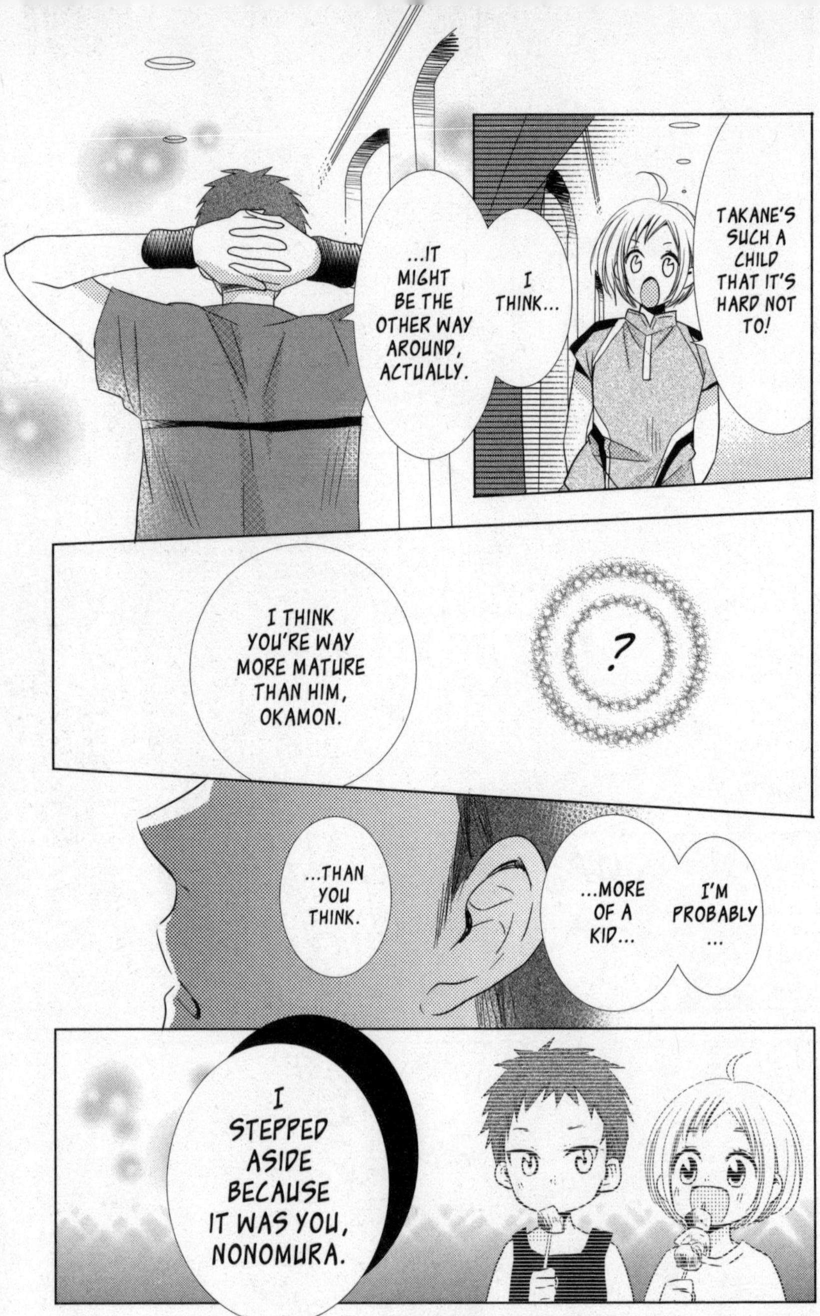
TAKANE'S SUCH A CHILD THAT IT'S HARD NOT TO!
I THINK...
...IT MIGHT BE THE OTHER WAY AROUND, ACTUALLY.
?
I THINK YOU'RE WAY MORE MATURE THAN HIM, OKAMON.
I'M PROBABLY ...
...MORE OF A KID...
...THAN YOU THINK.
I STEPPED ASIDE BECAUSE IT WAS YOU, NONOMURA.

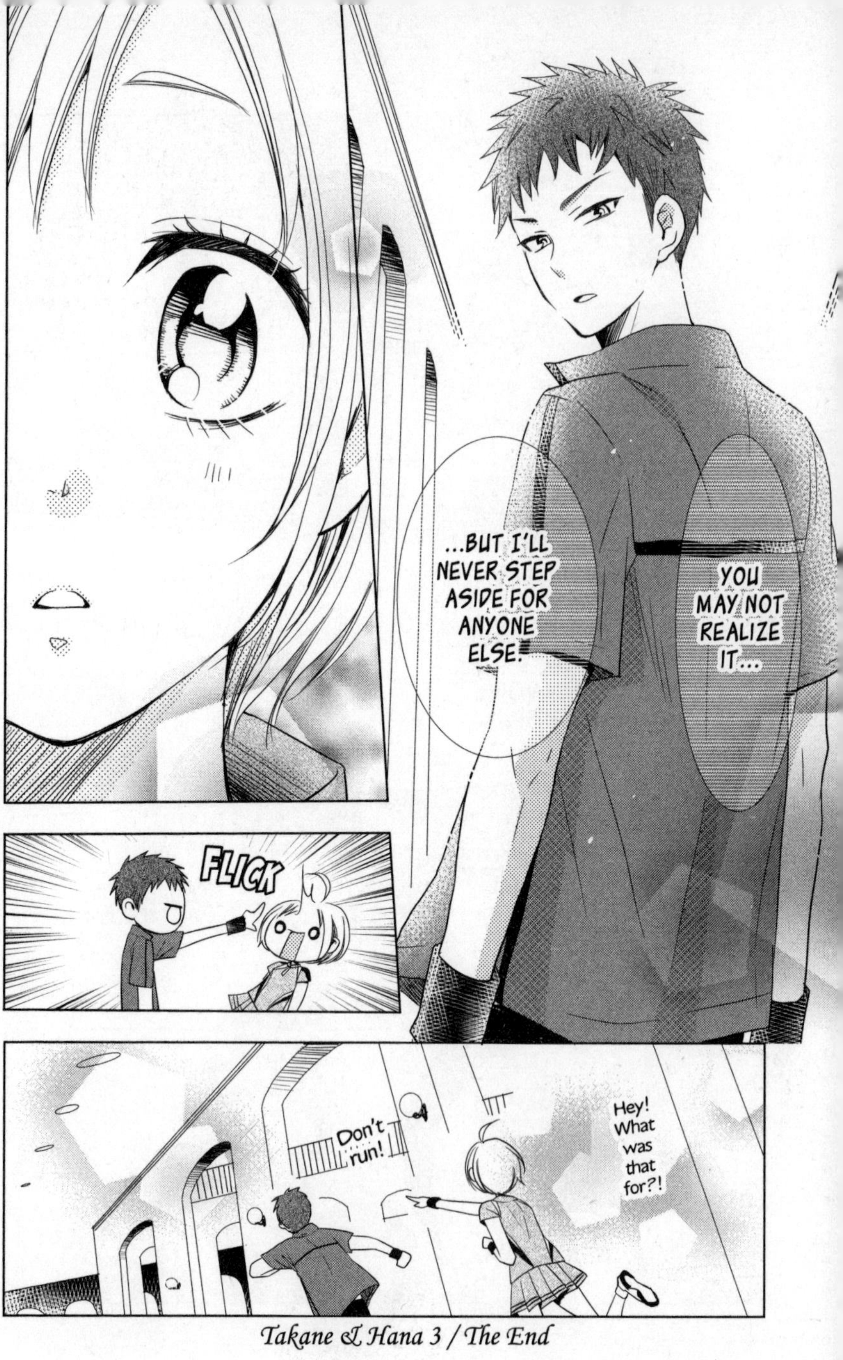
YOU MAY NOT REALIZE IT...
...BUT I'LL NEVER STEP ASIDE FOR ANYONE ELSE.
FLICK
Hey! What was that for?!
Don't run!

Takane & Hana 3 / The End

Special Chapter 1

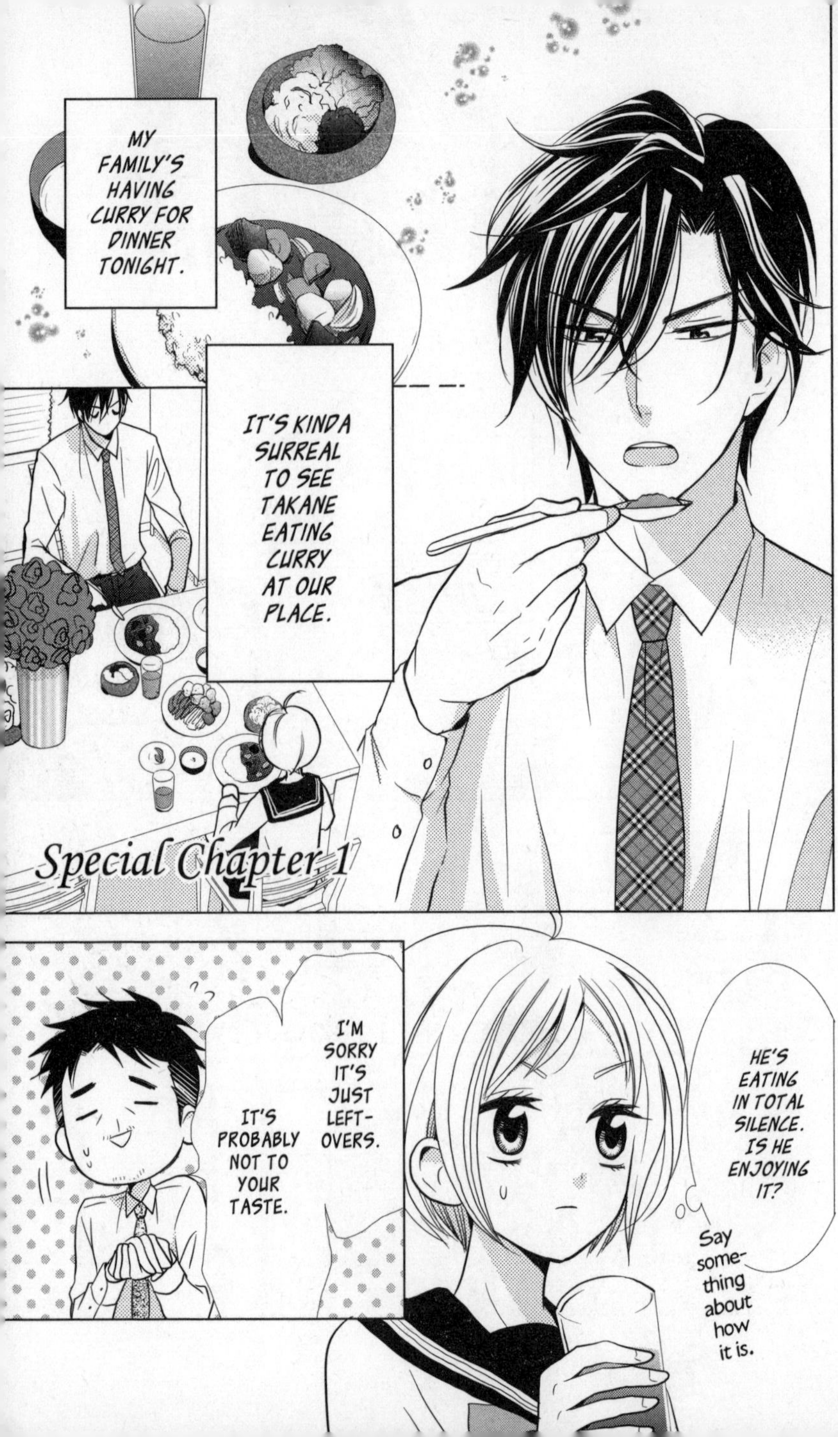
MY FAMILY'S HAVING CURRY FOR DINNER TONIGHT.
IT'S KINDA SURREAL TO SEE TAKANE EATING CURRY AT OUR PLACE.
HE'S EATING IN TOTAL SILENCE. IS HE ENJOYING IT?
Say something about how it is.
I'M SORRY IT'S JUST LEFTOVERS.
IT'S PROBABLY NOT TO YOUR TASTE.

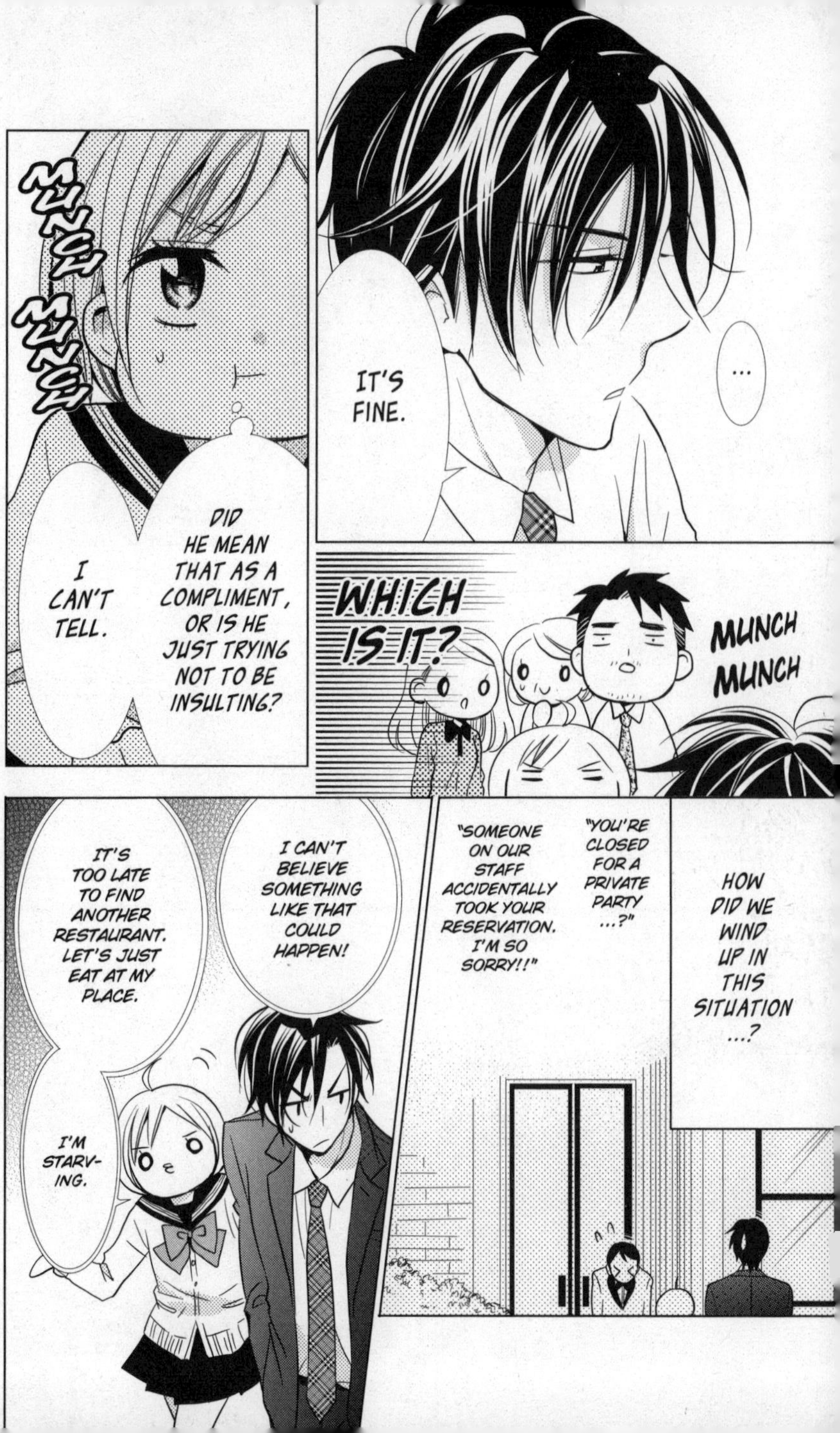
...
IT'S FINE.
MUNCH MUNCH
DID HE MEAN THAT AS A COMPLIMENT, OR IS HE JUST TRYING NOT TO BE INSULTING?
I CAN'T TELL.
MUNCH MUNCH
WHICH IS IT?
HOW DID WE WIND UP IN THIS SITUATION ...?
"YOU'RE CLOSED FOR A PRIVATE PARTY ...?"
"SOMEONE ON OUR STAFF ACCIDENTALLY TOOK YOUR RESERVATION. I'M SO SORRY!!"
I CAN'T BELIEVE SOMETHING LIKE THAT COULD HAPPEN!
IT'S TOO LATE TO FIND ANOTHER RESTAURANT. LET'S JUST EAT AT MY PLACE.
I'M STARV-ING.

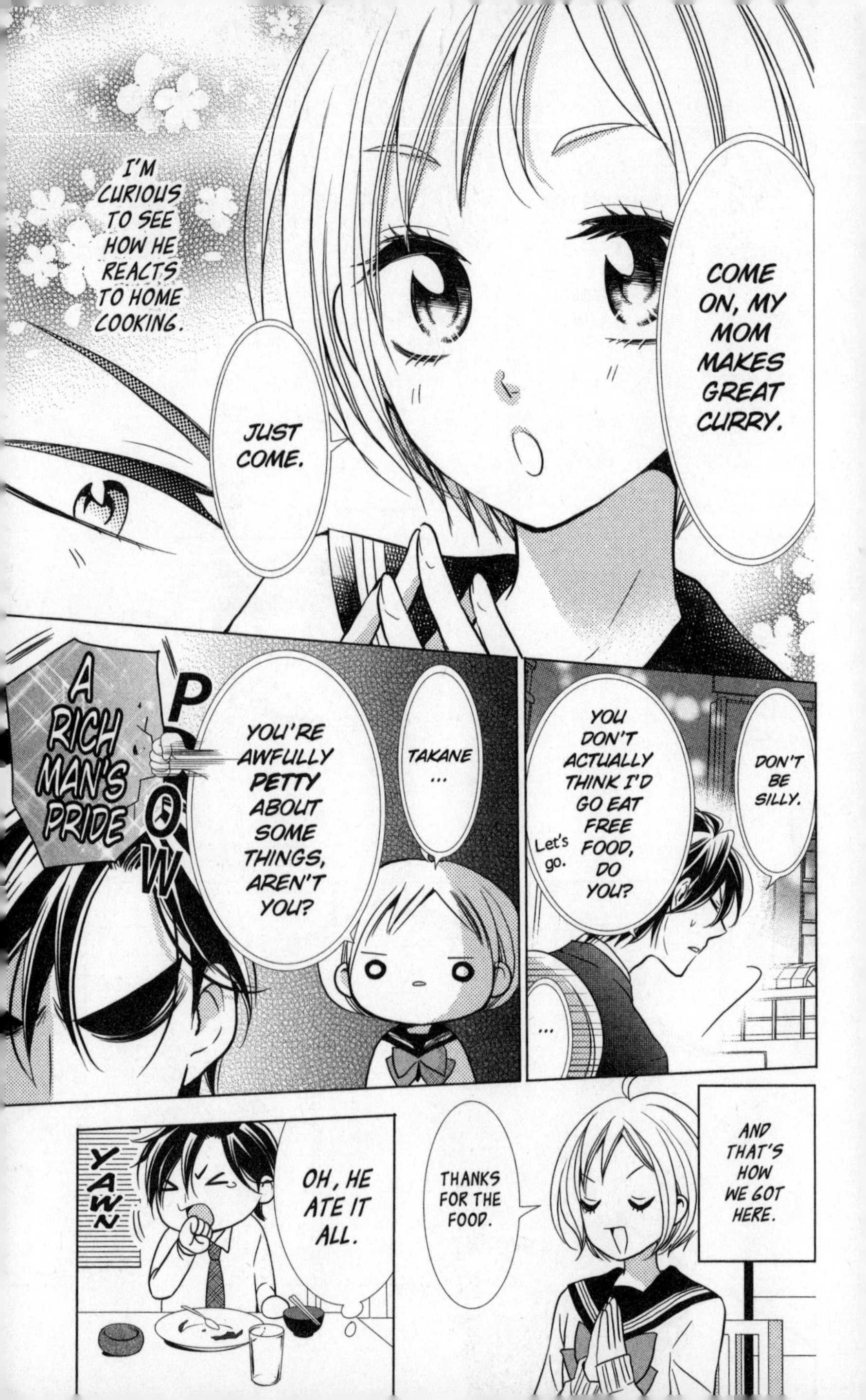
COME ON, MY MOM MAKES GREAT CURRY.
JUST COME.
I'M CURIOUS TO SEE HOW HE REACTS TO HOME COOKING.
DON'T BE SILLY.
YOU DON'T ACTUALLY THINK I'D GO EAT FREE FOOD, DO YOU?
Let's go.
...
TAKANE ...
YOU'RE AWFULLY PETTY ABOUT SOME THINGS, AREN'T YOU?
POW
A RICH MAN'S PRIDE
AND THAT'S HOW WE GOT HERE.
THANKS FOR THE FOOD.
OH, HE ATE IT ALL.
YAWN

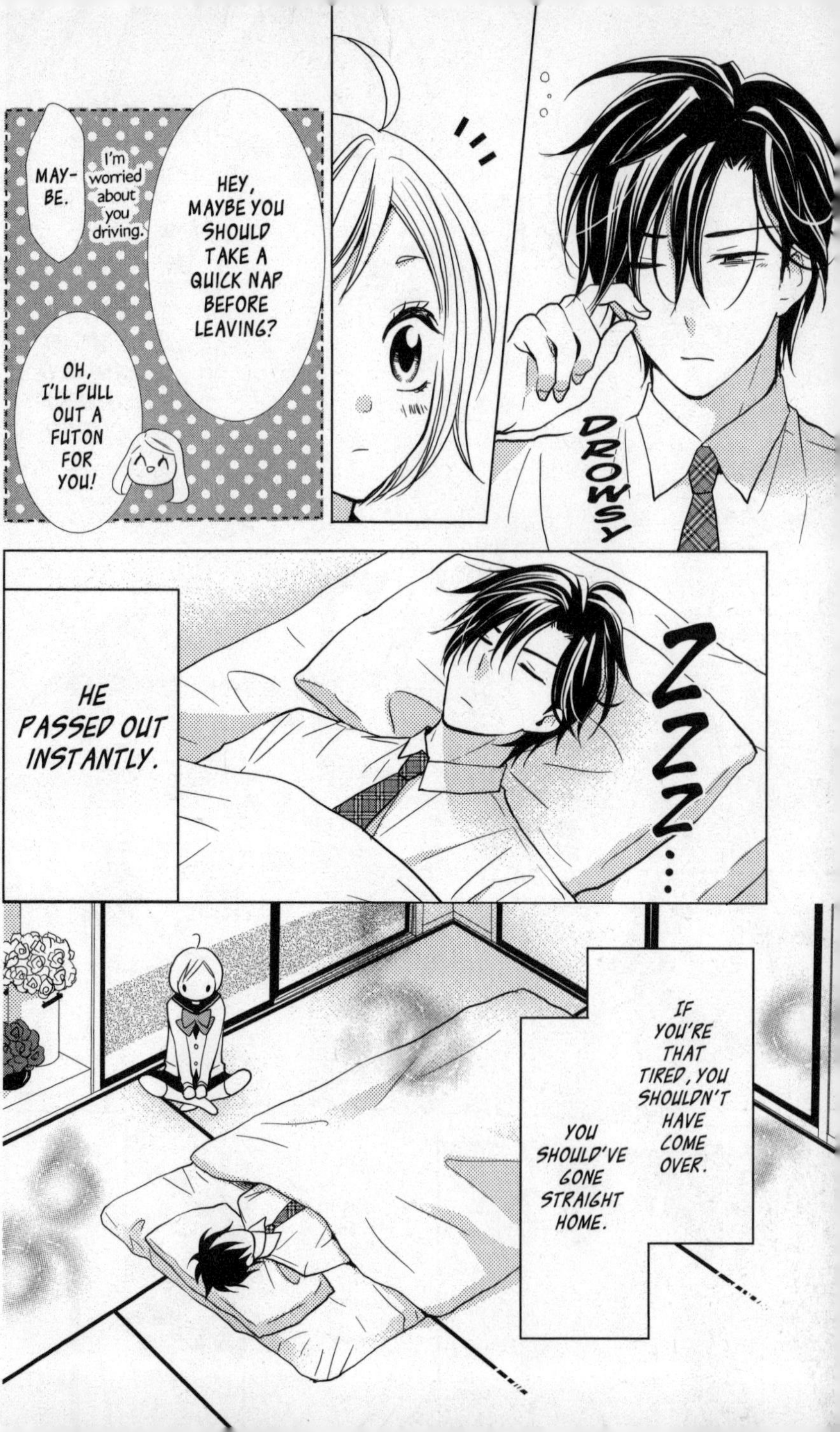
DROWSY
HEY, MAYBE YOU SHOULD TAKE A QUICK NAP BEFORE LEAVING?
MAY-BE.
I'm worried about you driving.
OH, I'LL PULL OUT A FUTON FOR YOU!
ZZZ...
HE PASSED OUT INSTANTLY.
IF YOU'RE THAT TIRED, YOU SHOULDN'T HAVE COME OVER.
YOU SHOULD'VE GONE STRAIGHT HOME.

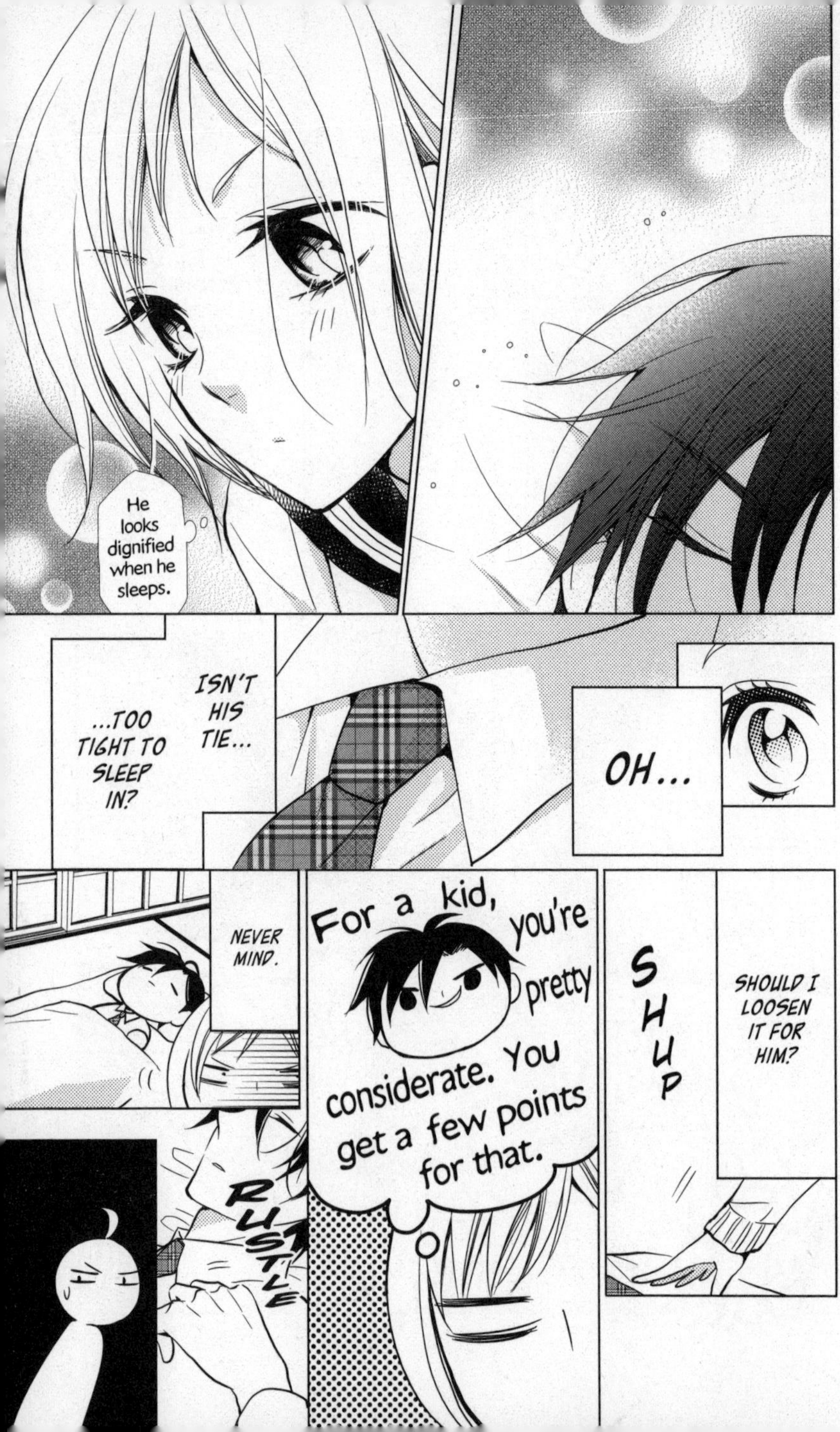
He looks dignified when he sleeps.
OH...
ISN'T HIS TIE...
...TOO TIGHT TO SLEEP IN?
SHOULD I LOOSEN IT FOR HIM?
SHUP
For a kid, you're pretty considerate. You get a few points for that.
NEVER MIND.
RUSTLE

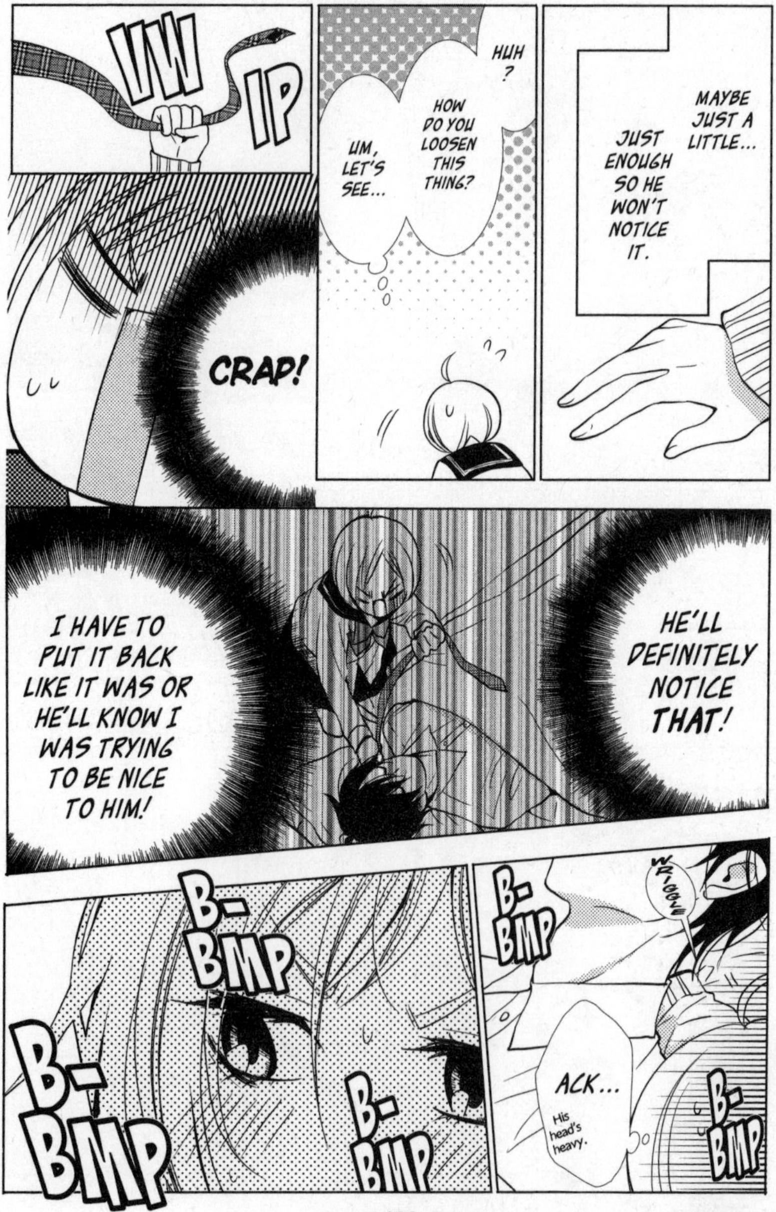
MAYBE JUST A LITTLE...
JUST ENOUGH SO HE WON'T NOTICE IT.
HUH?
HOW DO YOU LOOSEN THIS THING?
UM, LET'S SEE...
VWIP
CRAP!
HE'LL DEFINITELY NOTICE THAT!
I HAVE TO PUT IT BACK LIKE IT WAS OR HE'LL KNOW I WAS TRYING TO BE NICE TO HIM!
WRIGGLE
B-BMP
ACK...
His head's heavy.
B-BMP
B-BMP
B-BMP
B-BMP

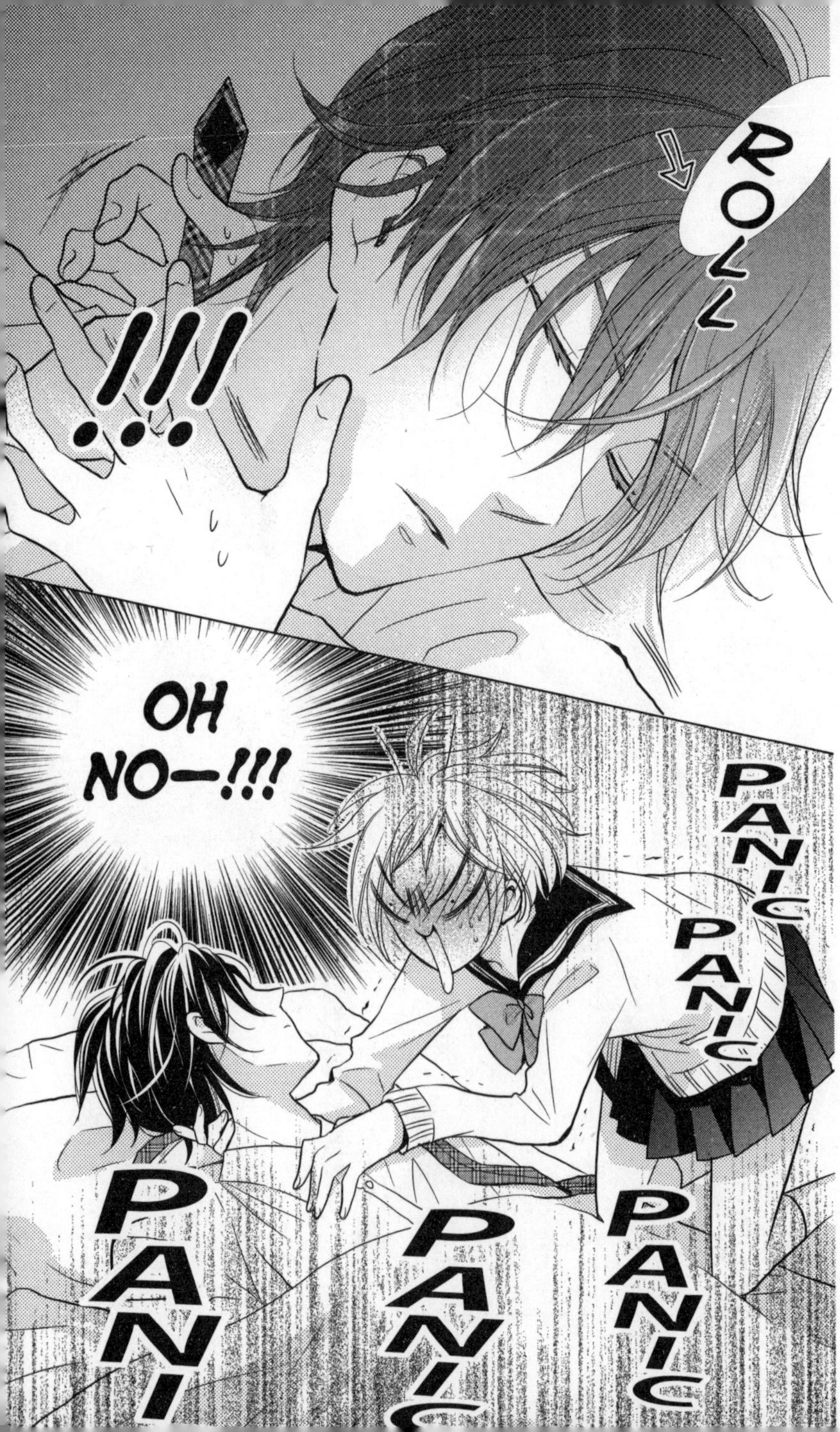
ROLL
...!!!
OH NO—!!!
PANIC PANIC
PANIC
PANIC
PANI

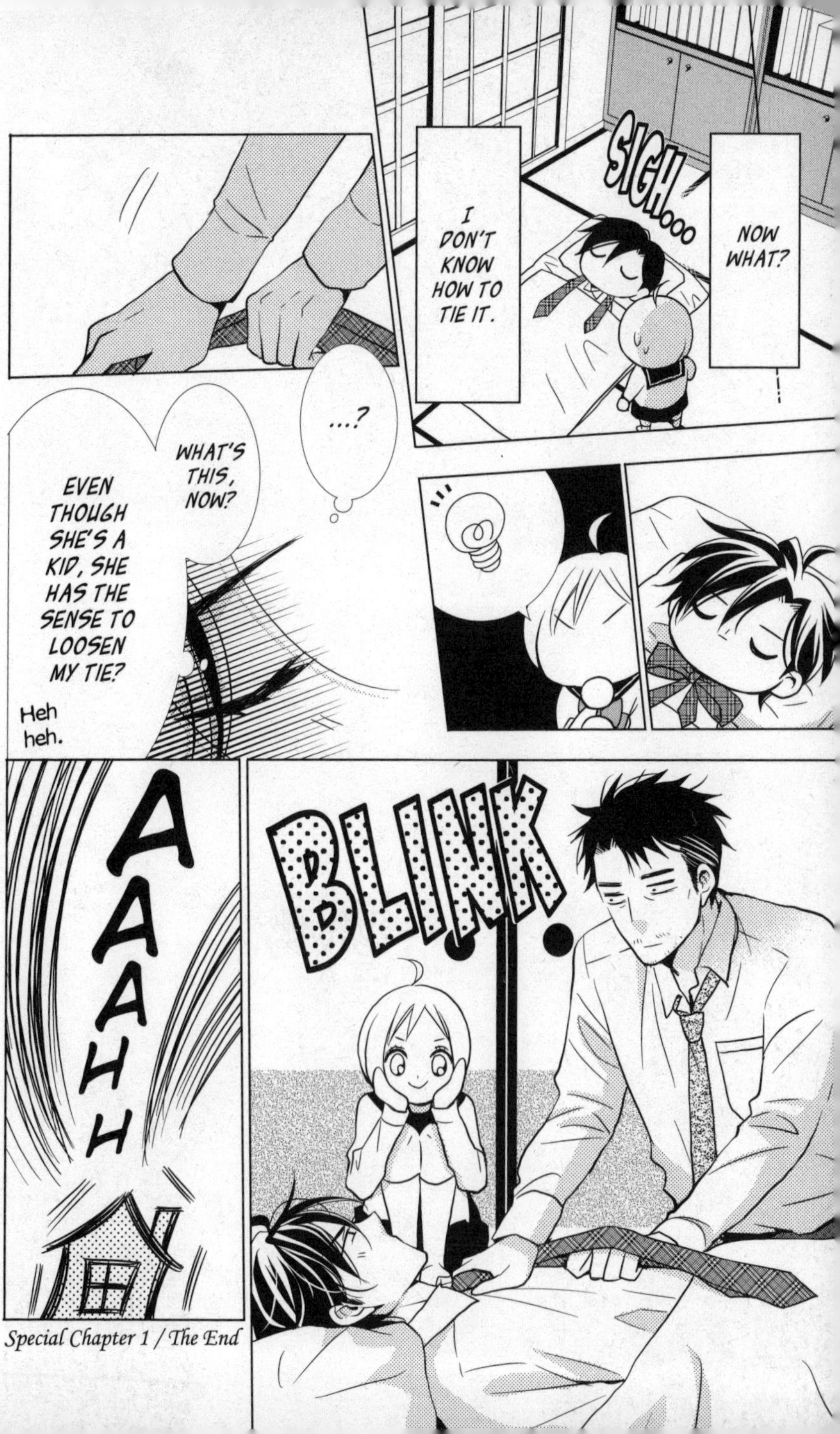
NOW WHAT?
SIGHOOO
I DON'T KNOW HOW TO TIE IT.
...?
WHAT'S THIS, NOW?
EVEN THOUGH SHE'S A KID, SHE HAS THE SENSE TO LOOSEN MY TIE?
Heh heh.
BLINK
AAAHH

Special Chapter 1 / The End

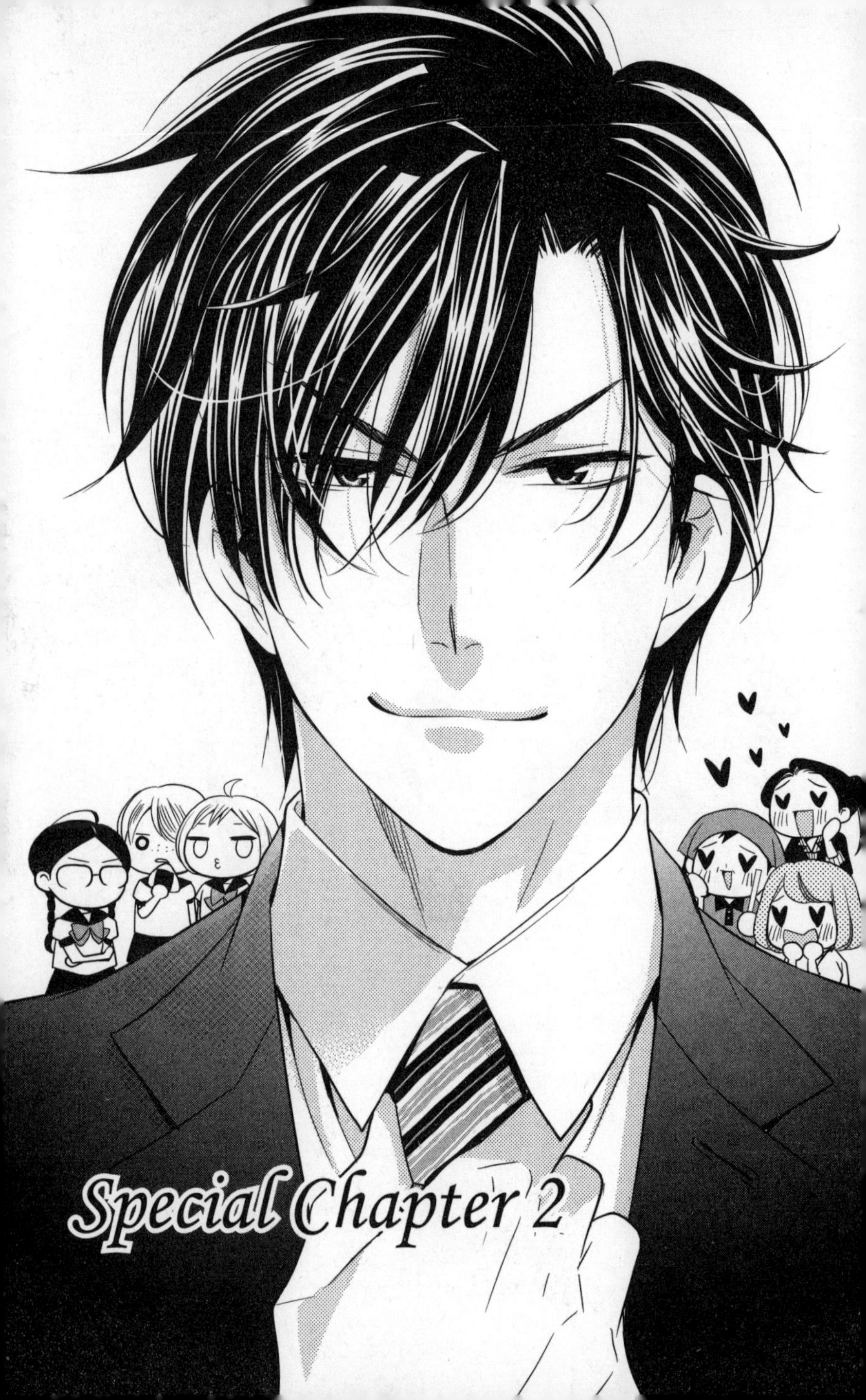
Special Chapter 2

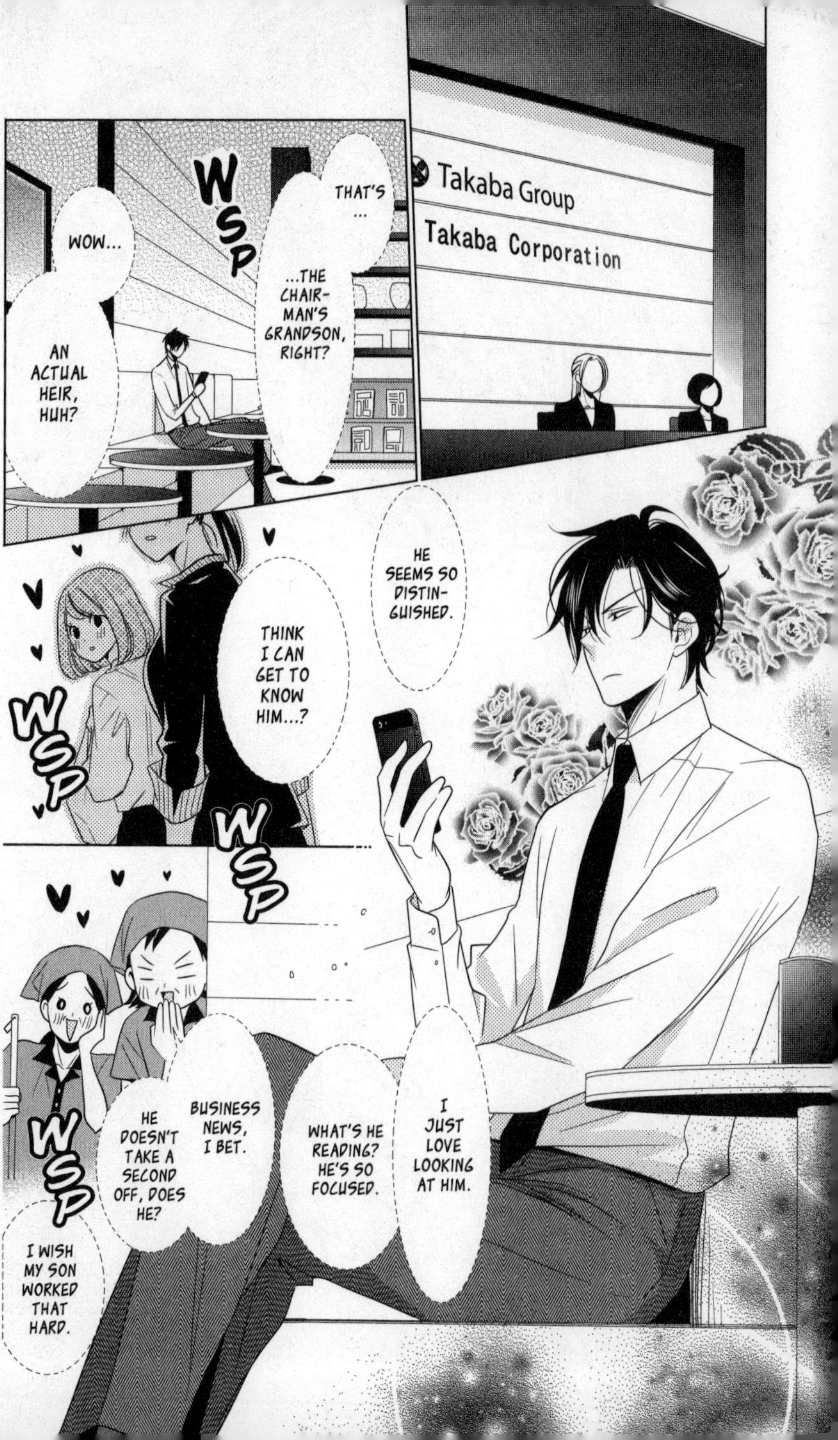
Takaba Group
Takaba Corporation
THAT'S ...
...THE CHAIRMAN'S GRANDSON, RIGHT?
WSP
WOW...
AN ACTUAL HEIR, HUH?
HE SEEMS SO DISTINGUISHED.
THINK I CAN GET TO KNOW HIM...?
WSP
WSP
I JUST LOVE LOOKING AT HIM.
WHAT'S HE READING? HE'S SO FOCUSED.
BUSINESS NEWS, I BET.
HE DOESN'T TAKE A SECOND OFF, DOES HE?
WSP
I WISH MY SON WORKED THAT HARD.

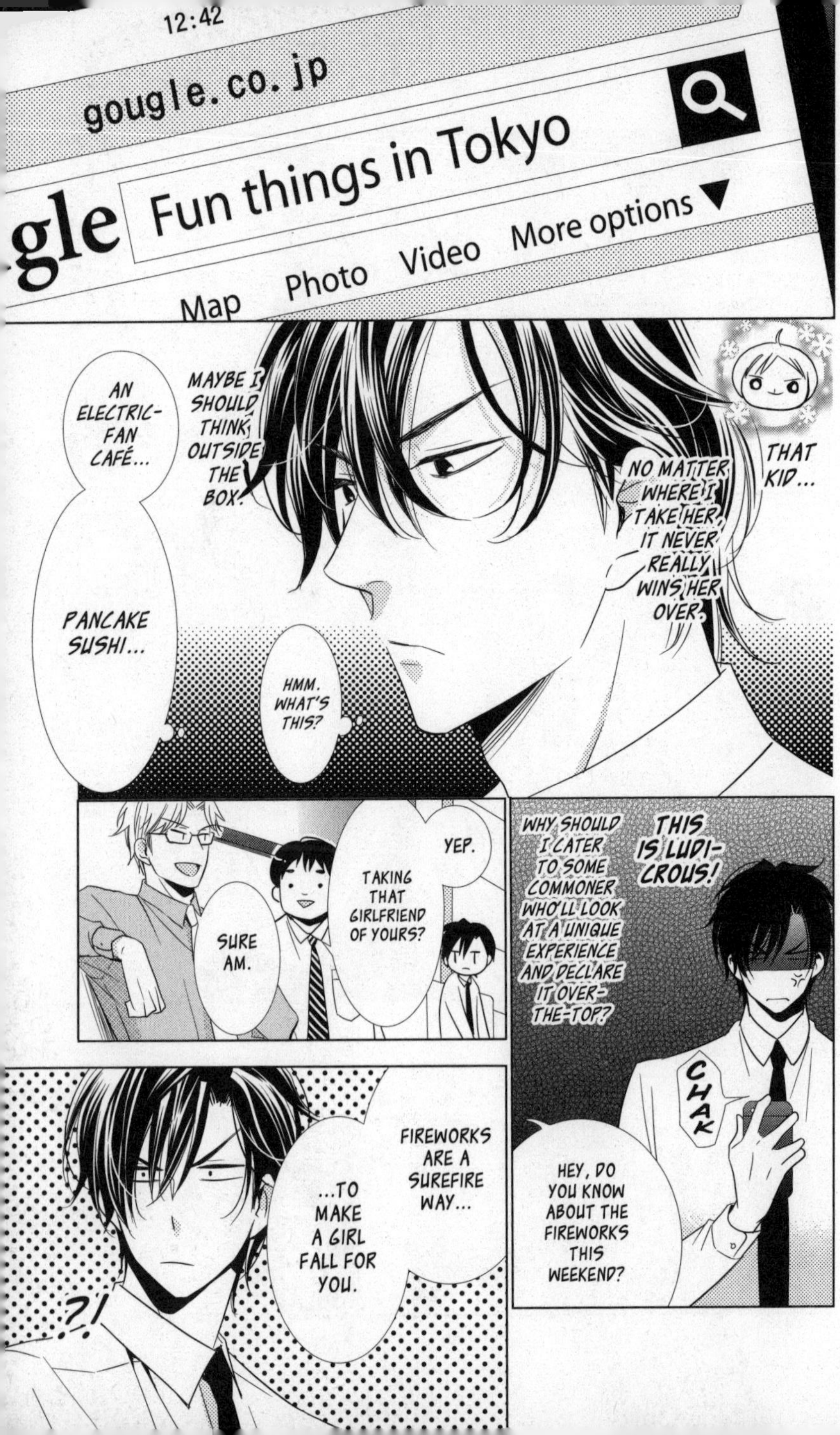
12:42
gougle.co.jp
gle
Fun things in Tokyo
More options
Map
Photo
Video
THAT KID...
NO MATTER WHERE I TAKE HER, IT NEVER REALLY WINS HER OVER.
MAYBE I SHOULD THINK OUTSIDE THE BOX.
AN ELECTRIC-FAN CAFÉ...
PANCAKE SUSHI...
HMM. WHAT'S THIS?
THIS IS LUDICROUS!
WHY SHOULD I CATER TO SOME COMMONER WHO'LL LOOK AT A UNIQUE EXPERIENCE AND DECLARE IT OVER-THE-TOP?
CHAK
HEY, DO YOU KNOW ABOUT THE FIREWORKS THIS WEEKEND?
YEP.
TAKING THAT GIRLFRIEND OF YOURS?
SURE AM.
FIREWORKS ARE A SUREFIRE WAY...
...TO MAKE A GIRL FALL FOR YOU.
?!

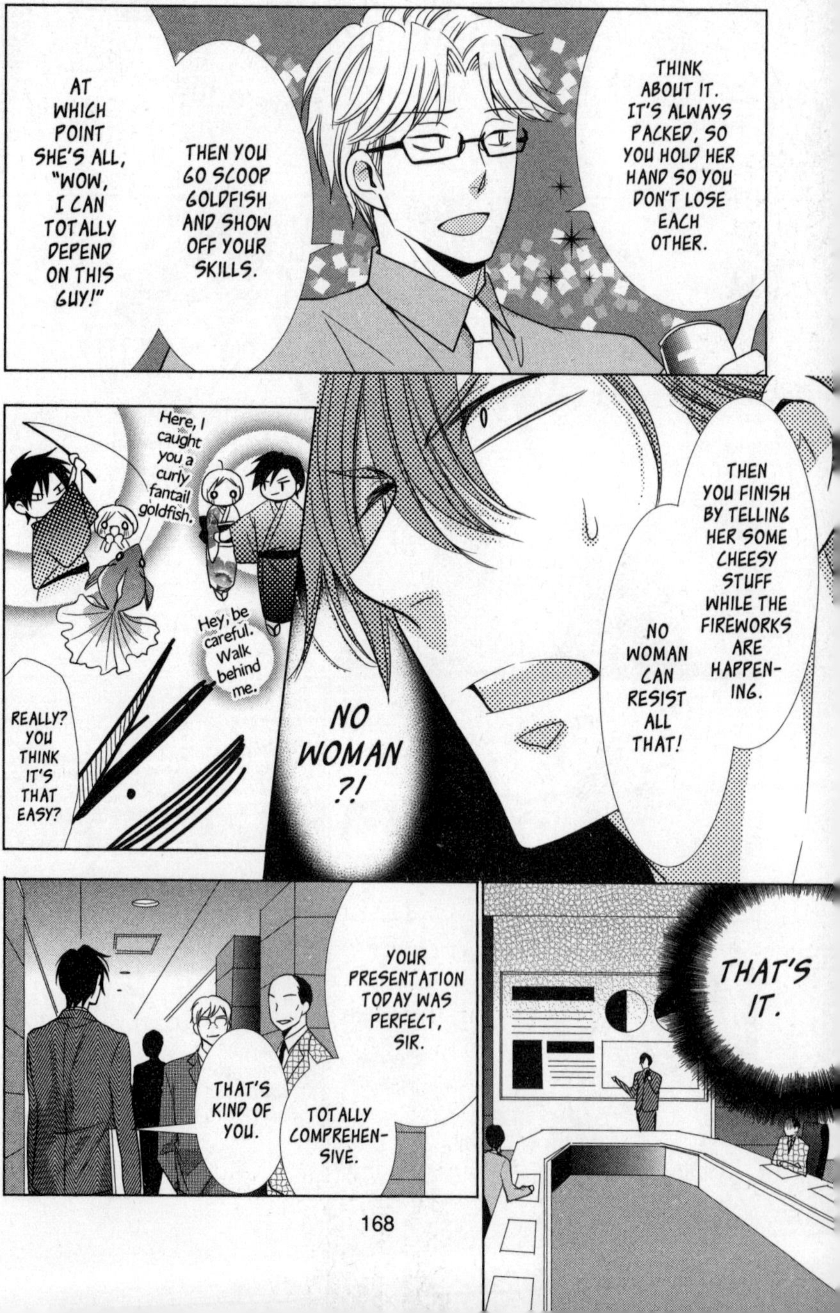
THINK ABOUT IT. IT'S ALWAYS PACKED, SO YOU HOLD HER HAND SO YOU DON'T LOSE EACH OTHER.
THEN YOU GO SCOOP GOLDFISH AND SHOW OFF YOUR SKILLS.
AT WHICH POINT SHE'S ALL, "WOW, I CAN TOTALLY DEPEND ON THIS GUY!"
THEN YOU FINISH BY TELLING HER SOME CHEESY STUFF WHILE THE FIREWORKS ARE HAPPEN-ING.
NO WOMAN CAN RESIST ALL THAT!
NO WOMAN ?!
Here, I caught you a curly fantail goldfish.
Hey, be careful. Walk behind me.
REALLY? YOU THINK IT'S THAT EASY?
THAT'S IT.
YOUR PRESENTATION TODAY WAS PERFECT, SIR.
TOTALLY COMPREHEN-SIVE.
THAT'S KIND OF YOU.

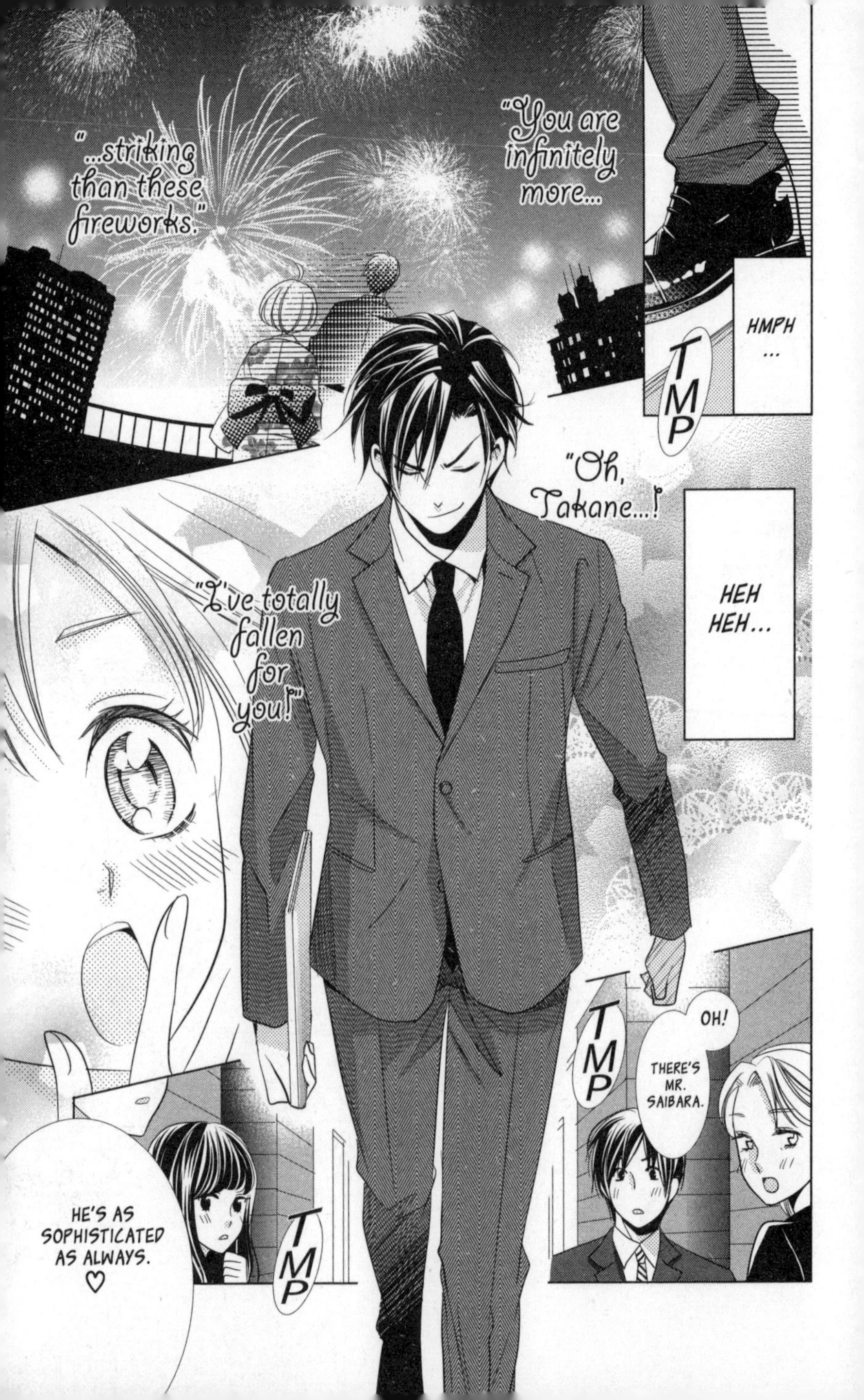
HMPH ...
TMP
"You are infinitely more...
"...striking than these fireworks."
"Oh, Takane...!
HEH HEH...
"I've totally fallen for you!"
OH!
THERE'S MR. SAIBARA.
TMP
TMP
HE'S AS SOPHISTICATED AS ALWAYS. ♡

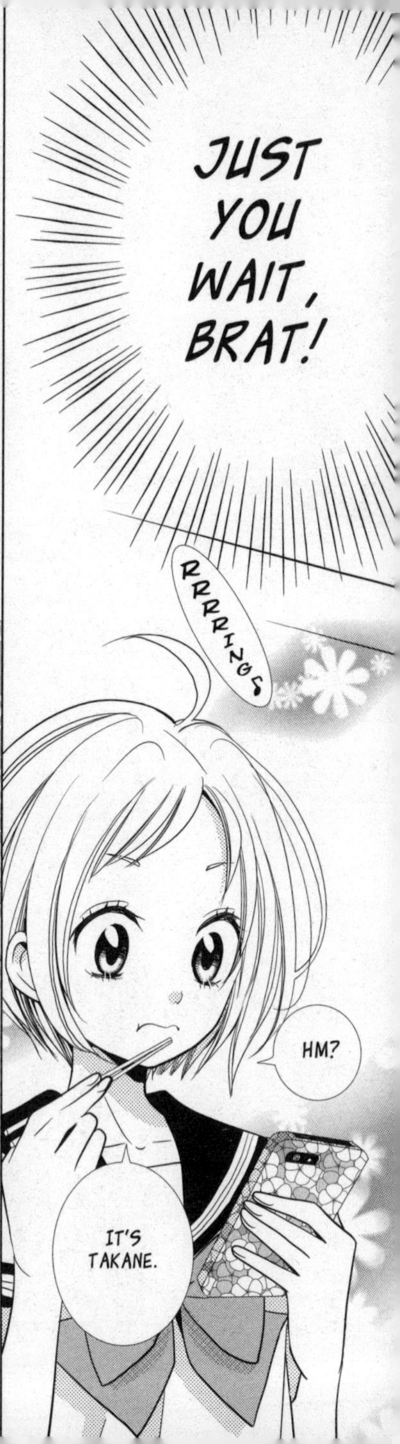
JUST YOU WAIT, BRAT!
RRRRINGS
HM?
IT'S TAKANE.

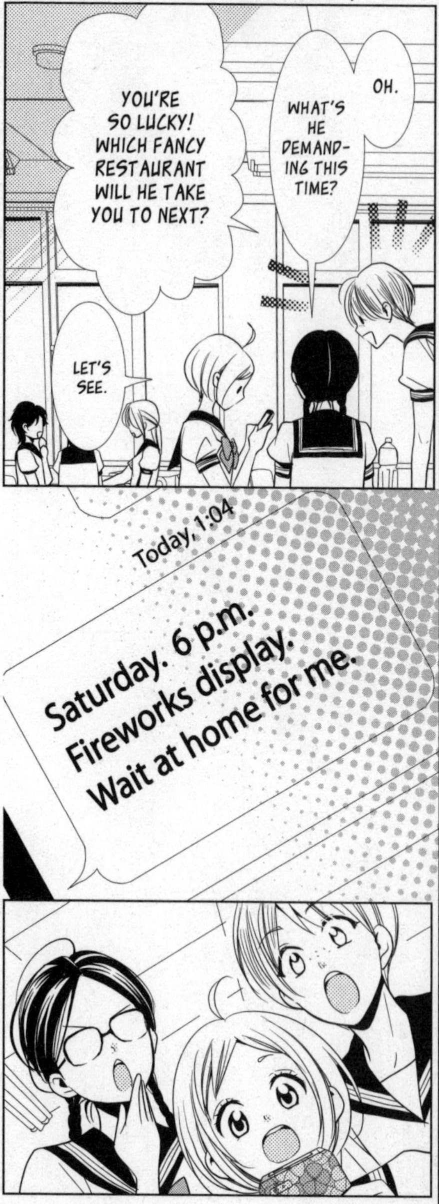
OH.
WHAT'S HE DEMANDING THIS TIME?
YOU'RE SO LUCKY! WHICH FANCY RESTAURANT WILL HE TAKE YOU TO NEXT?
LET'S SEE.
Today, 1:04
Saturday. 6 p.m.
Fireworks display.
Wait at home for me.

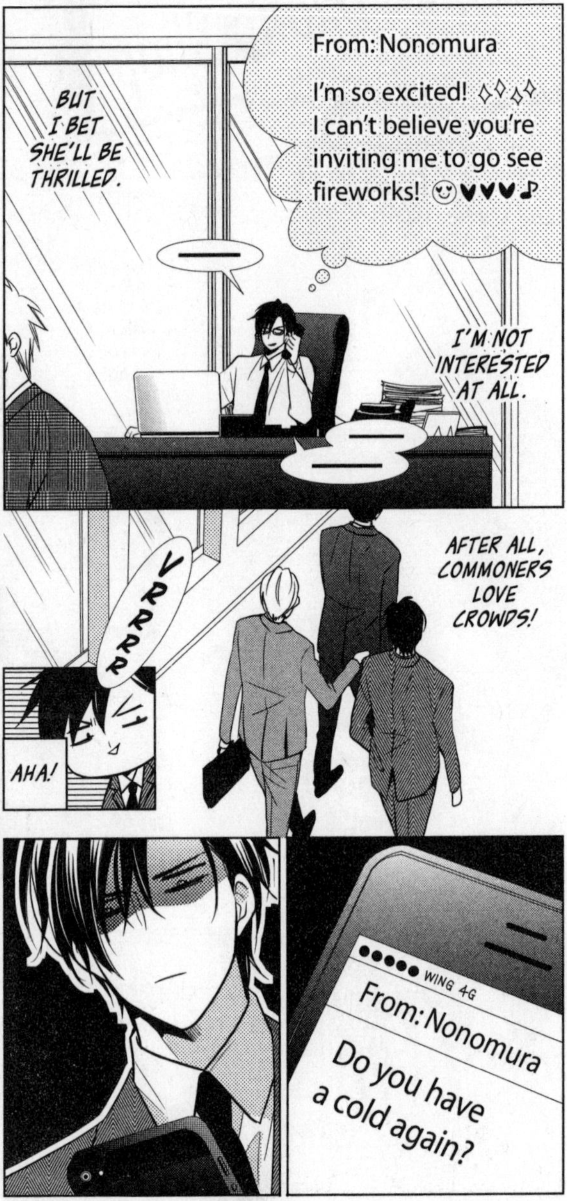
From: Nonomura
I'm so excited! ✧✧✧✧
I can't believe you're inviting me to go see fireworks! ☺♥♥♥♪
I'M NOT INTERESTED AT ALL.
BUT I BET SHE'LL BE THRILLED.
——
——
——
AFTER ALL, COMMONERS LOVE CROWDS!
VRRRR
AHA!
●●●●● WING 4G
From: Nonomura
Do you have a cold again?

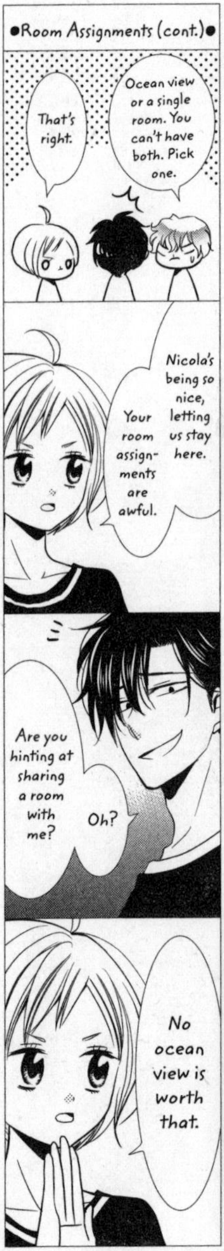
●Room Assignments (cont.)●
Ocean view or a single room. You can't have both. Pick one.
That's right.
Nicola's being so nice, letting us stay here.
Your room assignments are awful.
Oh?
Are you hinting at sharing a room with me?
No ocean view is worth that.

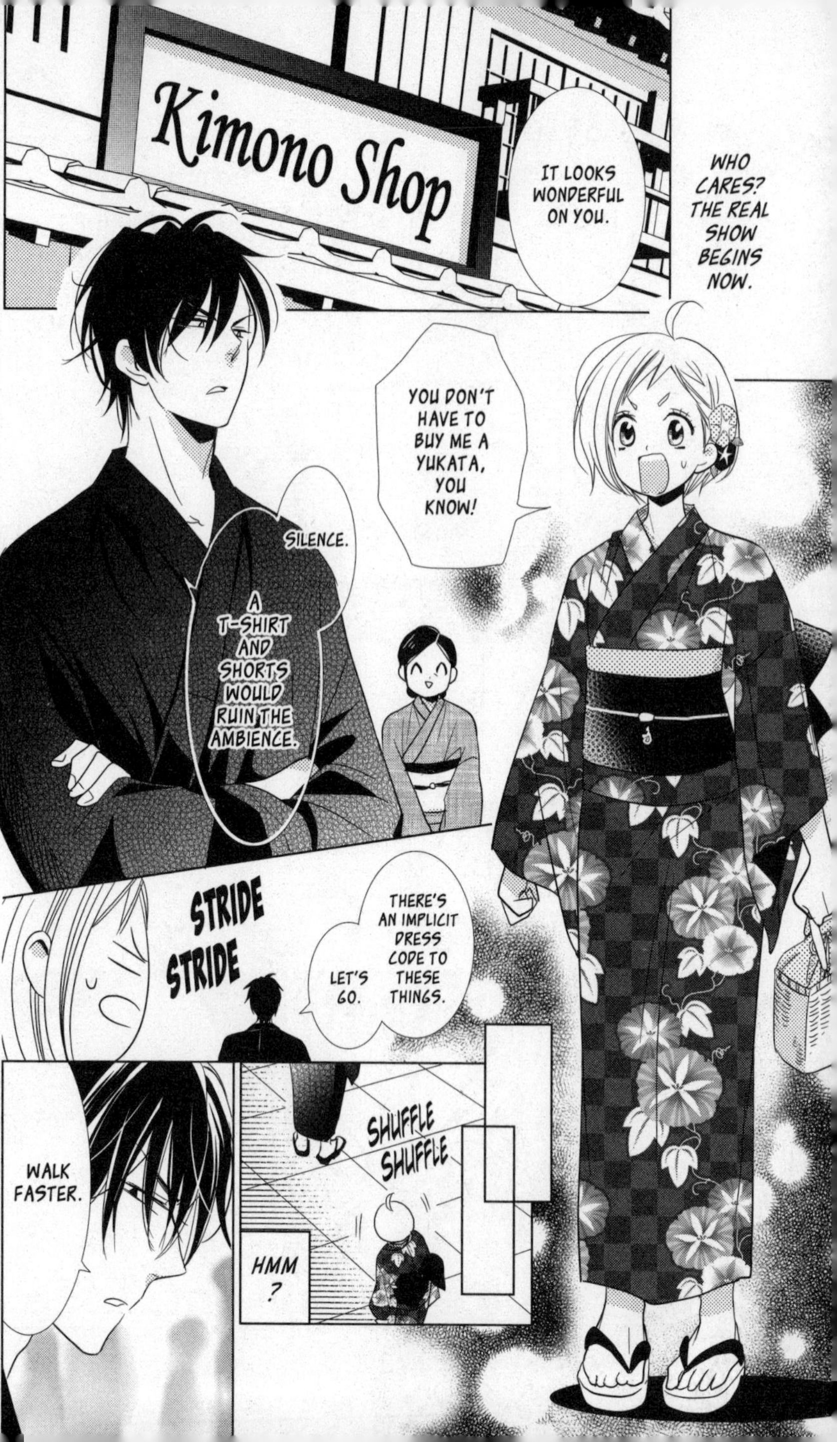
WHO CARES? THE REAL SHOW BEGINS NOW.
IT LOOKS WONDERFUL ON YOU.
Kimono Shop
YOU DON'T HAVE TO BUY ME A YUKATA, YOU KNOW!
SILENCE.
A T-SHIRT AND SHORTS WOULD RUIN THE AMBIENCE.
THERE'S AN IMPLICIT DRESS CODE TO THESE THINGS.
LET'S GO.
STRIDE STRIDE
SHUFFLE SHUFFLE
HMM ?
WALK FASTER.

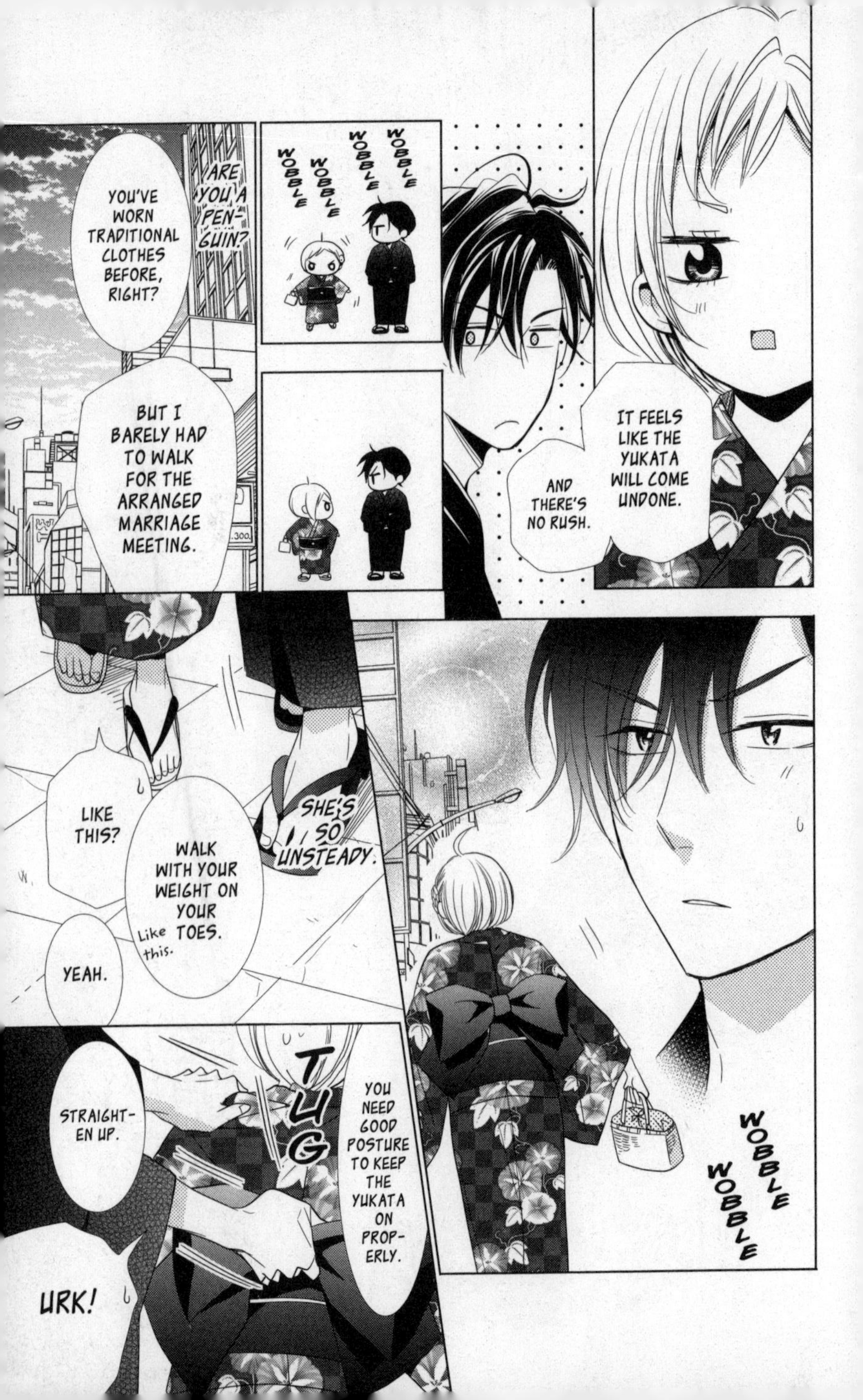
IT FEELS LIKE THE YUKATA WILL COME UNDONE.
AND THERE'S NO RUSH.
WOBBLE WOBBLE WOBBLE WOBBLE
YOU'VE WORN TRADITIONAL CLOTHES BEFORE, RIGHT?
ARE YOU A PEN-GUIN?
BUT I BARELY HAD TO WALK FOR THE ARRANGED MARRIAGE MEETING.
WOBBLE WOBBLE
SHE'S SO UNSTEADY.
LIKE THIS?
WALK WITH YOUR WEIGHT ON YOUR TOES.
Like this.
YEAH.
YOU NEED GOOD POSTURE TO KEEP THE YUKATA ON PROP-ERLY.
TUG
STRAIGHT-EN UP.
URK!

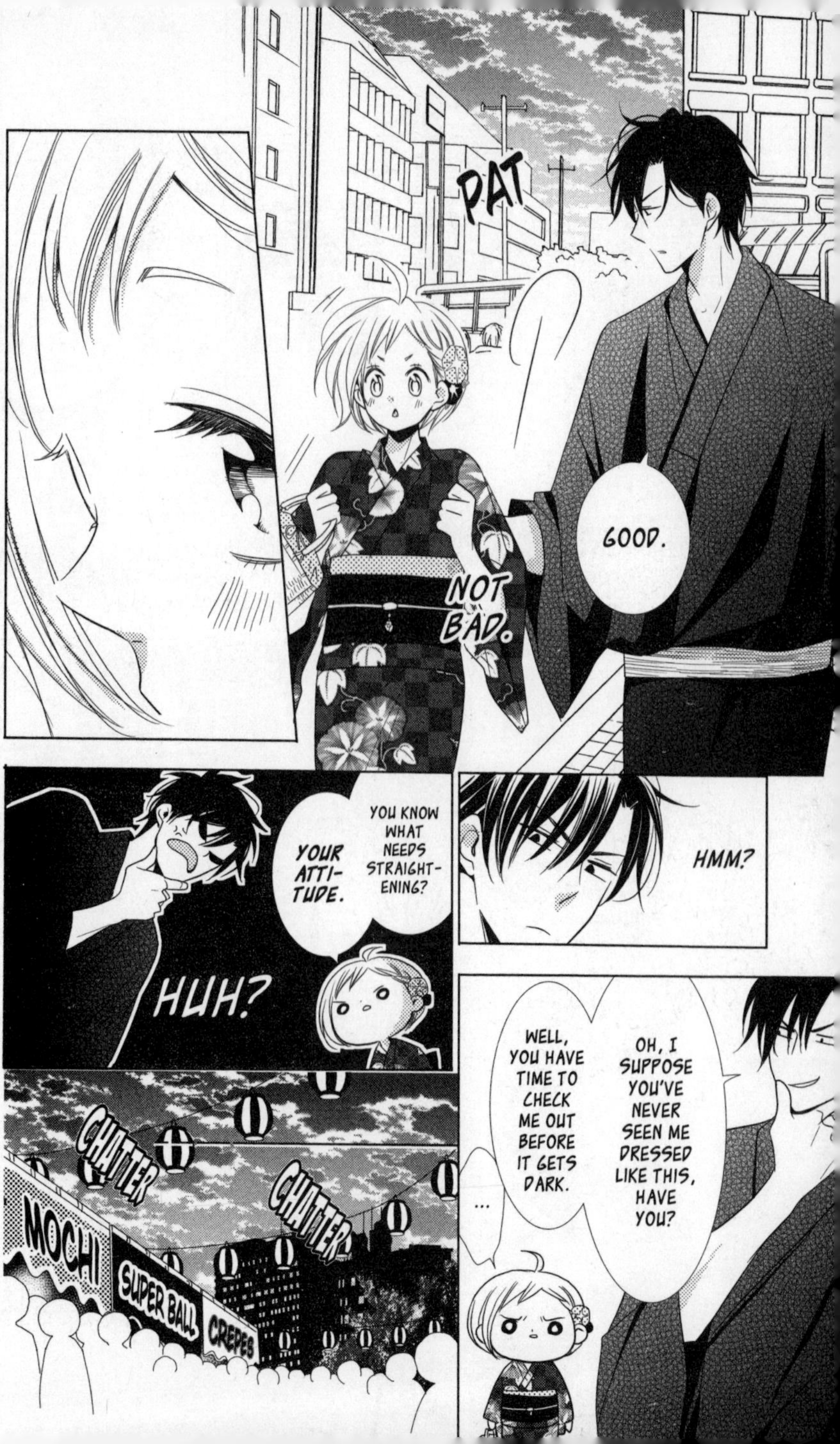
PAT
GOOD.
NOT BAD.
HMM?
YOU KNOW WHAT NEEDS STRAIGHT-ENING?
YOUR ATTI-TUDE.
HUH?
OH, I SUPPOSE YOU'VE NEVER SEEN ME DRESSED LIKE THIS, HAVE YOU?
WELL, YOU HAVE TIME TO CHECK ME OUT BEFORE IT GETS DARK.
...
CHATTER
CHATTER
MOCHI
SUPER BALL
CREPES

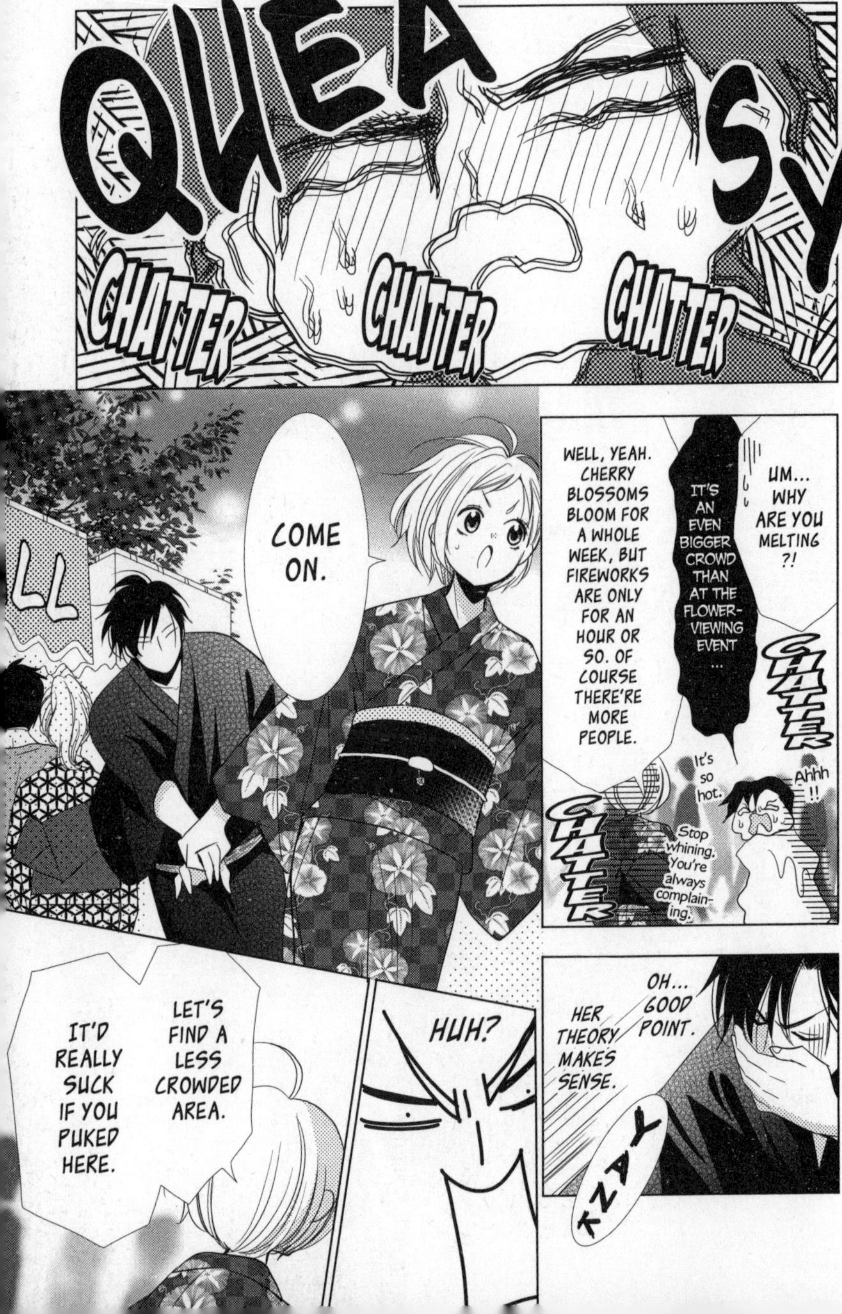
QUEASY
CHATTER
CHATTER
CHATTER
UM... WHY ARE YOU MELTING ?!
IT'S AN EVEN BIGGER CROWD THAN AT THE FLOWER-VIEWING EVENT ...
CHATTER
WELL, YEAH. CHERRY BLOSSOMS BLOOM FOR A WHOLE WEEK, BUT FIREWORKS ARE ONLY FOR AN HOUR OR SO. OF COURSE THERE'RE MORE PEOPLE.
Ahhh !!
It's so hot.
Stop whining. You're always complain-ing.
CHATTER
COME ON.
OH... GOOD POINT.
HER THEORY MAKES SENSE.
KZAY
HUH?
LET'S FIND A LESS CROWDED AREA.
IT'D REALLY SUCK IF YOU PUKED HERE.

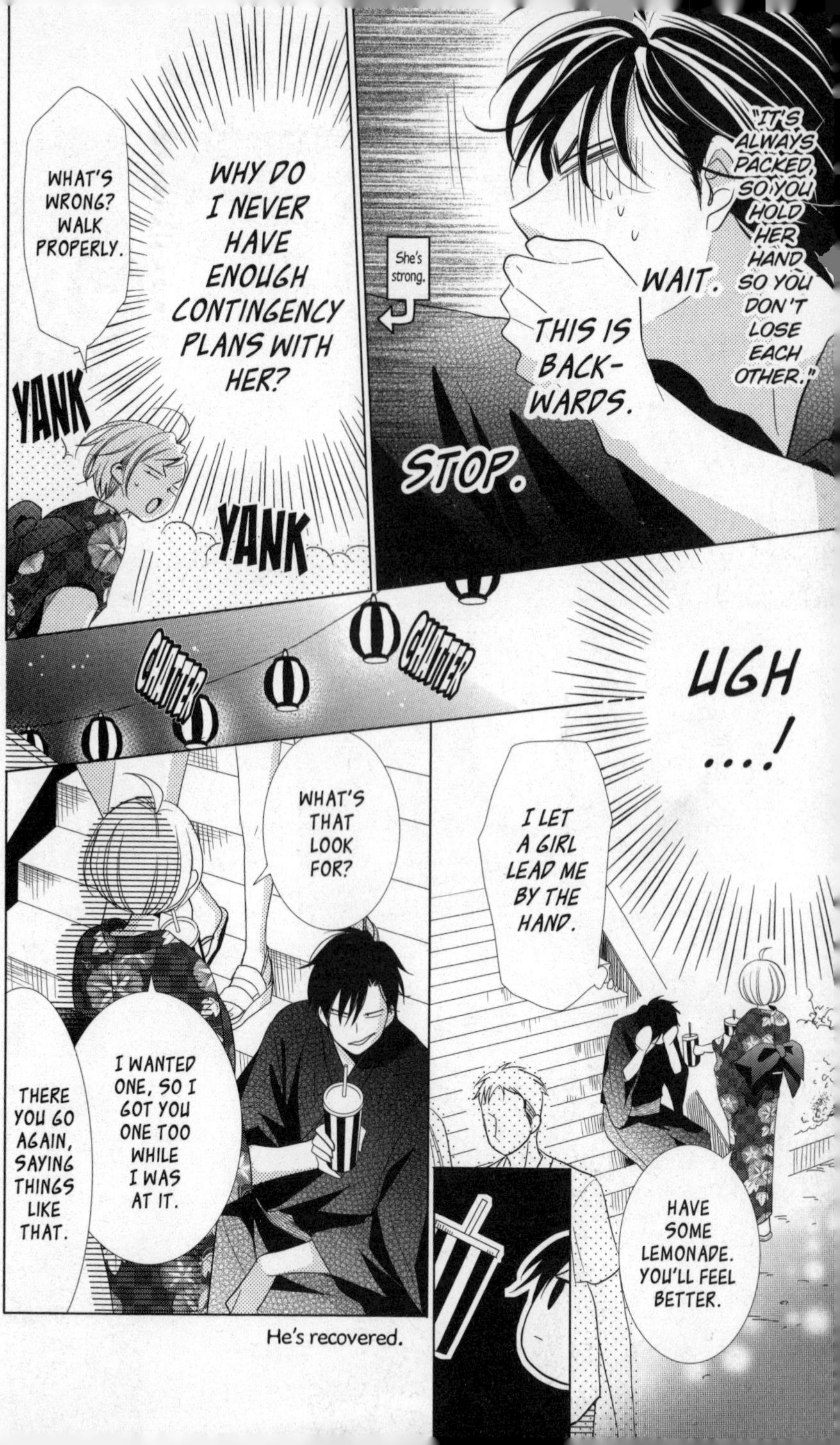
"IT'S ALWAYS PACKED, SO YOU HOLD HER HAND SO YOU DON'T LOSE EACH OTHER."
WAIT.
THIS IS BACK-WARDS.
STOP.
She's strong.
WHY DO I NEVER HAVE ENOUGH CONTINGENCY PLANS WITH HER?
WHAT'S WRONG? WALK PROPERLY.
YANK
YANK
CHATTER
CHATTER
UGH ...!
I LET A GIRL LEAD ME BY THE HAND.
HAVE SOME LEMONADE. YOU'LL FEEL BETTER.
WHAT'S THAT LOOK FOR?
I WANTED ONE, SO I GOT YOU ONE TOO WHILE I WAS AT IT.
THERE YOU GO AGAIN, SAYING THINGS LIKE THAT.
He's recovered.

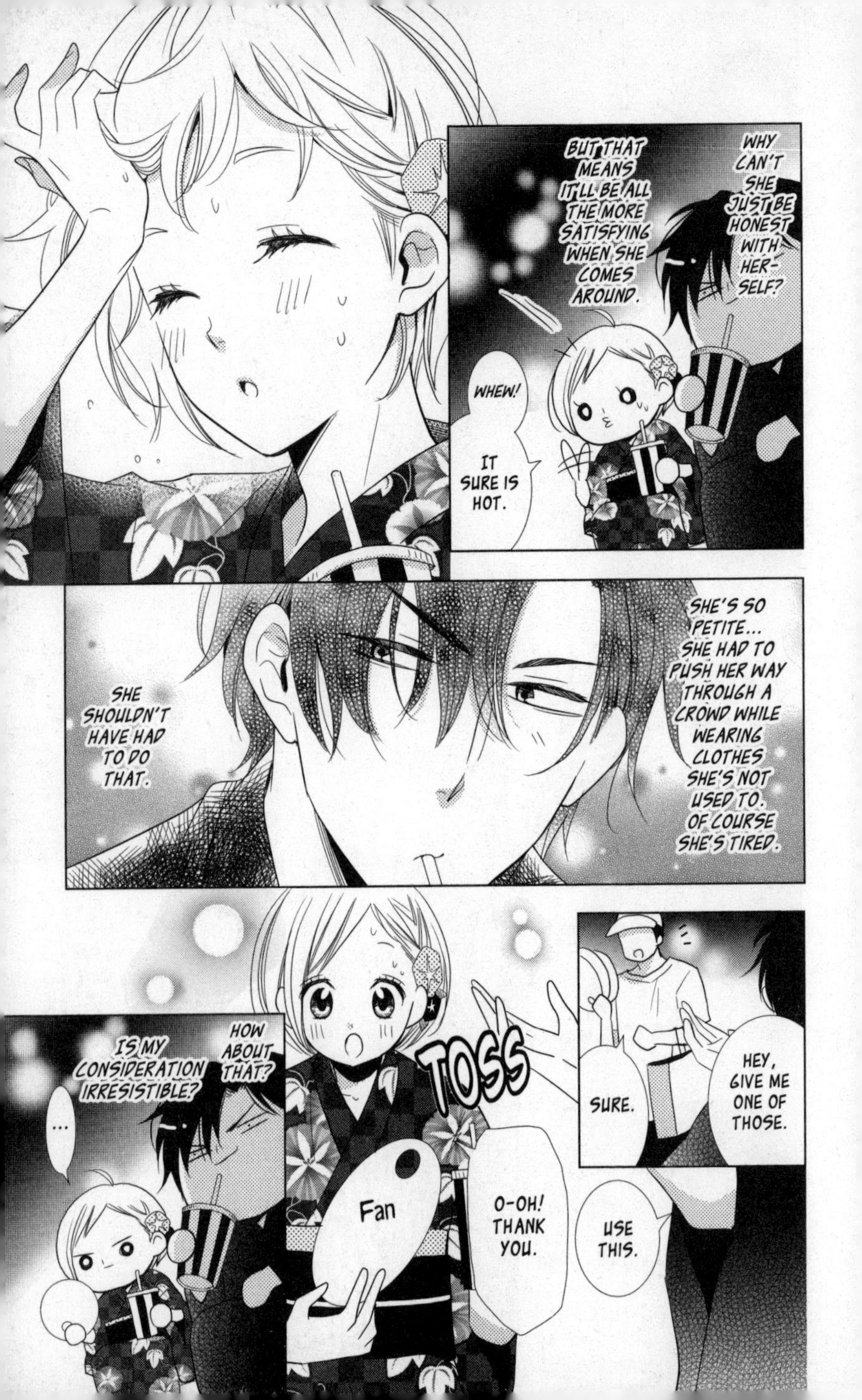
WHY CAN'T SHE JUST BE HONEST WITH HER-SELF?
BUT THAT MEANS IT'LL BE ALL THE MORE SATISFYING WHEN SHE COMES AROUND.
WHEW!
IT SURE IS HOT.
SHE'S SO PETITE... SHE HAD TO PUSH HER WAY THROUGH A CROWD WHILE WEARING CLOTHES SHE'S NOT USED TO. OF COURSE SHE'S TIRED.
SHE SHOULDN'T HAVE HAD TO DO THAT.
HEY, GIVE ME ONE OF THOSE.
SURE.
USE THIS.
O-OH! THANK YOU.
Fan
TOSS
HOW ABOUT THAT?
IS MY CONSIDERATION IRRESISTIBLE?
...

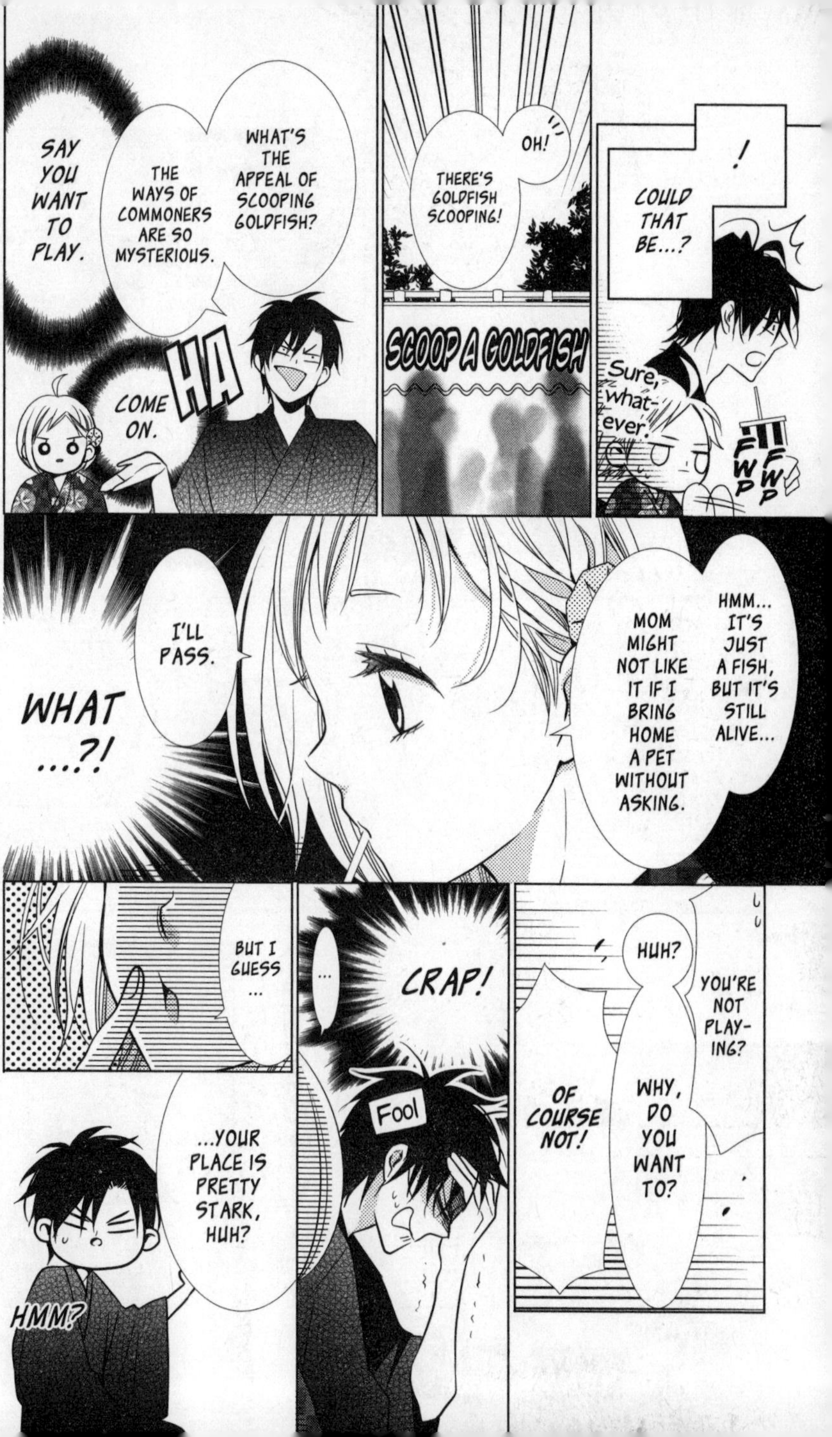
!
COULD THAT BE...?
Sure, what-ever.
FWP FWP
OH!
THERE'S GOLDFISH SCOOPING!
SCOOP A GOLDFISH
WHAT'S THE APPEAL OF SCOOPING GOLDFISH?
THE WAYS OF COMMONERS ARE SO MYSTERIOUS.
HA
SAY YOU WANT TO PLAY.
COME ON.
HMM... IT'S JUST A FISH, BUT IT'S STILL ALIVE...
MOM MIGHT NOT LIKE IT IF I BRING HOME A PET WITHOUT ASKING.
I'LL PASS.
WHAT ...?!
HUH?
YOU'RE NOT PLAYING?
WHY, DO YOU WANT TO?
OF COURSE NOT!
CRAP!
...
Fool
BUT I GUESS ...
...YOUR PLACE IS PRETTY STARK, HUH?
HMM?

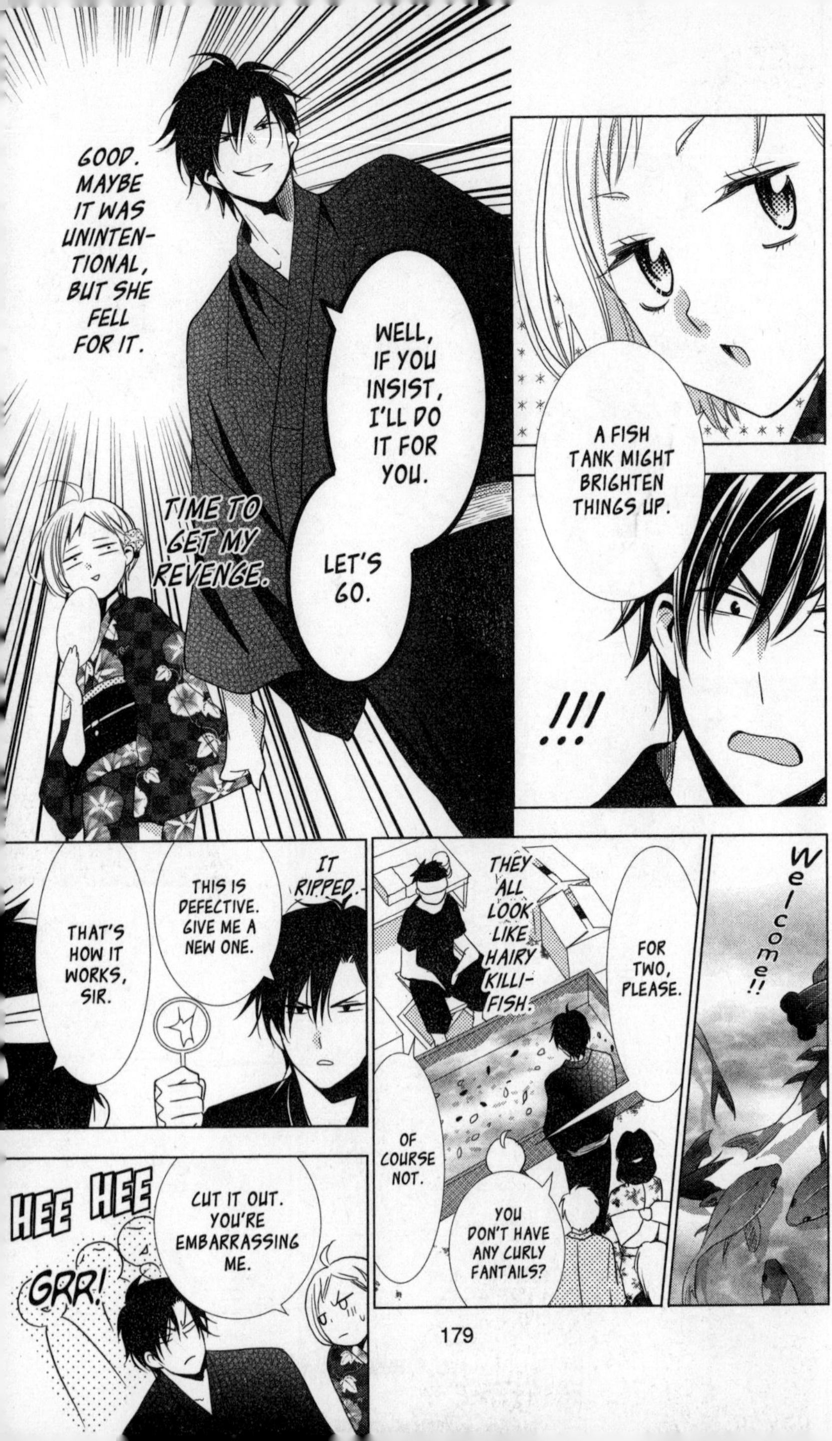
A FISH TANK MIGHT BRIGHTEN THINGS UP.
!!!
WELL, IF YOU INSIST, I'LL DO IT FOR YOU.
LET'S GO.
TIME TO GET MY REVENGE.
GOOD. MAYBE IT WAS UNINTEN-TIONAL, BUT SHE FELL FOR IT.
Welcome!!
FOR TWO, PLEASE.
THEY ALL LOOK LIKE HAIRY KILLI-FISH.
YOU DON'T HAVE ANY CURLY FANTAILS?
OF COURSE NOT.
IT RIPPED.
THIS IS DEFECTIVE. GIVE ME A NEW ONE.
THAT'S HOW IT WORKS, SIR.
CUT IT OUT. YOU'RE EMBARRASSING ME.
HEE HEE
GRR!

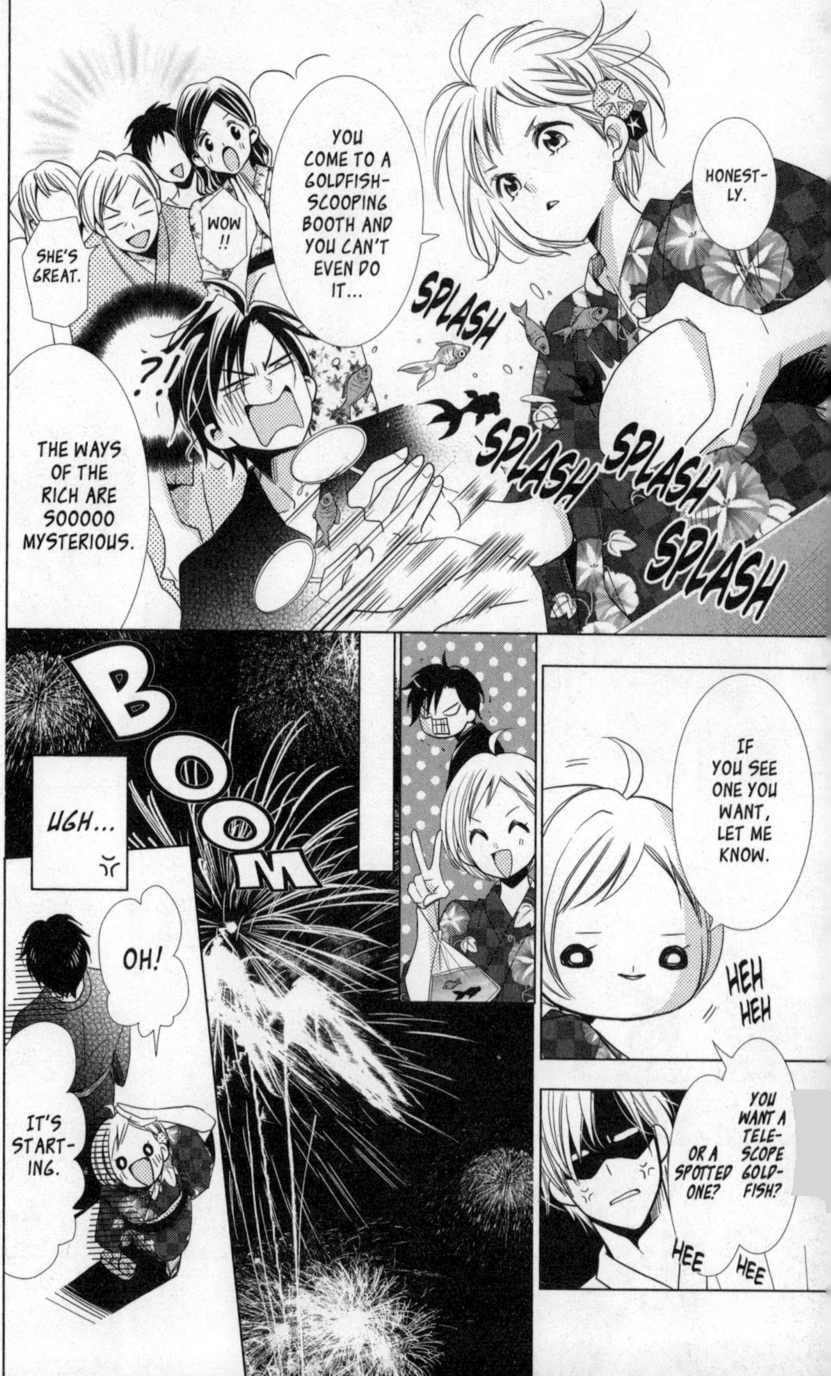
HONEST-LY.
YOU COME TO A GOLDFISH-SCOOPING BOOTH AND YOU CAN'T EVEN DO IT...
SPLASH
SPLASH
SPLASH
SPLASH
?!
WOW !!
SHE'S GREAT.
THE WAYS OF THE RICH ARE SOOOOO MYSTERIOUS.
IF YOU SEE ONE YOU WANT, LET ME KNOW.
HEH HEH
YOU WANT A TELE-SCOPE GOLD-FISH?
OR A SPOTTED ONE?
HEE
HEE
BOOM
UGH...
OH!
IT'S START-ING.

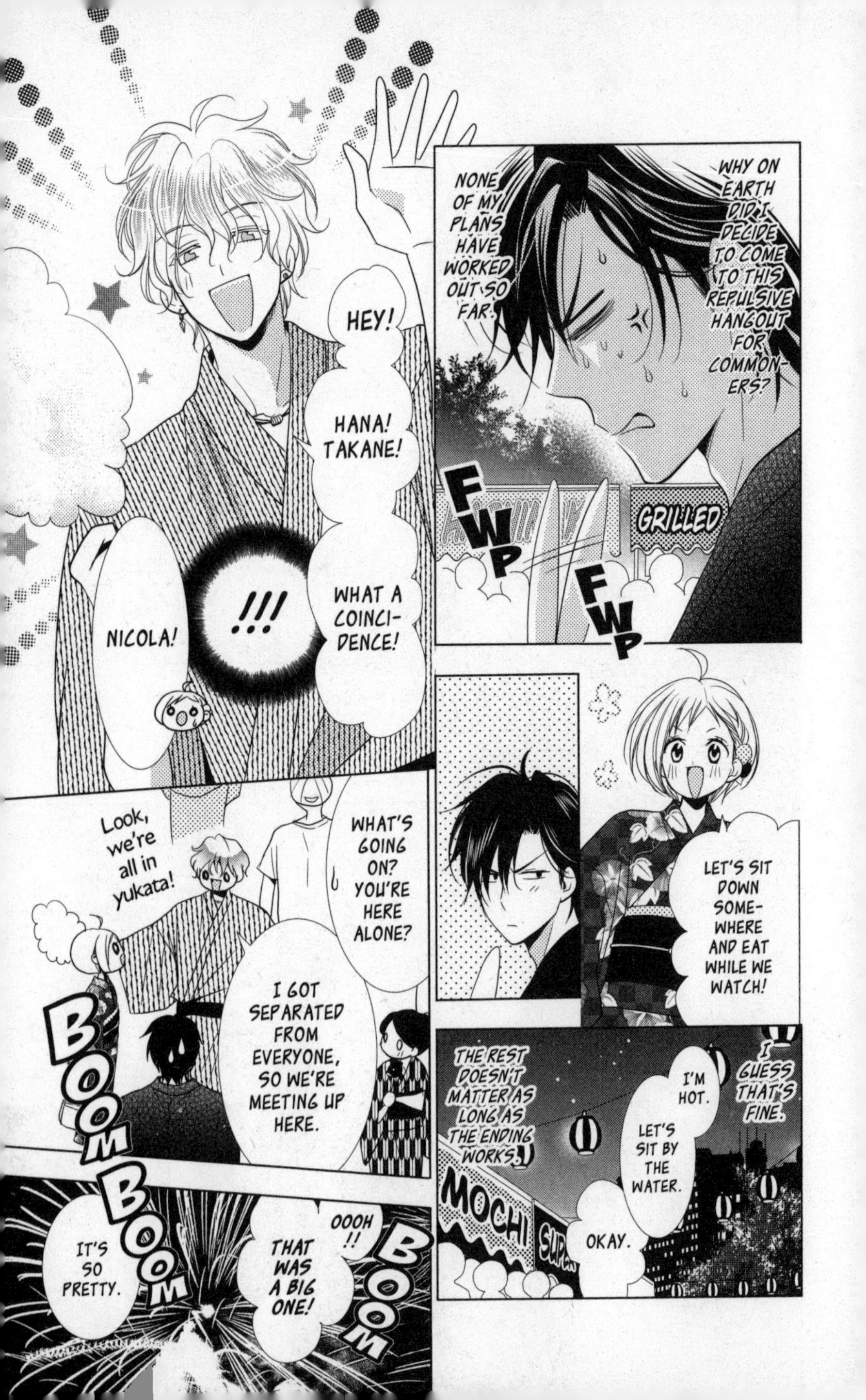
WHY ON EARTH DID I DECIDE TO COME TO THIS REPULSIVE HANGOUT FOR COMMONERS?
NONE OF MY PLANS HAVE WORKED OUT SO FAR.
GRILLED
FWP
FWP
LET'S SIT DOWN SOMEWHERE AND EAT WHILE WE WATCH!
I GUESS THAT'S FINE.
I'M HOT.
LET'S SIT BY THE WATER.
THE REST DOESN'T MATTER AS LONG AS THE ENDING WORKS.
MOCHI
OKAY.
HEY!
HANA! TAKANE!
WHAT A COINCIDENCE!
!!!
NICOLA!
WHAT'S GOING ON? YOU'RE HERE ALONE?
I GOT SEPARATED FROM EVERYONE, SO WE'RE MEETING UP HERE.
Look, we're all in yukata!
BOOM BOOM BOOM
OOOH!!
THAT WAS A BIG ONE!
IT'S SO PRETTY.
BOOM

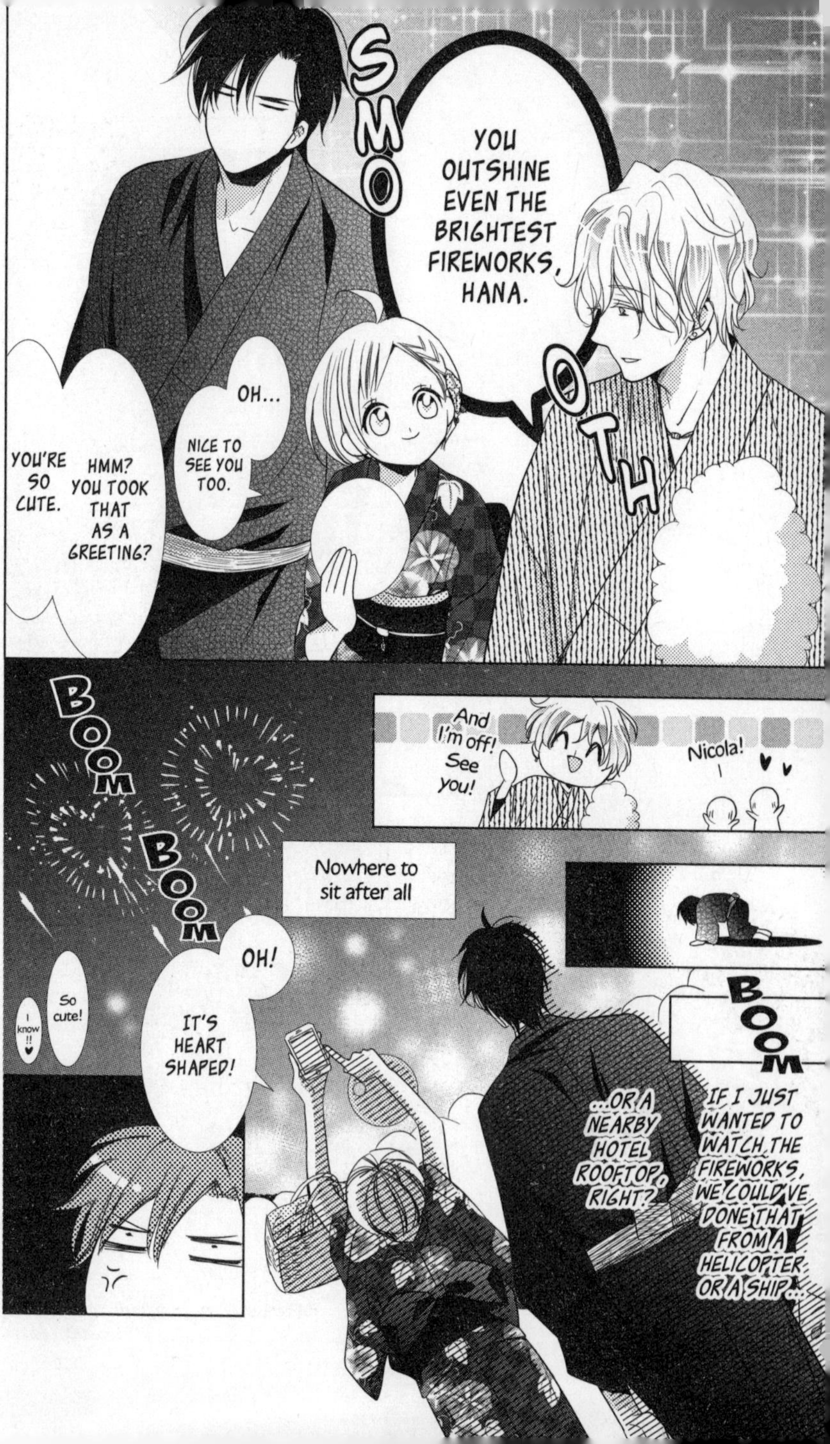
YOU OUTSHINE EVEN THE BRIGHTEST FIREWORKS, HANA.
SMOOTH
OH...
NICE TO SEE YOU TOO.
HMM? YOU TOOK THAT AS A GREETING?
YOU'RE SO CUTE.
Nicola!
And I'm off! See you!
BOOM
IF I JUST WANTED TO WATCH THE FIREWORKS, WE COULD'VE DONE THAT FROM A HELICOPTER OR A SHIP...
...OR A NEARBY HOTEL ROOFTOP, RIGHT?
Nowhere to sit after all
BOOM
BOOM
OH!
IT'S HEART SHAPED!
So cute!
I know!!

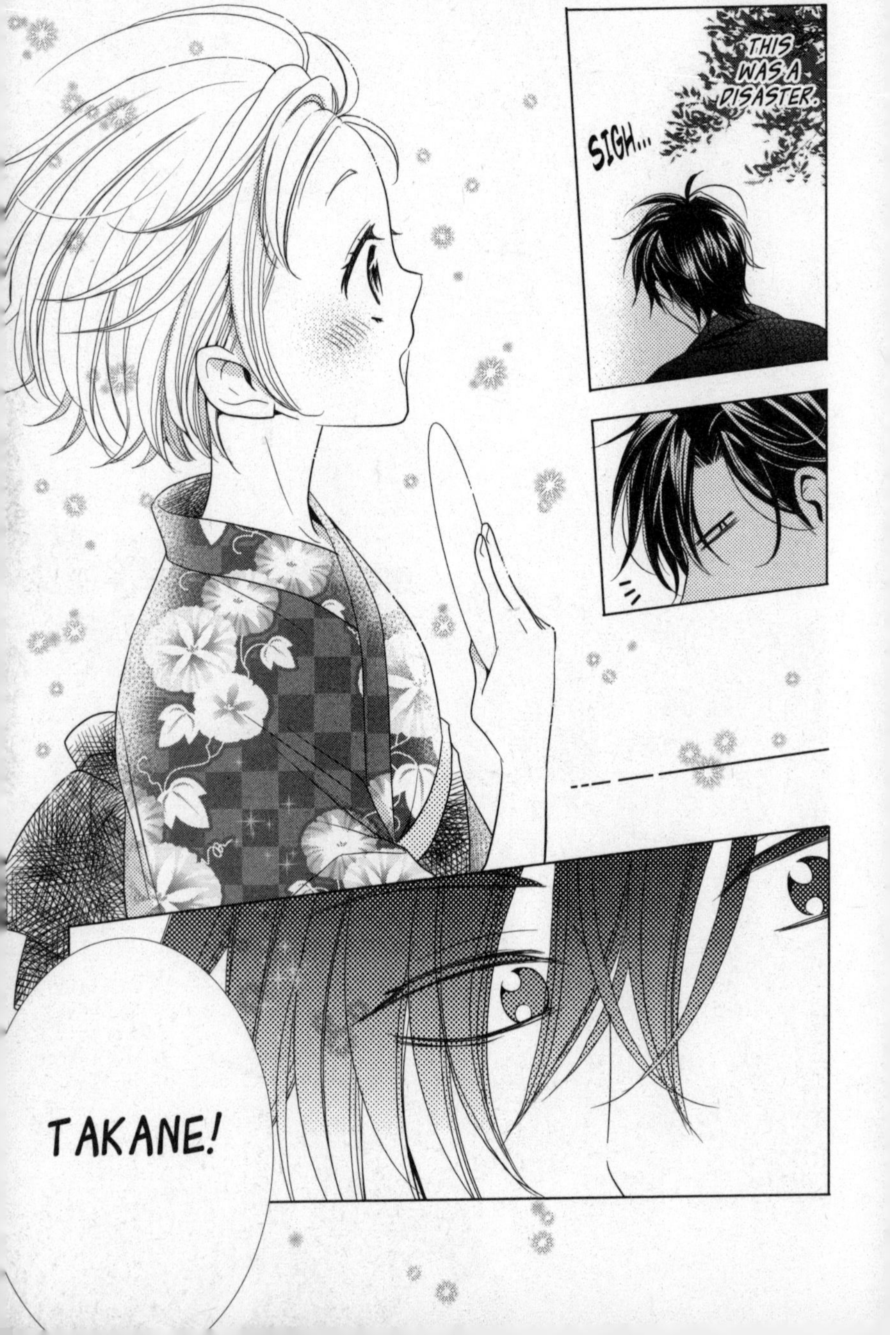
THIS WAS A DISASTER.
SIGH...
TAKANE!

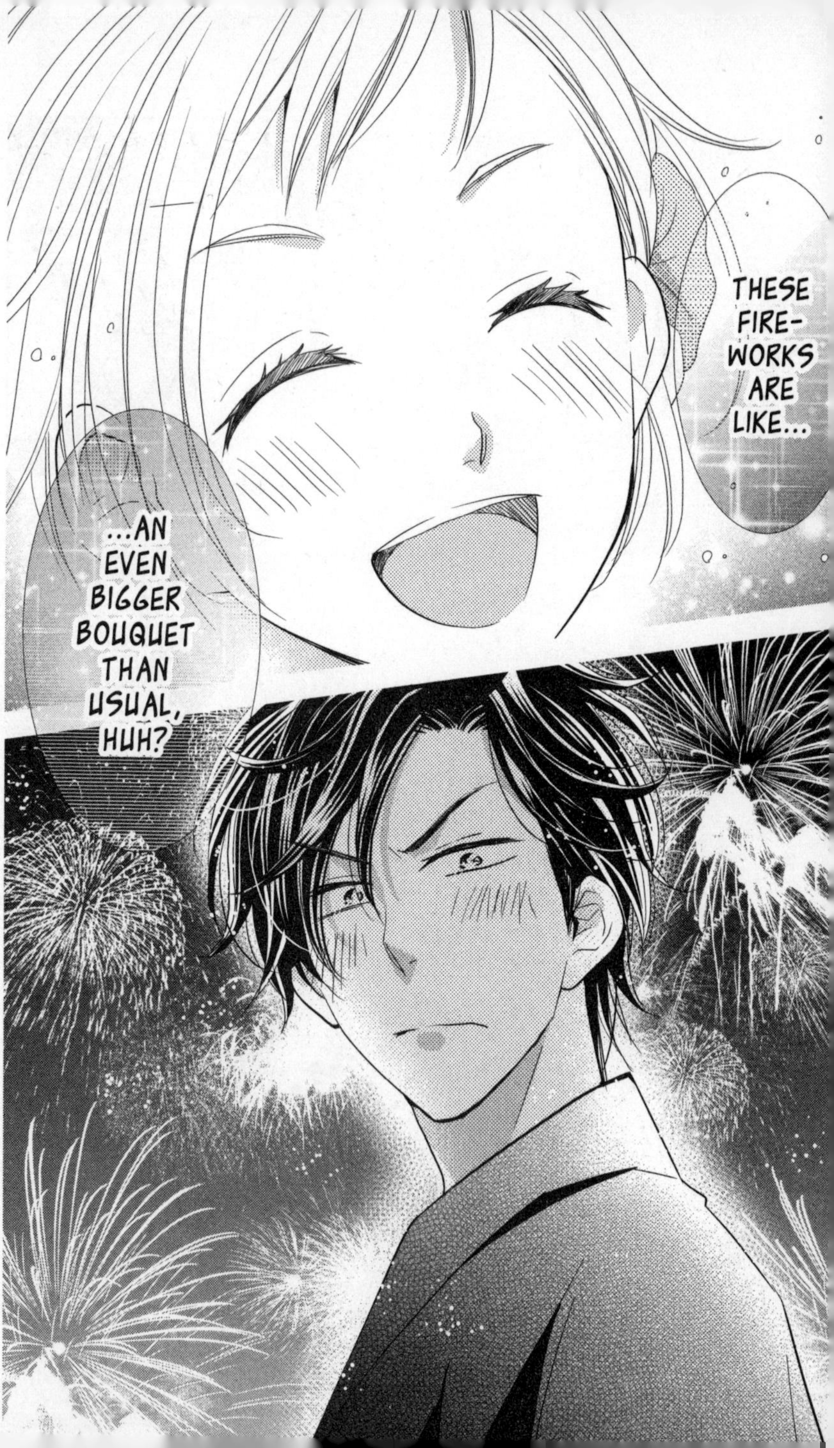
THESE FIRE-WORKS ARE LIKE...
...AN EVEN BIGGER BOUQUET THAN USUAL, HUH?

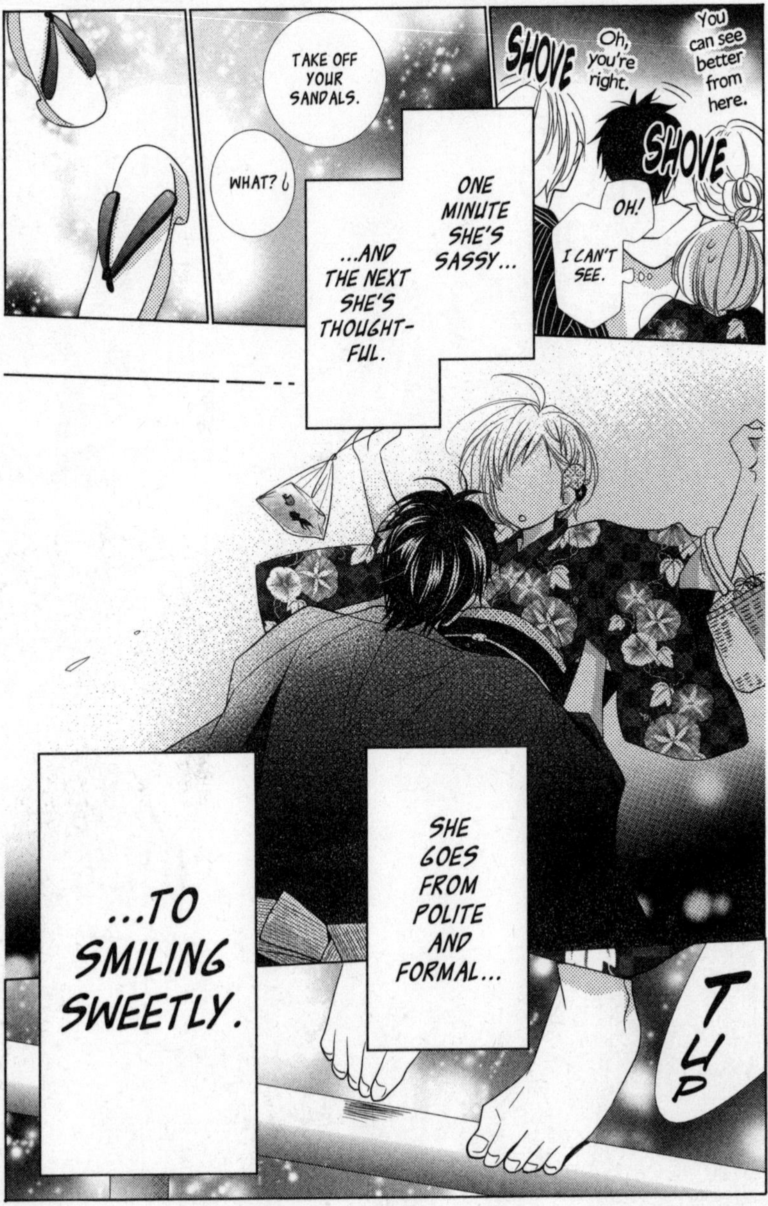
You can see better from here.
SHOVE
Oh, you're right.
SHOVE
OH!
I CAN'T SEE.
ONE MINUTE SHE'S SASSY...
...AND THE NEXT SHE'S THOUGHT-FUL.
TAKE OFF YOUR SANDALS.
WHAT?
SHE GOES FROM POLITE AND FORMAL...
...TO SMILING SWEETLY.
TUP

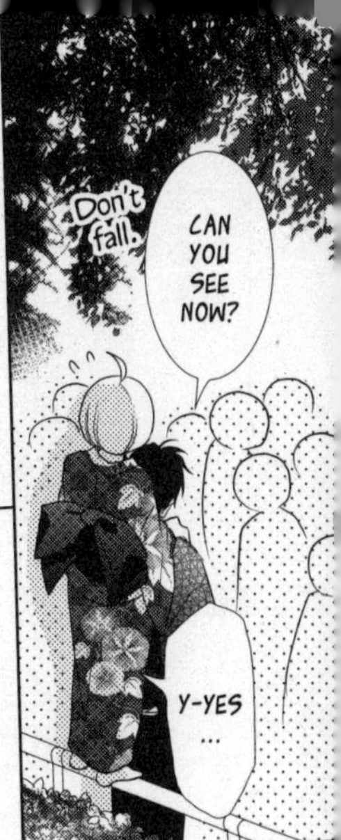
CAN YOU SEE NOW?
Don't fall.
Y-YES ...
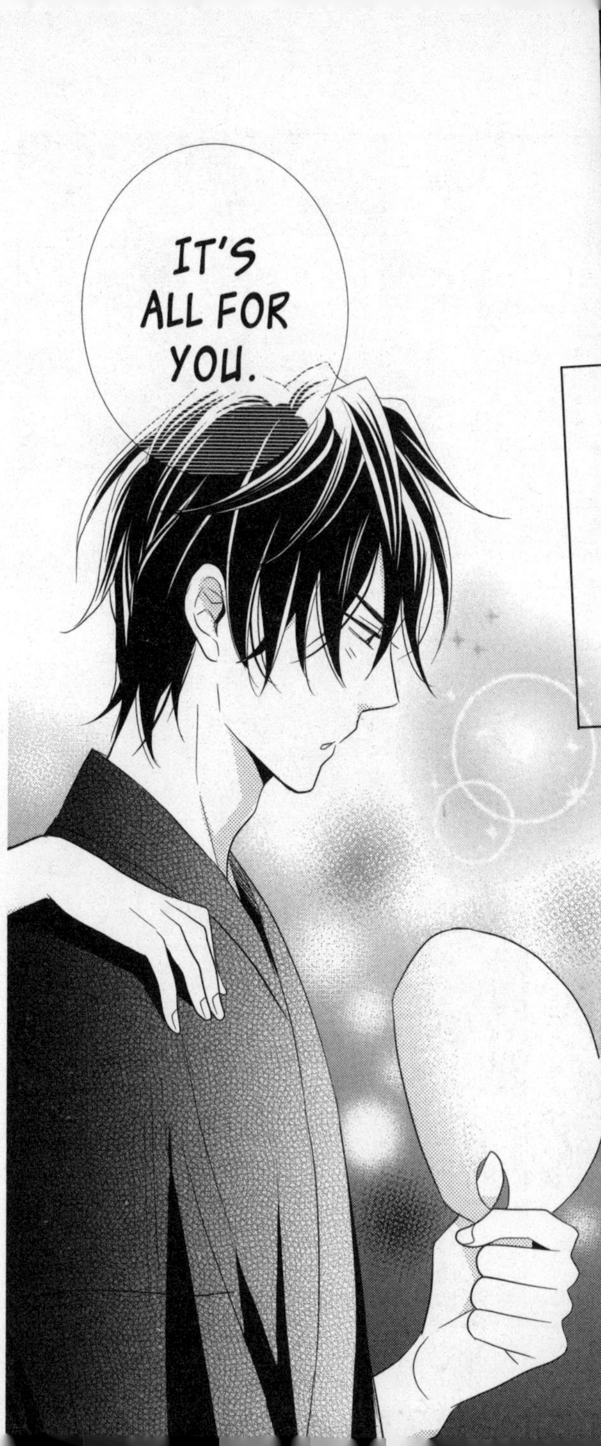
IT'S ALL FOR YOU.
ARE THERE STILL SIDES OF HER I HAVEN'T SEEN?

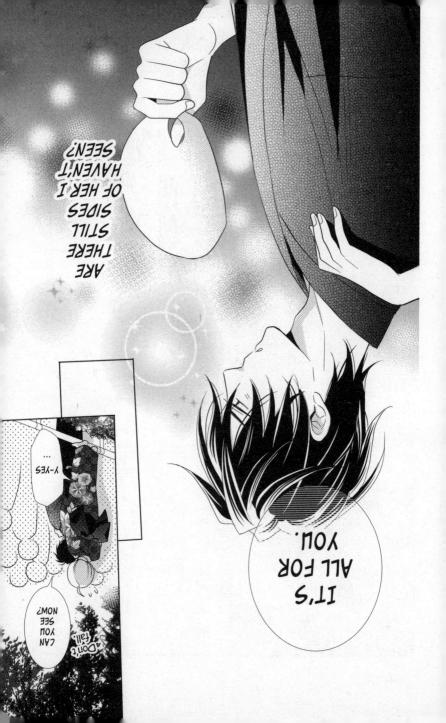

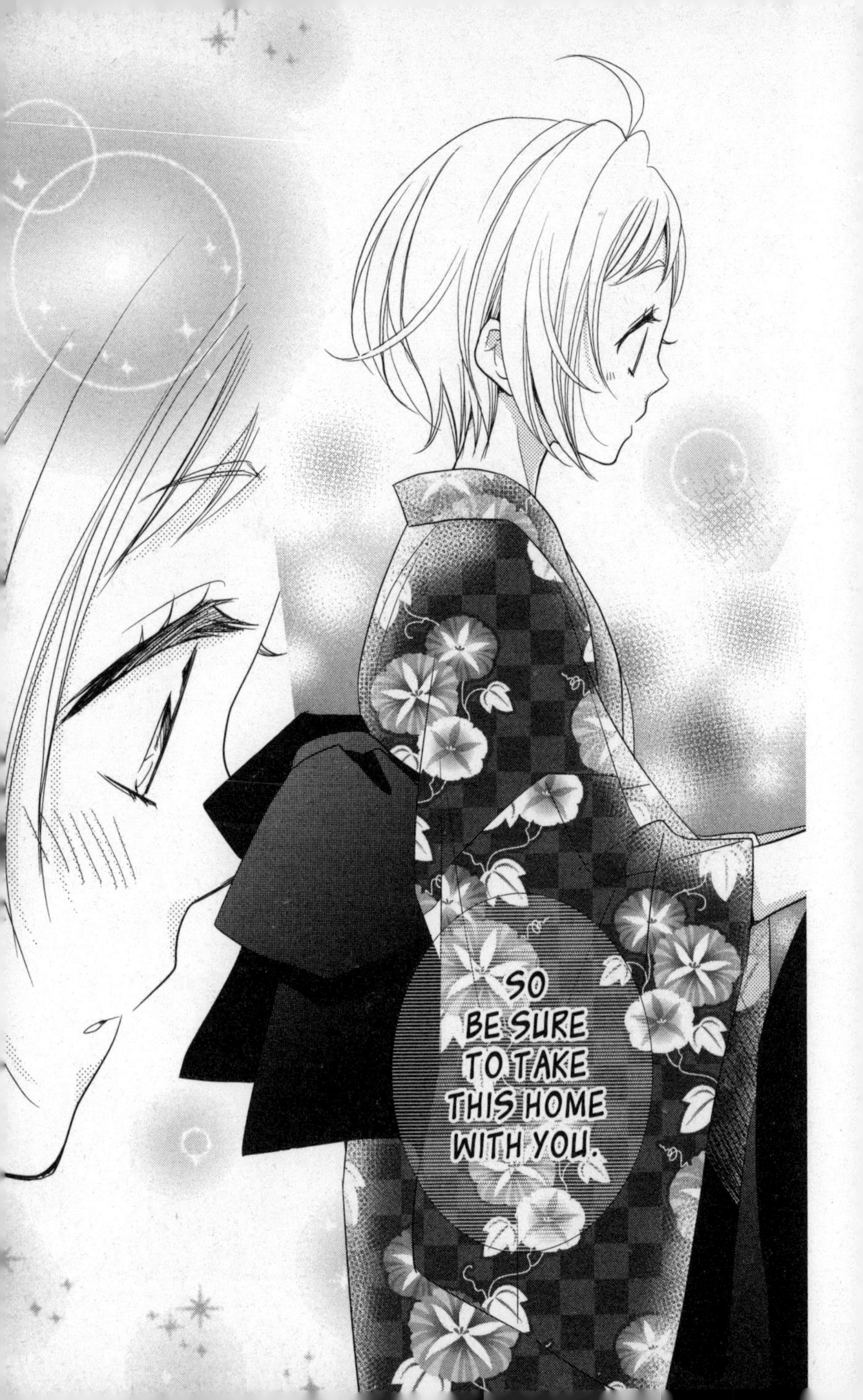
SO BE SURE TO TAKE THIS HOME WITH YOU.

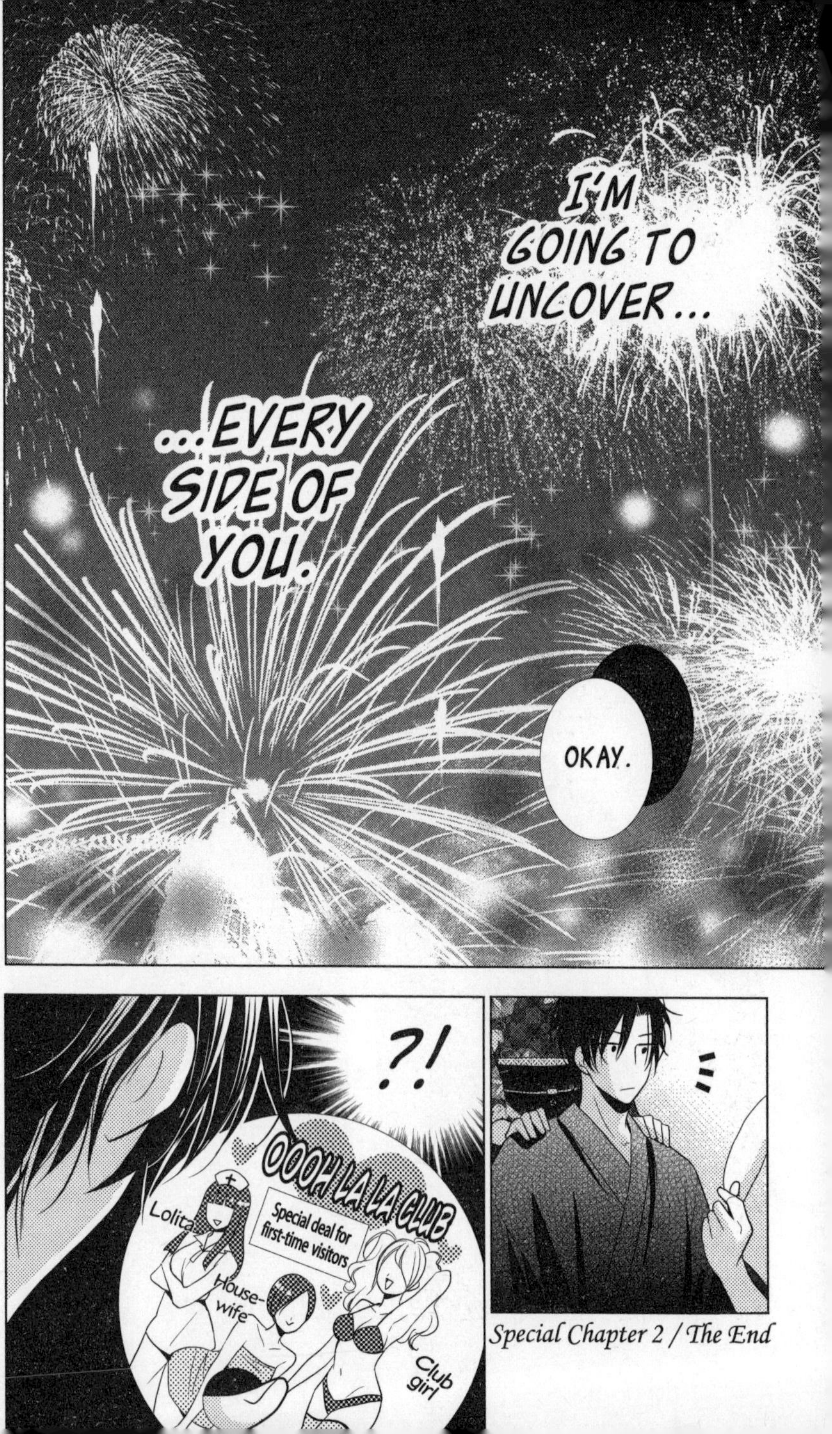
I'M GOING TO UNCOVER...
...EVERY SIDE OF YOU.
OKAY.
?!
OOOH LA LA CLUB
Special deal for first-time visitors
Lolita
House-wife
Club girl

Special Chapter 2 / The End

Goldfish

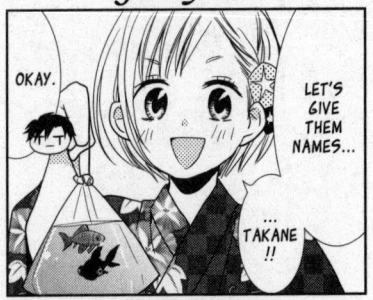

LET'S GIVE THEM NAMES...
OKAY.
... TAKANE !!
HOW ABOUT "ALTIS-SIMO" AND "LOUIS XIV" ?
TYPES OF ROSES
"HIDALGO" AND "PAPA MEILLAND" AREN'T BAD EITHER.
OH, BUT...
... "CRIMSON GLORY" HAS A NICE RING TO IT.
HMM...
LET'S NAME THEM "AKANE" AND "DEKAME."
DID YOU HEAR A WORD I SAID?
FINE. WE'LL SPLIT THE DIFFER-ENCE ...
...AND CALL THEM "AKANE GLORY" AND "DEKAME XIV."
"AKANE GLORY" IS FINE, BUT "DEKAME XIV" IS OUT.

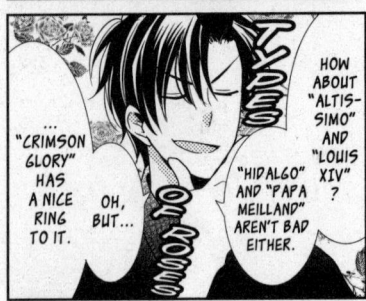

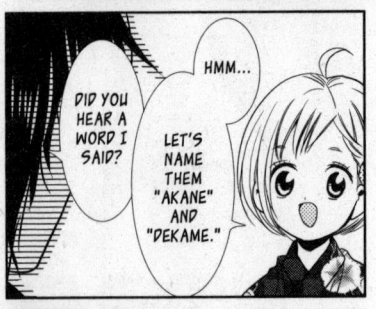

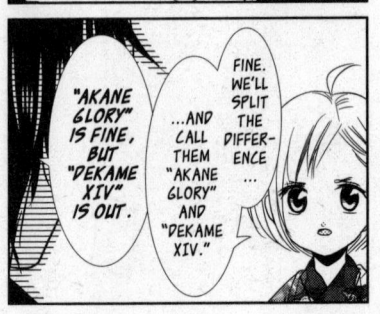

Bonus Story

Takane & Hana & Jr.

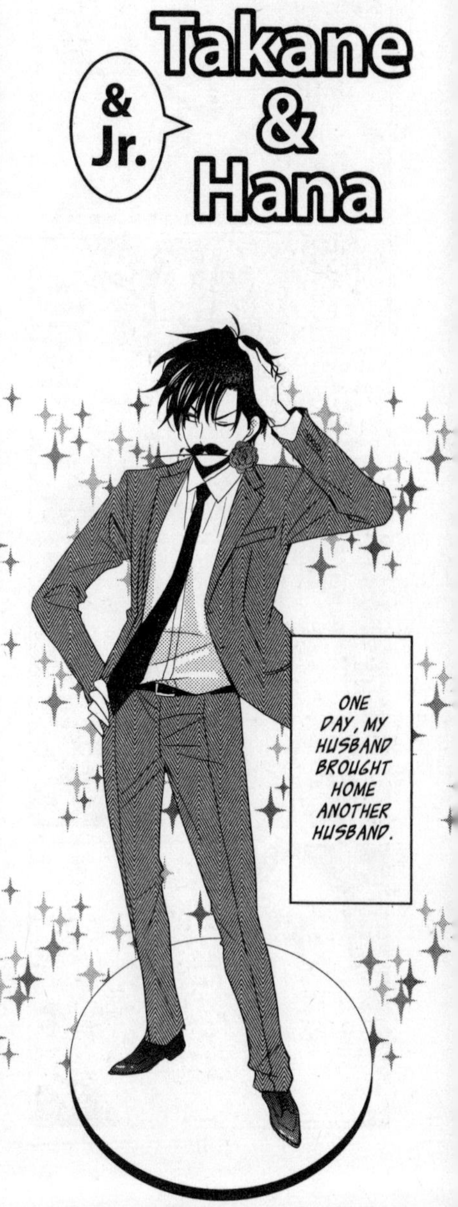
ONE DAY, MY HUSBAND BROUGHT HOME ANOTHER HUSBAND.

For Daddy's Little Girl

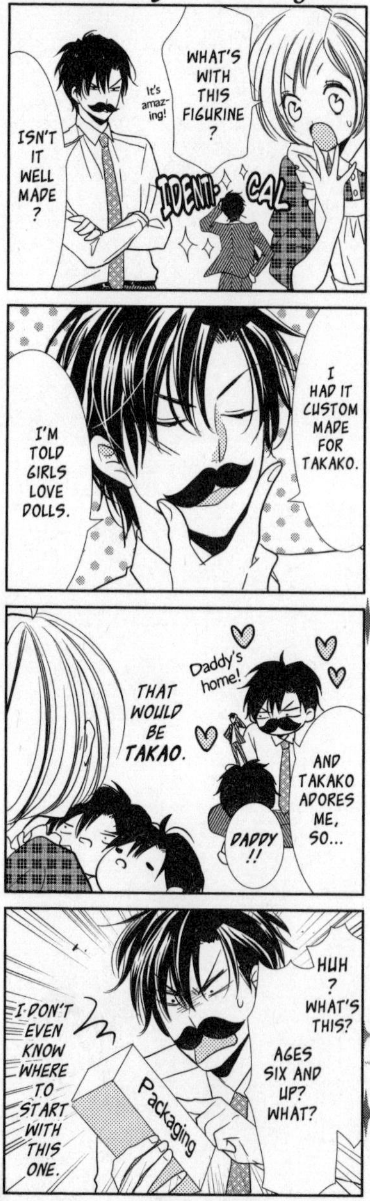
WHAT'S WITH THIS FIGURINE?
It's amazing!
ISN'T IT WELL MADE?
IDENTI- CAL
I HAD IT CUSTOM MADE FOR TAKAKO.
I'M TOLD GIRLS LOVE DOLLS.
Daddy's home!
THAT WOULD BE TAKAO.
AND TAKAKO ADORES ME, SO...
DADDY!!
HUH? WHAT'S THIS?
AGES SIX AND UP? WHAT?
I DON'T EVEN KNOW WHERE TO START WITH THIS ONE.
Packaging

And as for the Boys...

DON'T TAKE IT SO HARD.
IT'S MEANT FOR DECORA-TION.
WHY DON'T I PUT IT WHERE THE KIDS CAN ALL SEE IT?
RUSTLE
OH, I HAVE DOLLS FOR TAKAO AND TAKANORI TOO...
DOLLS OF YOU.
WHAT?
I HAVE A FIGURINE TOO?
RUSTLE
IT'S SO... PLAIN.
Not quite what I was pictur-ing.
THE DESIGN IS PERFECT! LOOK, THERE'S A WISP OF HAIR TO GRAB.
NON-SENSE!

The Fate of the Gifts

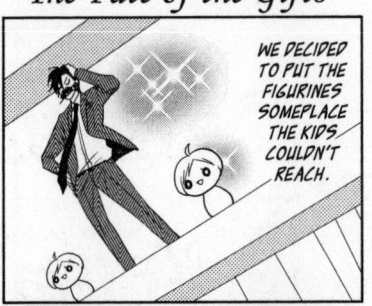

WE DECIDED TO PUT THE FIGURINES SOMEPLACE THE KIDS COULDN'T REACH.
COMMONER!!
COMMONER!!
AT FIRST WE THOUGHT THE CHILDREN WANTED THEM...
...BUT IT TURNED OUT THEY JUST DIDN'T WANT TO BE LOOKED DOWN UPON.
GRIN
OH!
YOU CLIMBED UP THERE AGAIN?
GRIN
GRIN
SLAM
I PUT THEM IN THE JUNK CLOSET.

Bonus Story: Takane & Hana & Jr. / The End

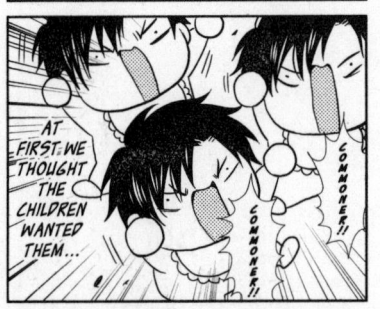

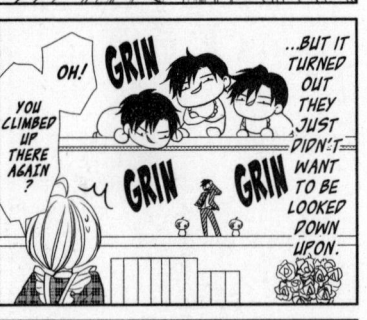

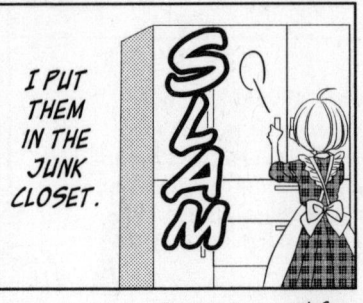

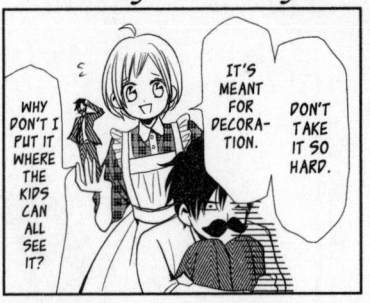

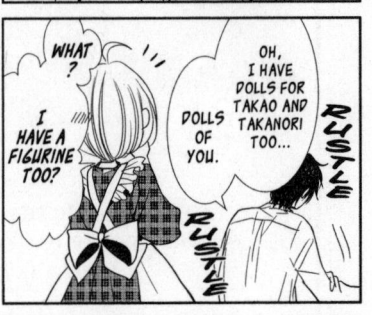

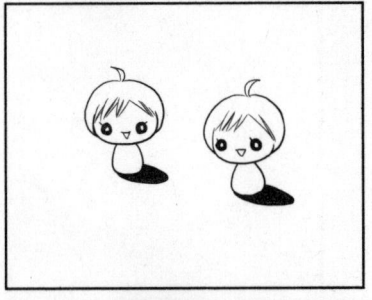

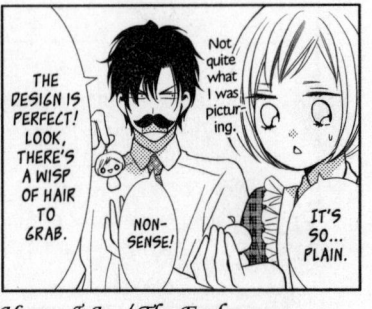

In keeping with the "bury the cover with stuff" theme, I chose to use tomatoes for this volume.

—YUKI SHIWASU

Born on March 7 in Fukuoka Prefecture, Japan, Yuki Shiwasu began her career as a manga artist after winning the top prize in the Hakusensha Athena Newcomers' Awards from *Hana to Yume* magazine. She is also the author of *Furou Kyoudai* (Immortal Siblings), which was published by Hakusensha in Japan.

Takane &Hana

VOLUME 3
SHOJO BEAT EDITION

STORY & ART BY **YUKI SHIWASU**

ENGLISH ADAPTATION **Ysabet Reinhardt MacFarlane**
TRANSLATION **JN Productions**
TOUCH-UP ART & LETTERING **Freeman Wong**
DESIGN **Shawn Carrico**
EDITOR **Amy Yu**

Takane to Hana by Yuki Shiwasu
© Yuki Shiwasu 2015
All rights reserved.
First published in Japan in 2015 by HAKUSENSHA, Inc., Tokyo.
English language translation rights arranged with HAKUSENSHA, Inc., Tokyo.

Printed in the U.S.A.

Published by VIZ Media, LLC
P.O. Box 77010
San Francisco, CA 94107

10 9 8 7 6 5 4 3 2 1
First printing, June 2018

 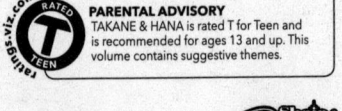 

viz.com

shojobeat.com

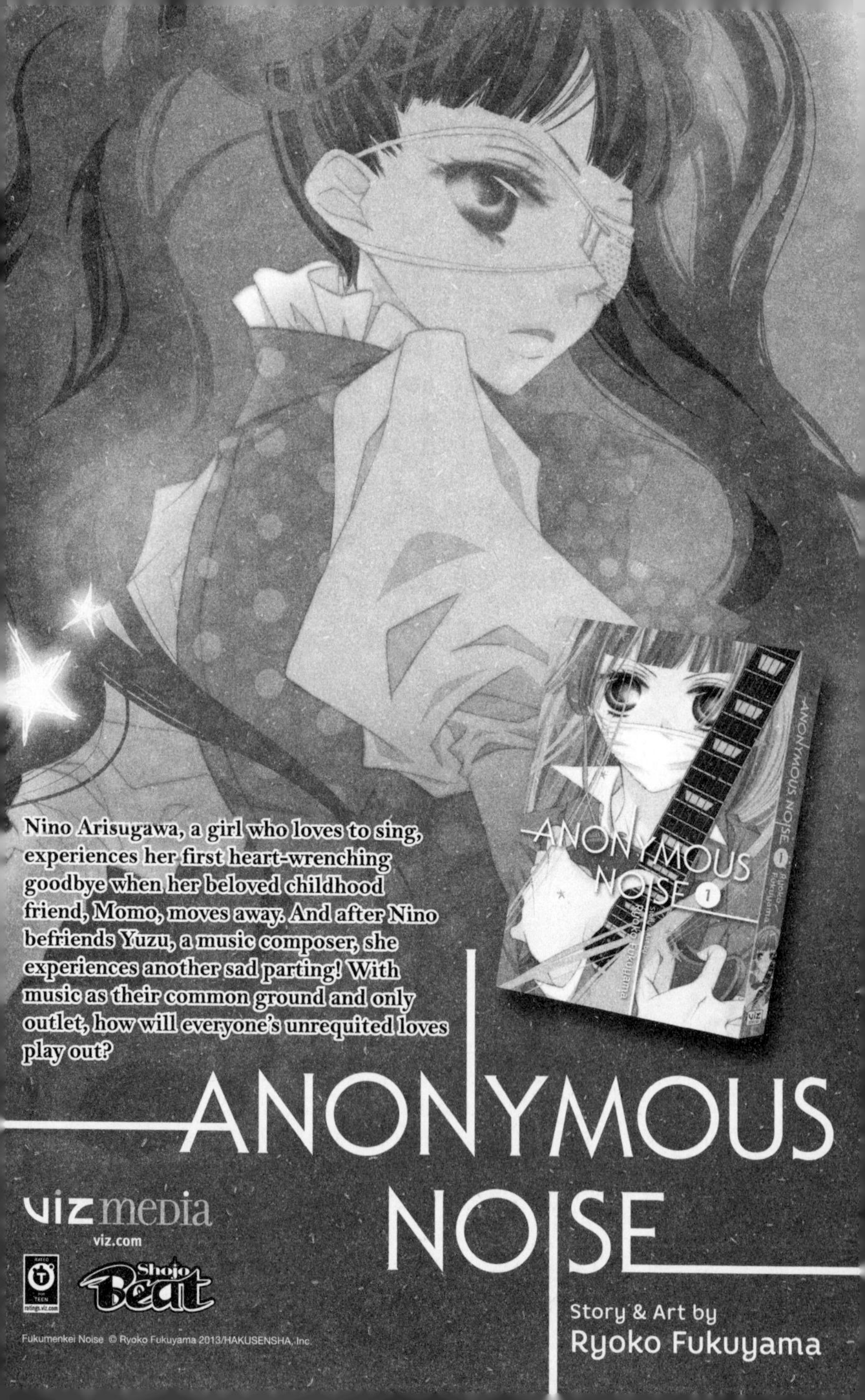
Nino Arisugawa, a girl who loves to sing, experiences her first heart-wrenching goodbye when her beloved childhood friend, Momo, moves away. And after Nino befriends Yuzu, a music composer, she experiences another sad parting! With music as their common ground and only outlet, how will everyone's unrequited loves play out?
ANONYMOUS NOISE
Story & Art by
Ryoko Fukuyama
viz media
viz.com
Shojo Beat
Fukumenkei Noise © Ryoko Fukuyama 2013/HAKUSENSHA, Inc.

IDOL dreams

STORY & ART BY
ARINA TANEMURA

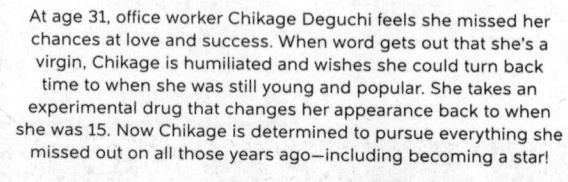

At age 31, office worker Chikage Deguchi feels she missed her chances at love and success. When word gets out that she's a virgin, Chikage is humiliated and wishes she could turn back time to when she was still young and popular. She takes an experimental drug that changes her appearance back to when she was 15. Now Chikage is determined to pursue everything she missed out on all those years ago—including becoming a star!

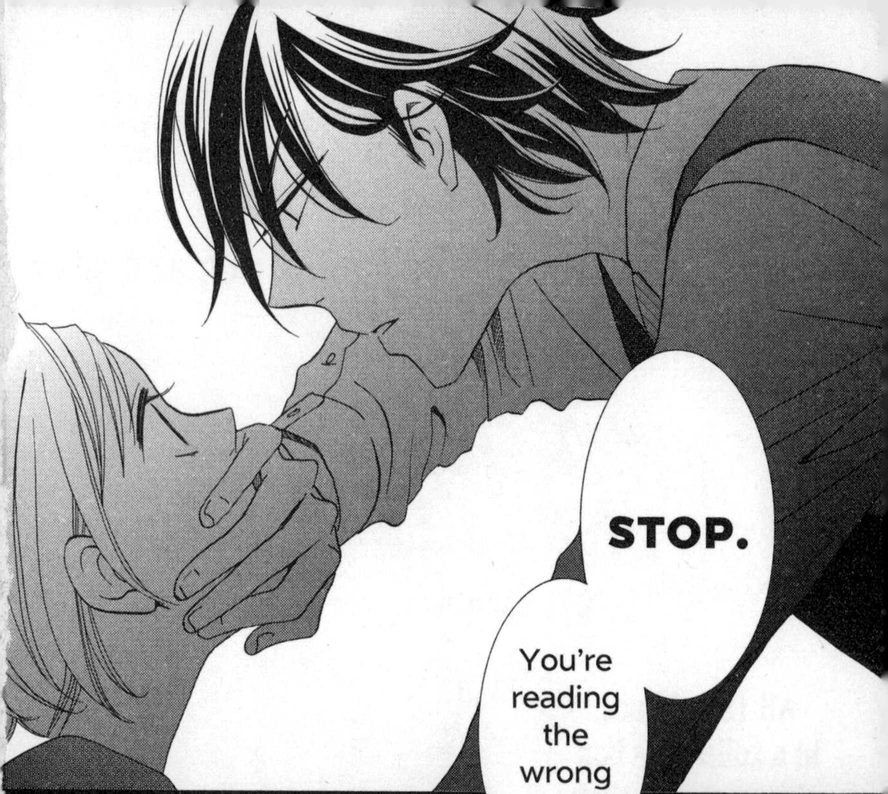
STOP.
You're reading the wrong way.

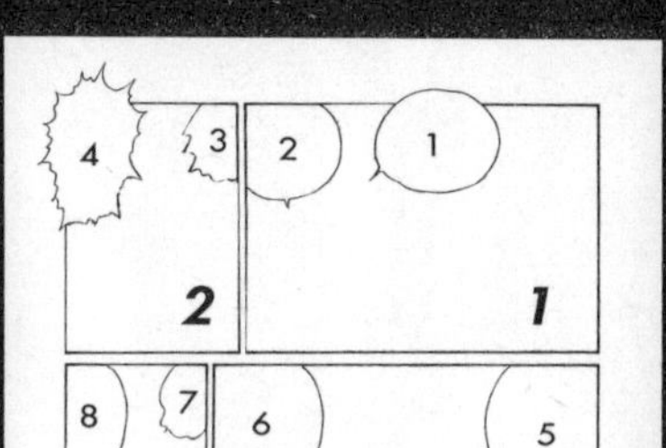
4
3
2
1
2
1
8
7
6
5
4
3
9
5
142

In keeping with the original Japanese comic format, this book reads from right to left—so action, sound effects and word balloons are completely reversed to preserve the orientation of the original artwork.

Check out the diagram shown here to get the hang of things, and then turn to the other side of the book to get started!